RULERS OF THE DEAD

More great stories from the Age of Sigmar

Sacrosanct and Other Stories
Various authors

Soul Wars
Josh Reynolds

The Realmgate Wars: Volume 1
Various authors
Contains the novels *The Gates of Azyr, War Storm, Ghal Maraz, Hammers of Sigmar, Wardens of the Everqueen* and *Black Rift*

The Realmgate Wars: Volume 2
Various authors
Contains the novels *Call of Archaon, Warbeast, Fury of Gork, Bladestorm, Mortarch of Night* and *Lord of Undeath*

Gods and Mortals
Various authors

Scourge of Fate
Robbie MacNiven

• HALLOWED KNIGHTS •
Josh Reynolds
Book 1: Plague Garden
Book 2: Black Pyramid

Hamilcar: Champion of the Gods
David Guymer

The Red Feast
Gav Thorpe

Shadespire: The Mirrored City
Josh Reynolds

Callis & Toll: The Silver Shard
Nick Horth

The Tainted Heart
C L Werner

Overlords of the Iron Dragon
C L Werner

Eight Lamentations: Spear of Shadows
Josh Reynolds

The Red Hours
Evan Dicken

Heart of Winter
Nick Horth

Warqueen
Darius Hinks

The Bone Desert
Robbie MacNiven

Audio Dramas

Realmslayer
David Guymer

Eight Lamentations: War-Claw
Josh Reynolds

Shadespire: The Darkness in the Glass
Various authors

The Palace of Memory and Other Stories
Various authors

The Imprecations of Daemons
Nick Kyme

The Denied
Josh Reynolds

Guns of the Black Eagle
C L Werner

RULERS OF THE DEAD

NAGASH: THE UNDYING KING • NEFERATA: MORTARCH OF BLOOD

JOSH REYNOLDS
DAVID ANNANDALE

BLACK LIBRARY

A BLACK LIBRARY PUBLICATION

Nagash: The Undying King first published in 2016.
Neferata: Mortarch of Blood first published in 2018.
This edition published in Great Britain in 2019 by
Black Library,
Games Workshop Ltd.,
Willow Road,
Nottingham,
NG7 2WS, UK.

10 9 8 7 6 5 4 3 2 1

Produced by Games Workshop in Nottingham.
Cover illustration by Igor Sid.
Internal art by John Michelbach,
Nuala Kinrade, Kevin Chin and Kari Christensen.

A CIP record for this book is available from the British Library.

ISBN 13: 978-1-78496-932-5

Printed and bound by CPI Group (UK) Ltd, Croydon, CR0 4YY

From the maelstrom of a sundered world, the Eight Realms were born. The formless and the divine exploded into life.

Strange, new worlds appeared in the firmament, each one gilded with spirits, gods and men. Noblest of the gods was Sigmar. For years beyond reckoning he illuminated the realms, wreathed in light and majesty as he carved out his reign. His strength was the power of thunder. His wisdom was infinite. Mortal and immortal alike kneeled before his lofty throne. Great empires rose and, for a while, treachery was banished. Sigmar claimed the land and sky as his own and ruled over a glorious age of myth.

But cruelty is tenacious. As had been foreseen, the great alliance of gods and men tore itself apart. Myth and legend crumbled into Chaos. Darkness flooded the realms. Torture, slavery and fear replaced the glory that came before. Sigmar turned his back on the mortal kingdoms, disgusted by their fate. He fixed his gaze instead on the remains of the world he had lost long ago, brooding over its charred core, searching endlessly for a sign of hope. And then, in the dark heat of his rage, he caught a glimpse of something magnificent. He pictured a weapon born of the heavens. A beacon powerful enough to pierce the endless night. An army hewn from everything he had lost.

Sigmar set his artisans to work and for long ages they toiled, striving to harness the power of the stars. As Sigmar's great work neared completion, he turned back to the realms and saw that the dominion of Chaos was almost complete. The hour for vengeance had come. Finally, with lightning blazing across his brow, he stepped forth to unleash his creations.

The Age of Sigmar had begun.

CONTENTS

NAGASH
THE UNDYING KING

Josh Reynolds

ONE

PLAGUE-FIRES

I still endure.

The skies weep, the seas boil, the ground cracks, but I still endure.

Let the stars gutter and the suns go cold, and still, I will endure.

The reverberations of my fall shattered mountains.

My servants are in disarray, bereft of my guiding will.

But I still endure.

I am death, and death cannot die.

It can only be delayed.

– *The Epistle of Bone*

The mountain air trembled with the squeal of splitting wood as the outer stockade succumbed to the greedy flames. The fire was not natural, for no natural flame burned the colour of pus. Natural fires left ash in their wake, not virulent, shrieking mould. It was a fire roused by sorcery, and only sorcery could snuff it. But there was no time. And, in any event, there was no one among the Drak who possessed the strength to do so. Not even their war-leader.

Tamra ven-Drak, voivode of the Drak, oldest of the highclans of the Rictus Clans, felt her soul wither as the great hall where she'd been born collapsed with a groan. Lodge poles burned like torches, and the skulls of three generations screamed useless warnings to their living kin from their rooftop perches. The fire spread like a thing alive, leaping from peaked log to thatched roof without pause.

'Back, get back,' she cried, shoving her clansfolk along, away from the creeping flames and towards an ornately carved stone archway. 'To the inner keep – go!' A stream of frightened faces surrounded her, pushing and shoving to escape the oily haze which preceded the plague-fires. The walls of the inner keep were high and sloped backwards, surrounding the lodgehouses of the highborn, as well as the great storehouses which fed her folk in the darkest months of winter, and the icy wells which drew fresh water up from beneath the earth.

The walls had been built in centuries past by greater artisans than her people now possessed. What few living warriors that remained to her clan were stationed there, loosing arrow after arrow at the invaders. Once the last of her folk were safely through, they would retreat down through the lichgates hidden beneath the lodgehouses and within the great wells, then along the secret paths that led into the surrounding wilderness. Those ancient paths had been carved for this very contingency after the black days of the Great Awakening, and they would be the salvation of her people – if she could buy them the necessary time.

Tamra held her ground, letting her clansfolk break and flow around her. The enemy would be inside the outer palisade in moments, and she intended to greet them with all due hospitality. She was a daughter of the Drak, and could do no less.

She caught the edge of her chest-plate and shifted it. The

armour was old and ill-fitting, digging into her flesh at inconvenient points. An heirloom from the Age of Myth, it had belonged to her father, and had been handed down from one voivode of the Drak to the next for generations. A stylised serpent, once a vivid red but now a faded brown, marked its faceted surface. It was the symbol of a fallen kingdom, and of lost glories.

Sister.

She glanced at her brother. His empty eye sockets burned with witchfire flames, and his fleshless fingers clutched the hilt of his barrowblade tightly. *You should go. They will be here soon.* His words echoed in her head like a freezing iron wind. *Your responsibility is to the living. Leave this to the dead.*

'No, Sarpa. We will meet them together.'

She recalled the day he'd died to an orruk blade, and the ceremony that followed. She'd left his body on a high slope, to be picked clean by scavenger birds and flesh-eaters. She had carved the sigils of rousing into his bones herself, as he would have done for her. As they'd both done for the dead who now surrounded them in a phalanx. The old dead, the loved dead, sons and daughters, fathers and mothers; the countless generations of the Drak, stirred to fight anew for hearth and home. Death was not the end for the Drak. They lived and died and lived again, to serve their people and their god, and they had done so since the coming of the Undying King and the Great Awakening.

And now the dead were all her people had left, in these final hours. They outnumbered the living two to one, with barely several hundred of her people left to flee. Most of their living warriors, and the hetmen who'd led them, had fallen, slaughtered in open battle by an enemy far stronger than them. But the dead held firm, and so would she. She could feel them fighting on the walls and in the streets. The majority of the dead were scattered throughout the outer keep and along the palisades, fighting to delay the inevitable. One by one, their soulfires were snuffed out as the enemy pressed ever forwards.

'We hold them here, until the outer village is empty,' she said. 'Then we retreat, no faster than we must. Let them blunt themselves on our shields. We are Drak. What we have, we hold.'

We hold, the dead echoed. The skeletons were armoured in bronze and carried weapons and shields of the same. Steel was precious, and carried only by the living; they needed it more than the dead. She could feel the flicker of soulfire animating each of the fleshless warriors, the brief embers of who they had once been. Such was the gift of the highborn of all the Rictus Clans. Only those who could stir the dead could lead the living.

Overhead, black clouds grumbled with the promise of a storm. The skies of the north were never silent, never peaceful. The snow had ceased for the moment, but soon it would be replaced by rain. Purple lightning flashed in the belly of the clouds, and she watched it for a moment. Then, the pox-flames parted and the enemy arrived in a rush.

The first to come were the hounds, their fur soggy with pus and their eyes faceted like those of flies. They bayed and loped forwards in a seething mass of rotted fangs and blistered paws. Bronze-tipped spears slid home, turning their howls to shrieks. Those beasts that made it through the thicket of spears died to swords and axes. As the hounds perished, their masters arrived, lumbering through the plague-fires. The blightkings were monsters, clad in filthy tabards over grimy war-plate marked with the sign of the fly.

They advanced with a droning roar, hefting outsized weapons in flabby hands. They struck the bronze shield wall like a foetid fist, and the line bowed inwards.

'Sarpa,' Tamra said, fighting to keep her voice calm. Her brother stepped smoothly towards the enemy. His barrow-blade sang a deadly song as it rose and fell, removing limbs and heads. The blightkings' momentum was broken in moments. They fell back, their droning song giving way to cries of alarm.

They retreated, seeking shelter in the plague-fires. But she could hear the distorted jangle of pox-bells and the thump of skin drums, and she knew more were coming. These had only been the most eager, the least disciplined. She looked around the palisade yard, watching as the last houses of her people were consumed, along with the bodies of the dead. Where the plague-fires burned, her magic was as nothing, and the dead were lost.

They are coming, Sarpa said.

'Fall back to the archway. Tighten the line.' She had learned the art of the shield wall from her father, and from his mother before him. Their spirits had whispered to her, in her infancy, and shown her much: the proper way to wage war, to raise walls, to lead. The dead had taught her the lessons of a thousand years. But they had not prepared her for this.

The lands claimed in millennia past by the Rictus Clans were far beyond even the northernmost cities and principalities of Shyish. They were harsh lands, clinging to the frozen coasts of the Shivering Sea. No enemy had ever come so far north in all the centuries since the coming of Chaos. Or at least none had survived the attempt. Those the cold did not claim inevitably fell to the shambling packs of deadwalkers who haunted the thick forests and ice floes in ever-growing numbers.

But these creatures – these rotbringers – were different. They easily endured conditions which had defeated even the most frenzied of the Blood God's worshippers. And now they were at her walls, battering down her gates. The remains of her strongest warriors hung from their flyblown banners, and the villages of her people were smoke on the wind.

This siege was the culmination of an assault on her territories which had lasted days. The rotbringers were marching north, and they seemed disinclined to leave anything larger than a barrow-marker standing in their wake. Her people had been driven steadily northwards from steadings and camps, until they'd had nowhere else to run. She hadn't had enough warriors, living or dead, to do more than delay the foe. And now, not even that.

How had it come to this? Was Nagash dead, as the southerners claimed? Had the Undying King truly fallen in battle? How could one who was as death itself die? Her mind shied away from the thought, unable to accept such a thing. Nagash simply... was. As inescapable as the snows in winter, as ever present as the cold, he had always been and always would be. To consider anything else was the height of folly.

Chortles of barbaric glee filled the night as scabrous shapes climbed the palisades. She looked up. These ones were men, rather than monsters, but only just. Clad in filthy smocks and rattletrap armour, they carried bows. Some of them might even have been Rictus, once, before they'd traded their souls for their lives. She'd heard from refugees that several of the lowland tribes had joined the foe, though whether freely or under duress no one had known. It didn't matter. Whoever they had been, they were the enemy now.

Shields, Sarpa said.

Bronze shields were raised with a clatter, covering Tamra, even as the dead continued to retreat. She heard the rattle of arrows, and saw one sink into a skull. A yellowish ichor had been smeared on the arrowhead, and it ate through the bone in moments. The skeleton collapsed, dissolving into a morass of white and yellow.

Tamra hissed in revulsion and flung out her hand. Amethyst energies coalesced about her fingers before erupting outwards in an arcane bolt. The palisade exploded, and broken bodies were flung into the air. As the echo of the explosion faded, the blightkings gave a roar and thudded forwards, supported by more of their mortal followers.

The dead reached the archway a moment later. 'Brace and hold,' Tamra said, as Sarpa pushed her back into the archway. It was the only route into the inner keep, short of knocking down the walls themselves, and these were not mere palisades of hardened wood. They were hard stone, packed by dead hands in better days. Sorcerous fire might eat away at them, but it would take time. Her people would be gone by then, scattered into the crags and hollows. There were hidden shelters in the high places, and secret roads in the low. Some of them would escape. Some would survive, and find safety among the other clans.

Axes crashed against shields for what felt like hours. The dead held firm. Sarpa stood beside her, waiting with eerie patience for what was surely to come. Tamra looked up at the archway, which rose high and wide around them. A hundred generations of Drak artisans had added to it, chiselling away cold stone to reveal scenes of life and history, great battles and small moments, the story of her people. She placed a hand against it. 'I will miss it,' she said.

We hold, Sarpa said.

'Yes,' she said. 'Hold.' That was what Drak did best. Come raiding orruks, marauding ogors or vengeful duardin, the Drak held. Their bronze shield walls had never been broken before today, and she was determined that they would not break again. Not while she drew breath. 'Hold, brothers and sisters. Set your feet and lift your shields. We are Drak.'

We are Drak, came the ghostly reply. The dead held, as they always did. She reinforced their will with her own, adding her strength to theirs. Bronze swords slid between locked shields, seeking swollen flesh. Bodies piled up before them, creating a second wall, this one of flesh. She considered drawing them back to their feet, but her strength was flagging. Best to save her power for holding this last phalanx together.

All around her, great maggoty axes hewed apart bone and bronze. Skulls fell to the snowy ground and were crushed beneath the tread of the enemy. The dead retreated, their line contracting. They left a trail of carnage behind them, but the enemy continued to press the assault. Tamra's breath rasped in her lungs as she spat darkling oaths. Amethyst fires seared pox-ridden flesh clean, as chattering spirits ripped warriors from the ground and sent them crashing into the stones. But it was not enough. Soon the spirits faded and the purple flames dimmed, leaving only the oily green of the plague-fires.

The archway cracked and crumbled as the dead were pushed back. The courtyard of the inner keep was empty of all save for those who had died on the walls. With a thought, she jerked them to their feet, though it repulsed her to do so. It was not right to animate the dead thus, not when flesh still clung to their bones, but necessity drove her. The deadwalkers lurched towards the foe, tangling them up, buying her a few more moments.

You must flee now, sister, Sarpa pulsed, his voice piercing the veil of pain that was beginning to cloud her thoughts. Her skull ached, and her heart stuttered in its cage of bone. She had never attempted so much magic in so short a span. All around her, the last lodgehouses of the Drak were burning. Stores of food, hoarded against the winter, were consumed by the flames. The ancient wells, which had served her folk since time out of mind, now vomited up a virulent steam, as the waters within turned foul and black.

She backed away, clutching her head. The back of her legs struck something. She turned. An immense wooden effigy, carved in the likeness of the Rattlebone Prince, stared down at her with empty eyes. As a child, she had prayed to Nagash, begging him for the strength to aid her people in battle. When she made the bones dance for the first time, she'd thought that he had answered her, that he'd blessed her. But where was he now? Where was the Undying King when his people needed him?

Tamra, her brother said. *Go.* Thunder rumbled overhead, as if in agreement.

'No. I will not leave you.' She flung out a hand, trying to summon the strength for another spell. 'I will...' She trailed off as a hush fell. The pox-worshippers had broken off their attack as they spilled into the courtyard, holding back, as if in readiness for something. 'What are they doing?'

Waiting, Sarpa said.

Tamra did not ask for what. She did not have to. She could feel what was coming easily enough. The flats of rusty axes thudded wetly against pustule-marked shields, and the droning song of the pox-worshippers rose in tempo. Their ranks split like a wound, disgorging a rotund shape, clad in foul robes. The newcomer waddled towards the dead, a leering grin stretched across his pallid features. Toadstools sprouted in his wake, pushing through the yellowing snow, and a cloud of flies swirled about his head like a halo.

Tamra could taste the fell magic seeping from him. A sorcerer. The same who had set the palisades alight and burnt the forests black.

'Well. Well, well, well. What have we here?' His voice was like mud striking the bottom of a bucket, and he flashed rotten teeth in a genial smile. 'Dead men walking.' He sniffed and looked around. 'This is the place for it, I suppose.'

He gestured, and a pox-worshipper limped forwards, cradling a grotesque banner in the crook of one bandaged arm. The creature set the banner upright. Plague-bells dangled from a daemonic visage wrought in iron. A pale liquid sweated from the face and pattered to the ground, causing virulent wisps of smoke to rise from the churned snow.

'I, Tulg, claim this place in the name of the Most Suppurating and Blightsome Order of the Fly,' the sorcerer said. He gesticulated grandly. 'Be joyful, for life returns to these dead realms.'

'This place is not yours to claim,' Tamra said loudly. Loose snow whipped about, as the storm grew in intensity overhead. Thunder rumbled. The crackle of the plague-fires was omnipresent. Somewhere, a hunting horn blew. She tried to shut out the noise, to focus on the enemy before her. If she could kill him, the foe might flee. Her people might yet be saved or, at the very least, avenged.

'Is it not? We seem to be doing a fine job, regardless.' The sorcerer looked around. 'I see no defenders of merit. Only old bones and a scrawny woman. If that is the best you savages can muster, our crusade will be easier than Blightmaster Wolgus claimed...'

'Kill him,' Tamra said. The dead surged forwards, their fleshless frames lent vigour by her will and fury. The sorcerer laughed and swept out his hands. Plague-fire consumed the remaining skeletons, one after the other. She staggered as their soulfire ebbed and her spells were torn asunder. The ache in her head grew worse, and she clutched at her scalp.

Back, sister. Sarpa shoved her aside as a claw of green flame swept down and he thrust up his shield to meet it. For a moment, he held it at bay, but the flames writhed around the edges of the shield and the bronze began to corrode. It blackened and sloughed away, and the flames poured down, engulfing her brother. He sank to one knee, his spirit groaning in her head. *Tamra... sister... run...*

Lightning flashed, searing the night. She heard the sorcerer utter a startled oath, and she screamed as her brother's soul was snatched away from her flagging grip. Smoke billowed, filling the courtyard. Coughing, she sank back against the statue of Nagash.

'I beg you help me,' she said, staring up at the effigy. 'Heed me, Undying King. Heed your servant in this, her hour of need. Help your people...' Her voice cracked and she slumped against the statue. Tears froze on her cheeks. 'Help us.' She saw the blackened hilt of Sarpa's barrowblade and snatched it up. As she lifted it in both hands, it crackled with the fading sting of lightning and burnt her palms.

'I do not know what sort of sorcery that was, but lightning or no, it will avail you nothing,' the sorcerer said, as he waved the smoke aside. 'I think I will chain you to my master's palanquin, corpse-eater. Or what's left of you. You do not need your arms or legs to stump along, awkward though it may be.' He coughed. 'And your scalp will look fine hanging from the banners of the Order of the Fly.' He clapped his pudgy hands together gleefully. 'So... arms, legs and hair. In that order, I think.'

'Come and take them, if you can,' Tamra said, forcing herself upright. Grief sat like a lead weight in her chest, along with not a little fear. Her brother was gone. But she was a daughter of the Drak, and death was to be embraced. She extended Sarpa's blade. She heard the winding of a hunting horn again, closer this time.

The sorcerer chortled and advanced, green fire dripping from his crooked fingers. 'Maybe I'll burn your tongue out as well. You seem like the type to curse overmuch.' The pox-flames flared bright and began to swell around him. As they did so, a shadow fell over him, and he glanced up, eyes widening. 'What–'

A flash of red and black descended. The ground shook, the flames were snuffed and the sorcerer vanished, his body abruptly pulped beneath the curving talons of the monstrosity which now crouched between Tamra and her foes. A long, whip-like tail of vertebral segments lashed with feline agitation as fleshless jaws sagged, exhaling a cloud of masticated spirits. The wailing spirits swirled about the beast, bound to its creaking bones by some fell sorcery. The blightkings drew back from the dread abyssal as it pawed at the snow, fastidiously scraping what was left of the sorcerer from its claws.

Its rider leaned forwards in her saddle, a mocking expression on her youthful face. She was beautiful, Tamra thought, though it was a deadly kind of beauty, like that of a fine blade. She wore black armour, studded with bones, and a tall headdress, in the fashion of the ancient kingdoms of the Great Dust Sea. Her exposed arms were the colour of marble, and her lips were blood red. Her eyes shone like those of a great mountain cat caught in the torchlight.

'Did we interrupt? My apologies – Nagadron grew impatient.' The rider's pale hand stroked the black iron bones of the dread abyssal's neck. At her touch, the monster stiffened and uttered a piercing shriek. 'I am Neferata, the Queen of Blood and Mistress of the Barrowdwell. And you... well, it doesn't really matter, does it?' Her thin lips stretched in a feral smile as she drew a long curved blade from a sheath on her saddle. 'After all, you'll be dead soon.'

The dread abyssal surged forwards, limbs clicking like the

workings of some great mechanism. Neferata leaned low, and at her gesture, the bound spirits boiled forwards. They rolled over the blightkings and their mortal followers like a malignant bank of fog. Spectral claws and blades separated heads from shoulders and spilled intestines into the snow. The blightkings tried in vain to strike back at their unearthly foes, but their blows chopped harmlessly through the smoky forms.

Nagadron slammed full tilt into the distracted blightkings, and Neferata's sword flickered out, capitalising on the damage done by her spectral warriors. She gave a shriek of laughter as the dread abyssal bore a bloated warrior down and bit off his head. An arcane bolt sizzled from her palm and zigzagged through the ranks of pox-worshippers, reducing them to smoking husks. As the slaughter progressed, Tamra heard the hunting horn once more, louder than ever, and felt the ground tremble beneath her feet.

The blightkings broke as Neferata savaged a path through their ranks, and they began to spill back towards the archway, seeking safety. But there was none to be had. A column of armoured riders astride coal-black horses speared through the archway and into the disorganized rabble. The newcomers wore black armour, and their pale feminine faces glared out from within baroque helms as they lashed out at the foe. They pierced the enemy ranks like a blade and the column split in two, encircling the pox-worshippers. The carnage which followed was brief and cruel. When the last of the blightkings lay dissolving in his own juices, Neferata turned her monstrous steed back towards Tamra. As she passed by it, she uprooted the plague-banner and tossed it aside. 'You are welcome,' she said, looking down at Tamra.

'Thank you, great lady,' Tamra stuttered. She had heard stories of the being known among the Rictus Clans as the Great

Lady of Sorrows, but seeing her in the flesh was something else entirely. The vampire radiated a terrible strength, as if her lithe shape were but a mask, hiding something infinitely more monstrous within. Eyes like agates bored into her own, and she felt as if her mind and soul were being peeled back bit by bit.

'You are of the Drak?' Neferata said. She gestured to her face. 'You have that look, something about the jaw.'

Tamra sank down to one knee, leaning against her brother's sword. 'Yes, O Queen of Blood. I am Tamra ven-Drak, voivode of these lands.' She looked up. 'Or I was.'

'Yes. You look a bit like dearest Isa. The eyes, I think.'

Tamra hesitated. Queen Isa ven-Drak had been dead for centuries, and her bones long since dust scattered on the wind. Neferata turned away as one of the black riders trotted towards her. 'The rest of our blightsome friends?' she asked.

'Scattered, my lady,' the vampire said as she removed her helmet. 'Or impaled, for those who follow to find.' She had been beautiful, once, and still was, if you ignored the hunger in her eyes and the stains of old gore streaking her ornately crafted war-plate.

'Ah, Adhema, your little jokes will be the death of you, I fear.'

'But not today, mistress.'

'No, not today. Today the Sisterhood of Szandor has won a great victory,' Neferata said. She looked back at Tamra. 'Where are your people? Some survived, I assume.'

'Fled into the crags and hollows,' Tamra said. She rose at Neferata's gesture. 'Where it is safe, my lady.'

Adhema snorted. 'There is no safety. Not here or anywhere else.'

'No. But perhaps we might make such a place.' Neferata raised Tamra's chin with the tip of her sword. 'Call your people back. They must go north, to the shores of the Rictus Sea, to the great redoubt there. You know it?'

'I... yes. Is-is this the word of Nagash? Has he returned? Is he to lead us in battle once more?' Tamra couldn't stop the questions from spilling out.

'Nagash?' Neferata said, looking down at her. She leaned over and spat in the direction of the effigy. 'That is for Nagash. And good riddance to him.'

Tamra watched the gobbet of crimson spittle slide down the statue's cheek. 'Where is he?' she asked, softly.

'Not here, sister,' Neferata said. 'I fear we have only ourselves to look to, in the dark days to come.' She gave a mocking smile. 'And what a relief it is.'

TWO

THE UNDYING KING

The Corpse Geometries are awry.
Their night-black formulae is rendered powerless by the madness of ruinous gods.
Order has been cast down, and Chaos reigns.
My kingdom shudders beneath a terrible lunacy, unfettered and ever changing.
But I still endure.
I will ever endure.

– *The Epistle of Bone*

On a basalt throne, far below the reach of any light, a vast figure stirred. A great hand, shrouded in a battle-marked gauntlet, reached up to touch a fleshless cheek as if to brush away some irritant. Immense bones, blackened by fire and scarred by blades, creaked in their housings as a massive head tilted upwards. Light flared deep within abyssal sockets, as consciousness returned. The Undying King awoke. Something had disturbed his slumber. A voice, calling his name, somewhere out in the dark.

No. Not one. Many. A thousand, a million. A storm of voices, crying out for him who had made himself a god; crying out for the Rattlebone Prince, the Great Necromancer... crying out for Nagash. And Nagash could not answer, for he lacked the strength.

A hollow laugh slipped from between tombstone teeth. This, then, was the true price for wresting divinity from the claws of fate: to hear, to see, and be unable to act. His mind shied away from the deluge of prayers, focusing instead on the one which had caused him to stir.

He cast his gaze about his empty throne room. Great pillars, made from the bones of entire generations, stretched upwards into the silent dark. Mosaics of onyx and amethyst lined the floors and walls, depicting his victories over the old gods of the underworld during the Age of Myth. So many victories. And one singular, inescapable defeat.

Now, spiders crept across his frame, spinning their webs between his ribs and over his eyes. Worms squirmed in the hollows of his bones. He snuffed out their lives with barely a thought and drew their deaths into him. It was not enough. Unfulfilled, he reached out and caught up one of the ghosts which clustered about his throne. The spirit struggled in his grip and came apart like a morning mist, flowing into the nooks and crannies of his form as Nagash devoured its soul-fire. Somewhat reinvigorated, his attentions turned outwards, following the voice which had awakened him.

Nine heavy tomes, each the size of a man and containing the accumulated wisdom of aeons, rose up around him, their heavy chains rattling loudly. The flabby pages of the books flapped with a sound like thunder as the Undying King hurled his fell spirit upwards, through the tangled caverns of Stygxx and the shadow-haunted palaces of the Amethyst Princes. Mile by mile, his consciousness crawled upwards, pulling itself along like a choking fog through the minds and husks of the dead which inhabited the underworld. In hidden redoubts and outposts, deadwalkers stiffened as Nagash's awareness suddenly occupied their rotting frames, if only for an instant.

His consciousness rode a flock of bats out of the lightless caverns, swirling up into the bloody skies. And then he was striding the night wind, bodiless and unseen. He crossed the brackish waters of the Sour Sea in the blink of an eye, and he raced above the great indigo veldts of Anku-Wat in the fleshless skull of a dire wolf. But no matter how far he travelled, or in what direction, the scenery was always the same – war, unending and all-consuming.

The armies of the Everchosen marched on the manses of the dead, and there was little Nagash could do save watch through the eyes of his servants and remember. He walked the fire-shrouded streets of Sepulchre as a shadow, and he saw the great tapestries of ghost-silk burn in flames of azure and cerise. In Morrsend, he watched through the poached eyes of a cooling corpse as a coven of soulblight vampires defended the living against the ferocity of the Blood God's worshippers, and were consumed by their own bloodlust.

Wrathful now, he roared silent curses as Crypslough stirred from its enforced slumber in the silent tombs of Yyr and shrugged off its chains. The zombie dragon, first and greatest of its kind, slid into the sky with a single beat of its ragged wings. It was not alone in its escape from Nagash's bindings. The black shape of the Syrnok Spinebat, huge and loathsome, emerged from the craters of the Wraith Moons, free to hunt the star fields anew. And everywhere, the gateways to long-sealed underworlds cracked wide and wept malignant spirits.

All that he'd built was beginning to crumble. The delicate precision of the Corpse Geometries had unravelled, and order overturned by chaos. Souls were spewed free and unbound into the skies, loosed from battlefields that had become monstrous abscesses of necromantic energy. The untended dead roamed in vast, ever-increasing hordes, endangering all who crossed their path. Those he had once counted as servants sought to carve out fiefdoms of their own from the carcass of his once realm-spanning empire. And all because of–

'Sigmar!'

Nagash turned. Burning towers stretched up towards the sky, casting a hazy radiance over the waters of the Bitter Sea. With but a thought, he was there, standing amidst the smoke and carnage, watching through the hundredfold eyes of the newly slain. He knew this city: Helstone. Its rulers had bended the knee to him, though they did not worship him. A proud people, mighty in war and cunning in trade. But not anymore. Now they were burning and dying, as the lords of Chaos ran rampant through the Ninety-Nine Circles. Nagash felt a flicker of satisfaction; perhaps if they had prayed to him instead, it might not have come to this.

'Sigmar!' the voice cried again. A prayer, perhaps, or a curse. Curious, the Undying King followed it, striding from body to body. Atop a crumbling tower, he found the speaker, and more besides. The one who cried out was a prince of the city, clad in iron and silks, fighting to hold a terraced tower. But there was another with him: Mannfred von Carstein, last prince of a forgotten kingdom. As ever, he glowed with spite and stank of ambition.

How many times had he chastised the Mortarch of Shadow for some scheme or other? He'd lost count. There was a certain joy to be had in conjuring new punishments for so deserving a creature, though he could not recall what the first had been, or the reason behind it. It did not matter. If Mannfred survived, there would be more betrayals and more punishments. It was his nature. As sure as death itself, Mannfred would always seek his own advantage. Such relentless drive was almost admirable, in its way.

Nagash watched as the vampire hacked down one roaring blood warrior after the next, fighting alongside his mortal ally with frantic courage. The tower creaked on its foundations, and the ancient stones burst as daemons and mortals alike scrambled up its sides. The mortarch fought back to back with the Helstone prince as red-skinned bloodletters loped towards them. Nagash turned away from the desperate conflict, his attention caught by another voice. A familiar one this time, not raised in prayer, but in invocation.

He left Mannfred to his fate and followed the voice across the vast mountains of the north, into the shattered ruins of the six kingdoms of Rictus, to the shores of the Shivering Sea. He remembered these lands, if only dimly. He had waged a war here, one of many. Those who should have been thankful for their status had instead used it to strike at him. Six kings of old, steeped in the arts he had dredged up from the deep wells of the underworld, had set themselves in opposition to fate. For six days and six nights, Nagash had fought and utterly destroyed the armies arrayed against him. And on the sixth day, he had taken the lives and souls of the kings, reducing them to blighted husks.

He had interred what remained of them in the crags overlooking the Shivering Sea, sealing their damned souls away within the rock until such time as he judged them suitably chastened. But the bindings he had looped about them had begun to grow weaker with every passing year since his defeat. Even now, he could sense the Broken Kings, rattling the bars of their cages and crying out for release.

As he passed over the great ice-rimed forests and snow-capped crags, the sky was riven by fire and storm. Lightning flashed, bringing with it the stink of the heavens. Was Sigmar watching, sealed away in his pitiful realm? Nagash hoped so. It was his dearest wish that the barbarian should be made to endure every torment inflicted upon Shyish thanks to his treachery. When he had become whole once more, Nagash would storm the gates of Azyr and drag the barbarian from his throne. He would cast him down. Aye, and Archaon with him.

All creation would bow before Nagash. All would be one, in Nagash. All would be well, because Nagash so commanded, and to defy Nagash was to defy death itself. And no living man or god could defy death. Not for long.

Far below, refugees struggled through waist-high snows, forging a path through the dark heart of the forests. The Rictus Lands had once been heavily populated, despite the harsh conditions. Now, plague and war had decimated the once-proud clans, reducing them to scattered bands, fleeing ever northwards towards the sea. He felt no sympathy for their plight. Had not their ancestors betrayed him? Had they not defied him? And yet, they were his – his to punish, or raise up, as it pleased him. They were his, like all those who dwelled in the Mortal Realms were, sooner or later. He would not countenance either their destruction or salvation in any name but his own.

Following close on their heels came the invaders, a motley column of despoilers stretching for countless miles, across fjords and floes, through forest and fen. No single army this, but several, joined beneath a solitary, flyblown banner. It resembled nothing so much as a wave of gangrene creeping across a shattered limb.

Rotbringers. The servants of the Plague God, usurpers of life and death both. In their wake, the natural order was undone. The snows melted, the barren scrub flourished with hateful life and the icy rivers became turgid with filth. Where they passed, the forest began to warp. The trees sprouted unnatural growths, or else sickened and died before crumbling to stinking mulch. Stones split to reveal slobbering mouths which panted hymns to the Lord of Decay, and the beasts of the crags shed their fur for coats of mould and scaly scabs.

A howl went up from the flanks of the monstrous column. The cyclopean plaguebearers and beasts of Nurgle who trudged alongside the mortal warriors had caught a glimpse of his spirit as it observed them. They could not truly see him, for he was far beyond the limits of their perception, but like all animals, they knew when a predator was near, and they brayed their fear to the skies. The mortal rotbringers would not understand. Not yet. But he would teach them.

He pressed on, hurtling through skull and skin, dragging himself along a chain of carrion birds and the bodies they fed on. As he neared the Shivering Sea, the voice which had called to him became clearer. Familiar.

'Master, I bid thee to appear. Your servant would speak with thee.'

The frozen sea was full of the dead and the things which feasted on them. A million bodies hung unmoving in a web of shattered ice-cutter galleys and trading vessels which stretched beneath the surface for miles in every direction. They had all perished at once, and suddenly. This had been the price of defiance. To defy death was to welcome it, to beg for it.

'Master, I feel you near. I humbly beg an audience with thee.'

The voice was insistent, yet respectful. Measured. Nagash rose upwards, climbing a ladder of the sunken dead, passing like a cloud of silt through thickets of broken spars and shattered masts. The thoughts of the Broken Kings scratched like mice at the underside of his awareness as he breached the surface.

Entreaties, implorations and demands swirled up through the bore holes of his mind. Even after so long, they had not learned their place. Or perhaps his current state had led them to grow bold in their confinement. He banished their voices with a twitch of his consciousness, and turned his attentions to the speck at his feet.

'Speak, my servant. Speak, my mortarch.'

Arkhan the Black, Mortarch of Sacrament, stood on the icy surface of the Shivering Sea and gazed up at the colossal horror which loomed over him. Nagash, the monster he had served for a millennia – and likely would for many millennia more – had appeared suddenly, like a strike of black lightning, streaking down from weeping skies.

The Undying King was impossibly vast, his towering form surrounded by a flickering corona which changed hues, ever shifting from green to black to purple and back again with painful rapidity. His shape had issued like smoke from the cracked ice, and it wavered in the cold wind which whipped across the sea.

An army of moaning spirits, the courtiers of Stygxx, swirled about Nagash, drawn helplessly into his hellish orbit. They blended together and broke apart in a woeful dance of agony. The wide skull, lit by its own internal flame, gazed down at Arkhan.

'My lord, you look... well,' Arkhan said. It was a lie. The Undying King's great skull was cleft from crown to jaw, and his armoured form was battered and twisted. Bones were broken, sections of armour missing, and a sickly radiance poured from a hundred wounds.

'Speak,' Nagash repeated. Ragged spirits squirmed from his maw as he spoke, joining those which swirled madly about him. Behind Arkhan, the crouched shape of his dread abyssal, Razarak, stirred. The creature scented the soul-stuff leaking from Nagash and growled hungrily.

'I crave a boon, O Undying King,' Arkhan said, gesturing for his steed to be still.

'There is an army coming,' Nagash said. The thunder of his voice made the ice beneath Arkhan's feet crack and shift.

Arkhan nodded, pleased by his master's apparent lucidity. It was a rare enough thing, these days. 'There are always armies, my lord. Grist for the mill, as you used to say.'

'Yes. They creep across my bones like maggots. I can feel them. I wish them gone, Arkhan. I wish all of it... gone.'

Arkhan paused, trying to parse the meaning to that statement. 'The forces of Chaos have no intention of leaving, I fear. They have come to stay. And your realm suffers for it. We must drive them from this place.'

Nagash said nothing for long moments. Then, he said, 'Do you know what "Nagash" means, my servant? It means absence. Nothing. Null. I am nothing, and yet I am everything. I am the end of all things, and the long night which follows the setting of the last sun.'

'So you have said, master.'

Nagash spread his long arms, as if to encompass the horizon. 'What is Chaos to me? It is nothing. As the fire is nothing to the cold which follows the snuffing of the final ember.'

Arkhan nodded sagely, as if he hadn't heard the same speech a hundred times before. Or some variation of it, at least. Nagash often liked to pontificate on the theme of power, and his memory was not what it once had been. His speeches were rote and almost ritualistic. 'But that ember must be snuffed all the same, my master.'

'And so it shall be. Chaos will devour itself. It must. Chaos is fire, and fire is not eternal. Only the cold is eternal. Only the dark. Only Nagash.' The looming shadow lowered its arms. It wavered, pierced through by falling snow and the bruise-coloured light of the setting sun.

'And what of your servants, my lord? What of those who seek only to serve you?'

'My servants? What are servants but extensions of my will? Your thoughts are my thoughts, your voice is my voice. You are but a shadow of a memory, given form and power by my will. Rejoice, Arkhan, for the burden of your destiny is not your own.'

This too was a variation on a very old theme, and Arkhan bore it as stoically as ever. More than once, over the centuries, he had considered rebellion. And more than once, he had discarded the idea as quickly as it had come. How does one rebel against a god? The answer, given all available evidence, was badly. 'As you say, my master.'

'A part of me desires only silence, to snuff out the light and let the dark rush in and fill the void which was once Shyish. Let the Three-Eyed King fight such an unravelling, if he would. I care not.'

Arkhan waited, but Nagash had fallen silent. He often did these days, no doubt lost in his own memories and the manifold perceptions of his fragmented consciousness. Finally, Arkhan said, 'And yet, we are still here, master. You have not snuffed out the light.'

Nagash looked down at him, as if only just recalling his presence. 'I have not. Why did you call me here, my servant?'

'A door to Stygxx forms beneath the sea, master. A gate to your redoubt. The enemy is coming here to take it. If they succeed, they will flood the underworld with their filth. I seek to thwart them.'

The Nine Gates to Stygxx were born anew every nine months, and they grew, aged and died in the same span, crumbling to dust before appearing elsewhere in an endless cycle of death and rebirth. That is why the Dark Gods had yet to find Nagash, for none could predict where and when the Nine Gates would open. That fickleness was one of the reasons Stygxx alone had remained inviolate, while the rest of Shyish shuddered in turmoil.

The other reason was Nagash himself. Of all the servants of the Ruinous Powers, only Archaon possessed the fortitude to face the Undying King in open battle. And Archaon was wise enough to resist the temptation to challenge Nagash – even weakened as he was – in the underworld. But others lacked such wisdom. Scenting blood, the scavengers sought the gates, and entrance to the underworld. When one was found, the slaves of darkness soon raced for it, each seeking to be the first to breach it in the name of their abominable patrons.

'And will you do so alone?' Nagash asked. He sounded almost amused.

Arkhan hesitated. 'Neferata is here. We will defy the foe in your name.'

Nagash's attentions began to wander. 'I saw Mannfred. He defies them as well, elsewhere. Alongside the living,' he intoned absently.

'Living or dead, all who call Shyish home serve you,' Arkhan said smoothly. 'All fight in your name.' Even if they were treacherous jackals like Mannfred von Carstein.

'A lie. Some worship falsehood, and deny the truth of my divinity. But they will know, soon enough. Soon...' The great shadow tensed as a ripple of something passed through it. Pain, perhaps, or anger. For Nagash, they were often one and the same, as well as constant. Arkhan studied the shadow the way a sailor might look to the sea, in an effort to determine how dangerous the next few moments were going to be.

'Soon, master,' Arkhan agreed.

The shadow twitched. The lamp-like eyes rolled away, staring out over the sea towards the indistinct horizon. 'Soon, I shall reach into the sky and close my fist about the stars. I will snuff the fire, one ember at a time. But not now. Not yet.' Nagash turned back. 'There is an army coming.'

'Yes, master. So you said.'

'What would you have of me, my servant?' Nagash stared down at him. 'You called, and I have come. Speak.'

'I ask that you aid us in this battle.' Arkhan lifted his staff. 'Bestir thyself, master, and show the foe what it means to challenge the Undying King in his place of power.'

Nagash said nothing. His form wavered and became a ragged, writhing morass. Then the titan shape dissolved into a flock of shadowy carrion birds, which sped away in all directions, screeching. Arkhan lowered his staff with a sigh. Only time would tell whether Nagash had understood. Nearly a century of having something close to the same conversation almost every day was beginning to wear on him. The Battle of Black Skies had broken Nagash in more than just body, and what was left of him raged anew each day, as stuttering fragments of memory coalesced briefly before flying apart once more.

Even now he was a hole in the world, an absence of heat, light and life given voice. More a force of nature than a god, he still possessed his share of foibles. Nagash had been something less once, and he was determined never to be that again. As such, he did not cope well with defeat. He could not conceive of it, and floundered in its wake.

Once, that would not have been the case. Arkhan could not say how he knew this, but he did. Once, Nagash had understood subtlety and the ways of guile. He had thought as a mortal thought, and persevered as only mortals could. But somewhere along the way, he'd forgotten. He'd become something else: a vast, irresistible force. Implacable and yet, as evidenced by his current state, all too fragile.

And now he was mad as well. Perhaps he hadn't always been so, but he was now. A mad god, gnawing his own vitals, trapped in a single moment of defeat and unable to move past it. That was Archaon's true victory. With one blow, the Three-Eyed King had undone all that Nagash had come to believe himself to be, and reduced him to but a ranting shadow.

It was only temporary. For all intents and purposes, Nagash was eternal. While Shyish endured, so too would Nagash. Destruction brought only rebirth. And a wounding, such as this, was only a delay at best. Nagash would recover, but it would be slow, and he would lose a bit more of himself in the process. In time, the Undying King might even ascend to the abstract and become one with the charnel mathematics of the Corpse Geometries.

Arkhan knew this as surely as he knew his own name. At times, he thought that he was not merely Nagash's servant, but was instead all those pieces of him which had been shed in his ascent to godhood. He was the mirror image of his master, and a reminder. For as Nagash became less an individual and more a force, so too did Arkhan become the reverse. 'And little enough profit has it brought me,' he said.

'Still talking to yourself, I see.'

'It is the only way I can converse with an equal. Hello, Neferata.' Arkhan turned. The Mortarch of Blood approached boldly across the ice, her dread abyssal pacing in her wake. His own steed growled softly in challenge. Like their masters, the dread abyssals did not get along. He laid a bony hand across Razarak's snout, calming the creature.

'Hello, Arkhan. I have gathered more survivors. The last of the Rictus Clans are arriving at the redoubt now. Those who have survived this long, at any rate.'

'And those who have not?'

She smiled, displaying a single, delicate fang. 'They're busy elsewhere.' She made an elegant gesture. 'I saw the shadow, and the carrion birds. Has he woken up again, our master?'

'He has.'

'More's the pity. This would be easier without him, I think.' Neferata looked up. 'What did he say?'

'There is an army on the way.' Arkhan looked at her. Once, he might have considered her beautiful. Perhaps part of him still did. But it was an icy beauty, inhuman and dangerous and, ultimately, untrustworthy. Neferata served only herself in this, as in all things.

She laughed. 'Well then, we should prepare a proper greeting, don't you think?'

THREE

POX-CRUSADE

The Three-Eyed King calls himself Godslayer.
His daemon-blade shattered my bones.
My rites and magics were torn asunder.
My body was left to the dust, and to the dust I returned.
But I stir once more.
I am death, and I contain multitudes.
Listen.
Believe.
I am death, and all are one in me.

– *The Epistle of Bone*

The blizzard had come up suddenly. The air was thick with snow, and for the third time in as many days, Festerbite wished he'd stayed in the Jade Kingdoms. At least it had been warm there, even if the trees did try to kill you every so often. His steed whickered harshly, snapping at the persistent flakes in irritation.

'Waste of effort, Scab,' Festerbite said. 'Save it for the flesh of our foes.' The horse-thing grumbled, and redoubled its efforts to take a bite out of the blizzard.

Hunched over in his saddle, snow pattering against the rust-rimmed holes in his helm, Festerbite whistled a mournful dirge. It did little to cheer him up. His mouth ached in that old familiar way. A new fang was coming in. He reached up under his helmet and scratched at the blistered bone of his lower jaw. The flesh had long since rotted away, and a thicket of yellow, glistening fangs emerged at random points from his jawbone.

Still scratching, he looked around. Shyish was an unpleasant realm, and this region of it doubly so. It was all ice and snow. Everything was either frozen or hard, or sometimes frozen hard. And it was far too quiet. In the Jade Kingdoms, the air throbbed with bird song and the hum of insect life. Here, the only sounds to be heard were the phlegm-choked laughter of his fellow knights, the clangour of plague-bells and the droning hymns of the faithful.

Nonetheless, it was an honour to be here. Blightmaster Wolgus had chosen Sir Festerbite from amongst the teeming hundreds who served the Most Suppurating and Blightsome Order of the Fly to be his second in command for this expedition. There were more experienced knights with greater glories to their names, but Wolgus – Hero of the Pallas Ghyredes, Breaker of the Cobalt Bastion – had chosen him, had asked *him* to ride with the pox-crusade and bring the fire of life to the cold lands of the dead.

Festerbite, eager for glories of his own, had not been able to say no. One could not deny the request of such a hero. Of the seven chosen blightmasters of the Order, those ordained by the Lady of Cankerwall herself, Wolgus was the youngest and the most energetic. He had carved out new territories for the Order in the wilds of Ghyran and Chamon, and he had matched wits and blades with the enemies of Nurgle wherever they might be found. It was Wolgus who had slain the Tzeentchian champion

Gog of the Twelve Tongues, and Wolgus who had broken the enemy's lines at the Black Cistern. And it would be Wolgus who led the Order to victory here, in these cold, dry lands. How could he fail, with such an army at his back?

The column, which comprised the main thrust of the pox-crusade, stretched both behind and ahead of Festerbite. Thousands had flocked to join this holy undertaking. Some were mortal; many were not. Most were capering zealots, clad in tattered robes and bearing the mark of the fly on whatever scraps of armour they had been able to scavenge. They beat drums and rang bells with carnival exuberance as they trudged through the snow in disorderly mobs.

Others were of a more professional disposition, dressed in hauberks made from toad-dragon hide and carrying wide iron-rimmed shields as well as festering blades and spears. These were the chosen armsmen of the Order, drawn from the blighted levies of Festerfane and Cankerwall, as well as from the smaller demesnes which sheltered beneath the aegis of the Order. They marched in orderly formation behind the steeds of their masters, chanting in low, steady voices.

Festerbite's fellow knights, all chosen by Wolgus as Festerbite had been, were towering brutes, clad in the thick maggoty war-plate of their Order. They wore mouldy tabards displaying the sign of the fly. Each of them had quested for and tasted the sour syrup of the Flyblown Chalice, delivered to their lips by the Lady of Cankerwall herself. They had taken the seven times seventy-seven oaths to the King of All Flies, and now rode for the glory and honour of Nurgle. Most sat astride bulky steeds like Festerbite's own, but some marched in the ranks, leading bands of putrid blightkings or brawling beastkin. Mounted or not, all were true knights, intrepid and bold.

The firstborn children of the Lord of All Things lurched,

squirmed and lumbered into battle alongside his mortal followers. Droning songs of war rose up from the squelching ranks of plaguebearers, accompanied by the buzzing of a million fat-bodied flies. Beneath their cloven hooves, snow melted and soil became vibrant with virulent hues. What little plant life there was beneath the frost bulged obscenely, roots thick with wormy pus. An invigorating miasma spread outward from the column, giving the land a more civilised texture.

A groan caught Festerbite's ear and he turned. One of the mad monks had collapsed, body black with cold. Festerbite turned his steed and urged it towards the fallen warrior, as the mortal twitched in his death throes. Sturdy as the servants of the Order were, this harsh realm was a fiercer enemy than many were prepared for. The trail of this pox-crusade was littered with the bodies of the faithful. The conditions claimed numerous lives, but there were other dangers aplenty in these unhallowed lands. The Order had faced deadwalkers, wrathful spirits and horrors without name since first crossing the Bridge of Scabs and breaching the Ithilian Gate.

As Festerbite drew close, several of the dying man's companions hunkered over the body, sawing at the flesh with rusty blades. Food was in short supply, and most had to make do when and with what they could. The mortal rotbringers were under a constant threat of starvation, and they had resorted to eating the weak when their supplies got too low.

'Leave him, you cackling jackals,' Festerbite barked, leaning over to slap a rotbringer with the back of his hand. The creature spun, diseased features twisted in a snarl. Festerbite's steed whinnied and snapped its teeth together inches from what was left of the pox-worshipper's nose. The robed pilgrim ducked away, bandaged hands lifted in acquiescence. 'Are you Bloodbound, to so greedily sup at a brother's flesh?' Festerbite demanded, before relenting slightly. 'Let him lie, so that his body might fertilise this parched soil, but take his weapons and armour if you must. No reason to let those go to waste.'

'Thank you, great one,' the leprous pilgrim gurgled, as he and his fellows fell to stripping the body. Festerbite watched them for a moment, and then wheeled his steed around.

'And thank you, Scab,' he murmured, patting the horse-thing's neck. Scab hissed and snapped good-naturedly at his hand. Festerbite dropped a fist between his daemonic steed's ragged ears. 'None of that now.' He twisted in his saddle as something caught his eye. He nudged Scab in the ribs and the horse-thing clopped away from the column.

A pole jutted from the icy ground like a grave marker. The weathered wood was slick with frozen blood, along with less savoury liquids. It stood upright in the snow, surrounded by heaps of shattered armour and broken weapons. Heads decorated the hollows carved into the pole's length. The cold had mummified these grisly remnants, reducing the flesh to little more than parchment stretched tight over bone. Some still wore helmets or tarnished circlets of office. There were brass horns twisted into the rune of Khorne, and the bird-shaped helms favoured by Tzeentch's chosen cat's paws. Whatever their origin, all were lit by an internal fire, visible through their eye sockets. And all still spoke.

A hundred voices, whispering softly, their words lost in the relentless moan of the storm. Festerbite found himself straining to listen, wondering what they had to say. Would they curse him, or were they trying to warn him? He nudged Scab closer. The horse-thing resisted at first, but a brutal thump of his heels inclined it to his way of thinking.

He drew close to the pole, one hand on the hilt of his rotsword. Behind him, the column trudged on. He leaned forwards, peering into the softly glowing eyes of what had once been a blood warrior. The Khornate killer had not died easily, to judge by the marks which decorated his skull. Broken teeth clicked in a twitching jaw as whatever force animated the skull continued to speak. Festerbite shifted in his saddle, trying to hear.

I... see... you!

He jerked back, eyes narrowing. Snow crunched beneath clumsy feet, somewhere just out of sight. Scab pawed the ground restlessly and whickered in discontent. Festerbite sniffed, suddenly aware of an all too familiar odour. With a curse, he jerked Scab's reins and turned back towards the column. Scab needed no urging to break into a gallop.

'Deadwalkers!' Festerbite roared, as he yanked on his mount's reins. 'Ware the flanks!' Behind him, the hungry dead staggered out of the swirling snow, a tide of rancid flesh and grasping claws. They spilled unsteadily towards the column. Arrows hiss-cracked into putrefying skulls and were left sprouting from crooked backs, but the dead swarmed onwards. It wasn't the first time the column had been attacked by the wandering dead, but their numbers increased with every assault.

'Sling your bows, fools – this is butcher's work,' Festerbite said, urging his steed back down the line. 'Molov, bring your axemen. Think of them as trees.' Around him, the column was falling into a battle line with practised speed. Spears rattled down, forming an improvised barricade. Zombies weren't that dangerous, if you could keep them at a distance.

'Trees don't bite,' Molov burbled. The blightking's antlered helm seeped noxious juices, which dripped down and turned the snow to pus as he led his obese god-blessed warriors through the ranks of the faithful, shoving aside the more fragile mortals. The putrid blightkings were bloated with the favours of Nurgle, their bodies swollen with holy corruption. They were slabs of fat and muscle bound in straining skin and armoured in rust-pitted war-plate.

'They do in the Jade Kingdoms,' Festerbite said. 'If it's any consolation, these shamblers smell a sight better than those piles of walking kindling. Make a prettier fire as well. Now shut your mouths, lift your axes and follow me.' He kicked his steed into motion. The horse-thing shrieked eagerly as its blistered hooves tore the earth. Molov and the other blightkings began to drone a hymn of war as they followed at a ponderous lope.

Festerbite drew his rotsword as he drew near to the closest of the deadwalkers, and removed its head with a single slash. That didn't stop it, of course. Bravado aside, the shambling dead were more dangerous than they looked. There were hundreds of them, more than enough to swamp the column and even shatter it, if Grandfather Nurgle chose not to favour them.

He pushed the thought aside and concentrated on hewing at the grasping corpses as they pressed close about him. His steed shrilled a challenge and reared, pulping skulls with its hooves and trampling the fallen into mush. 'That's the way, Scab,' Festerbite said, as he lopped off a rotting talon. 'Make them mulch for Grandfather's garden. For the glory of the Order of the Fly!'

But as he fought, a great shadow seemed to spread over the corpses, filling their shrunken limbs with strength. They attacked with renewed ferocity, and Festerbite felt a sudden thrill of fear. It had been so long since he'd felt such a thing that it took him by surprise. He hesitated, and paid the price. Rotting fingers clawed at his steed, tearing gobbets from the horse-thing's unnatural flesh. It screeched in pain and reared, hurling him from the saddle.

Festerbite fell heavily to the ground. His steed was bowled over by the deadwalkers and a wave of clawing, biting corpses washed over the struggling beast, hiding it from view. Incensed, Festerbite lurched to his feet and hacked at the zombies. He began to bellow a hymn to Nurgle as he fought, but the words caught in his throat as the head of every deadwalker turned towards him as one, their eyes glowing with an amethyst light.

He backed away, sword extended. The sound of the battle had grown dim, as if it were far away. The dead closed in on him, trailing bits of his unfortunate steed in their wake. They moved with unnatural purpose. Normally, they fought like the dullest of beasts, but these moved in unison. The ground trembled beneath his feet, and he saw the shadowy presence again, rising up over him like an avenging god. He heard the distant rumble of something that might have been a voice as the dead crashed against him.

Festerbite fought back, desperate now and without his usual confidence. They surrounded him on all sides, prying at his armour, gouging his flesh, hindering his blows. They were a quagmire of unfeeling flesh, immune to all save the most savage of blows.

One of the deadwalkers suddenly clutched at Festerbite's throat, its fingers tightening with inexorable strength. A strange fire burned in its ruined sockets, and sounds that might have been words slipped from between its ragged lips. He could almost hear a voice, like a bell tolling in the deep. His grip on his sword grew loose as the zombie's flickering gaze bored into his eyes, and deeper still, into the squirming malignancy of his soul.

I... see... you, it said. It was the same voice as before. A voice as black as the pit and as deep as the sea. The words shuddered down through him, and his heart convulsed in his chest. And then, the deadwalker's head was rolling free, and its eyes lost their hateful lustre. Festerbite sagged back, coughing. Hooves trampled the deadwalker's body into mush. The animal's rider laughed.

'What have I told you about letting them get hold of you like that? Here, give me your hand.' Wheezing, Festerbite caught the proffered hand and was hauled to his feet. He looked up into the murky gaze of Blightmaster Wolgus, and assayed a smile.

'He was quicker than I expected, blightmaster.'

'They always are, Sir Festerbite. The dead move fast, especially in these lands.'

Wolgus wore a halo of flies about his wide skull, and his body creaked with the power of Nurgle as he studied the battlefield. His battle-scarred, baroque armour was marked with stylised flies and leering faces. 'Well done, my boy. Made a proper mess of them I see. Grandfather is pleased.'

'And you, my lord?'

'Always, boy, always. Else I would not have sponsored you for knighthood.' Wolgus heaved himself from the saddle. The snow melted beneath his feet, turning to glistening slurry. 'The Lady of Cankerwall herself spoke as to the mighty deeds you might yet perform, in the name of the King of All Flies.' He caught Festerbite by the shoulders. 'And all of Festerfane will echo with the stories of what you and I accomplish here in these barren wastes.'

'As you say, blightmaster.' Festerbite bowed his head.

'As jolly as this is, I feel I must remind you that we have a schedule,' a deep, gulping voice said. Festerbite glared over Wolgus' shoulder at the massive shape shambling towards them. 'Not that I wish to interrupt such a touching moment, but, well... these poxes aren't going to spread themselves, you know.'

Wolgus sighed and turned. 'As ever, your counsel is most welcome, Gurm.'

'Of course it is. I am an endless fount of wisdom.' Gurm

leaned forward on his palanquin chair, knobbly fingers tap-tapping against the hilt of his balesword. The Herald of Nurgle was a bloat-bellied, lanky-limbed child of the King of All Flies. His grey-green skin writhed with maggots and rot-fly eggs, and his mighty antlers were fuzzy with a vivid crimson mould. He wore a battered breastplate over his sunken chest, a stylised fly painted on it.

Gurm was an ardent patron of the Most Suppurating and Blightsome Order of the Fly, and had fought beside its knights on a thousand battlefields. Even so, he was a daemon, and Festerbite put little stock in his loyalty to their holy creed. Daemons were fickle things and prone to treachery, even the jolly children of Nurgle. They sought glory in the eyes of their creator above all else.

As if reading his thoughts, Gurm gave a liquid chuckle. 'The dead do not tarry, Wolgus. And neither should we.'

'You'll forgive me if I choose to ensure our flanks are safe from further attack before we move on, I trust.' Wolgus dropped a hand to the pommel of his sword. 'This is not Ghyran, and these forests are full of worse things than tree-kin.' He gestured to Gurm's palanquin. It was crafted from the still-living bodies of four sylvaneth. The tree-kin were bound together by sutures of pus-coloured sap, and their withered limbs had grown into one another, forming the palanquin. A branch-wreathed head jutted from each corner, bark faces twisted in elemental agony. Their thick legs held the palanquin aloft, and glistening tendrils sporting poisonous thorns thrashed about them.

Gurm blinked his single eye. 'You sound as if you fear these lands, Wolgus.'

'I fear nothing that walks or crawls. But I see the world for what it is, not as I wish it to be.' Wolgus thumped his breastplate. Festerbite nodded in agreement. That was one of the central tenets of their order. Clarity was Nurgle's gift to his chosen: to see the world as it was, stripped bare of the tattered masks of desire and hope, leaving only a beautiful despair. There was comfort in surrender, and joy in acceptance. There was love there, at the heart of all endings, and serenity at the end of all things. And it was that bleak serenity which the Order of the Fly served. It was that serenity which they sought to impart to the ignorant and the savage.

'There is a better way than this. A softer road, and a gentler darkness,' Festerbite murmured, watching as the last of the deadwalkers were put down by Molov and the others. Wolgus chuckled.

'I know those words,' he said. 'I heard the troubadour, Onogal, sing them at the last gathering of the Order. How we applauded.'

'Would that he were with us now, for we could do with some gaiety in this fell place,' Festerbite said. 'The shadows loom close, even on the brightest day.'

Wolgus clapped him on the shoulder. 'I wish they were here as well. Brave Sir Goral, serene Dolorugus, and even bawdy Sir Culgus, who fought beside me at the Bridge of Scabs and held it for twelve days against the blood-mad hordes of Khorne. Glory is all the sweeter for being shared with one's fellows.'

'Speak for yourself, my lad,' Gurm said, with a phlegm-soaked chuckle. 'The scum rises to the top. And if we wish to be that scum, we must press forwards without delay. We must drive forwards, until the trees end and our prey find themselves caught between us and the sea.'

'And we will. As the Lady herself foresaw, in the stew of portent.' Wolgus grinned confidently. Festerbite saw no flaw in his reasoning. The Lady of Cankerwall was a seer without equal, and she could read the skeins of fate and moment in the effluvial smoke of her bubbling pox-cauldrons. Her will was as that of Nurgle, and the Order fought in her name as much as that of the Lord of All Things. From her noisome chambers, she orchestrated the sevenfold forces of the Order of the Fly, sending them where Nurgle decreed: to raze this forest, or build this citadel; to crush these foes, or conquer this demesne. And the Order did so, for to serve the Lady was to serve the Lord of All Things.

She was older than the Order itself, older even than the Jade Kingdoms some said, and had come upon the first of those who would become her blightmasters in the Age of Myth. Veiled and sitting astride a blightsome steed, she had drawn brave knights to her from across the kingdoms and anointed them in Nurgle's name. She had spoken to those first questing knights of honour in the service of Life itself, and her song had opened their courageous hearts to the sweet chivalry of despair.

It was the Lady who had set them on this course, for reasons they did not ask nor needed to know. That she had asked was enough. What true knight could resist the request of a Lady so great and fine as she who had guided them all these many centuries?

'If the Lady has foreseen it, so mote it be,' Festerbite said, piously.

'Hear hear,' Wolgus said. 'Our victory is assured. Else why would she have sent us?'

'Yes, well, no reason to laze about, is all.' Gurm sniffed and spat. He thumped his palanquin and the sylvaneth shoved themselves upright with wheezing hisses. 'Get them moving, Wolgus. Busy hands are blessed hands.' The palanquin tottered off, carrying the Herald across the battlefield and away.

'He's in quite the hurry,' Wolgus said, when the daemon was out of earshot.

'I've never seen him this insistent,' Festerbite said. Scab limped towards him, its scaly hide already healing. The horse-thing nuzzled him affectionately, and he patted its muzzle as he watched Gurm's palanquin jolt away. 'He's playing some game, isn't he?'

Wolgus nodded. 'Of course. That is his way.' He turned. 'Fear not, gentle Festerbite. Whatever scheme he is concocting, it will only be to our benefit. We alone possess the endurance to come so far into the hinterlands of this accursed realm. And we alone shall reap the glory of its conquest. The Lady has seen it.'

Festerbite thumped his chest in salute. 'For the Lady, blightmaster.'

Wolgus smiled. 'Yes. For the Lady, and the Realm Rotting.'

The air stank of sweet stagnation. In even the smallest death, there was life, and to Dolorous Gurm fell the pleasure of nurturing it. He left Wolgus and his knight to their mutterings of faith and chivalry and began his customary inspection of the battlefield. Everywhere he looked, rotbringers were hacking at the dead, ensuring that they would not rise again. Even the bodies of their fellow warriors were not exempt from this mutilation. To die in Shyish was to trade one master for another, and, as yet, not even the Dark Gods themselves could prevent the Undying King from raising up their fallen warriors for his armies.

This was not the first time, or even the fifth, that the pox-crusade had been forced to defend itself from the mindless dead since its arrival in Shyish. And since the dead seemed so eager to greet them, Gurm had decided to put them to good use. This newly sown field of corpses would yield fertile wonders, in time.

Everywhere, sour flesh swelled with newborn disease, and he gestured to his scribes. 'Note these buboes, and how they ripen,' he said, indicating one of the fallen deadwalkers. As his servants scrambled to do his bidding, he sank back onto his cushions with a sigh. Sprawled atop his palanquin, Gurm surveyed the battlefield and imagined the garden to come.

There was potential, here. Others might not see it, but he did. It would take time and patience, both of which he had in abundance. Ghyran was a veritable paradise compared to this – a realm fit to bursting with the stuff of life. Diseases needed no encouragement there, or barely any. Even the most fragile pestilence flourished in the hothouse of the Jade Kingdoms.

It took no skill. No talent. 'Quantity is the aim of the unimaginative,' the daemon gurgled, knocking a knuckle against the inflamed bark of his palanquin. One of the sylvaneth gave a raspy moan and shuddered. Pus-like sap bubbled up from between the cracks in the bark, and Gurm dipped a finger in it. He stuck the glistening digit in his mouth and sucked it clean. 'But quality – ah, quality – that is the mark of the true creative. One must have vision, if one is to stand out amongst the faceless hordes.'

And Gurm had vision to spare. This realm would be his canvas, upon which he would paint a virulent masterpiece. Papa Nurgle would raise him up for it, and bestow upon him all the choicest of compliments, as befitting a master craftsman.

Still, one couldn't be a craftsman of any sort without the proper tools. Gurm glanced over his shoulder. Wolgus stood in conversation with his inner circle, planning the advance. Doughty knights, all, and devoted to the King of All Flies. Gurm idly gnawed the blisters on his finger. It had been a fortunate day when he'd made the acquaintance of the Most Suppurating and Blightsome Order of the Fly. Rising from the blighted noble houses of the duchies of Festerfane, Cankerwall and the Pallas Ghyredes, the knights of the Order had fought at the forefront of Nurgle's armies in Ghyran since the fall of the Black Cistern.

Who else but the Order would have dared to leave the safety of Ghyran and cross the Bridge of Scabs? Who else would have challenged the feathered warders of the Ithilian Gate, and emerged victorious? They were staunch servants of Nurgle, though they valued their honour a touch more than Gurm felt was warranted. A good gardener was pragmatic, as well as inventive. The Order's chivalric ideals often got in the way of more practical concerns. But they made for excellent warriors, and were more trustworthy than braggarts like Gutrot Spume or ambitious fools like the Glottkin. Indeed, compared to their fellows, the warriors of the Order were almost... naive. They were idealistic nihilists, seeking to spread the sweetest of despairs. That idealism made them the perfect sort of shield. Other warlords might begin to question, to plot and scheme for their own glory. But not the Order.

It had been child's play to convince Wolgus, one of the seven blightmasters of the Order, to embark on a crusade into the wilds of Shyish, so that they might free it from the tyranny of death and raise its folk up in the ways of pox and sweet despair. And thus far, they had done just that. In the months since they'd passed across the Bridge of Scabs and pierced the Ithilian Gate, every force the primitive inhabitants of this land could muster had been smashed by the pox-crusade, and many of the native tribes had come around to their way of thinking. What profit in worshipping death, when life offered so much more, especially in regards to general longevity?

The pox-crusade had marched steadily north since their arrival all those months ago, guided by Gurm. He had led them into the glacial wilderness, where no other servant of the Ruinous Powers had yet managed to triumph. At his insistence, they had slogged through icy fens and across barren tundra into the Rictus Lands, driving the savage clans before them. Through blizzards, freezing rains and howling winds, he'd led them ever northwards, counting on Nurgle's blessings to see them through conditions which would have spelled disaster for lesser warriors.

Flies buzzed about his head, humming secrets. Gurm nodded sagely. 'Thank you, little ones,' he said. His flies had spread across these lands the moment they'd breached the Ithilian Gate. Their faceted eyes saw everything, and they reported it back to him. And what they reported was: Chaos. Everywhere, the membrane between realms was punctured. Realmgates vomited forth the servants of the Ruinous Powers, come seeking glory and conquest as they had in Aqshy, Ghyran and Chamon.

But the kingdoms of death were strong. It would take time to wear them down, and it would bleed the armies of Khorne and Tzeentch white. And while they spent themselves on the walls of Helstone, in the streets of Gravesend and amid the docks of the great port of Ossuary, Gurm would snatch victory from under their very noses.

Shyish was Nagash, and Nagash was Shyish. That much he'd learned from the delicately blistered lips of the Lady of Cankerwall, before their departure. For a mortal, she was most insightful. The seer had whispered to him of the Undying King. The king was the land, and the land, the king. Wound one, harm the other. Archaon had delivered the first blow, but another was required, this one to the very heart of realm and ruler both.

There was a path to the underworld close to hand. He could sense it, and his flies sought it. When he found it, he would lead his brothers into it. They would fill the underworld with a flood of bounteous filth and drown the Lord of Death in glorious fecundity. And it would be Dolorous Gurm who held his bony skull beneath the slimy waters. Gurm and no other. He glanced around at Wolgus, and chuckled.

He saw no reason to share his true aims with his mortal cat's paws. The Order of the Fly would shield him until such time as he reached his goal. Then, they would be dispensed with. If any survived the battle to come, he might induct them into his own service. Once he'd divested them of their foolish notions of chivalry and honour, of course. There was no place for that sort of claptrap in the service of the Lord of All Things.

Gurm knuckled his eye and chuckled again. Now was the time to strike, while Nagash was wounded and weak. Once he was destroyed or, failing that, bound, then Shyish would fall. Like Ghyran, it would belong to Nurgle, and the Lord of Decay would grow stronger yet. The garden would spread across two realms, life and death inextricably bound in chains of glorious rot.

Gurm shuddered in pleasure at the thought. The Three-Eyed King might be content to rest on his laurels, but Nurgle was always busy.

FOUR

THE RICTUS

The law of Nagash is this.

My will shall be the whole of thy desire, whether in life or in death.

You speak with my voice, and strike with my hand.

Refute all other gods, for what are gods to one who is death? Nothing, as you are nothing, save what I choose to make of you.

Nagash is all, and all are one, in Nagash.

– *The Epistle of Bone*

The assembled voivodes of the Rictus Clans stood in a wide circle, arguing. All save Tamra. It was the first time she had been to a conclave. Her brother had been to two before his death. He'd never seemed to have enjoyed them, and now she could see why. There was little fun to be had in watching more than a dozen old men and women bellow at each other for hours on end. But such was the way of the Rictus: all voices must be heard, all consideration made. From the lowest of the lowborn clans to the highest of the highborn, all had their say in a conclave.

There should have been more of them. The lands of the north were divided between six hundred clans, some larger, some smaller, but each with their own voivode. But there were barely more than twenty of them here now. There were whispers that some had joined the foe, forsaking old loyalties in the name of survival. Others had died in their steading, or fled into the deep hills. Those who remained, like Tamra, had retreated north to the Mandible.

The conclave chamber sat at the top of the highest tower in the redoubt known as the Mandible. It had once been the citadel of one of the legendary Broken Kings, though which one nobody knew. Few who lived dared to speak their names, and the dead were forbidden to speak of them. Whichever of them it had once belonged to, the redoubt was still a mighty fortress, as the Rictus judged such things. It had high sloping walls of quarried stone, reinforced with iron, and was shaped vaguely like a jawbone, as its name implied.

The ruins of the city outside the walls were of similar make, or had been, before fire and sorcery had torn them asunder. And beyond them lay the sagging, rime-encrusted remnants of the ice-docks, which had once played host to those who dared the frigid waters of the Shivering Sea, including traders from the Rime Isles and Helstone. The Rictus had ruled the north and all had sought their patronage.

Some said the duardin of the Cacklebone had built citadel and city both, in payment for an unspecified debt. Looking around, Tamra could easily believe it. The conclave chamber was open to the sky, and its walls had been ruptured by primeval calamity, but it still stood and showed no inclination to collapse any time soon. The worm-folk were great ones for working rock and stone, shaping them as easily as a child might shape ash and grease. What they built could not easily be knocked over. The weapons they forged were highly prized as well. Many a clan had bartered themselves into penury for the chance to own a duardin-forged blade or two. She glanced down at the barrowblade now belted about her waist, and ran her thumb over the heat-scarred pommel.

It was all that she had to remind her of Sarpa. Even the remnants of his soul were gone, torn from existence in some manner she didn't fully understand. It was as if he had been claimed by the storm itself. 'Foolishness,' she murmured.

'Oh, I agree, but one must allow for tradition, mustn't one?' Neferata said from behind her. Tamra glanced at the mortarch. Neferata stood a respectful distance from the circle, lazily watching the proceedings. Her dread abyssal crouched behind her, its skeletal chin resting on her shoulder. It growled as it noticed Tamra looking at it. Neferata reached up and swatted it on its muzzle. 'Quiet, Nagadron, I'm trying to listen.' She looked at Tamra. 'Why a circle?'

'All are equal, in life as well as in death. Rictus speak with one voice, or not at all.' It was an old tradition. One started by the Broken Kings, or so the stories said.

'As long as it's the right voice, I have no objection.' Neferata tapped her lip with a thumbnail. 'Still, we have precious little time for old men to shout about things they cannot change.' She stepped past Tamra and swayed into the centre of the circle, one hand resting lightly on the pommel of her sword.

The other voivodes fell silent, their eyes were on Neferata. Some of them were frightened, others wary. A few, challenging. All, however, were respectful. One did not rise to the rank of mortarch without first climbing a mountain of corpses, and it was Neferata who had brought most of them here, either by summons or personally. Tamra rubbed her cheek tiredly. She and those few of her folk she could find had followed the mortarch and her knights through the wilderness for days, until at last they had caught sight of the Mandible.

More refugees arrived every day, flooding in as the rotbringers laid waste to the north with pox and fire. Warriors from a dozen or more clans manned the broken walls, or saw to what repairs were within their power to make. If the Rictus were to make their final stand, the Mandible was a better place than most. The walls were high, the wells deep and it was defended on both sides by mountain and sea.

In the circle, Neferata cleared her throat. 'Voivodes of the Rictus, I greet thee in the name of the Undying King.'

'And we greet thee, Mother of Night,' said one of the voivodes. Arun of the Ung was the oldest of all of them, his face little more than a skull wrapped in parchment. He had seen a hundred winters more than any other man of the Rictus, and he looked as if every single one were weighing on him, hunched as he was inside a voluminous coat of furs and leaning against a staff of bone and wood. 'Have you brought his counsel, as well as his greetings?'

'Better,' Neferata said. 'I have brought myself, and my kindred. We will stand beside the Rictus in battle, as we once did, in seasons past.'

'Are we to stand then?' another voivode spoke up. Bolgu was the leader of one of the coastal clans, the Fenn. He was a big man, broad and built thick. He wore a cuirass of banded bone, marked with necromantic sigils, and the scars of old battles disfigured his fleshy features. 'To what purpose? No, better to flee across the ice. We will take our ice-cutter galleys and seek sanctuary on the Rime Isles, and wait for this pestilence to burn itself out. Let them fight the flesh-eaters and orruks, if they wish.'

'And when they follow you?' Neferata said. 'Where will you flee then?'

'We could seek aid from the duardin,' another voivode, Myrn, said. She was a frail thing, all skin and bones, her face tattooed with the tribal markings of the Wald. 'Their holds are under the shadow of the Great Enemy as much as our palisades.' She looked around. 'We trade furs and meat for iron and steel. Let us trade them for warriors instead.'

'The spirits have said that the high gates are closed and the deep drums are silent,' Arun said, his voice creaky with age. 'The duardin will not fight this war for us.'

'I suspect that they are busy fighting their own,' Neferata said. 'After all, where the followers of pox roam, the creeping ratkin are not far behind.' She wriggled her fingers for emphasis. 'Gnawing their way up, as the blighted legions dig down.'

'Then there is no hope,' Bolgu said.

'And what am I, then?' Neferata said, bemusedly.

'The servant of a dead god.'

The other voivodes murmured at this, though whether in agreement or shock, Tamra couldn't tell. Perhaps it was a little of both.

'And how do you know he is dead, mortal?' Neferata said, almost gently. 'Did he visit you? Perhaps to tender his heartfelt goodbyes?'

'We all know he is dead,' Bolgu said. 'We heard the thunder of his bones breaking, the scream of the souls loosed by his fall.' He tapped his chest. 'We felt the shattering of the Corpse Geometries, deep in our hearts.'

'How awful for you,' Neferata said. 'To have so little faith, I mean. Nagash cannot die. Nagash *is* death. He is this realm. The high mountains are his bones, the seas, his marrow.'

'Then where is he? Why does he not stand before us and speak these words?'

'And who are you, that he would deign to speak with you?'

Neferata laughed. 'You are maggots, grubbing in his flesh. Be grateful, and speak softly to me or not at all.'

Bolgu growled and Tamra felt the winds of death thicken. 'Mortarch or not, you are in our demesnes now, and it is you who will speak softly, vampire.' Ghosts congealed about him, clutching misty weapons. Bolgu could call the drowned dead as easily as another man might whistle for a hound. 'We will not be mocked. We hewed kingdoms from ice, and drew down the light of the moon to warm ourselves. We are Rictus.'

'Then act it, fool,' Neferata said. She spread her pale arms. 'I am the oldest of the old, and in me is the strength of time out of mind. I have weathered apocalypses beyond your imagining, and strangled newborn gods in their cradles. Would you pit yourself against me?'

Bolgu opened his mouth, and Tamra wondered whether he were suicidal or simply stupid. The Fenn plied the Shivering Sea, with all of its inherent dangers. Perhaps having faced the horrors of the deeps, the voivode of the Fenn could not conceive of someone as fragile-looking as Neferata being a threat. If that was the case, he was in for a nasty shock.

'Be silent, Bolgu, be still,' Arun said. 'The Queen of Blood is a guest here. We owe her courtesy, at least.' Bolgu subsided with a grimace. Arun turned his milky gaze on Neferata. 'You say you have brought yourself – what do you offer? Will you fight for us?'

'Yes, and more besides. I will teach you to fight, such as you never fought before.' She turned and clapped her hands. 'Adhema, Rasha... bring the maggot.'

The doors to the chamber slammed open, and two armoured figures, one of them Adhema, strode in, dragging a third in chains. Tamra couldn't say when they'd taken a prisoner. Perhaps at her steading, or even along the way. Some rotbringers had ranged far ahead of the bulk of their forces, acting either as scouts or merely following their debased whims. This one had been hard used by his captors, and the two blood knights were not gentle as they hauled him into the centre of the circle. They cast him onto the floor, and he lay gasping. Tar-like ichor dripped from his many wounds. It seemed inconceivable that he could still be alive. He gurgled something, and Adhema's boot found the side of his skull.

Tamra flinched at the sound. Adhema glanced at her and winked. The kastellan had spoken little to her since they'd arrived, which suited Tamra fine. Neferata was bad enough, but Adhema radiated a feral need for violence. For her, the only good kill was a bloody one, and all that lived was prey. Tamra had little doubt that if Neferata had not been there, Adhema and her warriors would have ridden down the Drak after finishing off the rotbringers.

'Why have you brought this... filth, here?' Bolgu demanded. He and the others stared at the chained rotbringer the way they might a mad dog. Tamra studied the leprous creature with more curiosity than fear. He was not a Rictus, or even a man of the south. His features were too round, too wide beneath the mask of boils and scabs. He stank, but not with the clean reek of decaying flesh. Old tattoos in the shape of weaving vines and ragged leaves marked the visible portions of his flesh, and his teeth were etched with runes.

'To get to the truth, one must dig,' Neferata said. She crouched beside the bound warrior and caught his chin. With the fingers of her other hand, she traced a line down his chest. Thick, oily blood beaded on his flesh, and he grunted in pain. The grunt became a cry as she twisted her claws into his chest. Adhema and the other vampire leaned close, eyes alight with interest, their hands on the hilts of their swords.

Dark liquid spattered the ground as Neferata indulged herself. Every so often she would pause and murmur a question, sometimes in a tongue that Tamra didn't recognize. It was a soft language and put her in mind of a summer breeze and rustling leaves. When the rotbringer answered, he spoke in a similar tongue, albeit more guttural. When he didn't answer, Neferata hurt him; quite badly, judging from his screams. Tamra was surprised. She'd thought the servants of Nurgle all but immune to pain.

Unable to watch for long, Tamra turned away. She looked out through one of the broken walls of the chamber and tried to ignore the screams. Her gaze was drawn to the high rock face which hung over the Mandible. Crags jutted like fangs from the looming shape of the Wailing Peaks, their uppermost tips hidden in the thick clouds which shrouded the skies. The Wailing Peaks extended from the coast and down into the southlands, stretching like a scar of rock across the body of the north. Besides the usual wild beasts, they were populated by tribes of savage orruks, bonesnapper gargants and roving packs of deadwalkers. In the fading light of the day, she could see flocks of carrion birds circling the lower crags. As the wind turned, she heard their raucous shrieks, and something else besides. A whisper of sound, like a voice calling from afar.

Free... us...

She blinked. She'd spoken to the dead often enough to know when a spirit was speaking. But she did not know these spirits, or recognize their voices. She tried to ignore them, but they persisted, their whispers growing more urgent. She heard a groan, and tore her eyes from the distant peaks.

The rotbringer was dead. Neferata stood over him, cleaning her hands with a rag torn from her cloak. 'Burn it, but be wary of the smoke. They can sicken the blood, even in death.' She looked around. 'Well? You heard. What say you?'

'It changes nothing,' Bolgu said. 'We knew they were coming. What use knowing their names or where they come from?'

'Knowledge is the key which unlocks the gates to power. I have eyes in every realm, and I see much and learn more.' Neferata tapped the side of her head. 'Knowing the name of your enemies is as good as knowing their minds. I have heard of this... Order of the Fly before. They are crusaders, like the ancient warrior-lodges of Gheist or the Brotherhood of the Ox in Helstone. They seek to convert their foes by fire and sword.'

'And?'

She smiled thinly. 'And it means that they will not stop until every last member of your race is dead or in service to the Lord of Decay, fool.'

A murmur ran through the gathered voivodes. Tamra barely heard it. The dead demanded her attention.

You call... we come. Unbind us, break our chains, free us…

Their voices echoed through her skull, flattening all thought beneath their hideous pressure. 'Who are you?' she hissed. Neferata glanced at her, but said nothing.

Free... us...

We hear... drums... war...

Break... chains...

Break them.

Break them.

Break them!

Bony fingers snapped. Tamra blinked. A skull, lit by hideous radiance, gazed down at her and she stumbled back, heart thudding. She had not heard Arkhan the Black enter the chamber. Neither had anyone else, if the looks the other voivodes were tossing their way were any indication. She had seen the Mortarch of Sacrament only at a distance since her arrival, but every necromancer among the clans could feel the harsh weight of his power beating on the wind, day and night. Up close, it was even worse.

'What ails you, Tamra ven-Drak?' Arkhan said, as he lowered his hand.

'The-the dead...' she began. Her mouth was dry, and her head ached with the muted thunder of their voices. 'Who were they?'

'Do not listen to them, child,' Arkhan said. Though he spoke softly, his voice reverberated through the marrow of her, and her fingers tightened convulsively on the hilt of Sarpa's sword. 'Pay the Broken Kings no heed. They are oathbreakers and thieves.'

The Broken Kings. The name pulsed through her like a deep ache. The last kings of the Rictus, bound in the dark with their armies by the will of Nagash. 'But surely we could use them,' she said, without thinking. 'We need men – we need armies. Why leave them bound in ice and rock?'

'For spite's sake. They broke the law of Nagash and must be punished, though all the world suffer for it. Without the law, disorder reigns.' Arkhan studied her with flickering hell-lit eyes. His skull was worn smooth by time and tide, and his black teeth gleamed in a fixed grin.

'I do not care about that,' she said, startling herself. 'I only care about my people, about their survival.'

Arkhan said nothing. His gaze dimmed, for just a moment. 'That is to your credit.' He stepped past her, and into the circle. The iron-shod ferrule of his staff struck the ground with every step, echoing like a funerary bell, silencing all conversation and argument.

'You squawk like hens,' he said, simply. 'Shall we flee? Where shall we flee? Across the sea? Where across the sea?' The liche turned, fixing his gaze on each of the chieftains in turn. 'Never considering that I stand between you and any route you might take.'

Silence. From the hasty glances, Tamra suspected that the mortarch was right. Neferata laughed. 'I did try to tell you,' she said. She set her elbow up on Arkhan's shoulder and smiled prettily at the Rictus. 'I am the sweetmeat and he the stick. Deny me, and you get him.'

'They will not deny you, I think.' Arkhan tilted his head towards her. 'Few can.'

'Flatterer,' she said. She pushed away from him. 'Two mortarchs stand with you. Nagash's eye is upon you. This is the moment you were born for, shaped for. This is the reason you possess the embers of power that flicker within you. Would you toss them aside? I thought the Rictus were black iron, but perhaps they are merely glass.' She glanced at Arkhan. 'Perhaps we should have gone east with Mannfred, eh? To Helstone. Maybe the Princes of the Ninety-Nine Circles are made of sterner stuff...'

Shouts of denial greeted her words. Tamra saw her lips curve in a slight smile, before blossoming into full mockery. Neferata threw up her hands and turned to face Arkhan. 'Do you hear something, Arkhan? Goats, I think. Stubborn and fearful, all at once.'

'They are right to be afraid. They are mistaken, however, in the object of that fear.' His eyes blazed brightly, filling the air with a shimmering amethyst radiance. 'They fear the enemy, when they should fear us, O Queen of Blood.'

'As well they should, O Prince of Bones,' Neferata said. She turned, scanning the faces which surrounded them. 'For if we so wished, we could simply slaughter them here and then raise them up. If they will not serve in life, they will serve in death.' She cocked her head. 'So, then, the question is before you – life... or death?'

'Both.'

Tamra hesitated. She hadn't meant to speak. Neferata looked at her and smiled. Tamra swallowed a sudden rush of bile and stepped forwards, drawing her brother's sword as she did so. 'I am Drak. What we have, we hold.' She flipped the blade and extended the hilt towards the mortarchs. 'And we will serve the Undying King in life and in death. For that is the law of Nagash.'

'That is the law,' Arkhan said, thumping the ground with his staff.

'Yes,' Neferata said. 'Quite.' She tapped the pommel of the barrowblade and pushed it back towards Tamra. 'Sheathe your claw, sister. You will need it soon enough.'

The rotbringers were within sight of the Wailing Peaks when the bone-giant rose up out of the snow with a great rending creak, startling a flock of carrion birds and uprooting a few scattered trees. Festerbite had thought it merely a hillock at first, one of the many which dotted these barren lands. Its enormous bones were marked with flickering amethyst sigils and shot through with twisting tree roots, and it wore a battered cuirass of curious design. It clutched an immense khopesh of bronze in its hands, which it raised over its skull.

Warriors scattered, leaving behind the chains and ropes attached to the great way stones which they had only half uprooted. The stones, like the hundreds of others they had torn down on their advance north, had been raised in honour of Nagash. Thus they were fit only for the toppling, but it seemed they had a guardian.

'Fall back!' Festerbite shouted as the khopesh descended through the curtain of falling snow with a thunderous hiss. The curved blade fell, and a blightking exploded from the force of the impact. The bone-giant wrenched the khopesh free of the bloody snow and swept it out in a titanic arc, bisecting men and beasts alike. The mortal adherents of the crusade scattered in panic. They fled in every direction, seeking to escape the undead monster's attentions as it strode into the midst of the fragmenting column. Supply wagons tipped as panicked animals reared and shrieked as their handlers lost control of them.

Armsmen attempted to make a stand, slamming together their shields and extending black-bladed spears. The bone-giant strode through them as if they were nothing. Limbs and heads flew as the khopesh thudded down and out. Zealots called out to Nurgle for aid, but their prayers went unheard as the construct slaughtered them. The winter wind rose wild, as if urging the monstrous construct on to greater feats of violence.

'Rally to me,' Festerbite snarled, yanking on Scab's reins. 'To me, fools.' Few listened, and those that did died soon after. The bone-giant rampaged through the ranks, slaughtering any who dared stand before it. The column split in two like a rotting chunk of wood. Festerbite gave up his attempts to rally the mortals and drew his rotsword. He thumped Scab's ribs, urging the steed towards the undead monstrosity as the rotbringers streamed past, fleeing. Other knights followed suit, seeking to claim the glory of battle for themselves, riding down fleeing armsmen and cultists alike in their haste. Horns blew and bells rang as they closed in from all sides.

'Too slow, Festerbite,' a knight crowed as his steed pounded past Scab.

'Cheat!' Festerbite snarled. 'You're a cheat, Oga!'

Oga laughed and hunched forwards in his saddle, a great filth-encrusted glaive clutched in one hand. He hewed at the bone-giant's leg, seeking to bring the titan to its knees. Instead, it twisted around and snatched the unlucky knight from his saddle. It was faster than it looked. Oga cursed and struggled, but to no avail. Festerbite winced as the giant squeezed its claw and popped Oga's head like a pimple. It then hurled the body in his direction, and he was forced to slide half-off his saddle to avoid the tumbling carcass.

Scab charged between the giant's legs, and Festerbite hacked at the bone. Out of the corner of his eye, he saw the khopesh slice out, leaving a headless knight galloping past, ichor spurting into the frosty air. Several others struck the bone-giant's legs and torso with their spears. The weapons splintered on impact but caused the bone-giant to lose a step. Festerbite raced out of reach as his fellow knights wheeled about. The khopesh thudded down, cracking the earth and throwing snow into the air. Scab stumbled, but retained its footing. Others weren't so lucky. Horse-things fell screaming, and their riders were tossed to the ground.

As the bone-giant turned its attention to the fallen knights, plaguebearers raced towards it, droning out a baleful war song. Festerbite readied himself to charge once more into battle, but a shout from Wolgus stopped him. The blightmaster gestured for him to fall back.

'But my lord–' Festerbite began.

'One side, one side, child. Let Papa Nurgle's own deal with this obdurate automaton,' Gurm said as his palanquin thudded past, accompanied by an honour guard of plaguebearers and beasts of Nurgle. Wolgus' steed cantered towards Festerbite.

'Let the Herald earn his keep, my friend. We need to reform the column, just in case this is but the opening thrust of an attack.'

Wolgus jerked his reins, turning his brass-scaled mount about. Festerbite followed him, swatting hesitant rotbringers with the flat of his blade. Armsmen reformed their lines, locking their iron-rimmed shields together in a rough wall. The less disciplined elements of the crusade would require more than a few bellowed orders and a swat from a sword to regain their courage.

He turned, prepared to say as much to Wolgus, but the blightmaster anticipated him. 'I know. A distraction. It will take us hours to reorganize the column. Delay atop delay.' He turned, roaring orders to chieftains, pox-abbots and hedge-sorcerers. The Order's subordinate commanders were doing what they could, but the bone-giant's attack had been well timed. The snow was falling thick and fast, and many men would be lost in the storm.

Festerbite whipped around as he heard a high-pitched yowl. A beast of Nurgle collapsed in on itself as the khopesh sliced through it. But its slimy secretions began to dissolve the ancient blade, and the bone-giant was forced to leave what was left of the weapon embedded in the ground. Gurm roared out a command and the remaining beasts of Nurgle galloped towards their new playmate, trailing mucus and other excrescences in their excitement.

The bone-giant staggered back as the beasts clambered up its frame, yelping jovially. Bone began to sizzle and burn as the acidic attentions of the beasts took its toll. For every one it flung aside, two more nuzzled at its form, eating through armour and sigil alike. After a few moments of murderous affection, the bone-giant collapsed into a suppurating heap, and the beasts rolled across the snow, yapping in surprise.

'And that's the way you handle that,' Gurm said, reclining on his palanquin. The sylvaneth moaned as they carried their daemonic master towards Wolgus and Festerbite. 'What chance have the dead against life unbound?'

'More chances than just that,' Festerbite said. 'How many did we lose?'

'There's always more pus in the wound,' Gurm said. He blinked slowly. 'Besides, what price expedience? If it makes you feel better, I will take my brothers and scout ahead.'

'Do that. We'll be making camp.' Wolgus forestalled Gurm's mutter of protest. 'The storm grows worse. We need shelter for the more fragile servants of our lord and master. We must make camp, else we'll have no army left come tomorrow.'

Gurm stared at him for a moment, and then nodded. 'As you say, blightmaster. I shall ensure that no more surprises await you in your chosen campground.' He thumped his palanquin and the sylvaneth bore him away. Daemons loped in his wake.

'He is angry,' Festerbite said.

'He is frustrated. Daemons live in the moment. They know little of the business of day to day. Gurm would have us march our army to death and then question why we failed to overwhelm the enemy when we find them.' Wolgus shook his head. 'He is a great help in battle, and a great annoyance otherwise.'

'If he hadn't been here, we might have lost more warriors than we did,' Festerbite grunted, watching as the last remnants of the bone-giant dissolved into a pale soup. Murky steam rose from it, and the snow had melted all around. Warriors prodded it with spears, as if to reassure themselves that it was no more.

'It accomplished what it came to do, regardless,' Wolgus said. 'Another delay, another day lost to this wilderness. Gurm says we must press forwards, and quickly, though that is what he has been saying since we arrived in these cursed lands. But I am inclined to agree, if only because our foes seek to hinder us so obviously.' He turned in his saddle, scanning the storm. 'Can you feel it, Festerbite? We are being watched. Gauged and measured.'

Festerbite could and did. He glanced around, wondering what other horrors hid in the swirling snows. One bone-giant had ruptured the column and delayed their holy work. What if there had been two, or three? The crusade might have ended here and now. His hand tightened unconsciously on the hilt of his sword. 'Let us hope we are not inadequate to the task, my lord,' he said.

Wolgus dropped an amiable fist on his pauldron. 'Fear not, my friend. The Order of the Fly has never met a foe we could not best in battle, or outlast in the field. Not the root-kings, in their halls of wood and stone, and certainly not the unquiet dead of these gloomy lands. We will free them from the tyranny of death, and teach their peoples the true glory of sweet despair.' He gestured to the half-fallen way stones. 'Take some men and see to smashing those stones. We will accomplish one task this day, at least.'

'Yes, my lord,' Festerbite said, not really listening. In the falling snow, he thought he saw something, a vast shape, thin and loathsome, with two hell-spark eyes, burning like torches. The eyes stared through him, peeling away all that he was or ever had been. Then, the indistinct shape turned and strode away into the murmuring depths of the growing storm and was gone, and Festerbite could not say that it had truly been there in the first place.

The blightmaster was right. They were being watched. Despite what Wolgus believed, Festerbite feared that they had already been judged, and found wanting.

FIVE

THE GATE BELOW

Every dead thing.

Every whispering shade.

Every rasping soldier of bone and gibbering carrion-eater is mine.

Every living bird, every breathing beast, every man, woman and child.

They all hear me, as you hear me, in your marrow, in your heart and quavering spirit.

Know this – whosoever believes in me, whosoever follows the will of Nagash, shall prosper.

Listen, and be joyful.

– *The Epistle of Bone*

Nagash stood, a black mountain amid swirling snows. The lands around him were dead, full of bare trees and frost-coated rock. He had drawn the last ergs of life from this place and into himself to further bolster his dwindling might. The embers of his power stirred in the depths of him as his shattered consciousness coalesced in fits and starts. His mind slipped and slid down rat warrens of painful memory, seeking the path to the present.

He heard again the clangour of war, as the armies of the enemy invaded his realm through the realmgates. Daemons and mortal warriors alike poured into Shyish in their untold millions. For every gate he closed, two more burst wide to vomit forth a ceaseless cavalcade of horrors. The dead were numberless, but the servants of Chaos were limitless. The air had crackled with magic as Chaos sorcerers strove against the black arts of his mortarchs. Chaos champions with blazing weapons and god-hardened skin had cut down the dead in their hundreds, only to be at last pulled under by a foe who could not die again.

The unstoppable force met the immoveable object, and Shyish quaked to its very roots at the fury of their struggle. Once more, he felt the impact of the daemonblade as it crashed down against his temple, splitting bone. Nagash was no more wholly a thing of flesh than he was of spirit, and such a wound, delivered by a normal foe, would have been as nothing. But the Three-Eyed King was anything but normal. Four gods had poured their fury into him, and he blazed with a hideous strength. The blade he'd wielded had chewed apart bone and soul alike with greedy speed, gnawing at all Nagash was and ever would be, seeking to unravel the story of him.

Iron claws dug gouges in ruined bone as the Undying King clutched at his skull. An echo of that final, fatal moment still reverberated through the hollow places within him, and his titanic shape shuddered.

'I am broken, and my realm with me.'

His words echoed through the sepulchral air. Dead souls scattered, frightened by the thunder of his voice. He paid them no heed. How many times had he felt that same moment in his darkest dreams, repeated across ages and worlds? It was not always a daemonblade. Sometimes it was a simple sword, enchanted beyond all measure; at other times, a hammer, glowing with ancient magic. But always, there was the blow to body and soul, and his mind... fragmenting, scattering, fleeing.

'And yet, I endure. Death cannot die. Not while the stars wheel and the suns burn.'

He was death, and death could not die, *would* not die. Let the realms spin apart and reality crumble. Nagash would endure, a black thorn thrust in the heart of worlds to come, just as he'd always done. But not without cost. There was always a price for survival, but it was a price he would gladly pay.

A sudden clarity pierced the fog. He recalled what he had come here to do, though not why. He would remember, in time – a moment, or a day. Time had little meaning to one who was outside its reach. And if he did not remember, loyal Arkhan would surely remind him. For now, he was content to simply act.

The enemy were caught by the storm he'd conjured, their momentum stalled in the lowlands south of the Wailing Peaks. Now was the time to strike a mortal blow. One iron claw extended. Amethyst lightning crawled along the crudely forged facets, before streaking off into the storm.

'Awaken,' Nagash said.

The snow whipped about him. The storm howled, and something howled with it, a cry of denial and lunatic frustration. 'So, you would pit your will against mine?' Nagash spread his talons, and veins of purple light stretched out, piercing the clouds of frost. Anger strengthened his will, and his mind stiffened. Lucidity sliced through his mental fog like a razor, returning in an instant. 'I defeated you easily in life. What chance do you have in death?'

Deep within the snow, something shrieked. It was a sound of equal parts hunger and fear. A good sound.

'Yes. Remember. Remember who is master here, and who is the slave. Now... *awaken*.'

Hollow eyed and wide mouthed, ogors lumbered out of the storm. There were close to a hundred of them, a once-mighty tribe, reduced to eternal servitude by the will of the Undying King. They slavered mindlessly as their frost-bitten limbs clawed uselessly at the amethyst chains which looped about their thick necks and torsos. Nagash lifted his hand, drawing the sorcerous bindings tight. Even so, they struggled, more out of stubbornness than anything else.

'In life, you sought to poach upon my domain, to eat that which was forbidden. In death, I bound your bestial souls to the snows, so that, like the cold, you might never be sated.'

The ogors – or rather, these things which had once been ogors – howled and gibbered. Whatever dim thoughts they might once have possessed were long gone now, lost to centuries of unending hunger. They were one with the storm, with the winter wind itself. Their simian shapes bled into one another, dissolving and reforming as they writhed in their chains. Nagash swept his hand out, dragging them to their knees.

'You will listen. I will loosen your chains. You will feed. You will glut yourselves.'

He spoke steadily, impressing his malign will upon the scattered flickering of soulfire. They shrieked and screamed, resisting with feral strength. Even dead, and mad, they were stubborn beasts. But he was the Undying King, and his will was as the will of the universe itself. He gestured, and the amethyst chains evaporated.

'Go. Feed and rejoice in my name.'

The horde of hungry spirits turned, their forms billowing and fading, to rejoin the storm. But the wind howled with purpose now, and Nagash turned his mind from it, satisfied. He could not call up an army such as he might once have done, but he could delay the enemy and deny them a chance to rest. He could bleed them. These lands were filled with the detritus of a millennia of wars and skirmishes, and he would employ it all.

The rest would be up to his mortarchs. He judged them more than equal to the task, whatever the quality of their tools. It was why he had chosen them to serve, after all.

He looked up at the mad iridescence of the Wraith Moons and, for a moment, lost himself in the contemplation of those elemental forces which held them suspended. In dim, distant days, he had made a study of the Mortal Realms. They existed concurrently, bleeding into one another like rivers running into the sea. They were separated by the thinnest of membranes or the thickest of walls. In Shyish, the membrane was thinnest.

All realms connected equally to his, for the dead, whatever their realm of origin, were drawn to Shyish and to his service. He could see the pathways into all of the realms: to the south, the warm green of Ghyran; to the east, the harsh coppery glow of Chamon; and above them all, past the Wraith Moons, the shimmering azure radiance of Sigmar's realm.

'Azyrite...'

The memories flowed up like blood welling from a wound. A hand, blazing like the heart of a star, dragging him from the cairn where he'd lain insensate for millennia without number. The mountain-crushing convulsions of the last of the Hydragors as he drove the ferrule of Alakanash, the Staff of Power, into its vast brain. His armour turning black from the blows of the volc-giants, and Zefet-nebtar, the Mortis Blade, growing impossibly warm in his grip as he hewed canyon-sized wounds in their colossal, continent-spanning bodies.

Back to back, he and Sigmar had fought against impossible

odds. They had been allies. Twin gods, one light, one dark, born anew from the corpse of a half-forgotten world. Side by side, they had sought to impose order on the chaos which beset the fledgling realms. For a time, at least. The fire flared anew, stirred by rage. He threw back his broken skull and screamed in rage.

Sigmar had betrayed him.

His allies had betrayed him. *Him*.

The living, aligned against the dead. It had always been thus. They feared him, as well they should, for his glory could not be contained to a singular realm. Nagash was death and death was a constant, whatever the realm. All souls were his, all life came to his kingdom in time, even that which was claimed by false gods and trickster spirits.

The fire at his core grew hot, and the halo of bruised light which surrounded him flickered. He drew strength from his rage, battening on spite. They had dared to cripple him, to weaken him and leave him vulnerable. Archaon would never have attempted to invade had the Azyrite not done so first, and thus left the way open. Sigmar had torn a wound in Shyish, and the infection of Chaos had slipped in.

Once, great cloud banks of souls had drifted peacefully into his grip. But now, the dead knew no peace. Souls were trapped, like detritus in the wounds between worlds. They did not come to him, save on rare occasion. Many were drawn shrieking into the realms of Chaos, or else lingered at their place of death, ignoring his summons with a tenacity which infuriated him. The Corpse Geometries were askew, and his calculations made false. He was no longer the Undying King, but a pretender to his own throne.

He hissed in rage, and the wind writhed in sympathy. He lacked the strength to summon his servants in all their innumerable ranks or to confront the foe openly. His hold on the upper world was tenuous at best. Until his body had recovered, he was confined to this wraithlike form, unable to affect the world, save indirectly. But he did not need a body to wage war. He did not even need a mind, or at least not a whole and healthy one. All were one in Nagash, and Nagash was all. The deadwalkers and the bone-giant had been but the first and least of his weapons. The spirits of snow and hunger were greater still. And he would use them all, from the least to the greatest.

He spread his arms, and his will extended like the tentacles of some immense kraken, reaching out to stir dim, guttering embers of soulfire across the wide wilderness. All dead things in the north stirred, whether buried, drowned or roaming. New fallen or older than the stars, they turned as one to heed him. Some with reluctance, others eagerly, but all turned regardless.

'Come.'

The word thundered through the marrow of the world. Broken limbs bent to the task. Mouldering paws scrabbled at hard earth and bodiless souls sped through bower and glen. The word of Nagash was inescapable and irrefutable. They would come, in their numberless legions, and fall upon the living. They would kill until there was only silence. The north would be at peace once more, undisturbed and as orderly as a tomb, at least for a time.

For this would not be the last invasion. Distantly, he could hear the enemy scrabbling in the dust of the cairn-lands, seeking to break the seals of the Starless Gate and flood into Stygxx. The gate was a massive edifice of stone and bone, wrought into a gigantic fortified entryway in ages past by the Amethyst Princes, as befitting the only open road into their deep realm. It was the single path by which the living might journey into Stygxx, and its winding length had once played host to merchant caravans from Helstone, Ossuary and the Scarab City.

Now, in the shadow of the gate, battle raged. The slaves of darkness fought each other, for want of other opponents, and their champions mocked the name of Nagash. Always they sought to undermine him, to undo all that he had accomplished. The Dark Gods feared him, for in him was the Great Inevitability made manifest. All things died – even gods. All things, save Nagash. Nagash alone was eternal. Inescapable. Unavoidable.

But their servants could not be allowed to gain entrance to the underworlds of Shyish, either through the Starless Gate or any of the nine lesser gates, whose cycles of birth and death were known only to him and his mortarchs. Nothing could be allowed to interfere with his renewal, or to slow his return.

Shyish was his. The dead of all the Mortal Realms were his. And he would defend what was his, even unto the destruction of all that was. He was death, and death could not be denied, only delayed. The storm roared up around him, its fury increasing with his own. And then, just as suddenly, it died down. The snows fell and the wind dipped. Lucidity shivered apart, leaving behind only numb introspection.

Lost once more in his memories, preoccupied by what had been, Nagash turned and strode north. His form spread across the sky and faded into the darkness.

'He is gone again,' Arkhan said, as the weight of Nagash's presence faded. He and Neferata stood on the ice, far from the shore and the broken citadel of the Rictus. The Shivering Sea spread out around them, a vast grey expanse of ice that stretched to the very horizon.

Neferata nodded. 'Of course he is. What was he up to, and

was it any use?' They'd both felt the call. Nagash had long ago dispensed with any pretence of subtlety when it came to dealing with the dead. His voice was the rumble of an earthquake or the roar of a hurricane, drowning out everything else for as long as he spoke. The cunning conqueror of old was lost now, perhaps forever, subsumed by the force of nature he had become.

'Some.' Arkhan turned. 'He stirs the spirits of snow and hunger, and the ancient guardians left behind by the Broken Kings – the malignants and deadwalkers as well. The enemy numbers are parsed and pared away, as I planned.'

'As you hoped,' Neferata said. She looked out over the ever-shifting, icy surface of the Shivering Sea. The crumbled remains of a once-massive harbour clung to the shoreline. Frozen ropes creaked in the wind and tattered sails flapped mournfully. Sea birds perched on every surface, squabbling amongst themselves.

Arkhan inclined his head. 'Either way, our task is made easier.'

'Easier, but still nigh impossible.' She stroked Nagadron's broad skull, as the dread abyssal rubbed against her. 'Before Archaon wounded him, this would have been but the work of a moment. Now...'

'You speak as if he is dead,' Arkhan said.

'Isn't he? You were at the Battle of Black Skies even as I was. I helped you carry what was left of him into the underworld. He is but a shadow of what he once was, and there is less of him every day. It is as if he is... fading, becoming no better than one of those spirits which cling to him like wailing barnacles.'

Arkhan was silent. Neferata stared at him, willing him to speak. Finally, she said, 'What happens when he's dead? Truly dead?'

'He cannot die. What is death to one such as him? A setback, nothing more. A moment of a thousand years and he is returned. You know this, and yet you persist in questioning him.' Arkhan looked at her. 'Why?'

'A better question might be – why do you not?'

'Faith.'

'I call it cowardice. Nagash is a lie, Arkhan. Like all gods, his power is built on falsehood. Comforting stories to convince the gullible.' Neferata turned away as the ice shifted slightly beneath her feet. The Shivering Sea had earned its name fairly. From shore to shore it was a mass of compacted ice floes. The air was alive with a constant, booming crackle as the frozen waters bobbed continuously underfoot. In a way, it reminded her of Nagash – cold, predatory and void of all humanity.

'You have witnessed his power for yourself,' Arkhan said.

'I didn't say he wasn't powerful, did I? Merely that his godhood is an unsubstantiated claim, and nothing more.'

'Now you sound like Mannfred.'

Neferata hissed. 'Low, even for you.'

'But true. It is your nature to question, I think. A simple predatory instinct to worry the throat and crack the bone, to dig for the softness within.' Arkhan gave a rattling sigh.

Neferata peered at him, eyes narrowed.

'Are you calling me simple?'

Arkhan laughed. 'Perish the thought, O Queen of Air and Darkness. Merely pointing out that you are as he made you. As Mannfred is, and as I am.'

'He made us treacherous, then, as well as ambitious?'

'Of course. I suspect that it is the thought of either you or Mannfred taking his throne which drives him. You are the whetstones which sharpen the blade of his purpose.' Arkhan looked at her. 'I fear that purpose slumbers now.

He is here, but he does not notice us. His mind was broken on the blade of the Three-Eyed King, and it is scattered across the realm.'

'But it is strongest here, in this place, isn't it? I can feel the weight of him on the air, like an oncoming storm.' Neferata looked around. 'Is he listening now, do you think?'

'Possibly.'

'Why did you insist on meeting here, Arkhan? Of what value is this place to us? There are better places for a last stand.'

'Like Helstone?'

'Yes, or any one of a hundred other citadels which yet remain standing. A half a dozen kingdoms to the south owe fealty to me, and they would gladly take to the field in our name. Instead, we come here, to a snowy waste, full of savages and ice. So there must be a reason. What is it?' She didn't expect an answer. Not truly. Arkhan could not resist being cryptic, even with her. It was his singular vice, if a dead man could be said to have such a thing.

'Call it whimsy.'

'Do not play the fool with me. I can feel it, Arkhan. As can you – a newborn gate to Stygxx, somewhere far below us.' Neferata tapped the ice with her foot.

'Yes. It was born a few months ago. Not long after the fall of the Basalt Reach.' Arkhan leaned against his staff. 'I suspect it is the reason for this sudden invasion. The north holds little else of interest for the followers of Chaos.'

'It could be a coincidence,' Neferata said. Arkhan looked at her. She shrugged. 'Don't give me that look, old bones. I breathe the very stuff of subterfuge, and even I know that coincidences can sometimes happen, especially when all of existence is in upheaval. Reality is dying a slow death, and such twists of fate grow ever more commonplace.'

'Does it matter? They come, and we must fight. At least until the gate ceases to be in a few months' time.'

'And what if it remains for a century? Will you stand here on the ice for a hundred years? Two hundred?'

'It will not. They only last for nine months. You know this.'

'And what if, by some magic, the Ruinous Powers hold it here? What if they prevent it from dying? How long will you stand watch?'

'I will stand as long as I must. As long as Nagash commands.'

'You sound like Tamra,' Neferata said.

Arkhan glanced at her. 'You take a special interest in that one, don't you?'

'She is powerful.'

'Is that the only reason?'

Neferata chuckled. 'Perhaps not. But it is the only one I care to share with you. If she survives, she will make a powerful piece in the games to come.'

'And is that all they are to you? Pawns on a board?'

Neferata eyed him. 'What are they to you?'

'Chattel,' he said.

'A lie,' she said. 'I know you, Arkhan. And I know that you are more kindly disposed towards the living than one might guess. They have a fire in them, one that has long been extinguished in you. You bask in their heat, seeking to rekindle that which you once were.'

'And so?'

'The fire inside burns hottest of all.' She leaned close. 'Be careful that you do not burn yourself, old liche.' Arkhan clicked his black teeth in dismissal. Neferata drew back. 'Well, don't say I didn't warn you.'

She looked up. There was no sign of Nagash, but that meant nothing. He was in the air and the cold. Despite her denials, she knew that Nagash permeated his realm in ways almost impossible to fathom. 'Do you think he will help us, when the time comes?'

'I suspect so.' He turned. 'Look.'

Neferata turned. The voivodes, led by Tamra, made their way carefully across the ice. They skirted the frozen timbers and tangles of ancient rope which marked the remains of the sunken wharfs and docks of the Mandible, and trudged directly for the two mortarchs.

'You have come to a decision, then?' the liche asked, as they drew close.

'We have, O Lord of Sacrament,' Arun called, shouting to be heard over the ice. 'We are agreed – the Rictus must stand and fight. If we are to be worthy of these lands, we must be prepared to defend them.'

'Well said.' Neferata clapped her hands.

'Maybe so,' Bolgu said. 'Or maybe it's a fool's gesture.' The burly voivode looked around. 'We do not have the men to make it more than that.' He glanced at Tamra. 'Even counting the dead.'

Neferata smiled. The other voivodes recognised their betters instinctively. And even if they had not, the rulers of the Drak were surrounded by the spirits of the drowned. Ghosts clung to her coat, weeping, or else leaning in close to whisper into her ears. It was said that where Nagash walked, the dead could not help but stir. Those who were strong in the ways of necromancy woke the unquiet dead without intending to.

Tamra's face was pale and strained. Neferata could hear the murmur of the ghosts from where she stood. The Broken Kings spoke to the voivode of the Drak, pleading their case. Arkhan had only confirmed her suspicions in that regard. Tamra ven-Drak was infinitely more useful than her fellows, and had the potential to be more useful still, should she survive the battle to come. Already a plan was forming in Neferata's mind. Perhaps this spot would serve for a final stand, and more besides.

She pushed the thought aside. She had fears to allay. 'Do not fear, you shall not defend them alone,' she said, looking at Bolgu. 'Reinforcements are all around us, in the deep waters and the high crags. We shall draw the foe in, and catch him in a vice of bone and flesh.'

'The high crags? You mean... you would seek out the Prince of Crows?' Bolgu said, with a start. 'That beast has been raiding our camps since before I was born. And they've only grown bolder in recent months. My sister had a child snatched through an open window.'

'Lucky woman,' Neferata said. 'Ancient enmities must be put aside if we are to survive. We all serve Nagash – living, dead or otherwise. The ghoul-tribes will join us in war, either as they are or as ambulatory corpses. There is no third option.' She glanced at Tamra. 'I will go into the hills tomorrow. You will accompany me. A representative from the clans should be there... as a show of good faith.'

Tamra ducked her head. 'As you will, O queen.'

'Such a nice girl,' Neferata said, glancing at Arkhan.

The liche looked away.

The undead wolves pierced the curtain of snow like black arrows. A few at first, then more, then hundreds, loping across the ice field towards the rotbringer camp with a speed no living creature could match.

Pus-veined horses reared, whinnying in fear as they yanked at their pickets. Sentries retreated into the camp, bawling for aid. The rotbringers had only just begun to settle in to wait out the storm. It had come upon them suddenly, not two days since they'd fought their way through the latest horde of stumbling corpses to come between the servants of Nurgle and their goal. The storm's fury was such that it had made pressing forward impossible – even the rotbringers' endurance had its limits. Barely a third of the tents were up, and warriors scrambled to retrieve their weapons.

Festerbite stepped into Wolgus' tent. 'Blightmaster, we are beset by wild beasts.'

'Not just beasts, I think,' Wolgus said, pushing past Festerbite. 'Beasts do not move with such discipline or come in such numbers.'

'Deadwalkers,' Festerbite said. The wind had grown fierce, and eerie howls slithered through the encampment. Snarls and screams filled the air, and low, gaunt shapes darted into tents and atop wagons, eyes burning with sorcerous malignity.

'Something very much like them.' Wolgus hefted his shield. 'Come, let us see them off.'

Together, the two knights trudged into battle. The snow fell thickly, making it impossible to see more than a sword's length ahead. Snarling lupine shapes sprang at them from every direction. Muffled though it was, Festerbite could hear the rattle of weapons and the sound of steel biting flesh – others were fighting back. There was no time to retrieve Scab; the horse-thing would have to protect itself as best it could.

The rotbringer camp stretched for miles in every direction. It was a massive, sprawling jungle of tents and wagons, crudely divided into seven circles. Each circle was under the overall command of one of Wolgus' subordinates, and under ideal circumstances any of them would be capable of repulsing an attack. While the fanatics and the beastherds made do with what they had, the tents for the Order's armsmen were set up in concentric circles, with rough avenues from the outer circle to the inner. Stakes dipped in pox-broth jutted from the outer perimeters, and heavy boil-encrusted pavises, each the height of two men, lined the outside of the outer ring of tents, protecting them from arrows.

None of this, however, deterred the wolves to any appreciable degree. They bounded past the stakes and winnowed between the pavises. They tore through tents, savaging those they found within. Horse-things galloped through the camp, harried by slavering wolves, and lone warriors soon found themselves overwhelmed and buried beneath a pile of hairy bodies.

Slowly, Wolgus and Festerbite were joined by others as they pushed through the camp: blightkings, armsmen, wild-eyed beastmen and even a few pox-monks, chanting frenzied hymns to Nurgle as they wielded mace and flail in his name. The growing band fought its way towards a light which blazed up from the camp's centre.

Warm and noxious, the light melted the snow on the air and provided a welcome beacon for the struggling rotbringers. Warriors flocked to it from throughout the camp, fighting their way through a snapping gauntlet of undead beasts. Plaguebearers stalked the edges of the light, hacking down any corpse-wolf that got too close. The Order's mortal warriors staggered between this unnatural barricade and fell panting to the ground.

Festerbite was not surprised to see Gurm at the light's heart. The Herald of Nurgle was still sat atop his palanquin. The twisted sylvaneth had sprouted jewel-like seed pods which pulsed with a baleful radiance, and the ground about them steamed.

'Wolgus, my lad...' Gurm chortled, waving them towards him. 'I am most pleased to see that you are not filling the belly of one of these curs. I was about to send my flies to look for you.'

'Your concern warms the cockles of my heart, Herald,' Wolgus said. 'These things are being controlled, aren't they?'

'How ever did you guess?' Gurm licked his lips. 'You can practically taste the death-magic on the air. And some of these beasts were dead before this realm was a gleam in its creator's eye.'

'Like the bone-giant earlier,' Wolgus said. 'A trap. They wanted us to camp, so that we might provide easy meat for these creatures...'

'Then let us show them we are not such easy prey,' Festerbite said. A plaguebearer squalled as a wolf knocked it sprawling. Before it could react, the daemon was dragged out of the light and into the hissing snows by the lupine zombie. Festerbite glanced at Gurm. 'Not all of us, at any rate.'

'We endure,' Gurm said, a trifle defensively. 'That is what Nurgle made us to do.'

'No. I will not stand here and die.' Wolgus hefted his sword. 'I am a blightmaster of the Order of the Fly, and I will not perish in so unworthy a fashion.' He glanced at Festerbite. 'Are you with me, my friend?'

'Where you lead, my lord, I shall always follow,' Festerbite said.

Wolgus nodded and stepped towards the edge of the light. 'I do not know what fell spirit inhabits these husks, but whoever you are – reveal yourself!' he cried, as he slapped a snarling wolf out of the air. 'Or do you lack the courage for anything other than half-hearted attempts at assassination? Show yourself. Face me in honourable combat, and perhaps Nurgle shall move me to grant you clemency!'

'I don't think they're listening,' Festerbite said, as a half-rotted corpse slammed into his shield, jaws snapping. The wolf looked as if it had been dead for months, and it smelled worse, although under different circumstances, Festerbite thought he might have enjoyed the pungent aroma. Its teeth shattered on his shield, and he cleaved the beast's skull in two.

'Oh, he's listening,' Gurm said. Pestilential vines had sprouted from the ground around his palanquin, and a quartet of nearby wolves was caught in their writhing embrace. The corrupted sylvaneth who made up Gurm's chair shrieked in fierce agony as they manipulated the whipping tendrils. The wolves thrashed as the vines pierced their mouldering flesh and inundated them. Eventually, the vine-shrouded shapes went still. Pus-coloured blossoms sprouted on them, and the vines snapped away from their issuers with a squelching hiss.

'He who?' Wolgus demanded. 'Who attacks us?'

'Why, Nagash of course,' the daemon said. 'I thought I made that clear earlier.'

Wolgus shook his head. 'Impossible. He is dead.'

'So are they,' Gurm said. He gestured to a broken-backed wolf as it dragged itself towards Wolgus. 'Everything in these cursed lands is dead or soon to die. It does not seem to hinder them overmuch.' Out in the snows, something howled.

'Nagash,' Festerbite murmured. The name tasted strange to him, like a curse whose meaning escaped him. It was said, in the seeping halls of Cankerwall, that the Lord of Decay and his brothers-in-darkness had sealed Nagash away in a crypt of forgotten moments, burying him in the weft of time itself. But he'd been freed by the false god, Sigmar, and together they had sought to impose hideous, unchanging stagnancy on the realms of men.

Wolgus stomped on the dead wolf's skull. 'Nagash is dead. The Three-Eyed King broke him, and his legions with him.' He chopped through the spine of another, his rotsword eating away at its bones.

'Death is not the end in this realm, not even for its ruler,' Gurm said.

'These are delays, nothing more. But why?' Wolgus said. He turned to Gurm. 'Speak, Herald. What does the King of All Flies say?'

'Only that you must press forward, blightmaster. Ever forwards, never backwards. That is the way of it. We must drag this place from its stupor and make of it a garden. And quickly. That is your charge, and mine.'

The last of the wolves had fallen, but the howls continued. Festerbite turned, scanning the camp. He could still hear the sounds of fighting, though dimly, and the screams. He blinked. For a moment, he thought he'd seen something larger than any wolf, prowling through the tents.

The howls rose with the wind. Full of need and rage such as he had never known, they pierced Festerbite clean through. He looked about and saw that he was not alone in this. Even Wolgus looked taken aback.

'What is it?' the blightmaster demanded. 'Speak, Gurm – tell me!'

'Something worse than a wolf,' the Herald said. The daemon rose to his feet and chopped through one of the glowing seed pods. He tossed it to Festerbite. 'Cast that into the snows. It will take root where it falls and give us more light.'

The seed pod convulsed in his hand like a thing in pain. Glowing pus dribbled down his armour as he stepped forwards and hurled it out into the storm. Where it fell, the snow instantly turned to steam, and foetid brambles sprouted. More glowing seed pods emerged from the fast-growing brambles, washing the area around them in hazy light.

Festerbite was so preoccupied by this sudden vibrancy that he failed to notice the enormous shape speeding towards him through the snow. A shout from Wolgus caused him to turn. Something massive caught him by the head. A moment later he was wrenched from his feet and slung bodily through a sagging tent. He hit the ground hard and lay for a moment, trying to catch his breath. As he forced himself to his feet, he found himself surrounded by the bloated shapes of ogors.

But they were unlike any ogor he'd ever seen. Their forms swelled and shrank with the storm, and their eyes were hollow with hunger. They'd gnawed their lips to tatters, and each was missing a portion of flesh and muscle from its bulky frame. They stretched cold-blackened fingers towards him. He swept his sword out, but it passed cleanly through the cloudy shapes. A howl bristled upwards as they closed in on him. Too-solid blows rained down on his shield, crumpling it with monstrous ease. Hands scrabbled at his head and ankles. With a growing sense of panic, he realised that while they could easily touch him, he couldn't say the reverse was true.

Festerbite ducked his head and bulled through the ghostly ogors, eliciting a howl of frustration as he slipped their grasp. More of the hungry ghosts appeared, floating or shuffling through the snow. He saw one slide its greedy fingers into the chest of a hapless blightking, removing the warrior's heart with a triumphant groan. Another descended on a fleeing rotbringer and swallowed him up whole, leaving behind a contorted corpse curled up in the snow as it moved on to its next victim. The camp echoed with the screams of dying men and the howls of the barbarous spirits.

Everywhere he looked, ogors moved through the camp, slaying any who stood against them. Even the plaguebearers were having difficulty. As he watched, one unlucky daemon was caught between two of the cannibal sprits and torn asunder with a wet squelch. He heard a voice call out, and turned to see Wolgus striding towards him, his sword burning with a malignant light. The ancient runes etched into the blade pulsed wetly as the blightmaster swept it out and removed the head of one of the murderous spirits.

'Sir Festerbite – look out!'

Festerbite whirled around, but it was too late. The spectral ogor caught him up in its semi-tangible paws and tore at him in a frenzy. It ripped his shield from his arm and dented his war-plate. Festerbite screamed and chopped at it, trying to break its hold. His weapon passed through it harmlessly, but even so, it hurled him aside. Bleeding, he shoved himself to his feet. The ogor reached for him again, but stopped as a black blade emerged from its chest. The spirit arched in agony and clawed at itself as its form came apart like smoke on the wind. Wolgus stepped through its fading shape and caught Festerbite's arm. 'Let's get you back into that light of Gurm's. It seems to pain them, somewhat.'

'Your sword...'

'I had this sword from the Festering Seers of Plax. The contagions woven into its steel affect even the dead. Plague-fire seems to work as well. Would that we had a few more sorcerers in our ranks.' He slipped Festerbite's arm over his shoulder. 'Come, good sir knight. I'll not leave one of my brothers to the mercy of such bestial spirits.'

Festerbite's limbs were mostly in working order by the time they reached Gurm and his light. More seed pods had been distributed, creating a makeshift barricade of pestilent foliage. The ogors cringed back from the light, gnashing their broken fangs soundlessly, before turning to seek easier prey.

Outside the circle of noxious light, the fell spirits continued to ravage the camp. Occasionally, Festerbite would glimpse a flash of plague-fire or hear an agonized howl. The spectres weren't having it all their own way; there were some in the Order who possessed mystical blades or sorcerous abilities which made them a match for the ethereal dead. But not many. Not enough. Festerbite dabbed at his wounds. 'Maybe we should have stayed in Ghyran,' he murmured. Heads nodded, and agreements were murmured.

'And leave this realm to suffer so?' Wolgus asked, looking around. 'No. This is a pretty trap, I admit. But we will endure it, as we always have.' He shook his head. 'You hear, spirits? You cannot break our will, for it has already been broken. And our bodies are made of sterner stuff than bone and meat. Come upon us in wrath or in silence, and still we will triumph. Delay us, and we will only fight all the harder. Death might be inevitable – but so too are we.'

Festerbite couldn't contain the phlegm-choked cheer that welled up in his throat. The others joined him, until all of their voices were raised in a cry of defiance. Outside the daemonlight, the dead continued their attack. But it would be over soon enough. The night always ended, and the storm always abated. Some of them would survive – enough to continue the crusade, enough to wipe the north clean, and make of it a garden fit for a god.

Wolgus thrust his sword into the ground and spread his arms, as if daring whatever force was controlling the dead to come and face him. 'Do you hear me?' he cried. 'Are you listening? This is the moment we were created for. We are the knights of the Order of the Fly, the chosen sons of Nurgle. And we are implacable as the passage of time itself!'

SIX

THE PRINCE OF CROWS

This realm is mine.

All that endures within it is mine.

Every soul, every mind.

All are one with the Great Necromancer.

I see through every eye, and speak through every voice.

My blood seeps through the broken earth, and the fire of my wrath ignites the sun.

– *The Epistle of Bone*

Tamra stood on the edge of the crag, surveying the horizon. The sky here was streaked with shimmering ribbons of coloured light. The Mandible was but a distant speck, limned by the white shore of the Shivering Sea. The great slopes below were thickly forested and blanketed in snow and ice. She could see the pale smoke of cooking fires and the vast black clouds which accompanied the foe. 'They are not far at all, are they?'

Neferata clasped her shoulder. 'No.'

'From here, I can see what's left of the old harbour. My

grandfather told me stories about it. About the riches and spices and strange animals that could be seen on the wharfs, in the days before the Great Awakening. Of violet-feathered birds from the Skull Isles, and the great bats which the men of Gheist bred for war...'

'Yes,' Neferata said. 'It was a thing of glory, in its time. Before Nagash came striding south and smashed it all to bits. A great docklands such as this part of the realm had never seen. It played host to the ice-fleet of King Elig ven-Fenn, which sailed to the Rime Isles and beyond, unto the very edge of the realm itself.' Neferata stretched out her hand, drawing shapes on the frosty air. 'The Rictus were mighty, in their day.' She looked at Tamra. 'They could be again.'

'I know this,' Tamra said. 'But I doubt I will live to see it.'

'Doubt is the whetstone of hope,' Neferata said. She squeezed Tamra's shoulder gently. 'Come. Time is of the essence. We must make ready, for the foe will be here soon.'

'How soon?'

Neferata hesitated. 'Hard to say. Days, maybe. A week. A month. But sooner, rather than later. The trap is baited, and now we must ensure that the jaws will slam shut properly.'

Tamra bristled at the thought of her people as bait, but she held her tongue. To serve in life and in death, that was the law. And she would serve.

She looked at the cave. 'Is this his lair, then? The Prince of Crows?' As she spoke, she heard a caw from the trees. Carrion birds waited in the branches, watching. It was said that such creatures were the eyes of Nagash, for wherever there were carrion birds, so too there were the dead. What they saw, the Undying King saw.

'That is what you call him, yes. I knew him by another name, once.' Neferata looked up at the birds, her expression unreadable. 'He will be a strong ally, if he can be made to listen to reason.'

'And if not?' Tamra asked.

Neferata smiled. 'Well, we'll see, won't we?' She turned away.

Tamra followed Neferata towards the mouth of the cave. It sat high and back on the crag. The entrance resembled nothing so much as a borehole, angled downwards into the depths of the crag. It was almost lost to view, hidden by a thick copse of scraggly trees. Skulls hung from the branches on ropes of hair and dried ligament, dire warnings carved into the weather-scoured bone. She could feel ghosts watching them, murmuring softly in ancient tongues. The wind stirred the skulls, and they clacked loudly. She stopped and stared.

'Scared, poppet?' Adhema purred. The blood knight sat atop her coal-black steed nearby, hands draped over the pommel of her saddle. 'You smell like it.' The other blood knights chuckled softly, crimson eyes watching Tamra.

'Fear keeps the mind sharp,' Tamra said.

Adhema smiled. 'Helps with the taste, as well.'

Tamra turned away. Adhema laughed.

'Quiet,' Neferata said. She stood by the mouth of the cave, peering into the dark. 'Wait here. No matter what you hear, do not enter these caves,' she continued, looking up at Adhema. 'We will return before the moons rise.'

The blood knight nodded, frowning.

'If you're certain, my lady,' she said.

'If I were not, I would not be doing it,' Neferata said. She crooked a finger. 'Tamra, come.'

Tamra followed the mortarch dutifully. She tensed instinctively as they entered the shadowed cave. The smell of rot was thick on the air, and bones littered the ground. Animal, mostly, but some all too human, and many of those little. She gagged.

The cavern sloped downwards. She heard the drip of water and the squeak of bats. As they descended, Neferata plucked a broken skull from the ground and breathed into it. The skull, now glowing with a pale radiance, lifted up from her hands and floated ahead of them. Its light cast strange shadows on the walls. Besides the water and the bats, Tamra could discern a shuffling, sliding sound. She gripped the hilt of her sword more tightly.

'Why didn't we bring the others?' she murmured, fearful of speaking too loudly.

'One doesn't introduce a new predator into another's territory without asking. It's dangerous, and rude besides.' Neferata smiled. 'That's why I left Nagadron at the Mandible. One must display politesse in these situations – a lesson you'd do well to remember, sister.'

'Why do you call me that? We are not sisters.'

'Are we not? We are both members of a great sorority, Tamra ven-Drak – the women who speak for the dead. Men drag the dead from their slumber and bind them, but we coax them up. We do not enslave. Instead, we command, as is our right.'

Tamra shook her head. If there was a difference there, she wasn't seeing it.

Neferata glanced at her and smiled. 'You are my sister because I have decided such. If it displeases you, I shall not call you that again. Does it displease you?'

Tamra hesitated. 'No,' she said, finally. 'It is a great honour.' And it was. For was Neferata not Mortarch of Blood, the Sword of Nagash and kastellan of his citadels? Her name echoed through the histories of every kingdom, and her hand had guided the fates of untold billions, both living and dead.

Neferata laughed. 'There are some who would disagree, I assure you.' The echoes of her amusement bounced from wall to ceiling, setting bats to flight. She stopped. 'Ah. Look, sister. What do you see?'

By the light of the floating skull, Tamra could see images painted on the walls of the cavern. They were primitive, but somehow recognisable. Drawn to them despite herself, she stepped closer. They showed wars, famines and feasts, victories and defeats, crudely rendered by uncertain hands. 'Are these… What are they?'

'A record of ancient times. The story of those who inhabit these caves, and how they came to be here.' Rocks clattered as Neferata continued on. Tamra turned to follow, though not without some reluctance. 'What do you know of those days?' Neferata asked. 'Of the foolish ambition of High-King Tarun and his five cousins, and their final stand here?'

'My mother told me tales of Queen Isa and her brother Rikan,' Tamra said, stumbling after Neferata. She could hear the whispering of the Broken Kings, rising up out of the dark. She and Neferata were close to where they had been entombed, and their voices were clearer now. She could also make out the words. Not the usual implorations these, but instead... warnings?

Neferata's hand on her shoulder startled her. The vampire had moved behind her so quickly that Tamra hadn't noticed. 'Rikan the Handsome and Isa the Wise,' the mortarch said. 'The children of Arek ven-Drak, left to rebuild his clan in the wake of Nagash's invasion. And what do you know of them?'

'Rikan vanished in the third year after the Great Awakening. Some say he tried to kill Nagash, in order to free his father's spirit...'

'Yes,' Neferata said. 'The handsome ones are always a bit foolish. The Drak were better left to Isa at any rate. They didn't call her "the wise" for nothing.'

'I am descended from her,' Tamra said, proudly. 'It was she who composed the nine rites of revivification, and taught us how to keep the deadwalkers at bay after the Great Awakening.'

'Mm. And I taught her,' Neferata said.

Tamra paused. 'How old are you?' she asked, before she could stop herself.

Neferata laughed. 'Older than these hills, and younger than the seas.' She frowned. 'And sometimes I think I am older even than that.'

Tamra made to reply, but a sudden thrill of cold ran through her. She stopped, eyes searching the shadows. Vague shapes, clad in ancient armour and robes of archaic cut, beckoned to her from out of the darkness. Their broken skulls glowed with witchfire, and their voices swelled like thunder.

Free us... free us, daughter of our daughter... free us... do not listen to her... queen of lies... free us...

'Be silent,' Neferata snapped. 'We did not come here to speak to the dead.'

The Broken Kings receded sullenly. Tamra had not thought that ghosts could be offended, but these plainly were. 'They are retreating.'

'You hear them as well, don't you?' Neferata asked. At Tamra's hesitant nod, she smiled. 'I thought as much. You are more sensitive than the others. They can call up the dead, but you can also hear them. That is good.'

'I wish they would be silent,' Tamra said.

'Why? If their cries bother you so much, tell them so. Silence them.'

Tamra looked at her. 'I do not have such power.'

'Don't you? If you can hear them, then they can hear you. Speak – bid them be silent, as I did. Here, I will help.' Cool fingertips were pressed to Tamra's temples. Her heart sped up as

Neferata leaned close and murmured, 'Relax your mind. Let them in. They cannot harm you. Not while I am here.'

Tamra closed her eyes and forced herself to do as Neferata said. In her mind's eye, she saw crackling amethyst skeins stretching down into the roots of the mountain and heard the rush of voices, like batwings fluttering against the inside of her skull.

Free... us...

'No. Be silent,' Tamra said, and Neferata echoed her. 'Be still.'

No... no... speak the words... shatter our chains...

'I said be still,' she grated, pressing back against the sudden surge of pressure. They clawed at her mind, demanding and pleading. She lashed out, letting her anger heat the blade of her disdain. A thin scream, as if from some animal, greeted her blow, and the voices receded with a sound like leaves whirling down a culvert. When she came back to herself, she was panting from the exertion. She felt wrung out, and every limb trembled. 'They are strong.'

Neferata released her and stepped back. 'In life, they were steeped in the stuff of death. The first of your folk to learn the secrets Nagash guarded so jealously, for so long. I suppose Arkhan told you to ignore them?'

Tamra nodded. 'He said that they were oathbreakers.'

'Of course he did. For Arkhan, the world is a muddle of absolutes. That is his prerogative, as the mouthpiece of a god. For the rest of us, well... things are not always that simple.' Neferata caught one of Tamra's braids and gave it a gentle tug. 'Once, six kings, brothers all and rulers of six mighty kingdoms, sought to challenge Nagash. They thought power was their due, that it was theirs by dint of the sweat on the brows of their forebears. And so, when Nagash claimed these lands for his own, they sought to hold what they had.'

'What we have, we hold,' Tamra said, softly.

Neferata smiled. 'Yes. Six stood against the Undying King. And six great kingdoms were broken into six hundred petty, squabbling fiefdoms. All that power, once concentrated, was diffused. A good policy for peacetime, but a bad one when the winds of war blow anew.'

'What do you mean?'

'It is time for that power to once again be consolidated. Not six hundred, not even six, but one.' Neferata held up her fist. 'The time for debate, for argument with equals, has passed. Now is the time for swift action. Do you understand?'

Tamra swallowed. 'No.'

Neferata chuckled. It sounded to Tamra like the contented rumble of a tigress, fresh from the kill. 'I think you do. You hear the dead, Tamra ven-Drak. So listen to me now. You alone of your fellow chieftains have stood firm against the enemy in the field. You alone have survived where countless others have fallen, never to rise again. It is you whom the Broken Kings beg for their freedom, not Bolgu or the witch, Myrn.'

'I will not free them,' Tamra said, quickly.

'Nor did I imply that you should. But do you not think that the fact is significant?' Neferata circled her, trailing long fingers across the nape of her neck. 'Love is earned, but power must be taken, sister. That is where the Broken Kings made their mistake, and where your fellow chieftains make theirs. They, like Arkhan, see the world as an absolute. Thus it is, and thus it must ever be. But when Nagash came, the old order was overthrown and a new order raised up.'

'And now?'

'And now, new is old, and must give way as its predecessor did.' Neferata leaned close, and Tamra shivered at the unnatural chill which radiated from the vampire's flesh.

'I will not break the law of Nagash. I cannot.'

'And what is the law? Serve Nagash, in life and in death. How will you serve him, as you are? Chieftain of a scattered tribe, one voice amongst many? You hide your power, refusing the path fate has laid out for you.' Neferata's fingers played across Tamra's throat and her cheeks, spider-light touches. 'I understand, more than you can know. But there is a time to rage against fate, and a time to accede to it.'

Tamra stepped away from the vampire. Neferata's eyes glowed like those of a beast in the dimness of the cavern. 'Even if I did, what would be the use?' she said, quickly. 'The Rictus have neither the numbers nor the discipline to make even a single army. Those days died with the Broken Kings.' Her words echoed strangely in the cavern, and she had the impression that someone or something other than Neferata was listening. She heard a soft skittering in the dark, and she felt her hackles rise in a sudden premonition.

'Did they? I think not. And even if they did, what is death to you or I?' Neferata laughed. 'Besides, the Rictus are greater than you imagine. Whole armies crouch in these lightless tunnels, waiting for the call to war.' She clapped her hands together, and all at once they were limned with an amethyst fire. Purple light swelled to fill the cavern.

Tamra stared about her in dawning horror. The sudden radiance revealed hundreds of monstrous shapes surrounding them, either on the floor or clinging to the walls. There was no need to seek out the ghoul-tribes, it seemed.

'The corpse-eaters,' she spat, reaching for her sword.

Neferata caught her wrist. 'More than that, Tamra ven-Drak. These are your kin. They too are Rictus, though greatly altered by time and the magic radiating from the tombs of the Broken Kings. Who do you think painted those murals? Now, be silent.'

Tamra did as Neferata commanded, biting back a denial. The Rictus respected death in all its permutations, but corpse-eaters were slaves to it. Her people occasionally consumed the flesh of enemies, but only in ritual fashion and at certain times of year. And they never cracked the bones or rooted in entrails like a forest pig. But ghouls were beasts, and worse than beasts. The Drak hunted them with dogs and fire in the weaning season.

'Who comes hither?' a guttural voice called out. 'Speak, lest we slay thee.' It spoke in an archaic dialect, and Tamra could only just understand it. She had not imagined such creatures could talk. The thought of it sent a shiver down her spine.

'You may try, by all means,' Neferata replied. 'Who are you, to demand my name?'

'We are Rictus, and these ramparts are ours.'

'And I am Neferata, Chatelaine of Gallowdeep Manse and Voivode of the Nightlands.' She spread her arms, her hands still wreathed in crackling purple flames. 'Do you still wish to challenge me?' A sudden hush fell over the scuttling shapes, and they drew back as one, away from the light and from her. Neferata nodded in satisfaction. 'I see you still know me. Good. That will make this easier. Where is he? Where is the Prince of Crows?'

'Here, O Queen of Blood.'

Tamra whipped around. The voice had come from close behind her. She drew her sword, but not swiftly enough. Strong hands gripped her throat and bore her backwards. She struck the ground painfully, and let out a cry. A monstrous face glared down into hers, every scar and wrinkle illuminated by the light from Neferata's hands.

'Isa?' the monster said, in evident confusion. 'Is that you, Isa?'

'Get off her, Rikan. She is not yours,' Neferata snarled. She booted the creature in the face, knocking it sprawling. 'Touch her again, touch anything I have claimed without my permission, and I will burn your pestiferous kingdom to ashes.'

Rikan swept out a long arm, driving Neferata back. 'Who are you to lay claim to anything, Queen of Lies? These lands are mine. I am High-King of the Rictus, son of Arek ven-Drak and last prince of the Sudden Reach.'

Tamra froze. It couldn't be, could it? She stared at the feral monstrosity, trying to discern his features beneath the filth of ages.

The ghoul-king righted himself and crouched, ready to attack. 'These lands are mine to guard, until such time as Nagash forgive us our trespasses,' he continued.

'And will that forgiveness be forthcoming, when you blithely attack his messenger?'

'Messenger?' The creature's eyes narrowed. 'Then he has absolved you of your crimes?'

'What crimes would those be, Rikan?'

The ghoul-king threw back his head and howled. The others joined him, until the cavern reverberated with their caterwauling. Tamra clapped her hands over her ears and squeezed her eyes shut, trying to block out the abominable sound. The ghoul-king lowered his head and spread his arms. 'You know your crimes, woman, even as I know mine. For them, I was left to make a kingdom here, in the dark, with the last of my father's courtiers. We stand watch over our fathers and keep them still.'

'Then you are doing a very bad job of it, for I've been hearing them for days,' Neferata said. 'Whining like whipped dogs, begging to see the light of the moons once more. High-King – pfaugh! You rule nothing. The world has moved on and left you in the dust.'

'Do not listen to her, Isa,' Rikan said, glaring at Tamra. 'It was her honeyed words which set our fathers on the road to ruin. It was she, the mistress of all lies, who pricked the ambition of the great kings and pitted them against Nagash. And all for what?'

'You tell me, Prince of Crows. It's your story, after all.' Neferata smiled serenely. 'And what a lovely fable it is. If I were at fault for even half of what I'm blamed for, surely Nagash would have struck me down long before now.'

'And where is Nagash?' the ghoul-king said. He lifted his crooked, ape-like arms over his bestial head. 'Not here. He too is dust, I think. As you will be, Queen of Lies.' He tensed. 'I will rend you and make bread from your bones to feed my people.' The ghouls set up a clamour at that, cheering on their monstrous king.

Tamra looked around, filled with an atavistic dread by the sound. The whispers of the Broken Kings returned, more urgent than before. If the ghouls attacked, she might have no choice but to free them.

Neferata spread her arms. 'Then step forward, by all means.' Her smile widened, and her fangs gleamed in the violet light bleeding from her hands. Rikan growled and stepped towards her, claws raised. All around them, the watching ghouls began to slap the walls and floor of the cave, filling the air with a harsh rhythm.

'No,' Tamra said, without thinking. She stepped between them, hands raised. 'We don't have time for this.' Heart hammering, she locked eyes with the Prince of Crows, willing him to listen. He snarled, but subsided.

'Step aside, Isa,' the ghoul-king said. 'I would not see you harmed on her account.'

'No one will be harmed here,' Tamra said. She looked at Neferata. 'We came for help, not to settle old scores.'

'Mind your tongue, sister. I am no duardin, to nurture petty grudges like a child. He insulted me, and I will not stand for it.' Neferata's hand fell to the hilt of the long, curved dagger thrust through her belt.

'And you insult me,' Tamra said, softly.

Neferata blinked.

'I understand now why you brought me. He calls me Isa, as you did. Did you think I would not remember?'

Neferata smiled and inclined her head. 'I am found out. I fear I've grown less subtle in these trying times. Or perhaps you are simply wiser than your years.'

Rikan lurched forwards, talon-tips digging into the sleeves of Tamra's coat. 'Do not listen to her, Isa. Her words are barbed to catch the unwary. She flatters with one side of her mouth, even as she curses with the other.'

Tamra forced herself to meet the demented creature's eyes. He stank of madness and spoiled meat. 'Maybe so,' she said, 'but she is our ally.'

'Ours?'

'You are High-King, and your people need you once more.'

'My... people?'

'The Rictus Clans stand ready to follow you, my lord. Our lands are beset by invaders from the south – spreaders of disease and worshippers of the plague. Their numbers stretch across the horizon, and the thud of their drums shakes the ice from the highest crags.' She spoke quickly, giving him no time to question. 'You've heard them, I know. Sound carries fast in these hills. They destroy all in their path and harry our people.'

'Invaders,' he repeated, dully. 'Who would dare invade us? Our lands are mighty, and our armies mightier still. No. No, this is a trick. I am king. And my royal decree is this – death. Take her,' he said, flinging out a claw to indicate Neferata. He hauled Tamra back. 'One side, sister. Our kin scream in the dark for the blood of she who betrayed them, and we will have our fair due.'

'No,' Tamra said. Desperate, she drew her sword and held the edge beneath his throat. The ghoul-king paused, eyes wide. 'Isa? Who taught you to use a sword?'

'My name is Tamra ven-Drak. I am not Isa, though I am descended of her line.' She reached out and gestured, calling on the spirits of those who had died in the caverns. The bones strewn across the cavern floor began to rattle. 'I am your ally, as is Neferata. You must listen.'

'Ally? We need no allies such as her. She is sand and fog. Better to scatter her to the night than seek to build upon her good nature.'

Neferata laughed. 'Your time grubbing in the midden pits has addled you, Prince of Crows. You think Nagash will forgive this?'

'Nagash is dead, and all his slaves with him, I think. Else you would not risk coming here and spinning pretty words of alliance. Nagash is dead. Thus, go all tyrants.' The ghoul-king leered at her. 'We are free.' He swatted Tamra's sword away with inhuman speed and leapt for Neferata. The mortarch shrieked and reached for the curved dagger sheathed on her hip as the rest of the ghouls closed in. Tamra stumbled back and flung her will out, into the bones, willing them to rise. They clattered upright, but only for a moment. She clutched her head and screamed, as her will was snuffed in an instant. The dead collapsed back into oblivion.

No.

The word echoed through the vaulted cavern, sending bats into panicked flight. Tamra staggered back against a stalagmite, her head aching. Ghouls wailed and fell grovelling, or else fled into the darkness as the walls cracked and stalactites speared down to splinter across the floor. A pale purple radiance spilled from the growing cracks in the cave walls.

No. Freedom is an illusion. An aberration. The natural order is maintained. You belong to me, Rikan ven-Drak.

'No...' Rikan mewled. He threw up his talons in denial as rock shifted, contorting itself into a new and more horrible shape. The intensity of the amethyst light grew, bathing the entire cavern. Tamra stared in horrified fascination as part of the cavern wall twisted into the shape of a titanic skull. The great jaws moved.

Yes. I see all. I hear all. Nagash is all.

'Nagash,' Tamra breathed. His will weighed on hers like a mountain, crushing all thought and desire into base servitude. She wanted to crawl before him, to grovel as the ghouls were doing. It was only that he had not yet noticed her that allowed her to retain her dignity. To be ignored thus seemed at once a blessing and a curse – how much more painful, more wonderful, must it be to have his full attention upon you?

'My lord,' Neferata said. 'A most timely intervention.'

Neferata. My Mortarch of Blood. My Queen of Mysteries. Why do you cloud your mind? What do you hide from me?

'A woman must have her secrets, my lord,' Neferata said. She did not look directly at the leering skull, Tamra noticed, though whether due to fear or simple caution, she couldn't say.

I could take them from you.

'Yes.' Neferata knelt, arms spread, head thrown back. 'Do as you will.'

The glow blazed brightly, but only for a moment. As it faded, Tamra felt the titanic presence fade with it. Rikan lay on the ground, curled into a ball and whimpering. Neferata rose slowly. She was trembling.

'You said he was gone,' Tamra said, her voice hoarse with fear.

'He is. Mostly.' Neferata shook herself. 'What remains is still impressive, however.' She nudged the insensate ghoul-king with her foot. 'Up, dog. We have a battle to plan.'

The rotbringer camp sprawled across the diseased remains of a village. Its former inhabitants had either drunk from the Fly-blown Chalice and accepted the blessings of Nurgle, or they now decorated one of the many impaling stakes which the Order's armsmen raised with much gusto and mirth about the camp. Great tents of hide, silk and scale squatted on the frozen ground, and in the largest of these, the knights of the Order gathered.

'The root-kings came for us then, in their tangled phalanxes,' Sir Balagos said, as he took a long slurp from his ranklewine. He held court amongst his fellow knights, as he often did, sharing tales of triumph and treachery. 'They erupted from the lower levels of the Palace of Roots like termites spilling from a mound. Ironwood shields arrayed in serpentine fashion, the ranks of the duardin undulated, curving forward and coiling back. We knew, with a certainty born of controlled despair, that they would squeeze us like a boil should they close with us. Here was a pretty challenge, and one we rose to meet.'

Balagos was a burly warrior, his immensity barely contained by the creaking facets of his rust-riddled war-plate. He commanded a troop of hardy knights and a scrum of rot-riders – savages from the veldts of Ghyran who spread sickness wherever they roamed. Balagos had fought alongside Wolgus in the Jade Kingdoms, rising to high rank after his part in the taking of the Palace of Roots. Festerbite had heard the story often enough, but it never failed to fill him with a vicarious sense of triumph. The root-kings had been deadly warriors, and the tangled beards of their champions still hung in a place of honour in Cankerwall.

Festerbite wasn't the only one eager to hear the rest of the tale. The other knights leaned forwards on their stools and benches, goblets and mugs clutched tight. It was good to hear a story of triumph, of past victories, in days like these. The inside of the command tent was pleasantly stifling. Servants poured murky water over banks of coals, filling the air with a bitter steam. Chaos hounds lazed on the ground, gnawing broken bones or hunks of rotting flesh. Playful nurglings squawked and fought with each other beneath the benches, or else climbed the legs and capes of the gathered knights.

It was the first chance they'd had to truly rest since the attack by the spectral ogors. The ghosts had faded with the storm, leaving behind hundreds of bodies and a wrecked camp. But the pox-crusade endured. They'd left more than a third of their forces scattered between where they now camped and the Ithilian Gate, but those who remained were more determined than ever. The plague-bells rang day and night now, and the rotbringers sang hymns to Nurgle's majesty with greater fervour than before. It would take more than hungry ghosts to deter the Order of the Fly from its holy task. Or so they told themselves.

'Well? Get on with the story,' Croga demanded. The warrior was a renegade from the lowlands, clad in battered furs and stained, mismatched armour. He'd led his people in sipping from the Flyblown Chalice the very day the crusade had arrived on his doorstep, after first bashing out the brains of his voivode. His skin was already starting to bubble with the blessings of Nurgle, and his warriors had proven to be excellent guides. Even so, Festerbite couldn't bring himself to quite trust the turncoat. A man who betrayed one oath might very well betray another.

'Patience is the gardener's virtue, my friend,' Wolgus said, stooping to enter the tent. A scrawny fly-monk entered behind him. The zealot wore rough, filth-encrusted robes, designed to inflame and infect the sores on his god-touched flesh. The sign of the fly had been cut into his cheeks and brow. Wolgus motioned. 'Please, brother. If you would...'

At Wolgus' gesture, the zealot slid his robes down, revealing a wealth of sores and pus-oozing wounds on his back. Festerbite was amused to see that the encrustations had taken the form of a crude map. The fly-monk knelt before them, proffering the seeping diagram for their perusal. Wolgus caught up a stool and joined them, shooing a nurgling away from the map. 'These are the lands ahead, as near as we can gather.' He nodded to Croga as he said it. 'The ground turns hilly here. High crags, thick forests and then, finally, the Shivering Sea.' He prodded the map, prompting the monk to squirm. 'The savages flee before us, racing to the sea.' He glanced at Croga. 'No offense, my friend.'

'None taken,' Croga said. 'They're not running to the sea. They're fleeing to the Mandible. A redoubt. High, thick walls with mountains on one side and the sea on the other.'

'I suspected as much,' Wolgus said. 'The attacks we've endured have been nothing more than delaying tactics, to keep us from reaching them before they're ready. It's to be a siege then, if we continue.' He leaned forwards. 'Something we lack the numbers for, I fear.' He looked around. 'Who are we missing?'

'Bubos and Phlegmaxius both went south a day ago,' Balagos said. 'Looking for plunder, most like.' They weren't the only ones. Half a dozen chieftains, captains and champions had gone missing, and their followers with them. Some had doubtless grown bored with the column's deliberate pace and set off to find what loot they could. But the others had likely perished out in the wilderness, eaten by deadwalkers or something worse.

'And Tulg the Wide has been gone for nearly three days,' Festerbite said. The sorcerer had vanished into the north, leading a raiding party against the Drak, one of the local tribes.

'Croga's woodsmen can keep an eye out for both him and the others, though I fear the worst.' Wolgus frowned as he spoke. 'I hoped to be the sword, piercing the breast of our foe. Instead, we are to be the cudgel, battering them until they fall.' He looked around. 'We need a place to make a stand. Our camps are attacked every night by roving corpses. We need walls and time to rest, to let our poxes wax anew.'

'My rot-riders spotted a fortress, or what's left of one, on a high crag two days' ride to the west,' Balagos said. He tapped the festering surface of the map with a blunt finger. 'It would make an ideal keep, with a few civilising touches.'

'You'd be dead in a week,' Croga said. He sniffed and spat. 'I know that heap... It's already inhabited, and not by anything we'd want to meet. Best give it a wide berth.'

'By the garden, are all you Rictus so cowardly?' Balagos said. He slapped the map, causing the zealot to whimper. 'Who are you to tell a true son of Nurgle where he might go?'

The tribesman grinned blearily at Balagos. 'Someone who knows which way the wind is blowing. And the wind from that keep blows foul. Nagash himself cracked those walls, and the spirits of the dead rise wild from its stones.' He looked at Wolgus. 'This is all Nagash's doing.'

'Nagash is dead,' Wolgus said. The words lacked the power they'd had only a few days ago. Festerbite shifted his weight, trying not to think of what he'd seen and heard since then. Nagash wasn't dead, or at least death wasn't slowing him up all that much. None of the others seemed convinced. They looked away from the blightmaster, refusing to meet his eyes.

On that note, the meeting ended. As the others retreated into their stories or a barrel of rot-wine, Wolgus gestured for Festerbite to follow him. He accompanied the blightmaster out into the yellow slurry of the camp. The snow here had long since melted, leaving only patches of scabrous dirt and fleshy, sweating flowers. Tents made of rawhide, filthy silk and tanned human skin flapped in the wind. The comforting hum of flies filled the air.

They'd moved further north since the last attack, and they'd lost more warriors since. It was no wonder the more fragile servants of the Dark Gods had quickly lost their stomach for such expeditions. Every night was full of new horrors. Great bats swooped out of the dark and snatched away horses and men alike. Mournful siren calls rose to brain-splitting shrieks just outside of camp, and come morning, dead sentries littered the perimeter.

Though he said nothing, Festerbite had noticed that Wolgus' earlier fire had begun to dim. The blightmaster was hard-pressed to keep the disparate elements of the crusade in line, and his mood suffered the worse for it. With warriors dying left and right, wandering off or simply disappearing, their once overwhelming force had shrunk considerably in the mere weeks since their arrival. Festerbite and the other knights did what they could to keep the grumblers silent, but it wasn't enough. They needed rest, and time for the mortals to regain their courage.

The heart of their current camp had once been a village, but it was in a sorrowful state. They couldn't stay here long. 'The hope of a moment is but the foundation stone of everlasting regret, and today's palace is tomorrow's ruin,' Wolgus said, looking around.

The village had been burned to celebrate their triumph. Despite the devastation, Festerbite could still see how primitive it had been. There were no great houses here, as there were in Cankerwall, no high ramparts or boil-domed temples. Instead, it was all huts of stone and fences of wood and bone. What few altars or totems were in evidence had been broken and scattered, or else daubed in those hues blessed of Nurgle.

'What manner of god would force his people to live such lives?' he said. 'They huddle in frozen caves, worshipping bones and devouring one another. There is no joy here, no life – only animal persistence.' He looked around. 'I cannot understand it. Why do they not welcome us? Are they truly so ignorant that they prefer such stark deprivation to the rank warmth and noisome beauty of Grandfather's garden?'

'They are savages, good Sir Festerbite, and know no better,' Wolgus said. He bent and retrieved something from the ashes. Festerbite thought it might have been a child's toy, before the flames had gotten to it. Wolgus dusted ash from it, and stood. Still examining it, he said, 'That is why we have come – to teach them, to turn them from their false god and to the worship of the true powers which rule the realms. As we have begun to do in Ghyran and in Ghur, so we shall do in Shyish.'

'Do you think they will thank us?' Festerbite asked. Already, thick creepers were winnowing through the snow, and blister-flowers were blooming in the ashes. Soon, the snows would melt away, and the air would grow warm and thick, the way it was meant to be. The dead on their stakes were rotting now, their flesh blighted by the very wood which pierced it, and the miasma which erupted from them would soon sweeten the air and soil.

Wolgus tossed the toy down. 'It doesn't matter. The thrust of our crusade, Sir Festerbite, remains the same – to free the living from the tyranny of the dead.'

'And a most glopsome endeavour it is, my friend,' Gurm said, as his palanquin shuffled towards them on creaking limbs. Plaguebearers shuffled in his wake, sewing the broken ground with mouldy seeds culled from the twisted sylvaneth. This place would blossom full in time, vomiting forth the pestilential flowers of Grandfather's garden. 'The Lord of All Things is pleased. Listen – the flies hum with his blessings.' The daemon put one claw to the side of his head in an exaggerated gesture. 'Such fertile soil you have tilled for me, Wolgus. I look forward to tending these gardens in the aeons to come, for they will yield such a magnificent bounty.'

'As it pleases you, Herald. We but serve Nurgle's wishes, as any true knight must.' Wolgus turned to the daemon. 'Croga's pathfinders say they fled north. Towards the sea.'

'Just like all the others,' Festerbite added.

The daemon glanced at him. 'And so? There is only ice there. Ice and snow.'

'And well they know it,' Wolgus said. 'So why do they flee there? And why do the dead seek to delay us so, rather than simply bring us to open, honourable battle?'

'Who knows why the dead do anything. Nagash is mad, and his puppets are madder still.' Gurm sank back into his cushions, cyclopean eye narrowed. 'Perhaps they lack the strength.'

'Or perhaps it's a trap,' Wolgus said bluntly.

'And so? That's no reason to let them get away, eh?' Festerbite grimaced. Most daemons had little understanding of strategy and tactics. They saw no reason not to blunder into a trap, as long as it allowed them to swiftly claim a few more souls.

'No,' Wolgus said. 'Neither is there any reason to hurry.' He scuffed the ground with his boot, drawing a ragged shape in the snow and ash. 'The land narrows to an isthmus. We control everything to the south, and can fortify the high passes, preventing escape...'

'And why would we waste time doing that?' Gurm asked.

'Because we have plenty of it. What is time to us? We contain them, until support can arrive from further south. Perhaps we shall even call upon my fellow blightmasters. We hold the Ithilian Gate, after all, and the lands around it. Reinforced, our crusade will surely cleanse the north in Nurgle's name. And while we wait, we will ensure that your gardens grow fast and strong.'

'And you think support is coming, do you?' Gurm leaned forwards, balancing his chins on the pommel of his balesword.

'Of course. Are we not Nurgle's chosen pestilence? Are we not his blessed infection, thrust deep into the flesh of this realm? Others will come to join our crusade. I ask only that we give them the time to do so.' Wolgus spoke so intently that Festerbite found himself nodding along with his words.

'And let them share in your rightful glory too, I expect,' said Gurm.

Wolgus hesitated, then nodded. 'Yes, if need be. The garden is large enough for all. Perhaps those who flee will come to see that, if we but give them time. Even the strongest affliction needs time to flourish. Time is our ally in this holy endeavour, Gurm. Our strength waxes as theirs can only wane.'

Gurm laughed. 'Your generosity does you credit, Wolgus. Grandfather would surely approve.' He sat back. 'But we have a schedule to keep. We are not builders, we are butchers. We must push to the sea and set this land alight with plague-fires.

We must make mulch for the garden, and harrow the land so that Grandfather's bounty might spread.'

'We lack the numbers to hold this land, Herald.' Wolgus gestured. 'These delays have cost us more than time – they have cost us warriors. Supplies. All that we have left, we carry. Our servants are starving, and not even your verdant bounty can keep all of them fed in these conditions. If we press on, we risk losing everything.'

'And I said we are not builders. We go forwards. Or I go forwards. It matters not at all to me, Wolgus. Cringe in fear, if you wish. I had thought your Order made of sterner stuff than that, but I see that once more Father Nurgle is let down by his mortal children. Oh, how he shall weep when I speak to him of this...'

Wolgus stiffened. 'You would dishonour me?'

'You dishonour yourself, with this moaning of numbers and fortifications. There is a perfectly good fortress waiting for us at land's end. Let us simply take that one, eh?'

'And if we cannot?'

Gurm scratched his chins. 'Then you are buried in a shroud of glory. Cankerwall will echo with the songs of your deeds, and those of your loyal knights. Is that not what every knight lives for?'

Festerbite felt a pang at the daemon's words, and he knew Wolgus did as well. To die gloriously, in Grandfather's name, was the secret yearning of every servant of the Order. For those who did would surely be reborn in Nurgle's garden.

Wolgus grunted and turned away. 'Fie on you, daemon. You prick my sense of duty.'

'As a thorn pricks the flesh of a gardener. A reminder of what is, and what shall be.' Gurm licked his blistered lips and grinned. 'Such is my burden, Wolgus. I am the voice of the

King of All Flies, and it is through me that you know his will. And his will is that we press on, further, farther and faster, until all of this realm is his.'

SEVEN

THE CROSSING

Nagash still endures.
While he stands, his enemies shall not prevail.
Where he strides, all schemes will come undone.
Where he sets his standards, so shall victory be assured for those who follow him.
Heed the words of Nagash.

– *The Epistle of Bone*

Tamra watched as children chased each other across the ruined forecourt, scattering what few goats and chickens remained in their heedless flight. She smiled, thinking of the days when she and Sarpa had done the same. The smile faded as quickly as it had come, and her hand fell to the pommel of his sword.

Even now it was warm with the touch of the lightning which had claimed him. Better the lightning than the plague-fire, perhaps. But he was gone either way. Sarpa was gone. Nagash was gone. The world was dying. She could feel it every time she called up the dead, or spoke to the spirits. It was all winding down, and there was nothing she could do about it. Nothing at all.

Free... us...

She closed her eyes and willed them to be silent, as Neferata had taught her. The Broken Kings subsided, if grudgingly. She would be glad when this was done, when she could leave this place and its captive spirits. Let them howl into the wind, if they wished. So long as she didn't have to hear it. Sighing, she looked up. The forecourt led to the seaward gate, and past it the ruins of the once-great docks were visible. The prows and masts of broken ships jutted from the ice like tombstones. In the dull light of midday, the Shivering Sea seemed to stretch on into an infinity of white and grey.

Somewhere, on the other side of infinity, were the Rime Isles: desolate, empty of all human life and far from the reach of the enemy. It was no wonder that Bolgu and the Fenn wished to flee there. The isles could support the Rictus, though only crudely. They could rebuild, grow and even prosper. Or perhaps that was nothing more than an idle fancy – if even these harsh lands had been invaded, was anywhere truly safe?

She walked as she thought. Warriors nodded as she passed and murmured respectful greetings. Clansfolk offered her choice cuts of meat, jugs of goat's milk and scraps of fine cloth as a show of ritual deference. She thanked them but refused their gifts, as was custom. The people did not serve their voivode. The voivodes served their people.

Outside the walls of the Mandible, the full force of the winter wind plucked at her. She shivered and pulled her coat close as she passed through the tumbledown wreckage of a once-proud city. She could smell the midden pits and the plague tents beyond them. The rotbringers sowed sickness on the wind, and some of the Rictus had fallen ill as they fled their lands. The sick were housed in tents far back from the walls, where they awaited their turn for their souls to be granted the mercy of death, and their tortured flesh, the release of fire. The strongest were tended by lesser shamans and root-witches, whose arts were those of life rather than death. They might survive.

She crossed the shore and stepped into the ruined docklands. Several of the ice-cutter galleys favoured by the Fenns were beached on shore, waiting for the order to shove off. The thick metal-shod prows of the galleys were curved like axes, so as to crack the ice which covered the water and provide ease of passage. If it came to it, the galleys would carry all those who reached them away from danger and to the safety of the Rime Isles.

Frost-encrusted wooden planks creaked beneath her feet as she moved along the docks. The remains of broken ships littered the landscape, protruding at odd angles from beneath the ice. When Nagash had come, he had smashed the fleet first, so that none could escape. Only those vessels which had already been at sea had escaped him. Of those that did, only a few survived the zombie merwyrms and frost-drakes which surged in the Undying King's wake. Some among the Fenn whispered that many of those undead monstrosities yet slumbered beneath the frozen waters, waiting for Nagash's call.

She stopped at the edge of the docks and looked out over the ice. She could make out the thin figure of Arkhan the Black, still standing where she'd last seen him, his dread abyssal crouched at his side. Beneath the omnipresent crackling of the ice, she could hear the rasp of his voice. He was chanting, though she did not recognise the language.

The Mortarch of Sacrament frightened her. Neferata did as well, but for different reasons. Arkhan, like Nagash, stood at an implacable remove from Tamra and her people. It was as if he were apart from the natural flow of things, and yet somehow more real than the world around him. She could feel the chill force of his power from where she stood.

'Going somewhere, poppet?' a voice called down. Tamra looked up. Adhema sat in the canopy of ragged sails and broken masts above, sharpening her sword.

'I wish to speak to Lord Arkhan,' Tamra said. The blood knight was always around where she was least wanted, or needed. Her fellow blood knights, at least, were helping prepare the Mandible's few remaining defences for the battle to come. But Adhema seemed to have no patience for such things.

'Now, why would you wish to do that, hmm?' Adhema stopped her sharpening and looked down. 'What could you have to say to that old bag of bones?'

'It is none of your affair.'

'No, it isn't. And yet the question stands.' Adhema lifted her sword and peered down its length. 'Are you plotting, poppet?'

'Do not call me that,' Tamra said.

'But that is what you are, poppet – a new plaything for our gentle queen.' Adhema dropped gracefully from her perch. Even in full armour, she made barely any noise when she landed. 'A puppet, a poppet, a play-pretty...' she said, in a sing-song voice.

'You sound as if you are jealous,' Tamra said. Instinctively, she reached out, gathering the spirits which wandered the ice and ruined wharves to her.

Adhema laughed. 'No. Why rage against fate, eh?' She leaned her sword over her shoulder. 'After all, soon enough you and I will be good friends, I think. And she'll have a new favourite, our sweet queen. Then we can commiserate over the steaming heart of a freshly slain enemy. Perhaps you'll even join my sisterhood.' She swayed towards Tamra. 'I'll teach you to use that sword of yours properly. Mayhap you'll teach me to call up the dead.'

Tamra flinched back as the vampire got close. Even protected by a cloud of dead souls, she could feel the predatory malice radiating from Adhema. Was this what association with Neferata led to? The Broken Kings, Rikan, Adhema... all made into monsters.

'You act as if I am bound to her,' Tamra said. 'But when this is done, I will stay and lead my people. That is my fate.'

'Keep telling yourself that,' Adhema said as she walked past. 'It might even come true.'

Tamra didn't turn to watch her go. Instead, she stepped onto the ice and made her way cautiously out to where Arkhan stood. Walking across the ice was treacherous, and more than once she almost lost her footing. It had ruptured in places, and freezing waters bubbled up. She could just make out the shapes of sunken vessels beneath its surface, and other less identifiable things. Once, she thought she glimpsed movement, and picked up her pace.

Arkhan was facing away from her, and he gave no sign that he'd noticed her approach. His dread abyssal had, however. The bone-coloured monster stirred and its infernal gaze brought her to a halt. It growled softly, and Arkhan said, 'Be at ease, Razarak. What is it you wish to say, Tamra ven-Drak?'

Tamra swallowed. She didn't actually know. It had been an impulse. She groped for a question, and settled on the most obvious. 'Why do you stand out here, my lord?'

'Where else would you have me stand, daughter of the Drak?'

Tamra repressed a shudder as Arkhan turned to look at her. There was a clarity to his gaze she found disconcerting. Usually the dead were... muted, somehow. But Arkhan was anything but. 'No, I mean...' she began.

'I know what you mean. I am communing with the dead.' He turned away. 'I wonder, do you hear them?'

Tamra swallowed. She did. Voices seeped up from below and dead fingers scratched at the ice which held them imprisoned. 'I do.'

'And what do they say?'

'They wish to be free.' She looked up. 'Just like the Broken Kings.'

'The drowned have better chance of freedom than those six.' Arkhan thumped the ice with his staff. It cracked, and cold water sprayed up. Tamra stepped back. 'Indeed, those the sea has swallowed will soon be spat out.'

'You are... drawing them up?' It seemed an impossible feat, even for a being as powerful as Arkhan. At her most powerful, she had only ever commanded a few hundred of the dead, and most of those had been family.

'Indeed. All the dead of the Mandible are stirring, ready to fight again, beneath your banner.' The liche studied her. 'And it will be your banner, if Neferata has her way.'

Tamra looked away. 'I don't know about that.'

'No. You do not wish to know.'

'These lands have been splintered since the Great Awakening. Nagash, in his mercy, broke us.' She heard a harsh rattle and peered at Arkhan. It took her a moment to realise that the sound was laughter.

'Mercy? No. Expedience. Nagash detests waste. Why wipe out your people when they can serve better as a lesson to any who might seek to emulate them?' He gestured. 'In those days, rebellions sprang up like flies. The lords of Helstone, the corsair-kings of the Skull Isles, even the duardin of the Helgramite Summit... All sought to deny Nagash his due. And all paid the price. But none so great as the Broken Kings.'

'I think... I think she wants me to free them,' Tamra said. She pulled her coat more tightly about herself as a cold wind roared across the ice. 'Neferata, I mean.'

'Games within games,' Arkhan said. 'It has ever been her way.'

'We have all heard the stories. The mortarchs are said to

speak with the voice of Nagash, but how can they – you? How can one so... so...' She trailed off.

Arkhan gave a raspy laugh. 'We are him, and he is us. But we were all someone else, once. In us is Nagash's power made manifest. But so too are his weaknesses. Neferata is his guile, Mannfred, his ambition, and I...' It was his turn to trail off. He looked out over the ice.

'What? What are you?' Tamra pressed.

'I am his loyalty – to others, to this realm, to those he claims as his own. What Nagash has claimed, he will hold until time's last gleaming, even if he must destroy it to keep it.'

'That is not comforting.'

'Nor was it meant to be.'

'Why are you telling me this?'

'Because I do not believe you will survive, Tamra ven-Drak. To stand beside us is to court death and worse. But if you do survive, I wish you to understand what it means to serve him. To fail him. To defy him.'

'Thank you,' she said.

'Do not thank me. It is not a kindness.' He looked at her. 'Neferata weaves schemes the way a spider weaves webs. Strand by strand, until you are caught fast and trapped.'

'And is that to be my fate?'

'If you think to ask, then it is already too late.'

Tamra inclined her head. 'I thank you for your indulgence, my lord. I shall leave you to your calculations.'

'As I leave you to yours, Tamra ven-Drak. But, let me say this – Neferata is right about one thing. When the time comes, and you find yourself at the moment, do not hesitate in your decision. The dead travel fast, and only the swiftest of souls can hope to keep up with us.'

Tamra left him there, and as she trudged back towards the

docks, she could hear his chant rise anew. Beneath her feet, dead faces pressed against the ice, watching her go.

'She is a fool,' Adhema said bluntly.

Neferata glanced at her and then back at the ancient map she held. Tattooed onto a now-crumbling stretch of tanned flesh, the map revealed the shape of the old city outside the Mandible. It was nothing but ruins now, of course. But it never hurt to know the lay of the land.

'Who is, sister?'

'The necromancer.'

'There are quite a few necromancers in this citadel at the moment. At least three of them are women.' Neferata traced the line of a side street with her fingernail. 'There's a sally port east of here. We could use that to flank them, if we can get them into position.'

'You know who I mean,' Adhema said. She glanced at the map and added, 'It's too far from the central avenue. It would take too much time to get into position.'

'Mmm, perhaps you're right. And yes, I know who you mean.' Neferata carefully rolled up the map and tapped Adhema on the chest with it. 'If she were a fool, I would not have spared her life. She is cautious – a good quality in a leader.'

'Too cautious.'

'That is a matter of opinion. And we both know that, in the end, only one opinion counts.' Neferata locked eyes with the blood knight until Adhema looked away. The mortarch relented slightly and stroked her second-in-command's cheek. It was in Adhema's nature to be blunt. There was little left of the young woman she had been, before Neferata had passed along the dark blessings of the soulblight. 'If we win – *when* we win – the Rictus will require a guiding hand. Someone on whom

I – we – can count. The other voivodes are decrepit, deceitful or, well, dullards. She is the youngest and the strongest.'

'So was I,' Adhema said softly.

'Yes. But you were meant for bloodier things, kastellan.' Neferata turned away. 'You wanted vengeance, Adhema. War and glory, like your sisters. And I have given it to you. The city state of Szandor might be dust on the boots of the Blood God's servants, but its highborn daughters live to wreak vengeance in its name.'

'And for that, we thank you, O Queen of Blood,' Adhema said, bowing her head. 'But she is still a fool. You cannot trust her to make the right choice.'

'Oh, but I think I can.' Neferata smiled. 'The enemy grow closer by the day. They will be bloody and battered when they arrive, but still formidable. They'll outnumber us three to one at least – more than that, in the end. There are sorcerers in their ranks, and where sorcerers go, there are daemons.'

Adhema grunted and turned away. Her fingers tapped at the pommel of her sword. 'Corpse-eaters, deathrattlers and deadwalkers. A pretty army. Why give it to her? Why not just use it yourself?'

'Who says I'm not?' Neferata gestured. 'You must think outside of the immediate, Adhema. We who are eternal must learn to play the long game. Our conquerors will grow weak, in time, as all their kind do. We will outlast them, and rise again when their grip on the Amethyst Realm slackens. The seeds we plant here today will have ripened by then, and grown fat on blood and war. The Rictus will march south on that day, and Tamra ven-Drak will be at their head.'

Adhema nodded in understanding. Satisfied, Neferata looked out over the ruins below, calculating the enemy's approach. The ruins of the city spread out along the shore and the lower slopes of the Wailing Peaks. Once, the Mandible had been a centre of trade, and the population of the city that surrounded it had been the highest in the north. Two thirds of its people had perished in what the Rictus called the Great Awakening, and their remains still littered the city below, or else stumbled through the surrounding forests as unusually persistent deadwalkers.

Neferata closed her eyes, letting her mind drift. She could still remember the smell of the Shivering Sea in the summer and the cacophony of the docklands. She remembered standing on the ice-wharfs, watching as galleys slid across the turgid waters, sails flapping in the cold wind. She remembered the cheers of the people, as the skeletal guard of King Elig ven-Fenn marched down the boarding ramps, returning victorious from the Rime Wars.

Heady days, those. A million little conflicts, all staged for her amusement. How she and Mannfred had conspired against each other then, instigating proxy wars at the tiniest provocation. Her pawns against his, and both of them against Arkhan, though in truth Mannfred had always taken those contests more seriously. Arkhan infuriated him on some deep, abiding level. Centuries of confidence and guile would be stripped away with a single rasping comment, reducing her fellow mortarch to spluttering savagery.

Nagash had left them to their games, his mind turned ever inwards, calculating the dread formulas of the Corpse Geometries. Sometimes, he would stir to speak a single word, and a country would die, its inhabitants reduced to raw materials to fuel his continuing studies. Even now, she could not grasp the implications of such acts. She did not understand why the Undying King would craft a continent-spanning pyramid of crystallised ash or build strange mechanisms from bone and viscera. Mannfred had confided to her his suspicions that Nagash was attempting to craft portals to new and stranger worlds, or perhaps create secret routes into more familiar realms.

Whatever he'd been up to, the coming of Chaos had put an end to both it and her intrigues with Mannfred. It saddened her to think of so many plots left undone, so many schemes never to be put into motion. Of course, some she'd adapted and put into play against other targets. The servants of the Dark Gods were... simplistic in their scheming. They substituted complexity and brutality for efficiency, prizing victory over every other condition. And they were almost too eager to turn upon one another, even when it served no purpose. But there was little sport in it, only a sort of satisfying monotony.

She longed to match wits with the Three-Eyed King. There was a foe worthy of her. One who could drive Sigmar back into his fortress-realm, crack the soul of the Great Necromancer and set all the Mortal Realms aflame was surely as cunning as he was dangerous.

But first, she had to win the war here.

War... here... came the hissing whisper of the Broken Kings. They fluttered at the edges of her consciousness like frightened birds, and she calmed them with a single word.

'Soon,' she said.

Festerbite was tired.

He'd dreamed of amethyst fires and a great booming voice, calling out to him from the dark. Those blessed by the contagions of Nurgle didn't need very much sleep, but they had to have some at least. And he hadn't had any in days. No one had. Even the animals were on edge; Scab had bitten him three times in as many hours, and Balagos had been forced to kill his own steed after it had tried to gut him. Luckily, there were plenty of spares, thanks to the attrition they'd suffered getting this far – too many empty saddles, too many gaps in the battle line.

Festerbite wondered if this was how the Order's previous enemies had felt when confronted by the unflagging durability of Nurgle's chosen. But now they'd met a foe they couldn't simply outlast, one whose endurance outstripped even their own.

'The dead – our dead – are following us,' Croga said. The renegade looked exhausted. He'd been in the saddle for three days, conducting raids or simply trying to see off the ravenous packs of deadwalkers which harried their march. Though he lacked any skill with necromancy, he knew the trick of putting the dead down for good. 'Every corpse we've left unburned and intact is marching in our wake. Luckily they are as slow in death as they were in life.'

They stood with Wolgus some distance from a frozen lake, clutching the reins of their steeds. The lake stretched farther than the eye could see, and the land around it was bare rock, covered in hoarfrost. Sparse trees dotted the snowy shore, and birds croaked in the trees. The remains of several great bridges marked the surface, and the ruins of what might have once been some form of fortification stretched out along the shore.

And as with every scrap of land in this grim region, there were the stones – enormous menhirs and way stones of all descriptions and sizes. Some were pockmarked with hollow crannies stuffed with skulls. Others were intricately carved with what Festerbite thought must be scenes from the history of this land. Rotbringers strained at them, seeking to topple them with ropes and tools. Those that could not be toppled would be shattered or defaced. Nothing which gave glory to the false god, Nagash, could be allowed to stand in their wake.

'Not luck, Croga,' Wolgus said. 'It is the hand of Nurgle,

stretched out over us. By the time our fallen brothers come seeking our life's blood, we'll be behind the walls of this Mandible of yours. Then it will be a simple enough matter to return them to Grandfather's garden.'

Croga glanced at Festerbite, who looked away. Since his confrontation with Gurm, Wolgus had become almost desperately optimistic. It was to keep the morale of their warriors up, or so he claimed. Festerbite suspected that it was as much for himself as anyone.

'Everywhere we look – glorious desolation,' the blightmaster continued. 'There, see these bones, the way they are compacted beneath the soil? A road, my friend. And that great menhir, half slumped in a copse of trees? A milestone. This was once an empire, if a crude one. And now it moulders in a tomb of Nagash's making, neither crumbling nor rising. That is what we fight, my friends – stagnation.'

'We were mighty, once,' Croga murmured, half to himself. Festerbite looked at him. The Rictus shook his shaggy head. 'Once, our clans were kingdoms and our kingdoms ruled the north. From the Shivering Sea to the black stones of Stregocev, we were feared and respected.'

'What happened?'

'Nagash,' Croga said, spitting the name. He made a gesture. 'The Rattlebone Prince strode down from the moon and smote the north, shattering it. He cleaved the land, so that the sea rushed all in, and he shattered our cities, driving us into the wilderness.' He scratched at a suppurating nodule on his cheek, picking parasitic flea eggs from the raw wound.

'And now you defy him again,' Festerbite said.

Croga shrugged and popped a squirming larva into his mouth. 'We have another god now. A stronger one. Besides, Nagash is dead.' He hesitated. 'Isn't he?'

'As coffin nails,' Wolgus said, clapping the warrior on the back. 'Shyish stands at the dawn of a new era, my friends, a time of life and growth that will wipe away the dust of death. And we shall plant the first seeds here, in the north.' He gestured to a group of plaguebearers. The daemons dug seeping trenches in the soil with their swords and sowed blighted seedlings, as they had every time the column came to a halt. As the old order was toppled, the seeds of the new were planted, and the comforting hum of flies was heavy on the air.

Still, Croga didn't look convinced. Festerbite couldn't blame him. Wolgus was doing what he could, but the whispers had been running through the column for days. Between the attacks and the dreams, the disappearances and the sounds in the night, the Order's once-famed discipline was fraying. They'd come further than any other servant of the Dark Gods, and won more victories, but they were paying for it with every step. Now, with the Mandible but a day's hard ride away, fate – or something worse – had thrown one last obstacle in their path.

'No bridge,' Festerbite said, studying the frozen surface of the lake.

'Not anymore,' Croga said, and spat. He gestured to the remains of a stone structure, half-buried in the ice and snow. 'In my great-grandfather's time, there were nine great bridges of quarried stone which spanned the Corpse Run, and towns on either side. But the last of them, bridge and building alike, collapsed during the Bonesnapper Wars, when the gargant tribes came down out of the Wailing Peaks seeking marrow and meat.'

'Who won?' Festerbite asked.

Croga looked at him. 'See any gargants?' he said, scratching at his cheek.

Festerbite laughed. 'Well, the ice might be solid enough to cross, if we tread carefully.' He hesitated. 'Or we could go around.'

'It would add days to our journey,' Wolgus said. 'Days we cannot afford, according to our esteemed Herald.' He gestured towards Gurm, who sat some distance away reclining in his palanquin, surrounded by chortling plaguebearers and a number of knights.

Festerbite frowned at that. There were too many in the crusade who heeded Gurm's urgings. They wanted to be done with this place, with its wandering corpses and screaming ghosts. They wanted victory, even if it meant death.

'Nor do I wish to camp here,' Wolgus continued, 'not when we are so close to our goal.' He caught Festerbite by the shoulder. 'We must cross here. But first, the ice needs to be tested to see if it can bear our weight.'

'May I have the honour of leading the way?' Festerbite asked, knowing that it was what was expected of him. The Order prized courage in its knights, and the King of All Flies looked with favour upon the bold.

Wolgus nodded. 'Go,' he said.

Festerbite nodded and swung himself into the saddle. He called out to a handful of other knights, those closest to Gurm, who eagerly joined him as he rode across the flat forecourt of stones which marked where the bridges had begun. The pillars and posts of the long-demolished structures still rose from the frozen surface, and they had become home to birds' nests and strange purplish mould. The ruins on the shore were in a similar state. Whatever they might once have been, they were now nothing more than heaps of crumbling stone.

'Slow and steady, as is the way of Nurgle,' Festerbite said, as he urged a reluctant Scab onto the ice. 'No need to hurry, brothers.'

Most nodded in agreement, but one didn't.

'There's every need, Festerbite,' this knight gurgled as he followed him. He was skinny, and his armour hung awkwardly on his starveling frame. Stained bandages hid his face, and he smelled of unguents and spoiled fruit. 'We've got savages to kill – or had you forgotten?'

'The thought is ever foremost in my mind, Rotjaw,' Festerbite said, 'but we are not Bloodbound, racing heedlessly into battle. However, if you want to gallop ahead like one of the Blood God's own and drown in icy water, more power to you.'

'No need to be insulting,' Rotjaw grumbled. Several of the others chuckled. Festerbite didn't. He held Rotjaw's gaze as they continued to ride across the ice. Such disloyalty needed to be dealt with at once, before it could endanger the crusade.

'You shouldn't listen to the daemon,' he said without prevarication. 'Any of you.' Rotjaw twitched in his saddle. 'Gurm is our ally, but he does not speak for the Order of the Fly. Wolgus commands us, whether to victory or defeat.'

'Gurm speaks with the voice of the King of All Flies. Even Wolgus says so,' another knight said. Sir Reculix was a brawny brute, with a crown of antlers rising from his corroded helm, and his distended intestines wrapped about his middle like armour.

'That doesn't mean he doesn't twist Nurgle's words to suit his own ends,' a third knight croaked. His rusty armour was shrouded in filth-stained robes, and beneath his hood he wore a mask of bone and iron.

'Sir Blistertongue is right,' Festerbite said. 'The daemon is our ally, not our friend. Remember your true loyalties, and the King of All Flies will smile upon you. Have we not all drunk deep from the Flyblown Chalice, after all?'

'Aye,' came the grumbling murmur. Festerbite nodded in satisfaction.

Scab reared suddenly, shrieking. As he fought to control the beast, Festerbite looked down. A great shadow seemed to spread beneath the ice, twin sparks of amethyst flickering in its depths. The sparks grew to suns as the shadow contracted, becoming a titan skull. The rictus grin split in a soundless scream, and the ice cracked with a hiss. Festerbite looked around wildly. The others seemed to be having the same difficulties.

The ice heaved and water spurted into the air to rain down across them. Five decaying gargantuan corpses rose wheezing from below the broken ice, scattering the knights. The bonesnapper gargants had perished in the water, and their bodies had been preserved by the cold. Bloated paws slammed down, smashing riders and steeds through the ice and into the dark waters below, Sir Reculix among them. Festerbite sawed on Scab's reins, turning the horse-thing about. He began to gallop for safety. It was a trifle cowardly, but being drowned by the water-logged corpse of a gargant wasn't his idea of a heroic death.

'Get off of the ice!' he roared, riding hard. 'All of you – fall back!' Scab's hooves slipped and slid on the ice as Festerbite urged the animal to greater speed. The ice cracked beneath them as they raced towards the shore, and he could hear the undead gargants smashing their way through the frozen waters in pursuit. On the shore, a shield wall was being hastily erected by the Order's armsmen.

'Loose,' Wolgus bellowed, from somewhere behind the wall. Plague-fire arrows hissed through the steamy air and arced over Festerbite and the others. Normal flames would have found precious little purchase in the waterlogged hides of the monstrous zombies, but the plague-fires began to burn greedily, consuming wet flesh as easily as dry. One of the gargants collapsed back into the water, its unwieldy form wreathed in oily green flame. But the remaining four ploughed on, groping for the fleeing knights.

Rotjaw screamed as a hand snatched him from the saddle. Ruined teeth snapped shut on the Chaos knight's skull, silencing his shrieks. Scab's hooves dug into the shore and the horse-thing charged through an opening in the shield wall. Festerbite jerked his steed around, Blistertongue and the other survivors following suit. The four gargants waded onto the shore, water pouring from their decaying carcasses. More arrows thumped into them, and one's whole head was ablaze. But they kept coming.

The shield wall held, though only barely. Festering spears and mucus-stained axes bit into the tree-trunk limbs of the gargants as they tore at the armsmen. A wheeled altar to Nurgle creaked forwards, pushed by chanting rotbringers. The sorcerers gathered atop it unleashed a flurry of arcane bolts. The crackling bursts tore one of the gigantic corpses apart, sending its smoking husk flopping back into the waters.

'Ware!' someone cried. Festerbite twisted in his saddle and saw more enormous corpses rise from the waters of the lake. Slowly but surely, they began to haul themselves towards the shore. In the trees, the carrion birds were croaking in unison, and the sound caused Festerbite to shudder as he recalled his dreams from the evening before. It was the same voice, he was certain of it, stretched between a hundred avian throats.

Rotbringers screamed as they were hurled into the air or pulped between colossal teeth. The undead gargants stormed through the ranks, kicking men aside or simply stomping on them. Plague-fires ate at rotting flesh, but not quickly enough. Two of the gargants lurched towards the war-altar and the half a dozen sorcerers who crouched atop it. Festerbite kicked Scab into motion. 'Blistertongue, the rest of you – follow me,' he said, and the knights raced to intercept the monstrous deadwalkers.

Wolgus appeared to have had the same idea. Even as Festerbite reached the altar, one of the gargants loomed over it. Before it could snatch up one of the cowering sorcerers, the blightmaster was there, rotsword in one hand and a mace in the other. Wolgus chopped through the frayed tendons of the gargant's wrist, severing its hand. His mace snapped out, catching the brute in the jaw. The corpse staggered back, and Festerbite let his blade play across the backs of its knees as he galloped past. The creature toppled over.

'Ha! A mighty blow, Sir Festerbite.' Wolgus sliced a finger from the hand of the second gargant, and then crushed the remaining digits with his mace. The gargant hunched forwards, jaws wide, but before it could take a bite out of the blightmaster, a lasso of thorny vines settled over its neck and skull. The vines pulled taut and the gargant fell backwards, crushing its fellow. More vines, hurled by cackling plaguebearers, lassoed the others who'd made it to shore.

Festerbite saw Gurm's palanquin trundle past. Plaguebearers tore strips of seeping greenery from the twisted sylvaneth and fashioned ropes from them. 'Must I do everything myself, Wolgus?' Gurm called.

'If only you had mustered the impetus to do it sooner,' Festerbite said, though not loudly.

Wolgus leapt down from the war-altar. 'Be not so uncharitable, my friend. Such magics take time to weave.' He sheathed his sword and laid his mace across his shoulders. The mortal rotbringers were falling back as the daemons dragged the struggling gargants towards the shore. Those corpses still wading out of the lake were met by plague-fire and balesword. Wolgus turned. 'Croga, Sir Balagos – get them regrouped and ready, just in case this trick of Gurm's doesn't work.'

'It will,' Gurm said. 'As we press forward, we bend this realm to our will. Behind us, we have left the seeds for a mighty garden. And here, we will make a feculent wellspring, to feed all the green growing things which will soon populate these lands. And, well, these carcasses will make a fine pontoon, I think.'

The daemon gestured. The corrupted tendrils pruned from the sylvaneth burrowed into the twitching zombies on the shore, dragging them towards one another, no matter how much they struggled. The gargants tore at each other mindlessly as the vines bound them inextricably together. Giggling nurglings squashed themselves into the gaps between bodies, spreading their filth into the champing jaws, while plague-fires melted flesh and bone, furthermerging the struggling corpses into a single entity. Slowly but surely, a crude bridge was taking shape.

At the water's edge, plaguebearers gurgled and nudged one another as they drove their swords into the broken ice. The water frothed and turned dark, like stew. Steam rose from the melting ice as corruption spread from the baleswords and through the waters. The gargants staggered as the streams of foulness began to consume their decaying forms. Smoke spewed from their bodies as they lost the ability to do anything more than thrash impotently. Bloated flesh sloughed from broken bones, plopping into the churning waters.

More nurglings surfaced in the liquid corruption. Squealing with pleasure, they began to clamber up the sagging husks of the gargants, squeezing into the holes in their torsos and skulls. The tiny daemons hauled on dissolving strands of muscle tissue and bone, forcing the gargants to slump forwards, adding to the growing bulk of the makeshift bridge.

'Not much longer now,' Gurm said, leaning on the pommel of his balesword. 'Look at the little fellows go. They do get in everywhere, don't they?' He laughed and used his sword to poke Festerbite. 'Eh, Festerbite? Don't they?'

'They do, my lord,' Festerbite said, grudgingly. He looked around, taking note of how many broken bodies littered the shore or floated in the corrupted waters. Once again, it wasn't force of arms that had won the day but daemonic cunning. They were no better than chaff, absorbing punishment until Gurm could work his schemes. He looked at Wolgus, and knew from his expression that the blightmaster was thinking the same thing. Was this what the Order of the Fly had come to in these nightmare lands?

'We endure,' Wolgus said, softly. 'In Nurgle's name, we endure.'

Festerbite made to reply, but stopped himself when he realised that the birds had fallen silent. Black eyes watched the rotbringers from every tree and stone. As one, the birds rose into the air with a great cry. As they filled the sky, they seemed to briefly coalesce into a horrid, familiar shape. Then they winged their way north.

Festerbite shuddered. He suddenly felt cold, for the first time in a long time.

EIGHT

LIFE-IN-DEATH

Let them come in their thousands, I will endure.
Let the skies weep fire and the earth groan.
Let all things perish and tumble into the dark.
Nagash endures.

– *The Epistle of Bone*

Tamra watched her people work with no small amount of pride. Under the watchful eyes of the voivodes, clansmen had emptied the great crypts and ossuaries which stretched beneath the Mandible. The bones of the beloved dead were now arrayed across the courtyard, and women and children moved to and fro among them, seeking to arrange head bone to neck bone and heel bone to ankle bone, in accordance with the ancient rites. The bones had already been marked with knife and ink by those who'd seen to their stripping and interment so long ago, and they were prepared accordingly.

More bones were added from heavy bark baskets and hide sacks. These additions had been contributed by those refugees lucky enough to have gotten away with such valuable heirlooms. 'A good army, if small,' Bolgu said. He observed the preparations beside her, his thumbs hooked in his wide belt. 'We have bronze aplenty, to arm and armour them.'

Tamra nodded. 'Lady Neferata calls to the deadwalkers in the hills and in the sea caves. They will flood the ruins and make them perilous for our foes.' She ran a hand through her hair. 'Arun has drawn down the bodiless spirits which linger here, and I have made compact with the corpse-eaters. You and Myrn and the others will see to the raising of our dead.'

'It doesn't sound like enough, does it?' Bolgu said.

'No.'

'My ice-cutter galleys stand ready. If the walls fall, some of our people will survive.' Bolgu looked at her. 'I doubt either of us will be there to see them off.'

'We might surprise you. I have no intention of dying here.' Tamra looked up. The clouds were roiling with suppressed fury. Lightning flickered in their depths. She thought again of Sarpa, stolen by the storm. Despite her best efforts, she had not been able to call up his soul again. Wherever it was, she hoped he was at peace. Bolgu followed her gaze.

'I'd ask the Undying King for a clear sky to fight under, if I thought he was listening,' he said. 'I'd give my left hand to see the sun – just once more, before the end.'

'You think he does not listen?'

They turned to see Arun hobbling towards them. The old voivode supported himself on a staff made from the bones of his predecessors. He wore a cuirass of tarnished bronze and a helmet made in the shape of a swooping bat. 'For shame, Bolgu,' the old man said. 'Nagash stands with us, even now.'

'I do not see him, Arun,' Bolgu said.

'Because you are not looking. Nagash is in us and around us. He is all things, and all things are one in him. He is death, and we must die.' Arun bent forwards, his body wracked by a coughing fit. Tamra caught his arm, supporting him until he'd recovered. He patted her hand. 'All things die, my friends. That is the way of it.'

'I just wish it wasn't today,' Bolgu said.

'What day better than today? What moment greater than this? Nagash asks that we stand, and so we shall. For the honour of the Rictus, and glory to our clans.' Arun forced himself erect. 'We die, and live forever in death. Isn't that right, child?'

Tamra said nothing. Her eyes were on the women and children, on the men too old to fight or too young to be warriors. Would Nagash raise them up as well? Would they become deadwalkers or wandering spirits, growing more twisted with every passing century? She closed her eyes and rubbed her head, suddenly tired beyond all measure.

Arun gazed at her with gentle eyes. 'Death and life are a single strand, child. The Great Awakening showed us that, and for that alone we should be willing to die for him.'

'Willing or no, we'll die all the same,' Bolgu said. He looked up, at the wooden walkways which lined the interior of the Mandible's walls. 'I don't think she cares either way, the witch.'

Tamra glanced up. Neferata stood on the parapet, her dread abyssal crouched behind her, watching them. Her gaze was unreadable.

'Should she?' Arun said. 'We are but motes in the eyes of the mortarchs. How many generations have risen and fallen beneath her gaze, Bolgu? And how many more to come, in the centuries ahead? She is eternal, and we are finite. That is why it falls to the dead to remember the living.'

Bolgu snorted. 'It's said there's a band of monks, somewhere north of Morrsend, who shed their flesh when they join their order. Their skeletons spend eternity recording all that is said and done in those ancient lands. I wish we had something like that here.'

'Maybe we will,' Tamra said. 'War is not eternal. It is a flame which burns hot for a time and then gutters to embers.' She patted Arun's withered hand. 'When it does, we will be here, the dead and the living alike. And we shall have to find new ways to occupy ourselves.'

'But for now, we need to get our brothers and sisters on their feet,' Bolgu said. He gestured to Arun. 'You are the oldest, will you lead us in this?'

Arun nodded. 'It is my honour and my duty.'

He stepped forwards, raising his staff. The other voivodes gathered around as Arun began to speak the words.

'And Nagash spake unto me, and he said, "Child, can these bones live?" And I spake unto Nagash and said, "Yea, my lord, if thou wish it, they shall live. Thou knows the ways and means of bone and marrow." And Nagash spake unto me and said, "I know them." And lo, did the bones stand, for after life comes death, and after death come life-in-death. All that lives must die...'

'And all are one in Nagash,' Tamra and the others recited, solemnly.

As the words echoed out, a shimmering radiance fell across the long-silent dead, and they began to stir. Twitching phalanges gripped long bones and twisted them into place. Skulls rolled closer to vertebrae, as spinal columns flexed.

'Hearken unto his words,' Arun continued. 'All that lives must die, and all that die are one in Nagash.'

The assembled voivodes raised their hands and staves, and the bones of the dead rose with them. 'All are one in him, and to die is to live.'

'What is your opinion of our forces, sister?' Neferata asked, watching the necromantic rite taking place below. Bones joined together and skeletons rose up, one after the next. When it was done, there would be a few hundred skeletons, ready to march. Not many, in the grand scheme of things, but enough to accomplish what was needed.

'They will not stand,' Adhema said, as she ran a whetstone over her blade. 'Barbarians never do.' The vampire sat atop the parapet, her helmet at her feet.

Neferata looked at her. 'Is that the voice of experience, or merely opinion?'

'They lack discipline.' Adhema smiled thinly. 'But that can be fixed.'

'Are you suggesting we kill them, and raise them as deadwalkers?'

'I will do as my queen commands.'

Neferata snorted. She stroked Adhema's dusky cheek. 'Wasteful, sister. Why bother killing them, when the foe will do that for us?' She smiled. 'Then we raise them. That way, we get more than one use out of them.'

'I bow to your wisdom, my queen.' Adhema held up her sword and peered down its length. 'What do you wish us to do? Shall we fight here, or...'

'No. The Sisterhood of Szandor is at its best in the open, with room to gallop. Lead them a merry chase, if you would. Carve them, stab them, bleed them. I want them staggering by the time they reach these walls.' She held up a warning finger. 'Do not engage them in open battle, however. I don't want them bogged down, just bloodied.'

'They will still be many left, even after that.'

'What are numbers to us? Grist for the mill, nothing more.' Neferata leaned over the parapet. Below her, the ruins stretched for leagues, almost to the distant shores of the Corpse Run. It was a forest of broken walls, tumbled rooftops and scattered masonry. 'They will fell the trees to make siege weapons.' She patted the parapet. 'They see the wall, and they will not be able to resist trying to take it. That is why I gathered the Rictus here.' She turned around and leaned back, fingers interlaced over her stomach. 'The enemy will make camp on the shore, where it is open, if we give them that time. So long as we keep their attentions here, the battle is ours.'

Neferata pushed herself upright and stretched a hand up. She could feel the power here. Necromantic energy had seeped into the very stones of the shore, and it hung thick on the breeze. The ice of the Rictus Sea hid an incalculable tithe of corpses. There were entire fleets beneath those frozen waters, just waiting for the right voice to call them back to the surface.

She closed her eyes and listened. She could just make out Arkhan's chanting from somewhere on the ice. Raising that many dead souls took time, especially with one of the Nine Gates in the vicinity. The gates distorted the normal flow of things in unpredictable ways. But it was simply a matter of time: the ice would crack, the dead would rise, and their foes – this Wolgus – would be caught in the jaws of a trap. She glanced at the crags which loomed over the Mandible, and wondered whether the Prince of Crows would truly honour his word. It was hard to tell with such creatures. Reality was an illusion to them, no better than a dream. If nothing else, the scent of bloodied flesh would draw the packs out of the hills.

Arkhan's chanting wasn't the only sound on the wind. She could hear the clangour of bells and the sound of phlegm-choked bellows. Her nose wrinkled as she caught a whiff of putridity on the air. The enemy were close, and drawing closer with every moment.

'Hello, poppet,' Adhema said.

Neferata opened her eyes and turned. Tamra had joined

them. She glanced nervously at the blood knight, and then at Neferata.

'They are here.'

Adhema rose to her feet and recovered her helmet. 'Finally,' she murmured.

Neferata gazed out over the ruins. 'Speak, sister.'

'They've been sighted just outside what's left of the old city by Arun's spirits...' Tamra flinched aside as Adhema stepped past her. 'They will be here in a few hours, if not less.'

Neferata nodded. The oldest of the voivodes had bound a number of ghosts to the crumbled remains of the city walls, to keep watch. A cunning tactic, and one she intended to use herself in the future.

'Good. The tall tower there is relatively stable.' Neferata pointed. 'You and the other voivodes who are not otherwise occupied shall go there, to direct the battle. I have drawn every deadwalker for a hundred leagues to this place. They and the hungry ghosts which inhabit these ruins will be yours to command.' She turned. 'Your best archers will take to the walls. Our enemies are durable, but mortal. When the time comes, the honoured dead will march to meet our enemies, who will be in some disarray.'

'And what of you, Lady Neferata?'

'I? I will go where I will, and do as I wish.' Neferata leaned close to Tamra. 'Surely you do not think that I will abandon you, sister?'

'You abandoned the Broken Kings.'

Neferata gazed at her, like a cat puzzled by the bite of a mouse. 'Did I?' she said.

'Rikan said...'

'Rikan is not half the man he used to be,' Neferata said. 'I told you not to give credence to his yowling. He is mad.' She shrugged.

'Besides, ask them yourself if you wish. You speak to them as well as I. Draw them from their icy tomb and put the question to them. Whatever their answer, we could use the reinforcements.'

'If you wish the Broken Kings freed, why do you not do it yourself?' Tamra asked.

'Did I say that I did?'

Tamra didn't look at her. 'I am not stupid, whatever you might believe. I have eyes and ears and a mind to understand what I have seen and heard. Why?'

Neferata was silent for a moment. 'Such is the law of Nagash. What he has done, his mortarchs may not undo. It is outside our remit, and beyond our power.'

'Then why–'

'Because it is not beyond yours, Tamra. We are his servants, bound by geas and darkling oath. He is in our blood and brains. We cannot deny him, save that he wills it. Do not mistake me – on occasion, he lets us slip our leashes. And these days, they are quite loose. But to gainsay him is beyond me. Beyond any of us. But you...'

'I am beneath him,' Tamra said.

'He pays no attention to you,' Neferata corrected. 'Not yet. That will change and soon, I think. We will need strength like yours in the days to come. Things will grow worse, before they grow better.'

'Then there is no hope.' Tamra slumped.

Neferata caught her chin and raised her head.

'There is hope in Nagash,' she said. 'Nagash is eternal, as is Shyish and all who dwell within it. All are one in Nagash...' How many times had she said these very words? Faith was an ever-useful tool, and the easiest to abuse.

'And Nagash is all,' Tamra said, automatically. 'If I break the law, I will be punished. My people will be punished.'

'Better punishment than extinction,' Neferata said. She set

her hands on Tamra's shoulders, and the woman flinched. 'Perhaps it will not come to that. Perhaps... Perhaps these old walls will hold. Perhaps the Prince of Crows will turn the tide, or the drowned dead. But our enemies are here, now, and this is only the beginning. After these, will come others – stronger, god-touched and more savage.'

Neferata could smell the noxious smoke of the plague-fires, the reek of pox-infused flesh on the wind. She could hear the drums and bells of the enemy in the distance, and she knew Tamra could as well. 'This is not the last battle,' Neferata whispered. 'It is the first. The north staggers. Shyish reels. Our realm bleeds. But it is not done yet.'

'What–what must I do?' Tamra asked.

'Survive. Adapt. Show yourself as worthy as I know you to be, Tamra ven-Drak. You will lead armies in the wars to come. The seeds of those armies are here, and if you but listen to me, they shall flourish, and you with them.' Neferata pressed the tips of her fingers against the woman's throat. 'Do you truly wish to protect your people?'

'Yes,' Tamra whispered.

'Then, when the time comes, you will know what must be done.' Neferata turned her around and studied her. 'I will show you such sights when this is done, sister,' she said. She lifted Tamra's chin with a finger. 'There is more to this realm than these dour crags. I will show you the hourglass-lined streets of the City of Lost Moments, and the sunken avenues of Yves in the Bitter Sea. You will stand among the elect of this realm, a true deathlord. You will be feted, and songs of your power will be sung from Morrsend to the Skull Islands.'

'I do not wish any of that,' Tamra said. She stepped back, out of reach. 'I wish only to save my people, to preserve them from the ravages of the enemy.'

Neferata frowned. The girl was stubborn. 'And so you shall. You have my promise.' She looked out over the parapet. 'But first... we have a battle to win. To your post, Tamra ven-Drak. And remember what I said – do not be afraid to do what you must.'

Tamra nodded stiffly and left the parapet. Neferata watched her for a time, and then she turned her attentions to other matters. People filled the outer courtyard: men and women and children, moving to and fro, preparing for the siege to come. Adhema and her knights had taught the Rictus the basics of siege craft. Baskets of heavy stones lined the walls, ready to be thrown at the enemy. Fire-pits were stoked, to fill the air with smoke and better protect the defenders from the biting flies which invariably accompanied the rotbringers.

Once, the Rictus would have had soldiers to do these things. Now, those tasks fell to women and children and the crippled. Neferata shook her head. It was a shame that it had come to this. If Nagash had not destroyed them, the six kingdoms of Rictus might have made for a potent weapon against the enemies invading the Amethyst Realm.

'One must make do,' she murmured. She snapped her fingers and Nagadron heaved itself to its feet, tail lashing. She slid into the saddle. 'Come, Nagadron. Let us see what the enemy has to offer us, eh?'

'Lord of All Things, bless and keep me,' Festerbite said, staring at the distant edifice in shock. The Mandible was as impressive as Croga had claimed. The fortress rose over the ruined city like a barrow of stone and timber. It was bigger than any fortress they'd yet encountered in the dead lands, and stretched from the shore up into the mountains.

'I told you,' Croga muttered, turning the spit. The sludge-maggot squealed in pleasure as the flames cooked its green flesh brown. The creatures didn't mind being eaten, though the same couldn't be said of those doing the eating. They provided little sustenance, but with supplies running out, and the land close to the fortress stripped bare by the fleeing Rictus, the warriors of the pox-crusade were forced to make do. Croga poked the creature with a knife, causing it to wriggle. 'It's almost ready.'

'I'm not hungry,' Festerbite said, still staring at the Mandible. The ruins rose wild around it, a great jungle of broken stone and splintered wood. Ragged shrouds flapped like leaves in the wind, and the streets were covered in snow and ice. Festerbite's hand fell to his sword hilt as he heard the telltale moan of a deadwalker, echoing up from the necropolis.

'It'll be our last chance to eat before battle. And there's no guarantee that there's anything worth consuming in there, if we make it over the walls.'

Festerbite glanced at Croga. 'There's always the dead.'

They sat with the other officers – knights, chieftains and blighted champions. Most looked impatient. It was hard to resist the urge to attack immediately when the enemy was in sight. But the Order fought as an army, not as a horde. They had waged numerous campaigns across the Mortal Realms and honed their tactics to a killing edge. So they sat and muttered among themselves, waiting for Wolgus' command.

Croga snorted. 'That's one way to keep them from coming back, I suppose.' The sore on his cheek had spread, and his teeth were visible through the tatters of flesh. Rot-fly larvae squirmed beneath the skin of his jaw and neck, and he idly squeezed at them.

Festerbite turned, scanning the makeshift siege-camp as it was cobbled together beneath the shattered outer walls of the fallen city. Plague-bells rang out and hide drums thumped.

Rotbringers made shuffling obeisance before war-altars, listening to the rumbling catechisms of pox-abbots and rot-monks. Nurglings clambered over everyone and everything, rubbing their juices against proffered weapons and armour, including the broad-headed arrows used by the Order's longbowmen. Beastkin danced and capered about plague-fires, inciting themselves into a murderous frenzy.

He looked away as a boil-covered gor hurled itself into the fire with a screech of pleasure. He examined the scrub forest which spilled down the slopes of the Wailing Peaks. The mountains were well named. The wind made odd noises as it curled through the crags and slithered down the slopes into the ruins. 'Plenty of trees, at least. We can make do for siege-weapons, if we need them.'

'If we get the chance,' Croga said. He sliced off a wriggling chunk of sludge-maggot and chewed thoughtfully. 'While we squat here, the army of the dead closes in. A thousand corpses or more, trudging towards us out of the black. Not to mention whatever's lurking in the city, waiting for us.' He pulled another strip of gelatinous meat from the roasting maggot and stuffed it into his mouth. 'And the corpse-eaters, of course.'

'Corpse-eaters?'

'In the mountains.' Croga waved his knife. 'Breed like flies in those crags. The battle will draw them down, sure enough.'

Festerbite nodded. 'Well, that'll make things interesting. What say you, blightmaster?'

Wolgus stood some distance away atop a broken section of wall, his hands clasped behind his back. The blightmaster did not break off his study of the sea as he spoke. 'I say, what will be, will be. The outcome is the same, victory or death. The garden will flourish, and Nurgle with it.' He gestured. 'Where our blood and pus spills, the ground is forever dedicated to the King of All Flies. That is victory enough.'

He turned and dropped to the ground. 'Those walls are more impressive at a distance, I'd wager. There are gaps in them, patched with piled rubble. The towers are broken, and the gate has collapsed. The Rictus have neither the numbers nor the stomach to properly defend that citadel for long. Croga – you will take your woodsmen and fell trees fit for battering rams. I would prefer quantity to quality. Slugtail!'

A bloated beastlord shuffled away from his packmates as Croga rose to his feet, hurriedly stuffing the last of the maggot into his mouth. Patches of piebald flesh showed through Slugtail's mangy fur, and his horns were thick with mould and fluted like fungal tubes. He wore a filthy tabard, crudely marked with the sigil of the Fly, over his barrel chest. The beastkin made an interrogative noise and Wolgus said, 'To you, brother, will fall the honour of the first sowing. Rouse your children and set them yelping.'

Slugtail threw back his head and yowled. Echoing cries rose throughout the camp, as the beastherds readied themselves for war.

Wolgus doled out commands with crisp precision. The rotbringers, in their robes and corroded armour, would follow the beastherds into war. Behind them would come the core of the Order's forces – the armsmen and the blightkings, marching slowly and with an eye to rooting out any foes hidden in the ruins. And to the knights of the Order fell the honour of warding the flanks against any potential counter-attack. The army would attack in waves, moving up through the city, slowly but relentlessly. By the time they reached the walls, Croga would have enough trees felled to make battering rams.

'We are like the waves of some dark sea, lapping against the shore,' Wolgus said to those who remained. These words were for the true knights of the Order alone. 'We are the scythe, and they, the wheat. Slow, steady strokes clear the field.' Heads nodded in understanding. 'But first, we must give thanks.'

A sigh went up from the gathered knights. An old ritual this, handed down to them by the Lady of Cankerwall, and to her by Nurgle himself. Festerbite felt a pang in his chest, as if his blackened heart had jumped in its cage of worm-eaten bone.

'Kneel, my brothers. Kneel and receive the gift of the Flyblown Chalice.' Wolgus lifted the chalice from his belt. The metal was tarnished and blackened, its gemstones replaced by pulsing insect pupae and throbbing buboes. The seventy-seven verses of the Feverish Oath had been etched into its surface by the great Lady of Cankerwall herself. Every blightmaster was given such a cup upon his ascension, a sign of favour from the King of All Flies.

Wolgus dipped the worm-eaten cup into a puddle. The water turned as black as soot and began to froth with maggoty shapes. The liquid in the cup was the colour of rust, and it steamed in the cold air. 'The very blood of Nurgle, vibrant with his feverish miasma. Drink deep, my brothers. Drink deep, ye knights of the Order, and taste the stuff of victory.'

The chalice was passed from hand to hand, and each knight gulped from it in turn. Festerbite swallowed the pungent liquid with relish. It seared his throat pleasingly, and he felt the warmth of Grandfather's garden fill him. He felt stronger than he had in weeks, and he longed for the chance to test his sword's edge against the bones of the foe. But the haze of satisfaction was soon punctured by a familiar voice.

'We are at their very gates, and yet again you choose to delay,' Gurm said. 'What am I to do with you, Wolgus?' The daemon rocked to and fro on his palanquin, causing the sylvaneth to whimper wretchedly. 'The camp is abuzz, but no movement, no advance... What am I to do?'

'I assume that you will complain incessantly, as is your wont,' Wolgus said. 'But I do not have the time to listen today. Thrice, I have ceded the battlefield to your desire for expedience. I shall not do so a fourth time. Not here, not now. You brought us here to take this place, and now you shall allow us to do just that – in our own way.'

'We do not have time for these childish rituals of yours,' Gurm said. 'Slurping from a cup is no substitute for slaughter, blightmaster.'

The palanquin creaked as he rose to his feet. Wolgus met his gaze calmly.

'We have nothing but time, Herald. We are at their gates, and the sea is at their backs. Unless there is some other reason we are here? One you have not shared with us?'

Gurm sat back down suddenly, eye narrowed. The plaguebearers surrounding his palanquin raised their blades and murmured in warning. Festerbite drew his sword and joined Wolgus. So too did Balagos and the others. Gurm eyed them warily.

'Woe be to him who strikes a Herald of Nurgle,' he said, after a moment.

'Woe is our lot,' Festerbite said firmly, the power of the chalice still singing within him. 'We are the chosen of Nurgle, and despair is the balm of our souls.'

'Well said, gentle Festerbite,' Wolgus said. He gazed steadily at Gurm. 'See to your own schemes, Gurm, and leave me to mine. We will take this fortress for you, never fear. Just as we will aid you in whatever other plot you have brewing in your skull. We swore an oath to free this land from the tyranny of death, and we shall do so – whatever the means, whatever the cost.'

Gurm grunted and, after a moment of hesitation, nodded. He stamped on his palanquin, causing it to turn with the sound of splitting branches. It stalked off towards the shore. Daemons followed, shooting dire glances at the mortals as they went. Wolgus shook his head.

'I fear our Herald begins to question his patronage of our Order. So be it. We shall win this battle, at least, on our own terms.' Wolgus looked at each of them in turn. 'Ride, my brothers. Ride for the glory of Cankerwall and the Order eternal. For the Order!'

'For the Order,' Festerbite roared, joining his voice to that of his brother knights.

Gurm sulked on his cushions and stared up at the towering wraith. Nagash had been standing in the sea for days, waiting. While daemons could not feel what men might call fear, they could feel something approaching trepidation. Gurm was feeling that now: a distinct and unwelcome reluctance to advance. Only he and his daemonic followers could discern the monstrous force looming over the Shivering Sea. To him, it appeared to be a crackling tower of night-black energy, leagues high and wide. An abominable skull surfaced in the black on occasion, and its burning gaze swept across the horizon, seeking and searching. Hunting for them, perhaps.

He'd felt Nagash's gaze before, at the fall of the Verdant Necropoli in the Jade Kingdoms. The dead had few citadels in the realm of life, but that had been the greatest. He'd felt Nagash's rage as he'd ordered his legions to tear the barrow-city apart, stone by stone, and found it good. But that had been at a distance, with a realm between them. This, in contrast, was not pleasant at all.

He heard a piteous howl and turned in his seat. One of the beasts had collapsed, trembling, before the intensity of the Undying King's idle attentions. The daemon whimpered like a wounded animal and rolled onto its back, tentacles thrashing helplessly as it squirmed through the snow. Gurm flicked his gaze to one of the mumbling plaguebearers in his honour guard. The cyclopean daemon grunted and lifted its sword over the quivering beast. At Gurm's nod, the blade fell, cutting the beast's fearful yelp short.

Weakness could be tolerated, at certain times. Now was not one of them. He could feel the malignant power of their enemy growing stronger the closer they got. Nagash was weak, yes, but even weak, he was akin to a cold black sun. He was a weight on the world, drawing all light and heat into him. Spirits flocked to him in their thousands, dragged screaming through the snow-addled skies above. Every tree and rock was limned with amethyst light, as if infused with his radiance. He'd hoped the Undying King would be weaker than he was.

Gurm gripped his sword more tightly. Trepidation gave way to agitation; he'd come too far to be stopped now. He'd chivvied Wolgus and his dullards along, helping them just enough so that they could bleed Nagash white while he conserved his powers for the struggle to come. Now, it was his moment, which made Wolgus' sudden defiance all the more infuriating.

He shook his head. He really should have expected it. The Order waged war the way a reaper cleared a field, with care and skill, but not with speed. If he wanted this farce over and done with sooner rather than later, he needed to act unilaterally. This was not to be a battle; it was to be a slaughter. And soonest begun, was soonest done.

Gurm stood in his palanquin and swept his sword out, carving flickering wounds on the skin of the very air. His form trembled with the power surging through it. Such a working threatened to render him useless for the battle to come, but it was a necessity. The Order could not take such a fortress unaided, at least not with the necessary speed. Nonetheless, he'd hoped to save such tricks for when they'd had the gate to the underworld in hand.

Still, a dashed hope was much like a scattering of seeds. In time, new hopes welled up from the remains of the old. Such was life. He slashed the air a seventh time, and it began to twist in on itself. Murky light bled from the wounds he'd made, and a familiar droning rose up out of some hidden depths. The air vibrated with the pulse of slick wings and the jolly chuckles of his brethren.

'Come, oh my friends and oh my brothers,' cried Gurm. 'Come fill the air with your rancorous reek – come. Our time is now. Come!'

With a sound like the bursting of a boil, the first plague drone erupted into view, its daemonic rider hunched over the rot fly's bristly head. More followed, leaving a trail of noxious fumes in their wake. They spilled towards the Mandible as Gurm sank back into his seat with a sigh of satisfaction. He rolled his eye towards the coven of sorcerers he'd gathered.

'Call the rest, cousins. Call the sevenfold divisions of decay, and let us bring this farce to an end. We shall drown them in rot and turn the sea red with their blood. Come, and be quick about it. Leave Wolgus and his fools to their play. I have more important matters to attend to.'

NINE

BATTLE OF THE MANDIBLE

Let my enemies advance upon me from the north and the south, east and west.

Let the Three-Eyed King rush fast upon me, and I shall cast him down.

Let Sigmar seek to stay my wrath, and I shall scour his starlit halls clean of all sound.

Stand not between the Undying King and his destined end.

Death is not a foe to be beaten.

Death simply is.

– *The Epistle of Bone*

The Undying King stood upon the ice and studied the battlefield which stretched below and around him. It was rare that he witnessed such dismal skirmishes first-hand, and he found himself curious. The rotbringers had begun to advance through the city he'd shattered so long ago. Mortals and daemons plunged towards the Mandible, chanting the name of their desolate liege. Nurgle himself was not in evidence – the Lord of Decay lacked the strength to do more than peer into Shyish as yet, and his attentions were fixed elsewhere.

It was just as well. Though every fibre of his being revolted at the thought, Nagash knew he was in no condition to face down one of the Ruinous Powers. Soon, perhaps. But not in his weakened state, and certainly not in this reduced, insubstantial form.

He could feel the scattered splinters of his divinity strewn across the width and breadth of his realm. They flickered like fireflies, scattered across the nine thousand kingdoms. With a thought, he called out to them, and they began to stir.

In far killing fields, bodies stumbled to their feet, beginning the slow trek of a thousand years. Pilgrims, stirred by prophetic dreams, lifted their sacred effigies onto their shoulders and began to march, chanting his name as their children – and their children's children – would unto the ninth generation. In devil-haunted ruins, his servants sought his holy fires, driven to claim them in his name. Slowly, the lost pieces of his consciousness would return to him down the black river of time. His patience was infinite, and soon he would rise anew.

For now, he watched as another hole was torn in the flesh of his realm. More daemons flooded into being, like pus squirting from an infected wound. They flew, loped and stamped across his land, injuring the substance of reality further. But they had been unleashed too soon. A mistake – overconfidence, perhaps, or desperation. It didn't matter either way.

'A cunning stratagem, my mortarch,' Nagash said. 'As you predicted, they have committed themselves too soon.'

Arkhan looked up. The Mortarch of Sacrament was but an ant to Nagash, standing far below. An ant, yes, but loyal. 'It was only possible with your aid, my lord. It is your strength which makes triumph certain.'

'Yes. Certain.' Nagash relished the word. These invaders had begun to infuriate him. No matter how many he'd killed, they kept coming. They had no more sense than the poxes they worshipped. He could feel the damage they'd wrought in their wake, like a slow ache somewhere deep within him. They had burned a scar across his realm, a wound which would fester for centuries, further weakening him. And now they even dared threaten an entrance to his refuge. He wished to punish them, to break them, once and for all.

'With your aid, I shall draw up the drowned dead and swamp the rotbringers,' said Arkhan. 'Let them see how much they like decay then.'

Nagash looked down at him. 'You ask much, my servant. Can you do nothing for yourself?'

Arkhan was silent, for a moment. Then, he said, 'Alone, I can draw up a third of those waiting here. But I wished to make an impression upon our foes, my master, so that any who survive might carry tales of your might back with them to lesser realms. Together, we can send a million corpses stalking southwards, carrying word that Nagash is best left undisturbed.'

Nagash pondered this. His power was steadily waning, and he'd exerted himself overmuch these past few days. It was growing harder to maintain his cognisance, and to affect the world around him. He required sleep – a century or more of slumber, to gather his strength for the battles yet to come. Once he might have considered a show of force to be beneath him. After all, was his power not obvious? But now such a display might buy him the time he needed to recuperate unmolested.

A scratching at his consciousness distracted him for a moment. He turned his gaze towards the Wailing Peaks and the souls interred within the roots of the mountains. They begged him for their freedom, for the chance to fight once more in his name, to serve their people. He silenced the Broken Kings with but a thought. Let them watch their people die on the altar of his greatness. It was only fitting that they bear witness to the final ruination of those they'd led in rebellion so many centuries ago.

And they would be ruined. The last dregs of the Rictus would be broken here, whatever the outcome. The last drops of their treacherous blood would be spilled in his name, as was his due.

'The mortals will break and flee,' he said at last.

'Yes, but not until the dead are ready to greet those who pursue them. Their lives are the coins we use to buy the chance of victory,' Arkhan said.

'Still the gambler, eh, my servant?' A curious statement. He did not know why he had said it, or where the thought had come from. He brushed it aside as unimportant.

'I am but as you made me, my lord.'

'And Neferata?'

Arkhan hesitated, for a fraction of an instant. 'She knows what must be done.'

Nagash pondered this equivocation. Arkhan spoke with the voice of Nagash, in all things. Arkhan was the aleph: the central, unchanging facet around which all of the other mortarchs and deathlords moved. It was Arkhan who threw their petty schemes into disarray when necessary, and Arkhan who kept them from inciting the fury of the Undying King. And it was Arkhan who asked for leniency in regards to those whose treacheries were as numberless as the dead.

Arkhan, who had been with him since his first stirrings, whose voice had been one of those which had comforted him in the dark. There had been other voices there as well, and memories besides. He remembered the coarse feel of sand, and the taste of sweet blood. He remembered the screams of dying gods as he devoured them, one prayer at a time. Now they were a part of him, as Arkhan was.

All were one in Nagash. To serve Nagash was to be Nagash. Arkhan and the others could not defy him, any more than the Undying King could defy himself. And yet they did so, in a thousand small ways.

'I created you,' he said. It was almost a question.

'Yes, my lord.'

'I raised you up from dust and the memory of dust.'

'As you say, my master.'

'You are me.'

'All are one in Nagash, master.'

Nagash stared down at him. 'You are merely the cup into which all unnecessary things have been poured. I shaped you and I have filled you. Do not forget that.'

'All that I am, I owe to your benevolence, my lord. I persist but to serve you. As does Neferata, and as do the clans of the Rictus.'

Nagash looked down at his servant. Then, back out over the battlefield. The air hummed with the sounds of war and death. It was music to him. Souls rose over the Mandible, newly freed from their sheathes of flesh. He pulled them to him and consumed them.

'Very well,' he said. He let his hold on the world slacken, and descended into the depths.

The drowned dead were already stirring – that much Arkhan had been able to accomplish on his own. An impressive feat, but Nagash was more powerful yet. His cloudy shape began to thin and split. And soon, the dead began to do more than stir.

Tamra watched in growing horror as the armies of decay marched on the Mandible. The forces of the enemy stretched from shore to mountains, and came on with an air of carnival exuberance. Snorting, stamping beastkin loped ahead of bell-ringing zealots and renegade tribesmen, flying the banners of a dozen smaller clans. And beyond them, the true iron of the enemy – stolid warriors, clad in hauberks and carrying heavy iron-rimmed shields, marching in formation. With them came the bloated blightkings and creaking war-altars, which spewed noxious fumes into the snowy air.

Stomach roiling, she stepped back from the edge. 'Nagash preserve us,' she said.

No one responded, though she had little doubt that they were all feeling the same way. The ruined tower the gathered voivodes occupied was close to the outer wall. Once, it would have been manned by clan-archers. Now, Arun led the strongest of the voivodes in a communal chant. Between them, they would be able to control the numberless hordes of deadwalkers which stumbled through the ruins. It was easy to drag a body to its feet, but substantially more difficult to make it do what you wanted. In most cases, it was enough to point zombies in the right direction. They would instinctively lurch towards the closest source of flesh.

But today required precision, rather than instinct. The deadwalkers would be employed to flank the enemy and hem them in. That meant keeping them all moving in the same direction, at roughly the same speed. Tamra's skin crawled as she joined her voice with the others, trying to block out the hellacious babble of the enemy. She wove the ritual gestures by instinct. She could feel the unnatural hunger of the animated corpses, and the dull animal agony which marked their wretched persistence. Though their souls were gone, their flesh still functioned, still felt the phantoms of hunger, thirst and pain. In trying to control them, her mind was open to theirs. She and the other voivodes were forced to endure the ache of splintered bones and rotting flesh, and the gnawing, unquenchable desire for living meat.

'There are so many of them,' Myrn said. The leader of the Wald looked spent already, her eyes hollow with exhaustion. 'So many...'

'It doesn't matter,' Tamra said. 'Our people are counting on us. What we do now, we do for them.' As she spoke, she could hear the murmurings of the Broken Kings, stronger now with all of the magic swirling about the air.

Free us... for them... free... us...

'I cannot,' Tamra hissed. 'I will not.'

Myrn looked at her. 'What?'

'Nothing. The enemy are upon us. Do you hear?' Tamra felt a jolt as the dead sighted the living. The black hunger asserted itself and the zombies lurched forwards with a communal moan. Through their eyes, she could see the front ranks of the foe drawing close. She slackened her hold on the dead-walkers, allowing them to surge forwards.

Arrows rattled across the stones. The bows of the rotbringers were heavier than those of the few clansmen occupying the walls, and they had a longer range. A voivode cursed and gestured. In the ruins below, packs of long-dead hunting dogs loped silently towards the archers. The enemy was bogged down, caught halfway to the walls by the charnel horde. They would have to hack themselves a path through a thicket of clawing hands and teeth.

Tamra gestured, and the smoke rising from one of the braziers in the tower coalesced into the snarling features of the Prince of Crows.

'How do you fare, sister?' he growled.

The ghoul-king still had her confused with his long-dead

sister, Isa. Tamra had given up trying to convince him otherwise. She suspected some part of him knew the truth regardless.

'We have stopped the advance for now. You know what you must do?'

'Aye. We shall fall upon them as we swore. The city shall not fall, sister. And soon, we shall be reunited, and my people made whole again.'

Tamra nodded tersely and broke the connection with a gesture.

'He's mad,' Myrn said. 'Can we trust them?'

'He is, and we can.' The corpse-eaters would come, because Nagash had commanded it. Tamra had said nothing of Nagash's presence in the caves to the other voivodes. Neferata had insisted that she claim sole responsibility for the act – another strand of her web. Tamra pushed the thought aside. Now was not the time for worrying about the future; the here and now was dangerous enough.

She glanced at the sky, wondering where Neferata was. They could use the mortarch's strength, if only to alleviate some of the burden on themselves. As she looked up, she heard a deep droning sound. The voivodes' chanting faltered.

The sky was full of flies.

The Sisterhood of Szandor waited in the lee of a hostelry wall alongside the main avenue for their moment to strike. For five centuries, the blood knights had waged Neferata's wars on three continents and across two realms, and they were the very picture of martial discipline. They had been trained by the Blood Dragon himself, and had forgotten more about war than most could learn in a lifetime. And yet, even for them, waiting was the hardest part.

Or so it was for Adhema. The gift of the soulblight had done little to curb the kastellan's natural impatience. War was her art, and she was ever keen to practise it upon the enemies of her queen. She sat atop her restive steed, kneading the animal's muscled neck with her iron-shrouded fingers, watching as the battle unfolded.

Neferata's plan was elegant in its simplicity. They needed time to call up the drowned dead and for the ghouls to muster, and for one other element besides, so the enemy had to be caught and held in the ruins. They had to be delayed by hours, or days if possible – battered, bloodied and bruised until the time was right.

Adhema glanced towards the far crags of the Wailing Peaks. Though she was weak in the arts of sorcery, she could feel the pull of the souls trapped there well enough. An army of the dead and damned, imprisoned by Nagash and unlikely to be freed, save in the right circumstances and by the right person. 'Poor little poppet,' she murmured, with bleak amusement. Neferata's gambits were as fire, burning all in reach. She shook her head and turned her attentions back to the matter at hand.

Outside the remains of the hostelry, deadwalkers flooded the ruined streets. They stumbled towards the advancing rotbringers in ever-increasing numbers, spilling out of broken hovels and clambering out of hillocks of rubble, responding to Neferata's call. Few mortals, living or dead, could resist the whispered entreaties of the Mortarch of Blood. A fact Adhema had learned, much to her own cost.

She could hear the clamour of the foe's bells, and the bellicose roars of beast-things drawing near. The beastmen hacked at the staggering dead with futile abandon, trying to chop themselves a path straight towards the Mandible's main gate. They were joined in this vain enterprise by mortal rotbringers. The frothing zealots chanted the sevenfold name of their god as they smashed zombies to the ground with shields and cudgels. More than one were dragged down and torn apart, or devoured where they stood.

Similar battles were raging on either side of the avenue throughout the ruins. Thousands of deadwalkers pushed southwards like a living wall, stymieing any attempt by Nurgle's followers to advance or slip past. Swarms of bats fluttered about the heads of the sorcerers who crouched on the war-altars the zealots pushed forwards, distracting them. Screeching spirit hosts issued from dry wells and broken buildings, swirling about those who'd invaded the city where they'd died. Everywhere, in the ruin with no name, the dead strove savagely against the living.

Adhema tapped the pommel of her sword, considering her options. A charge now would break the mortals and send them running back along the main avenue. But the true might of the foe was still plodding along. Those were the ones she wanted.

'Taking their time,' she murmured.

She glanced skywards, searching for some sign of Neferata. It was rare that her queen participated in open battle; Neferata was not one to sully her hands, if she could help it. The Rictus, fools that they were, had expected her to lead from the front, as their own voivodes did. She suspected that the mortarch was out on the ice somewhere, waiting for the inevitable. It was on the ice that this matter would be settled. The death-throes of the Rictus were but a sideshow to Neferata's true purpose.

'The air smells foul,' a blood knight said. Others murmured agreement.

'Daemons,' Adhema said. Only daemons had that particular odour. Strange yowls broke out. The rotbringer ranks dissolved into confusion as heavy slug-like bodies barrelled through them, slashing the air with pulpy tendrils.

Adhema watched the slobbering daemon-beasts flounder through the packed ranks of the deadwalkers. The daemons put her in mind of her father's kennels, in happier days before the fall of Szandor, and of the yapping pups of his hunting hounds: all enthusiasm and no brains. The ranks of corpses split and flowed around the daemons, stumbling on to meet the regrouping rotbringers.

'Now, sister?' one of her knights asked eagerly.

'Not yet. Let the offal earn its keep a few moments more.'

She cast a glance at the walls of the Mandible. Somewhere up there, Neferata's new favourite was controlling the dead. Her lip curled back from a fang, and she looked away. In truth, she bore the mortal no ill will. She could not help what she was, or that Neferata was interested in moulding her into something more useful to the mortarch's long-term goals. Nonetheless, it was irksome to endure such manoeuvrings. Luckily, she was in the right place to work out her frustrations.

A low droning sound filled the air. She peered up and saw dozens of large, winged shapes hurtle overhead. She'd fought the servants of Nurgle before, and knew plague drones when she saw them. The daemonic insects sped towards the walls of the Mandible in their hundreds, bypassing the deadwalkers entirely.

'That bodes ill,' she said absently. But it wasn't her responsibility. The Mandible would fall, sooner or later. It wasn't up to her to protect it. Her role was only to bleed the foe, and savage them where she judged best.

And one other thing besides. A little thing, but annoying nevertheless. Her freedom to enjoy the song of war would only last until the walls fell. The moment the Mandible was taken, she was to lead her sisters back to seek out and keep safe the object of Neferata's immediate affections. The voivode of the Drak was key to victories not yet born, or so her queen insisted. That one deathmage, however powerful, could be so important exasperated Adhema.

Her hopes of enjoying herself for a good long while before then, however, were few. The dead faltered as the blight flies reached the walls and began their attack. The voivodes controlling them were obviously distracted. It would likely be their undoing.

Adhema peered over the morass of battle and saw mounted warriors guiding their scaly steeds forwards through the snowy ruins, in support of the marching shieldbearers. Chaos knights, bearing the blighted blessings of Nurgle. They were the prey she was after, and she intended to claim them before it was too late.

She kicked her steed into motion. 'Now, sisters. Time to bleed them a bit.'

The blood knights exploded from the hostelry and galloped into the disorganised mass of rotbringers who packed the avenue. Bodies were sent flying or else crushed beneath iron-shod hooves. Adhema leaned over in her saddle and removed a beastman's head. Her sisters' lances pierced bloated torsos and gouged great wounds in those fortunate enough not to be impaled. The hooves and teeth of their nightmare steeds added to the toll of destruction.

Adhema laughed as she led her warriors through the ranks of the enemy. The ruined walls to either side of the avenue were splashed with ichor. Few living things could resist the charge of the Sisterhood of Szandor. Deadwalkers stumbled in their wake.

'The ones with the shields,' she called out. 'Let us crack them wide.'

Iron-rimmed shields splintered as they struck a hastily erected shield wall. Adhema laid about her on either side, cleaving skulls and chopping through upraised blades. The blood knights carved a red path through the ranks, and the mortals broke in the face of such fury, streaming away from the rampaging vampires. But Adhema had already forgotten them. Her true prey was in sight. With a roar, she led her sisters towards the knights of Nurgle.

Adhema shouted for joy as they met in the centre of the avenue.

Rikan ven-Drak loped through the frost-limned trees, sword in hand. His warriors moved in loose formation around him, clutching their own weapons. They descended the slopes of the Wailing Peaks in their hundreds, eager to give battle. The call had come, and they had answered, as he'd sworn. His sister needed his aid, and he intended to give it. The High-King could do no less, recognised ruler or no. He glanced towards the Mandible and cursed.

The monstrous flies swarmed over the fortress in great numbers, and he could hear the droning call of daemons in the ruins. The enemy had come in even greater strength than he'd been led to believe. He found he didn't mind. More enemies meant more to kill.

'Come, warriors of the Rictus. There are foes aplenty.'

His brave warriors gave a cheer and charged down towards the rotbringers working to fell trees. They scattered, seeking weapons and shouting warnings to their fellows. Rikan led from the front, and he caught one of the startled creatures a hard blow with his sword. It flipped head over heels and collapsed into the snow.

His warriors fell upon the others, biting and clawing – no, why had he thought that? He shook his head, trying to dislodge the image of gaunt, grey shapes hacking, smashing and gouging victims with claws and bone clubs. His men were rough, it was true, but they were not beasts. Not like the creatures they fought; not like the one now roaring and slapping his men aside like flies. The monster had been a man once, but now he was a bloated thing, his flesh bulging with abominable larvae.

'Turn, monster, turn and face the High-King,' Rikan roared, as he surged towards the creature. The beast spun, and Rikan was forced to swerve beneath the sweep of an axe. He lunged up, catching the haft of the axe and halting its swing. 'I smell the blood of kinsmen on you,' he said, as he strained against his opponent. 'Are you of the Rictus?'

'I am Croga, beast. First of my clan to accept the blessed miasma of the King of All Flies,' Croga roared, shoving Rikan back. His axe flashed down, splitting the ground where Rikan had been standing.

Rikan leapt over him, causing the renegade to whirl.

'A traitor's death, then,' Rikan hissed, as he bulled full into the renegade. Croga screamed as Rikan's claws – no, *his hands* – pierced his chest and slammed him against the ground. Rikan's jaws gaped wide and he sank his fangs into Croga's throat. With a jerk of his neck, he tore his foe's jugular out. He spat the lump of tainted flesh aside and lurched up and away from the twitching corpse, clutching his head.

The appearance of the warriors around him wavered, revealing pale flesh draped in rags and rotted armour, rather than furs and bronze. Bearded faces bled away into feral, fang-studded maws, and determined gazes became mad. Rikan blinked and shook his head.

'Are you well, milord?' one of his warriors asked. Gazbrul ven-Wald – a loyal and true servant. But to Rikan's confused gaze, the man's expression was at once a querulous snarl and a grimace of concern. He seemed to have two faces, and Rikan could only guess as to which was the true one. He rubbed his eyes, trying to banish the delusions.

'Aye, Gazbrul, my friend,' he said, clasping his man on the shoulder. 'Some effect of the foul miasma which accompanies our foes. It distorts my senses, I fear.'

'No less than ours, I suspect,' Gazbrul said, with a shake of his shaggy head. 'For a moment, milord, I thought you some great beast.'

'The only beasts here are these rotbringers,' Rikan growled. 'They seek to take our lands from us, something not even the Undying King could do. And I intend to show them why.' His men let out a raucous cheer, and Rikan straightened. 'Come, brothers... shall we leave our kin at the mercy of these monsters?' He pointed his sword towards a band of approaching armsmen. There were many of them, which was good.

He was quite hungry.

The plague drones filled the air, blotting out the grey light of the Ghost-Sun. The hum of their wings was as thunder, and the stamp of daemonic feet caused the earth to shake. Daemons flooded into the ruins, hewing bloody pathways through the dead. It was everything Gurm had hoped it would be, and more: life against death, fecundity versus stagnation.

'Look at my lovelies fly, Wolgus – have you ever seen a more majestic sight?' Gurm called out, as he caught sight of the blightmaster riding towards him at full pelt.

Wolgus sawed back on his mount's reins, causing it to rear. Hooves slashed out, and nearby plaguebearers scattered with grunts of alarm; Gurm's palanquin stumbled, nearly tossing him to the ground. He caught himself on a branch and gave it an irritated twist. The sylvaneth squealed, in a voice like snapping green twigs.

'You could have just said no,' Gurm said, glowering at Wolgus.

'I did say no. Did I not say that we would take this fortress?' Wolgus had his mace in hand, and the haft creaked in his grip. His personal armsmen had joined him, and the mortals warily faced the daemons over the rims of their shields. Behind them, the camp echoed with the sounds of battle and the cries of ghouls.

Gurm looked towards the camp, and then at Wolgus. 'Then why aren't you out there, taking it? Instead you take your ease here, while your knights ride out to reap glory.'

Wolgus didn't flinch this time. He'd drunk from the chalice, and he was firm in his convictions once more. 'It is for a blightmaster to oversee the tides of battle, not splash in its embrace. Lines must be bolstered, ranks firmed, retreats sounded. Such is my burden. Why do you seek to steal my victory, Herald? You have cast my tactics into the dust, and rendered my strategy meaningless.'

'Actually, you told me to keep to my schemes. And so I have.' Gurm reclined on his cushions, his balesword across his knees. 'You know the camp is under attack, I trust.'

'I am well aware. My warriors fight to contain it. Unlike you, they are trustworthy.'

Gurm clutched his chest in mock pain. 'I do not have time to waste, watching you play master-of-sieges, boy. There's more at stake here than your pride.'

'Then why bring us?' Wolgus demanded.

'Someone must pay the blood toll for getting me here. You were my shield, blunting those attacks which would have sapped my power. Now, I cast you aside and unsheathe my sword for the killing blow. That is war, isn't it?'

Wolgus shook his head. 'You have no idea what war is. Nor do I have time to teach you. Is this all for glory, then? Is this to be Gurm's victory, rather than the Order's?'

'It is to be Nurgle's victory,' Gurm said. 'For we serve him in this, as in all things.'

'But to what end?' Wolgus pointed his mace at Gurm's head. 'What is in that fortress that you cannot wait for us to take it?'

Gurm licked his jowls thoughtfully. Wolgus thrummed with resentment. His honour had been pricked wide, and now bled freely. His warriors marched on the final redoubt of those they'd come so far and endured so much to make war on, and the moment was being snatched from them. Necessary, all of it, but... risky.

'Perhaps I was overhasty,' Gurm said. He spread his palms in apology. 'I was overcome with fervour, Wolgus. Surely you understand. The King of All Flies speaks, and we can but obey.'

'What does he say, Gurm. And none of your homilies this time – why are we here?'

Gurm sucked on his fangs, debating with himself. If he removed Wolgus' head now, there would be an outcry. The problem with the Order was that they took the business of war far too seriously. While it was rare, it wasn't unknown for the servants of Nurgle to turn upon one another for silly reasons. Life was competition, after all. But there was no time for that now. He still needed Wolgus, if only to keep the Order in the fight.

'A gate,' he said. He leaned forwards. 'To Stygxx.' Wolgus stared at him. Gurm sighed. 'The underworld, Wolgus. Where Nagash resides.'

'Nagash is dead,' Wolgus said automatically.

'So he is. And what is left of him hides in the underworld. I would seek those aberrant remains out, and fill the guts of this realm with Nurgle's squirming legions.' He extended his sword towards the sea. 'There – do you sense it, Wolgus? A hole in the world, somewhere below the ice. It is there I must go. But I must shatter this fortress to do so.'

'Why did you not tell me this before?'

'Few men are willing to march into the jaws of a god, even a dead one,' Gurm said. A lie, of course. But Papa Nurgle would forgive him.

'A holy crusade indeed,' Wolgus said, absently. He stared out at the sea. 'To conquer the underworld in Nurgle's name would bring great honour to the Order.'

'Indeed it would, my friend, indeed it would.' Gurm leaned back, pleased. After all, there was still plenty of time to shuck the Order and claim victory for himself. 'And together, you and I will do just that.'

TEN

FALL OF THE RICTUS

The great bells of Ossuary shall sound nine times,
and the seas of all the realms shall dry up.
I will stride across the empty oceans, and the drowned dead shall rise at my call.
I will crack the earth and shatter the mountains.
Nine words shall I speak.
And nothing more shall ever be said.

– *The Epistle of Bone*

Aged Arun was the first to fall, a scabrous arrow left sprouting from his eye as he stood chanting atop the ruined tower. He slumped with barely more than a sigh. Tamra watched in horror as his skull collapsed in on itself, eaten away by the rot emanating from the arrow. His body began to twitch a moment later, like a side of meat eaten hollow by maggots. Something giggled tinnily as Arun's bat-winged helm rolled away with a clang. A moment later, tiny bloated daemons spilled out of the old man's body and scampered across the tower.

Myrn and the others yelped and cursed as they were forced to turn their attentions to the tiny daemons and away from the battle below, and from the buzzing hordes approaching from above. Tamra stamped on a nurgling as it clawed at her leg. Arrows tore her coat, and she narrowly avoided the slash of a rot fly's stinger. The insect screeched as one of the other voivodes lanced it with an arcane bolt and sent it tumbling away, wreathed in purple flame.

Everywhere that arrows thudded home, nurglings sprouted. The tiny daemons bubbled up from the slime-tipped heads of the arrows and ran every which way. Tamra snatched up a brazier and scattered burning coals across the closest pack of the tittering creatures. As they screamed and crisped, she looked out over the fortress. The air above the Mandible was full of plague drones. The daemonic riders cut men from the walls with gleaming baleswords, or else hurled fiery skulls.

One of the skulls struck the base of the tower and erupted into plague-fire. Something swelled within the flames and stuck to the stones. Greasy tendrils of smoking wood crept upwards, clutching the tower like a creeper vine. More patches of insidious plant life crept across the walls or spilled across the courtyard, growing in the heat of the plague-fires. Obscene blossoms sprouted from the tendrils, spewing a noxious pollen into the smoky air.

The tower began to shudder as the tendrils that were wrapped about it tightened. Tamra gestured, and a howling cavalcade of frenzied spirits raced to strike at the writhing vegetation. She heard a scream from behind her, and whirled to see Myrn sag, a plaguebearer's blade in her back. The daemon yanked the weapon free and charged towards Tamra, chuckling evilly. She dragged her sword from its sheath as it reached her, and black lightning snapped as their blades met.

She staggered, thrown off balance by the force of the blow, and then stumbled further, as the tower groaned and began to turn on its base. Stones clashed and timbers burst as the tendrils crushed the base of the tower and sent the entire structure slewing towards the wall.

Instinctively, Tamra leapt. There was no time for anything else, not even to shout a warning to the other voivodes. Heart thudding in her chest, the world spinning about her, she screamed. Spectres streaked upwards at her call, and caught her in cold claws. They swarmed about her like a cyclone and carried her roughly to the ground. She hit the earth hard and rolled, barely holding on to her sword.

The tower crashed heavily against the wall, crushing ancient masonry beneath it. Dust billowed as the tower continued its descent, striking the ground with an echoing boom. The wall collapsed inwards, carrying men and daemons with it. She covered her head as shrapnel struck the ground around her. Daemons poured through the newly made gap in the wall, attacking any who staggered into their path.

The dead lurched through fire and smoke to meet the invaders. The skeletal warriors had been meant to counter-attack when the rotbringers drew close to the walls. But now, they marched forwards, battling against the daemons who thrust themselves through the weak points in the walls and spilled into the courtyard. Spirits swept shrieking through the air, duelling with the buzzing plague drones. But the dead were too few, and the daemons almost limitless.

'Do you live, Drak?' someone coughed. She rolled onto her back and looked up at Bolgu. Blood stained his furs and warplate, and ichor smoked on the blade of his axe. He gripped her arm and dragged her to her feet. 'On your feet, woman. We must flee.'

'The walls,' she said, fighting for breath. Everything hurt, and she was bleeding from a graze on her cheek. Plague-fires roared up, casting sickly shadows across the courtyard. She could feel their heat in her bones, and suddenly she was back in her own steading, and her home was burning again before her eyes. Bolgu shook her, snapping her back to the present.

'The walls have fallen. As I said they would. Come on.' He half-dragged her towards the seaward gate. People were streaming through it, carrying nothing save children or weapons. A phalanx of skeletal warriors was arrayed before the gate, warding off any enemy who got too close. Tamra jerked her arm free of Bolgu's grip.

'I will not flee,' she said. 'Not again.'

Not... flee... free us... free us...

The Broken Kings howled in her head, pounding at the walls of her consciousness.

He glared at her. 'And who will lead our people if we die here? Those who can will flee to the galleys. My crews have orders to cast off as soon as the holds are full. If we are not on those ships, they will leave us.'

'Then go, if you must. I will stay.' She turned and drew her blade. 'Someone must hold them back.'

Hold them back... call us forth... free us...

'Let the dead do it,' said Bolgu. 'Our responsibility is to the living.'

She hesitated, remembering old hopes and old voices. She looked at Bolgu.

'Let's go.'

Festerbite shoved his way through the broken seaward gatehouse, past knots of giggling nurglings. Scab was dead, thanks to one of the monstrous knights who'd engaged him and his brothers in the central avenue. He'd been thrown from the saddle, and by the time he'd recovered, a dozen brave knights, including Sir Balagos, had joined Scab in death.

He'd engaged one of the creatures, spearing it with a broken standard. When the walls had fallen, the remaining vampires had fled, like the cowards they were. He looked forward to hunting them down later, when the battle was won. There was much honour to be gained by purging the realm of such perfidious creatures. For now, he would content himself with the joys of executing their mortal followers in Nurgle's name.

A skeleton stumbled towards him, its limbs weighed down by giggling nurglings. He took off its head with a single blow. More of the fleshless dead filled the courtyard, battling Gurm's legions and the Order's warriors. Mortals fought, too. They were brave, if misguided, and he felt some touch of pity for them. Their world was coming to an end, and they could not conceive of the better one which awaited them.

Several black-fletched arrows ricocheted off his armour, startling him. Clansmen scurried along the walls above, firing as they fled for more stable ground. The short recursive bows of the Rictus were as toys when compared to the longbows of the Order's armsmen, though he was forced to admit they had their merits at short range when one last arrow sank deep into his arm. There was no pain, but it was inconvenient.

As he paused to pull it loose, he scanned the shoreline. The savages were fleeing for the iron-prowed galleys being shoved onto the ice with great booming cracks. There were not enough vessels for all of them, and some of the savages had turned back to face their pursuers with looks of hopeless desperation. Others fled for the rocky slopes, or sought shelter in the ruins of the once massive docklands which dominated much of the waterfront.

It mattered little where they ended up – all would be brought to heel eventually. Those who would not sip from the Flyblown Chalice and accept the blessings of Nurgle into their hearts would be made into mulch for the garden. But that didn't mean they would be allowed to escape unscathed. Daemons flooded onto the ice in pursuit of the galleys, accompanied by the remaining knights of the Order and the quickest of the rotbringers.

He caught sight of Wolgus' personal banner flapping in the wind, and he felt a moment of elation. The blightmaster was leading the charge, as was only fitting. This was a great victory for the Order of the Fly – perhaps the greatest in its history. Troubadours would sing of this day, and the tapestries dedicated to the long march from the Ithilian Gate would hang in Cankerwall. Wolgus would be heralded as the greatest of the seven blightmasters, and the Order would have a foothold in the realms of life and death.

Chuckling to himself, Festerbite started towards the docklands. He would leave pursuit of the galleys to those with steeds, and to Gurm's daemonic followers. Instead, he would content himself with cleansing these ruins of savages. He was joined by blightkings and frothing zealots as he entered the tangle of docks, jetties and capsized galleys. He was glad to see Molov still alive, and the blightking nodded to him in greeting.

'A fine day, eh, Sir Festerbite?'

'The finest, my friend,' Festerbite said, with a laugh. 'Come, let us bring the warmth of the garden to these cold souls.'

Mortals fled in terror before them, squeezing like rats through frozen timbers. Some turned to fight, but fell to heavy blades, maces and cudgels. Hot blood slopped across the ice, and Festerbite rejoiced. They had spent too long in the wilderness, fighting things which didn't bleed. 'Don't kill all of them – take those who surrender,' he shouted to Molov. 'We're not beasts, after all.'

As he said it, warriors burst from the shadows and attacked.

A spear grated across his helm, and he caught the haft. Wrenching it from its owner's grip, he cut the hapless savage down. 'Yield, and you will be spared,' he roared, kicking the twitching corpse from his blade. 'Submit to the Lord of All Things and find your soul's salvation.'

An axe sank into his arm, and he spun, stabbing the man who'd wielded it. The Rictus staggered back, clutching at his stomach. Festerbite reached for the wounded man, but found himself distracted by a painful blow on the back. He sank to one knee, wheezing, as his attacker circled him and caught up the wounded man.

The woman glanced over her shoulder as she dragged her bleeding burden into the shallows, retreating into the forest of wreckage that had once been docklands. Her narrow features were tight with fear.

Festerbite heaved himself to his feet and stomped after her. 'You cannot escape me, woman,' he called out. 'Yield, and I will grant you mercy. There is no need to die today. Death is the enemy. Seek salvation in life!'

'Quiet,' Tamra whispered. 'Quiet.'

Behind her hand, Bolgu was trying to scream. The wound in his gut was festering far more quickly than she'd expected. Fat maggots squirmed beneath his ravaged flesh, and his eyes were wide with pain. The pox-knight who'd wounded Bolgu had followed them into the wreckage of the shallows, and was still searching for them with his fellows. The creature bellowed words of mercy and surrender, even as he struck down those who drew too close. She winced with every blow and scream.

They'd been heading for the galleys when they'd seen the rotbringers attacking those seeking shelter in the frozen docks. Despite himself, Bolgu had been unable to ignore their cries.

There was more to the voivode of the Fenn than she'd thought, and she felt a pang of regret that she wouldn't have the opportunity to know him better.

Bolgu grabbed her wrist. She looked down at the injured voivode.

'What? What are you trying to say?'

Bolgu clawed at the hooked knife in his belt, and she understood. The rot was in him, eating him hollow the way it had Arun.

'Life in death,' she said, as she drew the knife. He sagged in relief as, with only a moment's hesitation, she sank the blade to the hilt in his chest. He shuddered once and died. She rolled his body away and wiped her hands on her trousers, feeling faintly ill. Bolgu had been the last. As far as she knew, all the other voivodes were dead.

Neferata had been right. Arkhan, as well. And now the moment she'd dreaded was upon her. Past the wreckage, she could see daemons pouring onto the ice. Some pursued the fleeing ice-cutter galleys. Others raced towards Arkhan the Black, still standing his lonely watch. Hundreds more were occupied slaughtering those who sought shelter in the Mandible, or in the forests above it. The walls had fallen and the battle was lost, but her folk were still fighting, still struggling against the inevitable.

And it was inevitable. She saw that now. Victory had never been an option. They were meat, bait to lure in the beast. Neferata waited, somewhere, to capitalise on the rotbringers' exuberance and ensure that the jaws of her trap snapped shut at the proper time. The dead could afford to be patient. Tamra felt no anger, only fatigue.

'I will serve him in life and death,' she murmured. Her hand fell to her sword.

Smoke was rising from the Mandible. The plague-fires burned freely. She could hear her people screaming… fighting… dying. Some of them were still alive. Some of them could still be saved. But she couldn't do it alone.

We... can... save... them, the Broken Kings whispered. *Let us save our people, daughter... let us help them... free us...*

Their voices reverberated in her skull. Her head throbbed, full of visions and faces, of scenes from the past, or perhaps from the future. The air stank of milk and spoiled meat. The ice cracked beneath her feet. Her breath burned in her lungs, freezing her inside and out. The edges of her vision pulsed black as she stretched out a hand towards the distant crags.

Free us... free us... free us.

'Yes.' It was easy, once the intent was there. Just as Neferata had said. The bindings were weak, and the ghosts were strong. They wanted freedom, and they pushed while she pulled. So very strong. She heard a gruesome crack, and a roar of stone and ice.

She felt empty as she staggered back against the frozen wood. The pox-knight that had wounded Bolgu whirled at the sound and stormed towards her, chopping through ice-sheathed ropes and frost-blackened wood in his haste.

'There you are,' he gurgled. 'Thought you could hide, eh? An admirable attempt, but the game is done now.'

She got her sword up just in time. The force of his blow knocked her skidding. Bones aching, she fumbled to her feet. She felt like a wrung-out rag. Her head pounded with the rumble of hooves and the rattle of armour. She avoided her opponent's next blow, and the third. She raised her sword and backed away, panting. The pox-knight stalked after her, a throaty chuckle slithering from his fleshless, fang-studded jaws.

'Yield, witch. Yield and perhaps I'll spare you.'

'I have been made that offer before. I did not yield then. I shall not yield now.'

The pox-knight stopped. He inclined his head. 'As you wish.' He swung his blade up in a salute. 'You are brave, woman. Your suffering shall be swift.' He advanced, the ice cracking beneath him with every plodding step.

'Yours will be anything but.'

The pox-knight looked up as a heavy form descended in a shower of snow from the tangle of canvas and nets, smashing him from his feet. The knight's sword flew from his grip, and a clawed hand drove his head through the ice and into the chill waters below.

'Do you yet live, Isa?' Rikan growled, as he held the struggling warrior's head beneath the ice.

Over his shoulder, she saw the other rotbringers swarmed by ghouls. The sounds of their screams almost drowned out the cacophony in her head. The pox-knight's thrashings grew weaker as long moments passed. Tamra didn't speak until he'd fallen still and silent.

'I live. The others?'

'They flee across the ice like cattle. You broke his law, Isa. I felt it in my soul.' Rikan left the body where it lay, half in the ice, and padded towards her. 'I can hear them riding up from the dark hollows of the earth, and all the souls who dared follow them into the black are riding with them.' Black blood ran down his gaunt, grey form. Broken arrows jutted from his broad back and shoulders, and seeping sword cuts marked his chest and arms.

'My name is Tamra...' she began. The pressure in her head had slackened. But she could still hear the Broken Kings roaring in triumph as they swept down from their mountain prison. She could see the rotbringers in the Mandible fleeing before them. She could feel the shock of a tomb-blade biting into corrupted flesh. She shook her head, trying to clear her mind of the unwanted images and voices alike.

We are coming, daughter... we are free... free...

'I know what your name is,' the ghoul-king snarled, catching her by her coat. He slammed her back against a wooden strut. 'I know. I know who you are, and I know what you have done. You have freed our father and his brothers, and Nagash will *punish* us.'

'I did what I had to do. He will understand. Neferata...'

Free... free... free...

'Neferata lies!' Rikan's voice was nearly a shriek. 'I told you that. They all lie. We are lies wrapped in flesh. Nagash's lie. Nagash's flesh. And you have broken Nagash's law.' He released her and stepped back, gargoyle features twisted in anger. 'Why?'

'To save our people,' Tamra said. She snatched up her sword. 'I am Drak. What we have, we hold. I have my people, and I will hold them.'

We will save them... save them...

Rikan stared at her, crimson gaze unreadable. 'I thought as you did, once. And now, I think that I am mad.' He plucked a broken arrow from his flesh. 'I love you, sister.'

Tamra's hand tightened on the hilt of Sarpa's sword. 'I love you, brother,' she said, the words like ashes in her mouth.

Our people... we will save them...

'How sweet.'

Tamra turned. Adhema grinned at her. The kastellan looked the worse for wear: her armour was tattered and bloodied, and wounds marked her visible flesh. But she still held her sword, and it was still as sharp as ever. Several of her warriors stood behind her, or crouched in the wreckage, and their red eyes gleamed hungrily.

'You stirred them up, didn't you, poppet?' Adhema said. 'I felt it in my marrow. Even as she planned.' She extended her sword towards Rikan, as he snarled at her. 'How does it feel, to be a cog in her great machine? Is it all that you hoped?'

Tamra said nothing. What was there to say? Adhema was right. 'Did you fight your way through the foe just to taunt me?'

'Don't flatter yourself, poppet.' Adhema pointed her sword at Tamra. 'I came to protect you, to ensure that you survive your foolishness.' She smiled thinly and spread her arms. 'You see how much she cares for you?'

Gurm nodded in satisfaction as the walls of the Mandible fell. The skulls that the plague drones carried had been specially prepared for him in Ghyran, pickled in the sap squeezed from corrupted trees. Already the stinking heat radiated by the great tendrils was melting the snow to slurry and blistering the stones. The contaminated plant life would inundate the fortress, converting it into something more pleasing to Nurgle's eye. Soon it would do the same to the Wailing Peaks themselves, coring out the harsh stone and replacing it with moss, mould and agreeably rancid spoilage.

'Life against death,' he said, glancing at Wolgus. The blightmaster rode alongside Gurm's palanquin. Together, they traversed the corpse-strewn avenue which led to the main gate of the crumbling fortress, leading a band of daemons and rotbringers.

'Life against death,' Wolgus echoed. 'I admit, your way is the faster.' He didn't sound happy about it, but Gurm hadn't expected that. Wolgus was practical, if nothing else. He knew better than to poke a gift rash on the scab.

'I did say,' Gurm chortled. His honour guard of plaguebearers echoed his amusement. Behind him, the sounds of battle rose from the siege-camp. Packs of ghouls scuttled through the ruins, attacking isolated warriors. Gurm paid it little heed. Let the beasts have their fun while it lasted. Soon enough, the Order would put their warrens to the torch and hunt them down with bow and hound. Whatever plan the mortals had had, he'd put paid to it.

'The fortress is ours, and the way to our true goal is open,' Wolgus said. 'This is a great victory for the King of All Flies.' He gestured, and the armsmen who followed them broke into a lope, streaming towards the shattered gates. There was still fighting going on within the fortress, and there would be for some time. But the way was open, and the foe was on the run.

'Indeed it is. And with it comes the utter ruination of all our enemy's hopes. He cannot hide from us for long. We shall beard him in his lair, and drag his broken bones back to Cankerwall.' Gurm shook his fist at the distant ice. The spectre of Nagash had vanished. Gone back to Stygxx to cower in fear, he suspected.

But he could still hear the chanting. He'd heard it since their arrival, and had assumed it was coming from the Mandible. Now he wasn't so sure. It was coming from somewhere out on the ice. A grim voice, echoing up to the sky above. It had not faltered, not even when the Mandible had fallen. And he could feel the skeins of magic in the air tightening, as if a great working were nearing its completion.

The looming peaks rumbled, as if an avalanche were in the offing. He glanced over, curious, but saw nothing save the play of fading light across distant snows. He turned his attentions back to the Shivering Sea.

Something was happening, out on the ice. Some last ditch scheme to deny them victory. But it was too late: the north had fallen, and soon all of Shyish would follow suit. The realms of death would become a new garden for Nurgle to enjoy, and the name Dolorous Gurm would be whispered by every blighted blossom.

He thumped the point of his sword against the floor of the palanquin, encouraging the sylvaneth to greater speed. The ice, and the gate to Stygxx, awaited.

'Come, Wolgus – we have a gate to claim, and a god to humble!'

ELEVEN

NAGASH RISES

There are nine gates and behind them wait my ninefold legions.

Nine is the number of the books which contain my wisdom.

Nine is the number of my mortarchs.

And I shall speak nine words before the final gate, and cast it wide.

And all shall be consumed in darkness, as the light of every realm is snuffed at the ninth, and ultimate, hour.

– *The Epistle of Bone*

Neferata sat back in her saddle and watched as the Mandible collapsed and the Rictus fled to their galleys. She frowned. The battle she'd spent so much time engineering should have taken days, not hours. The daemons had thrown her calculations off. She'd thought that the disgusting creatures would wait until they had the gate to Stygxx in reach to unleash their full power. Instead, they'd burst like an overripe pustule and thrown all her plans into disarray.

'That's the problem when dealing with the stuff of Chaos, Nagadron,' she said. 'It's impossible to predict, even for one as skilled as myself.' The dread abyssal growled and she knocked her knuckles against its skull. 'Ah, well... Even the best laid plans are soon ruined.' She swept her staff out, and murmured softly. The air around her thickened with soul-stuff. Wailing faces took shape, and murmuring spirits clutched at her.

Arkhan would raise the flesh. But she still had the spirits of the drowned and recently dead to manipulate. While the rotbringers were busy chasing the living, the dead would have their way. The strongest of them shot away from her like comets, spiralling towards the swarm of plague drones which spread through the skies above the Shivering Sea.

She urged Nagadron down, swooping over the ice and the fleeing mortals, followed by a writhing tail of spirits. The Rictus had served their purpose admirably, even though they'd let her down in the end. She was inclined to save some of them at least, if only for Tamra's sake. Nagadron slammed into a plague drone, tearing at it. Neferata whirled her staff and drove the weighted ferrule into its rider's single eye. The daemon's head popped, and she wrenched her staff loose. She swept it out, setting the air alight with the gesture.

Burning plague drones fell twitching to the sea like raindrops about the fleeing galleys, whose iron prows carved a watery path as their oars thumped the breaking ice, shoving the vessels along. Neferata nodded in satisfaction.

Not all of the galleys had been so lucky. Several had been caught, and their passengers and crew fought frantically against the beastkin and rotbringers clambering aboard. She considered lending them aid, but only for a moment. She'd saved a few. That was enough. She had better uses for the dying. She whispered, and on the decks of an overtaken galley, the butchered dead rose again to attack their killers.

Free...

The word echoed through her head, followed by a twisting feeling. The sensation speared through her, and she turned towards the distant peaks instinctively. Her keen hearing soon picked out the screams of those rotbringers still in the Mandible. Bellows of triumph quickly turned to cries of panic as a new foe fell upon them with all the fury of the damned. The Broken Kings were free at last.

'Ha! She did it!' Neferata clapped her hands in glee. At least one facet of her plan had fallen properly into place, if a bit earlier than she'd expected. It had been a stroke of luck that one of the Nine Gates had decided to sprout here, necessitating her presence. And even luckier that the Rictus had produced a deathmage capable of doing what she herself could not. She'd hoped the terrors of a grinding siege might encourage Tamra to see her point of view in time, but she supposed imminent extermination served her purposes just as well. Either way, the Rictus Lands once more had an army worthy of the name, and all it had cost her was a ruined fortress and a few unruly tribesmen. A bargain.

'Oh my sister, the glories we shall reap together,' Neferata said. 'The triumphs we shall see, with your hand in mine.'

Let Mannfred play the hero of Helstone. Let Arkhan stolidly follow a senile god. She would settle for dragging order from chaos and putting right what had been allowed to go wrong. This was but the first step on a long road to victory. With the armies of the Rictus Lands at her back, she would sweep south and drive the servants of Chaos back to the Ithilian Gate and beyond. She would salvage what she could, and bolster those kingdoms loyal to her. A new empire would prosper in the darkness. *Her* empire.

'Nulahmia,' she murmured. She shivered in anticipation.

The rotbringers and daemons pouring onto the ice had not yet noticed the newly arisen enemy to their rear. She intended to see that they didn't, not until it was too late. The rotbringers would be caught in the open, between the drowned dead and the Broken Kings. 'Down,' she whispered to Nagadron, and the dread abyssal shrieked in acknowledgement.

Nagadron plunged downwards, swooping low over the ice. She aimed the dread abyssal towards a group of battle standards, and hunched low in the saddle. Nagadron hurtled towards the standards at great speed, faster than any plague drone, and the dead, both Rictus and rotbringer alike, stirred in its wake. Neferata dragged the dead to their feet as she passed, casting the enemy ranks into further confusion. She spat incantations, shattering the ice beneath the hooves of mutated steeds or setting them aflame. As they swept over the standards, Nagadron banked, twisting in the air. A troop of Chaos knights galloped across the ice below her.

She smiled. It had been too long since she had fought on foot, amid the carnage, and smelled the blood of her enemies as it dappled her flesh. Decision made, she thrust her staff through the back of her saddle.

'Go, Nagadron – kill, with my blessing,' Neferata said, as she slipped gracefully from the dread abyssal's saddle.

She plummeted downwards, jerking Akmet-har from her belt as she did so. The curved blade of jet purred in her grip as she slashed out, opening the wattle throat of a plague drone's rider. She kicked the daemon's body off of the great fly's back. Spinning her blade about, she drove it into the daemonic insect's head and twisted. Thrashing in its death throes, the rot fly fell towards one of its fellows. As the two crashed together, Neferata leapt onto a third, splitting the rider's skull with her dagger.

The rot fly twisted in mid-air, trying to sting her. She caught its proboscis and slashed open its bulbous thorax, emptying its guts over the battle below and drenching an unlucky knight in a wash of acidic fluid. She vaulted from the dying creature and dropped into a crouch on the ice.

Darting forwards, Akmet-har held extended in front of her, she cut through the stringy tendons of a mutated horse, spilling its rider onto the ice. Before the rotbringer could right himself, she was atop him, the tip of her blade sliding through his visor. Laughing, she jerked the blade free and turned, seeking new prey. She caught hold of a passing stirrup and, with a jerk of her shoulder, tore both saddle and rider from the running horse. She slammed the knight down, through the ice, and watched as he was dragged into the depths by the weight of his armour.

A monstrous daemon-steed reared above her, slashing the air with its thorny hooves. She gestured, and a bolt of crackling purple light snarled from her hand. The creature screamed as the arcane bolt tore through its skull, and it sank down, tossing its rider. He was a bulky one, and his battle-scarred armour was more ornate than the others. The breastplate was engraved with a leering face, and the pauldrons were moulded in the shape of stylised flies. Real flies circled his wide head in a humming halo. His face was a mass of scar tissue and weeping sores, but his eyes blazed with malign intelligence.

He was on his feet more quickly than she'd anticipated, and the heavy mace he carried snapped out. She ducked beneath the blow and then was forced to twist aside as the sword he held in his other hand hissed towards her. She stepped back, out of reach. Her spirits swirled about them, preventing any who might have done from coming to his aid. She extended her dagger as she circled him.

'Scars are stories,' she said, 'and I see whole volumes etched upon that reeking war-plate of yours. Do I have the honour of addressing Ocander Wolgus, Blightmaster of the Order of the Fly, Hero of the Bridge of Scabs and Master of Festerfane?'

He hesitated. 'You know me?'

'I know many things,' Neferata purred. 'I know you won your spurs at the Black Cistern, and that you struck the head from the King of Thorns in the Verdant Necropoli.'

'I know you as well, witch. The people of Hallowgrave call you the Ghost-Queen, and the primitives of the Ithilian Vale know you as the Blood Maiden. You are the darksome whelp of Death himself, and a mockery of all that lives.'

Neferata gave a mocking bow. 'It seems we know each other, then. Just as well... I do so hate to kill a stranger.' She set her feet and languidly stretched out a hand. 'Come, good sir. Prithee, do come and dance with me.'

'Have at thee, leech,' Wolgus said. The ice cracked beneath his feet as he charged at her. Neferata slipped beneath the blow and spun, drawing a rush of ichor from his side. Her obsidian dagger cut through his armour as if it were paper. Wolgus staggered, and clapped a hand to his side. 'That actually hurt,' he grunted.

As he turned, Neferata leapt. Dagger gripped in both hands, she thrust it down. The blade pierced Wolgus' armour, but it became lodged in the corroded metal. She released it and dropped down behind him. Before he could turn, she slashed out with her leg and caught his ankles. He gave a bellow of surprise and toppled forwards. Neferata pounced. He swept his mace out, and she let it smack into her palm. She tore it from his grasp with a hiss, flinging the baleful weapon away. Her palm was scorched black where she'd touched it. She tore her dagger free of his armour and flung up a hand, conjuring a mystic shield as he slashed at her with his sword. The iridescent oval of light cracked when the blade struck it. Grisly runes flared bright along the blade's length and her shield exploded, knocking them both from their feet.

Neferata clutched her aching head. It was never pleasant when a spell was broken, though she'd suffered worse in her time. She'd dropped her dagger somewhere, and now flailed blindly for it. A hand caught her by her throat.

'Would that your allegiance was not seared into your blood, sweet lady,' Wolgus grunted, as he dragged her to her feet. 'For you would find a sure home amongst our Order. Alas, 'tis not to be.' He drew a filth-encrusted poniard from his belt and made to thrust it into her heart. Neferata's hand flashed, catching his wrist and halting the tip of the blade a hairsbreadth from her breast. She grinned as he goggled at her.

'Alas indeed, you lump of spoiled meat,' she said. She caught his other hand and rocked forwards, slamming her brow into his face. Bone crunched and Wolgus staggered, blood in his eyes. Freed from his grip, Neferata twisted, dragging his arm to the limits of its extension and simultaneously driving a foot into his torso.

Wolgus flew backwards, bouncing across the ice. Neferata paced after him, enjoying herself more than she had for many years. As he regained his feet, he scrambled for his sword, reaching for where it lay sticking from the ice. She leapt for him just as he snatched it up. The rotbringer spun, more quickly than she'd expected, and the point of his blade was waiting for her when she landed. The sword tore through her armour and the flesh beneath, narrowly missing her heart.

She fell with a feline scream, tearing the sword from Wolgus' grip. She writhed on the ice, coughing up black blood. She could feel the cancerous enchantment woven into the steel trying to find purchase on her unnatural flesh. Luckily for her, Nagash had made his mortarchs of sterner stuff – any other vampire would have been consumed by the blade's sorcerous power. But she was still weak, and growing weaker. She clutched at the hilt, trying to pull it from her chest. Pain spasmed through her, forcing a shriek from her lips.

'Head and heart, the stories say,' Wolgus said. He stalked towards her. 'Pierce the heart and remove the head.' He flexed his fingers. 'I've done the one, now it's time for the other.'

He advanced, and Neferata squirmed backwards, spitting hoarse curses.

Daemons galumphed towards Arkhan the Black across the ice, howling eerie dirges. He'd ceased his chanting when they had arrived. There was no more need to draw their attention, after all. They were coming to him, as he'd planned. He could feel Nagash at work in the depths, driving the dead to the surface, and he allowed himself a moment of satisfaction. He'd hoped such a threat to his refuge would provoke Nagash into something approaching lucidity. So long as the servants of Chaos feared Nagash, Shyish would never be conquered. Not fully. A victory here would resonate through two realms.

Overhead, Razarak duelled with the monstrous flies which had preceded the tide of daemons. The dread abyssal could easily hold its own, and Arkhan left the creature to its fun. He had his own affairs to consider.

The leader of the filthy horde was easy enough to spot; Arkhan would have identified him even if he hadn't known who he was looking for. The ghosts of ice and snow had whispered the name of the Herald of Nurgle to him, and it was a familiar one. The dead of three realms knew it: Dolorous Gurm, the Garden-master. Gurm, who had uprooted the restless dead of the Verdant Necropoli in Ghyran and made a bonfire of their bones. Gurm, who had infected the mindless deadwalkers of the great forest of Fangnettle in the Realm of Beasts, and made them carry poxes and plagues into the camps of the living. Gurm, enslaver of the Dreadmere sylvaneth.

It was this last act which had convinced Arkhan that Gurm was a sickness which needed purging. The tree-kin of the Dreadmere had long cared for the dead who sheltered beneath their roots, and it was they who had guarded one of the secret routes between the realms of life and death. To see them bound in such a manner infuriated him to a degree that he found surprising. They did not deserve such torment. The birth of one of the Nine Gates below the Shivering Sea had given him the opportunity to avenge the insult and shake Nagash from his stupor.

It had been a simple enough matter to let the daemon discover the existence of the gate, and to leave the Rictus Lands relatively undefended by any save mortal forces. All to lure Gurm in, and deal with him, permanently. As the first rank of daemons reached him, Arkhan traced a spiteful gesture on the air, and the disgusting creatures crumbled to dust. Their dissolution opened a path to their master, revealing the Herald of Nurgle in all his foul glory.

Arkhan motioned, and amethyst lightning crackled from his palm. The tortured shapes of the sylvaneth which formed the daemon's palanquin twitched and screamed as their diseased bark began to crack and crumble. Their newly freed spirits whispered in gratitude as the palanquin tipped, toppling its rider to the ice. Gurm fell with a cry of frustration, and his honour guard surged forwards with a droning howl.

The mortarch set himself and swept his staff out, setting the ice aflame. The daemons' howls turned to agonized squeals as the fire devoured their putrid flesh. One by one, they were reduced to greasy motes of ash. Gurm pushed himself to his feet and leapt, springing high over the flames. The Herald of Nurgle crashed down on the other side of the fire, cracking the ice and knocking Arkhan back a step. Arkhan began to chant another incantation, but Gurm lurched after him, sword tearing a ragged hole in the liche's robes.

'A pretty song, bag o' bones, but it ends here,' Gurm cackled. The daemon swept his balesword out, but Arkhan caught the blow on his staff.

'I have not yet begun to sing, pus-belly.' Arkhan twisted his staff, driving the tip of Gurm's sword into the cracking ice. The liche drew his sword with his free hand and opened a steaming wound in the daemon's side. 'How do you like the melody now?'

Gurm shrieked and yanked his sword free in a spray of slurry. Their blades crashed together with a dolorous clang. Arkhan's feet slid back as Gurm leaned into the blow. Inhuman muscle squirmed like worms beneath his flesh, and the daemon's single eye blazed with fury. 'I will derive great pleasure from using your bones to stir my plagues, liche.'

'I would settle for seeing you cease to be,' Arkhan said, locking his feet. 'Care to wager odds on which is more likely?'

Gurm roared and forced Arkhan's sword down. The daemon lunged, jaws wide. Arkhan jerked forwards, slamming his skull into the daemon's maw. Rotting fangs splintered, and Gurm staggered back, clutching at his mouth.

'Bit off more than you could chew, eh maggot?' Arkhan said, bits of daemonic dentition dotting the front of his skull. He paced after his foe. 'I know you, Dolorous Gurm. Boastful daemon, slave of an idle god. You might have found Ghyran to be easy pickings, but this is Shyish, and we are stronger than that.'

'Life or death, beast or metal, it does not matter. All things rot, and Nurgle is rot made manifest,' Gurm gurgled, brushing ichor from his face with a knobbly knuckle. 'I will warm these frigid waters and stretch a bridge of decay down into their heart. Nurgle's children will walk a road of my making into the unblemished depths, and they will spread his foetid word through the guts of your realm...'

'Not while I stand,' Arkhan said.

'Then fall,' Gurm said, darting forwards. Their blades connected again and again as they spun in place, stamping and cursing. The ice, already weakened by Arkhan's sorcery and the weight of the battle taking place across its surface, ruptured with a sudden thunderous scream. Spars, prows and shattered masts thrust upwards, piercing the air. A blow from Gurm knocked Arkhan back against the splintered remains of a galley's prow.

The liche murmured a single word, and the waterlogged wood twisted, wrenching itself into a new, more monstrous shape. The spirits of Gurm's enslaved sylvaneth rejoiced fiercely as Arkhan gave them the chance they'd been longing for. The wood exploded into splintery tendrils which snared the Herald of Nurgle, savaging his rubbery flesh. Gurm howled in pain and hacked wildly at the twisting serpentine shapes. Before Arkhan could aid the spectral sylvaneth, the surviving plaguebearers closed in on him, baleswords hissing out.

He parried a blow with his staff, and removed a horned head with his tomb-blade. The liche twisted out of the path of a bone-shattering blow and spat a spell. A plaguebearer wailed as it was reduced to ash by the force of Arkhan's magic. But for every daemon that fell, two more rose to replace it. Arkhan was alone against an army. They clambered gracelessly through the newly sprouted forest of wrecked vessels, their hooves skidding on the ice.

He heard a rasping scream, and saw Gurm chop his way free of the possessed wood. The agonised spirits of the sylvaneth fled at last, unable to bear the touch of Gurm's blade for a moment longer. The Herald chortled, despite the bubbling wounds which marked his hide.

'A pretty trick, that, but ultimately useless, bag o' bones. You stand alone. Your god has abandoned you. Nagash is nowhere to be seen, and Nurgle is with me.'

'I am used to solitude,' Arkhan said. 'Even alone, I am more than a match for every daemon in your pestilential horde. Summon more, if you will. Call up flies and beasts by the score, I will outlast them all.' He set his staff and extended his tomb-blade towards the ranks of plaguebearers which surrounded him. 'I am the right hand of death, little pus-bag. Test me at your peril.'

Gurm raised his sword in a mocking salute. 'Have at thee, then.'

At his signal, the plaguebearers lunged forwards in a stinking mass. Arkhan backed away, fending them off with spell, staff and blade. From above, he heard the screech of Razarak, and knew that his steed was equally beset. The creature would have to fend for itself. Daemons pressed close, and baleswords darted in at him from every direction.

As he countered a blow, he felt the familiar hum of ancient spells suddenly rise to a strident screech. He turned, eyes fixed on the distant shape of the Wailing Peaks. To his eyes, the crags glowed with an unnatural light. He felt a pulse of sympathy for Tamra ven-Drak. She had made her choice; only time would tell whether it had been the correct one.

Arkhan staggered suddenly. He heard the furious scream of Nagash roar through him, curdling the marrow in his bones. If the Undying King hadn't been paying attention before, he certainly was now. Gurm gave a shout and lunged through the press, seeking to take advantage of the mortarch's moment of distraction. His blade pierced Arkhan's robes and slipped between his ribs. Arkhan stumbled back, the enraged cries of Nagash still pounding in his skull.

'Where are your boasts now, liche? Your defiance is as hollow as your head.' Gurm twisted his blade, causing it to grate against bone. Arkhan shuddered. Beneath his feet, the ice did likewise, but more violently than before. Even Gurm noticed, and his gloating laughter trailed off as he realised that something had changed. He looked down, his single eye narrowing in confusion. 'What is making that infernal racket?'

'Nagash,' Arkhan said, simply.

Gurm looked sharply at him, eye widening. But whatever he'd been planning to say was lost in the roar of bursting ice. A tangle of drowned corpses heaved to the surface, arms flailing, their hands grabbing at the Herald of Nurgle and dozens of his fellows, pulling them down into the frozen waters with a single, convulsive jerk. Gurm screamed as he vanished beneath the water, his lanky frame pulped by a hundred fists, his flesh gnawed by a hundred mouths.

A second mass of bodies rose, dripping. It rose up, up, like some hideous column of rotting meat. The remains of wrecked ships were fused with the dead flesh of the drowned, and the eyes of every tangled corpse glowed with an unholy radiance. A hundred mouths moved as one.

'The law of Nagash has been broken, my servant. Is this your doing?'

'No, my lord,' Arkhan said. The quagmire of bodies continued to rise, until it towered over the ice and its shadow stretched to the Mandible itself. Slowly, it split, resolving itself into a vaguely humanoid shape. Nagash had done more than raise the dead – he had used them as raw materials to craft himself a new body. A body held together by blackest sorcery and the iron will of the Undying King.

'I will find the one who has broken my law. None may defy the will of Nagash. Even the stars themselves are slaves to my will.' A skull made of squirming corpses and shattered ships' hulls gazed down at the army of daemons spilling across the ice, as if noticing them for the first time. 'But first... an example must be made.'

Nagash spoke, and the world shook.

'Hear me, bringers of rot. Hearken, servants of a lesser god. Heed the words of He-Who-Is-Death. I am come round at last, and all thy souls are forfeit.' The great voice boomed out over the ice, drowning out the sounds of battle and the clatter of bones and wood. 'I am Nagash. Bow down and weep. Thy hour of doom has arrived at last.'

Wolgus could only stare upwards in horror as the typhoon of corpses and wreckage continued to swirl and swell. Threads of amethyst lightning shot through it, and the tumbling bodies clambered towards one another. Massive cracks shot through the ice, and water roared upwards, consuming unlucky warriors.

'What... what...?' Wolgus croaked.

'Behold, the Undying King in all his hideous strength,' Neferata hissed, dragging the sword free of her chest. Wolgus whirled about, but he was too slow. She lunged, driving his own blade into him. She forced him back, pinning him to a spar. Wolgus howled and slapped her aside. He clawed at the sword, trying to pull it free.

'No,' he gurgled. 'A trick – it is a trick. Gurm said...'

'Did you honestly think that you could kill death itself, little man?' Neferata wiped blood from her mouth as she rose slowly to her feet. 'Let alone in this realm?' She laughed and leaned forwards, pressing her palm against the pommel of the sword. She began to push against it. Wolgus writhed in pain. The blade sawed through his hands as he fought against her. 'You lost the moment you set foot in Shyish. The only garden which will grow here is one of bone.'

'G-Grandfather...' Wolgus moaned.

'Shhh. Rest now.' Neferata leaned her full weight against the blade, thrusting it all of the way through him. Wolgus stiffened. Black ichor spilled from his mouth and splashed steaming to the ice. Neferata stepped back, smiling slightly. 'You are done.'

She looked up. Nagash had crafted himself a body from the corpses of the drowned and the wreckage of the larger ships. The ice shuddered as he waded through it, striking out at the horde of daemons and rotbringers with a thousand hands. A purple radiance blazed within him, and his voice shook the air. Hundreds of shrieking spirits swarmed around him, bound by chains of crackling power, and these malignant souls swarmed eagerly over daemon and mortal alike as Nagash advanced towards the shore.

'I told you that he would aid us.'

'So you did,' Neferata said, turning. Arkhan's robes were blackened and torn, revealing his scarred bones. He sat slumped atop his dread abyssal, leaning wearily against his staff.

'The daemon?' she asked.

Arkhan chuckled harshly. 'Nagash has it in hand.' He looked at Wolgus, hanging slumped on the spar. 'The warlord?'

Neferata glanced lazily at the body and brushed her fingers against the rapidly healing wound in her chest.

'He fought like it.'

She turned as Nagadron landed nearby, splintering the ice beneath its paws. The dread abyssal padded towards her, grumbling in a satisfied manner. Ichor stained its talons and jaws. She swung herself into the saddle in a single, smooth motion.

'Well then. Shall we join our lord and master in advancing upon the enemy?'

Arkhan gestured. 'Lead on, O Queen of Blood.'

'My thanks, O Prince of Bones.'

The two dread abyssals loped forwards and, as one, launched themselves into the air, carrying their mortarchs into battle.

TWELVE

THE LAW OF NAGASH

I have pulled down the sun.
I have cracked the seals of the underworld.
I have dried the seas and burned the grasses.
I have humbled my enemies and cast the earth into the sky.
I have been walking to and fro in the deep places, and I gather my strength anew.
Listen.
Understand.
I will return.
I cannot die.
Nagash will rise.

– *The Epistle of Bone*

Nagash rose.

The battle ended soon thereafter. Caught between the dead on the shoreline and the towering abomination stalking inland from the sea, the warriors of the Order of the Fly made their final, fatal stand in the shallows, amongst the wreckage of the docks. As certain as their victory had seemed, now their defeat was a foregone conclusion.

Rotting claws reached from beneath the water to drag down the unwary as those who sought safety in the ruins of the docklands were pounced on by packs of ghouls. The few who fought their way to shore were met by the silent armies of the Broken Kings, arrayed for war with a discipline no living warrior could match. The deathrattle legions advanced slowly, grinding their enemies beneath them inexorably. Skeletal horsemen ran down fleeing rotbringers, and heavily armoured skeleton warriors slew any who tried to make a stand.

The Broken Kings themselves marched at the head of their armies beneath tattered banners, surrounded by desiccated warriors. Their ragged standards were so badly faded that it was hard to tell one king from another. All were clad in furs and iron war-plate, tarnished by the silent centuries spent buried in the depths of the mountains. Black-bladed axes and swords licked out, stealing the life from floundering rotbringers as the armies of the dead marched on.

All of this Tamra watched from her perch on the ruined deck of a frozen galley, Rikan standing protectively at her side. Some few survivors had gathered around her, seeking the protection of her magic and the swords of Adhema's remaining blood knights. Several galleys had escaped, carving their way across the cracking ice and into the mists of the Shivering Sea. She hoped that they made it to safety, if such a thing existed anymore.

Others had not been so lucky. At her command, spirits guided those who survived the overtaken galleys to her. Men, women and children trudged hurriedly across the splintering floes, weeping with relief and fear in equal measure. It was no pleasant thing to see one's god.

'He is as monstrous as I remember,' Rikan said, staring at the titanic horror. 'The dead are but tools to him, to be used and discarded.'

Nagash carved a path through the ice, wrecked vessels rising in his wake – the sea was giving up its dead as the Undying King made his way to land. His voice boomed out, shaking the frost from the rigging above her head, and cold fires swept through the remaining daemons, reducing them to motes of greasy ash. His vast hundredfold hands reached out, scattering the swarms of plague drones and crushing them. The quivering souls of the mortal rotbringers were torn from their savaged flesh and drawn irresistibly into the maelstrom of Nagash. She turned away, unable to stand their screams any longer.

Adhema smiled at her. 'You should be proud, poppet. This is your victory, as much as his.' The kastellan leaned close. 'How do you like being a deathlord, eh?'

'I am not,' Tamra said hollowly. 'I am my people's voivode. Nothing more.'

As she said it, she cursed the uncertainty in her voice. She hugged herself, trying to squeeze some warmth into her flesh. She had been cold since she'd freed the Broken Kings, since she'd heard Nagash's scream of rage. She risked a glance at the Great Necromancer. She flinched as the monstrous visage turned briefly in her direction. The glow within the twisted eye sockets grew brighter for a moment, and she stumbled back. Rikan reached out to steady her.

'Isa... look. Our father comes.'

She shoved the ghoul-king's claw away and looked over the rail. Six figures strode across the shattered ice towards their refuge, only vaguely distinct in their panoply. Whatever differences they'd had in life had been worn away by death and captivity. Now they walked as one, fought as one and spoke as one. The Broken Kings gave no notice to the shifting of the floes or the surging waters in their approach. Their voices pulsed in her ears.

'*Daughter of our daughter... You called and we have come.*'

Even now, they spoke as one, with a dissonant merging of voices. She swallowed a rush of bile. There was none of Sarpa's kindness in these revenants. They were harsh things, cold and sharp as blades. The fire of their souls was black, and it hurt her to see them so close.

'I... thank you, fathers of my father,' she said.

Six fleshless skulls turned upwards, studying her with witch-fire eyes.

'*You have freed us from an eternity in the dark, daughter. We stand in the open air because of you. And so, we shall serve you, until the end of all days.*'

'No, I do not want that,' she said. 'No, please...' She stretched out a hand, but it was too late. As one, the ancient kings of the Rictus drew their blades and presented them up to her, hilt first, as they knelt. 'No, I did not free you for this... I just wanted to save my people.'

'And so you have,' Neferata called out, as her dread abyssal dropped to the deck. Survivors scattered as the great beast let out a screech. Neferata slid from the saddle as Arkhan's mount slammed into the mast. The liche's dread abyssal clutched the frost-coated wood with its talons, as Arkhan dropped to the deck with surprising grace.

Neferata stalked towards Tamra, arms spread. 'Look – see! Your people live, sister. Some of them, at least. All because you had the courage to make the right choice.'

Tamra stepped back out of reach as Neferata drew close. The mortarch stopped, frowning.

'What is it? Are you not pleased?'

'*Neferata. Queen of Lies. Schemer*,' the Broken Kings whispered.

Rikan stepped between Tamra and the mortarch.

'You hear, witch? They know what you did to them. To us.' The ghoul-king shook his head. 'I may be mad, but I recognise that much.'

'And what did I do?' Neferata asked. She peered at Tamra. 'What am I guilty of, save aiding you in your time of need?' She stretched out her hand. 'Come, sister. Take my hand and all will be well. I will teach you to be a queen, to better rule your people.'

Tamra hesitated. She looked around, at the frightened faces which stared at her. There was fear in their eyes, but also... hope. She thought of the ice-galleys, speeding towards the Rime Isles. The clansfolk on those ships would need her, if they were to survive. Her people – what few of them remained – needed her. She lifted her hand.

Rikan caught her wrist. 'No. You do not need her, Isa. Please...'

'Silence,' Neferata snarled.

Tamra looked at the ghoul-king. She stroked his gore-stained cheek. 'My name is Tamra. Isa is long dead. But I am alive. And our people live.' The monstrous vampire closed his eyes and shuddered. He released her and stepped back.

Tamra looked at Neferata. 'You used me, didn't you?'

Neferata inclined her head. 'Of course. I use all of the tools fate supplies me. The foundations of the realm crumble, and someone must keep them suspended. But I promised you that I would raise you up, and so I have.' She twitched her fingers. 'Take my hand, sister.'

'Neferata... be silent.' Arkhan's voice rolled across the toll of a bell. Neferata glanced at her fellow mortarch. Tamra felt the galley shudder down to its frozen roots, and she turned.

Nagash was approaching.

'We will tell him it was the only way,' Neferata said, and there was something that might have been frustration in her voice. 'Surely he will realise...'

'He realises, but he does not care. Such is the way of Nagash.'

Arkhan looked at Tamra, and the fire in his sockets flickered. She wondered if that was pity in his eyes. The cold inside her was worse. It clung to her bones, and she felt her soul curdle within her. She felt the faint stirring of what might have been trepidation from the Broken Kings.

'Tamra ven-Drak.'

Tamra turned. Her folk were weeping, praying, whimpering. The face of the Undying King was not pleasant to look upon. She flinched back from the blazing, hellish gaze.

'Do you know me, woman?'

'I know you, oh Undying King. I am your servant, in life and death.' She sank to her knees and lifted her sword on her palms.

'Then why have you defied me, my servant?' A great hand gestured and the Broken Kings screamed as one. The wight kings were drawn into the air by chains of crackling amethyst light. They writhed in Nagash's grip, and the echoes of their agony made her gasp. She crumpled to her hands and knees. 'Why have you freed these treacherous souls from their prison?'

'M-my people… I had to save my people,' Tamra gasped.

'Your people? You have no people. All souls, living or dead, belong to me.'

The glowing chains flared. The wights screamed more loudly, and Tamra screamed with them. She fell to the deck in agony. She felt as if she were being eaten away, from the inside out.

'And so, mighty Nagash, she has preserved what is yours from those who would take it,' Arkhan said, as he strode to her side. 'She serves you, even in her defiance. Will you punish her for seeking to do your will?'

'Yes. None may defy death. Death is inevitable.'

'Better a death in your service, than death at the hands of your enemies,' Neferata cried. 'I will teach her, oh Great Necromancer. I shall make this land a bastion in your name. She shall be a weapon, wielded in your name. Spare her, I beg thee.'

'You... *beg*?'

Tamra raised her head and saw Neferata sink to one knee beside her. 'I beg. Spare her, forgive her, as you have forgiven me, and Mannfred in his turn. Forgive her sins, and she shall serve you as a deathlord. She is strong in the ways of death.'

Nagash was silent. For long moments, all Tamra could hear was the thudding of her heart and the scream of splitting ice. Then, the Undying King said, 'Yes. Look at me, Tamra ven-Drak. Look at me, Queen of the North.'

Tamra struggled to meet the infernal gaze. The heat of it beat at her mind and burned away the cold, filling her with fire instead. Her blood boiled in her veins, and her muscles cramped painfully. The thunder of his voice soured the marrow in her bones.

'You say you broke my law to save your people. But they are my people, to save or abandon as it pleases me.'

'I-I merely wished to keep them safe,' she whispered.

'And so they shall be. For forever and a day. Behold.'

As one, every living Rictus aboard the galley – man, woman and child alike – screamed, as did those still on the ice. An arc of amethyst lightning leapt from person to person, growing brighter with every addition. Their screams rose, spiralling up, higher and higher. The lightning streaked out and away, across the ice. Somehow, Tamra knew it was heading for the ice-galleys which had escaped. She wanted to cry out, to beg the Undying King to stop, but all that came out was a groan. She had broken the law of Nagash. And now, despite Neferata's promises, her people would pay for her crime. Nagash looked down at her. One great claw rose, wreathed in a blinding light. She cowered back, unable to bear it.

'I hold your people's lives in my hand. Do you see?'

'Please,' she cried. 'Punish me, not them. It was my crime… my weakness… not theirs!'

'Punish them? I do not punish them. I am saving them, as you wished. I give their lives to you, to protect for all your days, unto the sinking of these lands. Rejoice, child. Nagash has answered thy prayers.'

Nagash stretched his claw out over her. The light blazed brighter and brighter, until she could see and feel nothing save the unendurable heat of it. The screams of her people roared through her head, until she thought she would go mad from the sound. And then, just as suddenly as it began, it was done. The old familiar cold flooded through her, worse than ever. She felt hollowed out and scraped empty, save for the voices of the dead which echoed through her more strongly than ever before.

To her horror, she saw that the deck and the ice were littered with smoking skeletons. On their pale bones were etched deep runes. Not the familiar sigils of her clan, but older bindings, ancient and unbreakable.

'Rise, my people,' Nagash said. The bones of the Rictus rose with a whispery sigh. 'And rise, deathlord. Rise and greet your people. They await your command, as they did in life.'

Tamra rose, wishing to weep but unable to do so. Her mind felt as if it were full of ashes, and her heart hung frozen in her chest. The dead looked at her without recognition, without hope or fear or anything save dull obedience.

'Why...?' she whispered.

'You wanted them to be safe, and so they are.' Nagash stared down at her. 'You sought to usurp my dominion. But I am a merciful god. Now, you will protect them, and lead them into battle in my name. You will serve me in life and in death, as you proclaimed.'

Tamra looked up, unable to comprehend what had occurred. After everything they had endured, this was to be their reward? She stumbled, and sank to her hands and knees again, clutching her chest. She wanted to scream, to howl her disbelief to the skies, but no sound came. Grief, like joy, was now denied to her. Nagash had hollowed her out and filled her with his power. She could feel it burning away all that she had been. What would be left of her, when it was done?

'Yes. Now you understand. Such is the mercy of Nagash. Remember, and learn what it means... to... defy... death...' As he spoke, his conglomerate form began to come apart, body by body. The corpses thumped to the deck or smashed on the ice as the amethyst glow faded. Soon the echoes of his voice faded as well, leaving only a terrible silence in its wake.

'He returns to Stygxx, to the slumber of ages,' Arkhan said.

Tamra barely heard him. She knelt on the deck, hunched over, a scream stuck in her throat. She felt it would stay there forever. She flinched as a bony hand touched her shoulder. She could feel the power of him, more than ever before. It sparked against something inside her, as if she and Arkhan and even Neferata were part of the same great flame.

Arkhan looked down at her. 'Stand, deathlord. The chosen of Nagash do not kneel, save in the presence of Death himself.'

Tamra rose awkwardly. She stared blindly at the remains of her people, still trying to understand. 'Why?' She turned to Neferata. 'You told me they would be safe.'

'And so they are, sister. Safer now than ever before. I told you that I would make you a queen, and I have done so.' Neferata looked around. 'Perhaps not in the way I intended, but a small price to pay.'

'They are dead.'

'As am I. As are we all. The dead are strong. Why else would the Rictus have worshipped them? And now, thanks to you, they are one with them. Why do you not thank me, sister? Are you not pleased?'

Tamra stared at the Mortarch of Blood. 'Thank you?' she said. She raised her barrowblade. The remains of her people stiffened at her gesture, their empty eye sockets turning towards Neferata and her followers. Tamra felt the Broken Kings as they gathered about her, their ancient souls flickering with an old hate, a hate that she now truly understood. 'They were right about you. I thought you came to help us, but you sought to help only yourself. You are no longer welcome in these lands.'

Neferata laughed. Tamra made to raise her blade, but found it blocked by Arkhan's own. The Mortarch of Sacrament shook his head.

'No,' he said. He looked at Neferata. 'Leave. Now.'

'Who are you to tell me when I must leave?'

'I am the right hand of Nagash. Your game here is done. Go find a new one.'

Neferata smiled mockingly, and gave an elegant bow. 'If such is the command of the right hand of Nagash, I must obey.' She looked at Tamra. 'In time, sister, you will understand what I have done for you. You will see that it was for the best. And perhaps then I will return, and together we will lead your people to war.'

The mortarch turned away and went to her dread abyssal. She climbed into the saddle and the beast leapt into the air with a shriek. Neferata sped away. Adhema and her knights followed in the direction of their mistress, their steeds galloping across the broken ice. Tamra watched them go. She looked up at Arkhan, a question on her lips.

'We serve him in life and in death,' he said, before she could speak. 'Such has it always been, child. Your people look to you for reassurance.' He pointed, and she could see the shapes of galleys approaching, through the ice. There was nothing living aboard those ships, nothing left of all that she had fought so hard to preserve. Only bone and ashes.

'She used me,' she said. 'I knew... I thought...' She thrust her fists against her eyes, fighting to regain control. She longed to lash out, to use her newfound strength. She shuddered and dropped her hands. She looked at Arkhan. 'I thought he would forgive me.'

'He did,' Arkhan said. 'His mercy is a poison few can stomach. But you are strong. And your people still need you, Tamra ven-Drak. Perhaps now more than ever.'

She turned and the dead knelt as one. 'No,' she said, softly. 'No, do not kneel.'

At her words, the dead rose. She felt a flicker of something in them. An ember of what had once been. It was small, but it was there. And perhaps, with time, it might flourish again. She felt the murmur of the Broken Kings brush comfortingly across her mind. They would serve her, as they had promised. Together, they might even rebuild a simulacrum of what had been lost. She looked around.

Rikan met her eyes and inclined his brutish head, his gaze unreadable. 'You are High-Queen now, sister.'

'Yes,' she said, and knew that it was true.

Arkhan was right. Dead or alive, her people needed her. She would serve them, as she had in life. What was left of them, what she had, she would hold.

She was a daughter of the Drak, and could do no less.

NEFERATA

MORTARCH OF BLOOD

David Annandale

My purpose is domination.

Domination of enemies. Domination of realms. Domination of events, of time, of fate, of chance, of self. Domination prevails. All else falls away. There are no limits to the sacrifices I will make in its name.

The past, the present and the future roll into one another endlessly, locked and grinding like vast mill stones, turning and turning and turning. The powers of the realms rise and fall, rise and fall, yet the passions of the living and the dead are constant in their nature. Hatred, revenge, ambition, desire, fear... they do not change, and their constancy makes them useful to me. They are my arsenal. So is disaster. When the sweep of events overwhelms all other calculations, the only choice is disaster. I embrace it, because through it, as through everything else, runs the tide of blood. Ebbing and flowing, rushing and stilled, it is constant yet changing. And it has always been mine.

– A Call to Purpose

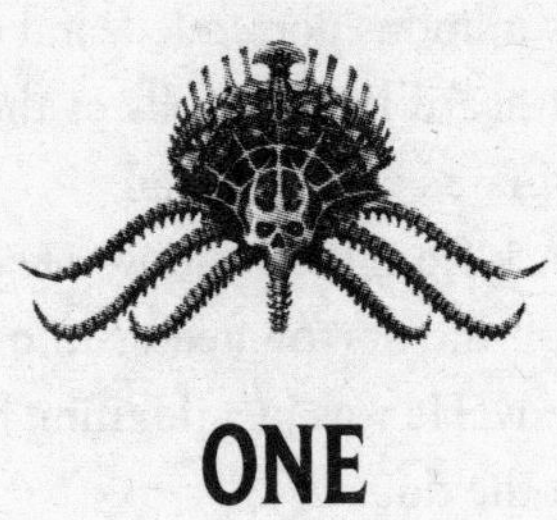

ONE

AGE OF MYTH
THE SEASON OF LOSS

Snow the colour of ash fell over Nulahmia. It was the grey of abandoned hopes and forgotten graves. It gathered upon rooftops like torn shrouds, their tatters sweeping onto windowsills. In the streets, mounds formed. Gazing down at them from his chambers in a corner turret of his family's palace, Mathas Helezan thought the mounds looked like huddled bodies. Cold death descended from the sky to blanket the city of tombs. Mathas felt trapped between the dooms of sky and land. He couldn't breathe. He yanked at the casement and opened the windows. The wind of sepulchres keened into the room, stinging his face with the grey flakes. The cold braced him, and he filled his lungs. He choked, swallowing fragments of pain. Bent double over the sill, gasping, he heard the hammering at the palace doors. The sound shocked him back to calm. The knock was heavy, a mailed fist slamming against bronze three times.

Three reverberating booms, the tolling of a bell reaching up through the night for him. At first he was surprised he could hear the knocking from the far side of the palace. Then he realised what the summons portended, and of course he heard it. Every Hellezan heard it. The walls of the palace trembled with the impact of fate coming to call.

Mathas stood back from the window. He crossed his chamber, passed through the narrow recess into his armoury, and began to make ready. He was just donning his helm when his father appeared at the doorway.

'It is tonight, then,' Mathas said.

Verrick Hellezan nodded. He was pale, and his eyes were stricken.

The Culling of the Firstborn was upon them.

'You aren't grieving, are you, father?' Mathas asked. 'We knew this moment would arrive. We have been preparing for it.' The Mortarch of Blood had cursed mortal houses of Nulahmia with the tradition centuries before.

'Yes, I know.' Verrick's voice trembled with fear and the anticipation of sorrow. 'I did not think it would be this night.'

'Would another night make a difference?'

'No,' Verrick admitted.

'She knows I am about to ascend to command of the house, father,' said Mathas. 'There is no hiding that from her.' Like all other firstborns in his position, he must go to the Palace of Seven Vultures. 'It is my time to be tested.'

'I had hoped we might have been able to discover the nature of the test before this moment.'

Mathas smiled. 'It is deadly. We know that much.' The Culling was real. Most firstborn never returned, except in coffins. Their mutilated remains were presented to their families, and the biers were carried in mocking silence by a cortege of skeletons.

'If you fall...' Verrick began.

'I won't. But if I do, you *will* go on.'

'Will we?'

Mathas could already see, in his father, the same despairing face he had encountered so often in the kin of the lost firstborns. 'The Hellezans can survive,' he said. 'The others have.' More or less. Weakened by the losses, some houses failed, decapitated by the death of the firstborn. But others continued to exist, diminished and humbled, taught the futility of resisting the blood queen, often even before the idea had been whispered in the halls. The grieving leaders of these houses bent their knees and bowed their heads before Neferata, entreating her that this son, or this daughter, should be a full and sufficient sacrifice.

'But you won't have to just *survive*,' Mathas said. 'I will return. I will return as *myself*,' he emphasised, as he saw the shadow of a greater horror pass across Verrick's eyes.

Some firstborn did not return in coffins. Shrouded by darkness, their flesh cold and pale, their eyes red with ancient, unquenchable thirst, the new vampire thralls of Neferata crossed their thresholds as destroyers.

'You weren't at the home of the Salveins,' Verrick said. 'You didn't see what Harvath did to them. He painted the walls with their blood. And the bodies...' When Verrick shook his head, it seemed to Mathas that he sent a tremor down his entire frame. 'They filled the corridors, and we couldn't count them. Such butchery. So many pieces.' He closed his eyes for a moment, squeezing them tight against the vision of the charnel halls. 'Harvath just stood there, the blood of his family dripping from his mouth. I don't know if he even saw us.'

'That won't be me, father. You know it won't.'

Verrick smiled sadly. No matter what Mathas said, it seemed, the old man refused to be comforted. 'I know,' he said. 'You might be more restrained.'

'Like Wrentis Nalvaux?' He had been merciless in his bloodletting, killing his family members who needed killing, turning those who would be of use, and subjugating everyone else. And so another house had become Neferata's, controlled by her will as surely as if her terrible presence resided in its chambers. 'No,' Mathas said. 'I will return, and we will all rejoice. This is not the moment of doom. This is our chance to strike.' He paused. 'We *want* this,' he said softly.

'I know,' Verrick said, without conviction.

Mathas clasped his father's shoulder. Verrick had devoted himself to the struggle, and the effort of the decades had told on him. His frame had withered. His bones seemed frail under Mathas' touch. His eyes were sunken in his sallow face.

'You've done well, father. You've brought us this far. It is time I took up the torch. This night, I will.' He had been in training for his entire life, waiting for this very night. He, his parents and their allies had not known when the summons would come, but they had known it was inevitable. Mathas was a first-born, and as mercurial as the queen of Nulahmia could be, she had never spared anyone marked to take part in this ritual.

Why would she? Mathas thought. *It is so useful for her.*

He left his quarters and made his way through the palace. Verrick walked at his side, seeming to age with every step. The wall sconces burned brightly in the halls, casting a defiant light over the great portraits of the Hellezan line. Gold inlay on the columns and gold leaf on the ceiling gleamed, rich with the pride of a family that had carved out a wealthy life in the kingdom of death. *Withstand and Prevail*: that was the Hellezan motto, and Mathas believed in it. He would prove its worth and his own tonight.

His armoured boot steps echoed down the halls, the only sound in the palace, though everyone was awake. Servants clustered in doorways to watch his passage. The household seemed to be holding its collective breath. His mother, his brother and his sisters were waiting for him at the main entrance. Teyosa of House Avaranthe, his wife, stood beside them holding their infant son, Kasten.

The doors were closed, but Mathas could sense the dark beings waiting on the other side. Two men-at-arms stood at attention, ready to pull the doors open when he gave the signal.

Mathas embraced his mother. Glanath's lips were pressed together tightly, her face taught with strain. The years had been hard on her too. It was his responsibility now to make sure his parents' sacrifice had not been in vain.

Nor would they be the only ones depending on him. There were other families whose fortunes would rise or fall because of this night. In truth, he believed that the fate of all Nulahmia rested on his shoulders. There was solemn pride, but no vanity, in that belief. If he succeeded this night, everything would change. If he failed, someone else would have to take his place, and someone surely would, because the struggle was too important. There was no alternative, other than the despair of complete surrender.

'I won't fail,' he said to Glanath.

'I know you won't,' she said. 'You march from our palace to a greater one, and to your destiny.' Her voice trembled only once. She spoke quietly, but with incantatory fervour.

Mathas turned to Teyosa. 'I will return to you,' he said. His hand hovered over the sleeping head of Kasten. 'I swear it.'

'You should not have to fight alone,' said Teyosa.

'Yet I must.'

'I could...' she began, but trailed off as he shook his head.

'If you tried to follow, they would kill you before you had taken ten paces from our gates. You are second-born. Your family has already paid its tithe of blood. And we need you here.'

Teyosa looked down at Kasten and nodded. 'You will pass by my family's house,' she said.

'Yes,' said Mathas. 'I will learn what I can as we do.'

In the last week, rumours had reached the Hellezan palace that a plague had come to House Avaranthe. Silence had fallen over the family, but there had been no way to learn the truth, no way to know if Neferata had discovered that they were part of the plot against her. If the worst had happened, there could be no open contact between the two houses, especially now that the attention of the dark queen had fallen on the Hellezans.

The days and nights of the Hellezan palace had been consumed with the dread anticipation of Mathas' summons. The Culling of the Firstborn came to every house. Since there were no exceptions, the summons was predictable. It was possible to prepare for it. Mathas had. The threat stiffened the resolve of the Hellezans and the families with whom they forged quiet, whispered alliances. They vowed to break the chains Neferata had thrown over Nulahmia. The city may have been her creation, but it was time it was freed from the grip of its creator. As plans were laid and the kernel of an organised resistance slowly, almost imperceptibly, came into being, the links between the families had become, on the surface, more distant. If the Avaranthes had been found out, and punished, the appearance of that distance was all the more vital.

Teyosa understood. Yet Mathas knew she feared for her family and grieved in the expectation of tragedy. Knowing one way or another might help. Mathas needed to know, too. Everyone in House Hellezan did.

'I'll find out,' he promised, determination growing. 'Good news or ill, I will come back, and I will hold you as I tell you.'

'I can ask no more,' said Teyosa.

Mathas nodded to the guards, and they opened the doors.

The wind shrieked into the entrance hall, blowing grey before it. The snow whirled about the Hellezans. Verrick winced and brushed the flakes from his shoulders as if trying to shed himself of a dark omen. Three Black Knights stood on the portico. Their heavy armour gleamed dully in the reflected lights of the hall's torches. The cold breath of the night whistled through their empty eye sockets, and the chill of the grave worked through the seams of Mathas' armour and clutched his face with a numbing grasp. The blast of the snow storm surrounded the Black Knights, but another, more frigid wind blew from the undead warriors themselves.

Mathas took in the eroded crests on the trio's armour and bowed. The skeletons were nobles from houses that had been powerful when their families were alive, and were even greater now they were dead.

The middle Black Knight cocked his head as if amused by Mathas' display of courtesy. *You aren't fooled*, Mathas thought. *You sense my loathing. Good. But I will walk into the dark with honour. Do not think you can take that from me.* He stared back into the knight's empty sockets. After a few moments, the skeleton turned and strode away, armour creaking, bones grinding together. The other two waited for Mathas to come between them. When he did, they fell into step on either side, an escort of doom.

At street level, the mounds of snow looked even more like bodies, huddled in agony against the building walls. Though the night was freezing, the shapes were melting, heated by the unnatural alchemy that governed their existence. Where the grey was piled high enough to take on the curves of agony, it began to bleed. The masses sank down, rotting, turning to blackened slush, then running in crimson streams down the cobblestones, washing against Mathas' boots.

The Black Knights took him down a wide boulevard that ran between towering mausoleums. The black walls were hundreds of feet high. Rank upon rank of huge, snarling gargoyle maws covered the facades. Behind every gaping mouth was a stone throat, leading into the structures and the tombs within. The mausoleums held tens of thousands of coffins. Few of their occupants slept soundly.

The grey snow fell past the gargoyles. It gathered on Mathas' shoulders. It settled onto the street, and was swept away by the streams of blood.

Everything in the night shouted to Mathas that only death could triumph in Nulahmia. He was going to prove the night wrong. They did not know it, but the Black Knights were giving him the opportunity to make that attempt. He would spill blood, and he would kill. But it was one death in particular he sought. One death, to bring the hope of life to the mortals of Nulahmia. Or, no – not a death, for he did not pretend he could kill what was already dead. Destruction, then. He lived to destroy one being.

He was going to destroy Neferata.

Mathas recognised the folly of the quest. He knew he was not the first mortal to make the attempt. What did his two decades of training mean compared to her countless millennia of existence? The hubris of his attempt was without measure. *But one of us will bring you down*, he thought. One of these times, the blade would strike home. He refused to believe that she was eternal. She, too, was guilty of pride. What was happening to him this night was proof of that. She was inviting destruction over her threshold. One day, the invitation would be accepted.

Your hour is coming, he thought.

They reached an intersection of many avenues. The land here was on a steep slope, and Mathas beheld a vista of the sweep of this quarter of Nulahmia. To his right, the city sloped downwards. To his left, it rose towards the great mass of Neferata's palace. The enormity of what he intended struck home. Ending the being who had commanded Nulahmia into existence was madness.

It is an honourable madness, he argued. *One worth dying for.*

The Black Knights and Mathas crossed the wide expanse of the intersection. There were no other mortals on the streets at this hour. They had fled the grey snow as they would a fall of death from the skies. The city was not silent, though. In the shadows below and in the greater darkness above, Nulahmia groaned and rang with endless creation. The hunger of Neferata's will was never satiated, and it urged the city into transformation. No structure or configuration of streets was eternal. There were monuments a thousand feet high and vaults as big as mountains, and they too would vanish, as if melting into air, at the command of the queen. Death and Neferata were the only constants. Death came for everything.

Mathas looked up at one of the soaring monuments before him. Engravings marked the deaths of a million souls in a distant battlefield. The towers rose from the corners of the intersection where, he recalled from his childhood, there had once been homes. *Every change is death*, he thought. In Nulahmia, creation's only purpose was, in the end, to be washed away by blood.

Movement at the top of one of the towers caught his eye. A ragged glow, the colour of sorrow, rushed down the face of it with a howl that seemed to drag claws across his soul. A banshee floated a short distance above Mathas, its wizened face gaping at him in mockery and grief.

'Proud Hellezan,' the banshee hissed with a voice of crumbling earth, 'joined to the proud Avaranthes. So much pride. Such nobility. How do they serve you now?'

Mathas did not answer. He stared straight ahead and kept walking.

'Tell me of your defiance!' the banshee taunted. 'Sing to *me* of hope!' The banshee kept pace with him. '*Hoooooooooope!*' it shrieked, and then it rushed ahead, up the hill, wailing. It stopped by high iron gates, flowing in and out of the bars. 'Hope,' it repeated. 'Hope. Come and tell *me* of hope, proud Hellezan.'

Mathas knew those gates. He tried to brace himself for what he would see when he drew near. But when he beheld the grand mansion beyond the gates, his eyes widened. He stumbled, shaken by sudden distress.

The rumours were true. Death had taken House Avaranthe. The light that came from the broken windows did not come from torches or lanterns. The glow was sickly green, the phosphorescence of wraiths that flowed, wailing, through gutted corridors. Skeletons swarmed over the façade, unmaking and changing. The roof was gone. A fell nimbus rose from the interior to meet the falling snow. It coiled around the walls, and seemed to work in conjunction with the skeletons. The corpses toiled to unmake the mansion and turn it into a new thing. Mathas could not make out the nature of the transformation, beyond the death of what had been. The new building was taller. Its gables reached out into the air, turning into clawed wings of stone, as if the structure would soon take flight.

The skeletons still wore shreds of clothing. It was falling in rotten tatters as the labours of construction continued. In the spectral light, Mathas could just make out enough of the designs that remained. The dead were the Avaranthes. The undead creatures they had become now slaved to destroy the home. Before long, no trace of the family would exist.

The banshee laughed with grief.

Mathas' legs were numb. He could not feel the ground under his feet. He and Teyosa had feared for her family, and though he was not surprised by what he saw, the shock was immense.

The Black Knight in the lead had paused and was looking back at Mathas, skull cocked. Mathas did not know if it was amused or curious. He suppressed a shudder as he felt the cold evaluation of the eyeless gaze. He wanted to pull his sword and charge. *For Hellezan! For Avaranthe! For life!* The words were huge in the back of his throat, demanding to be shouted. He choked them back. Such defiance would betray the families and all they were struggling to bring about.

Does she know? he wondered. *Did Neferata have the Avaranthes killed?* She might have, but then again, it might really have been the plague that felled them. Even if Neferata was behind the destruction, she could have commanded it for any of a hundred reasons, or for no reason at all. No, Mathas decided, the conspiracy had not been discovered. If it had been, doom would have come for all of the Hellezans, and not just for him.

And if he was wrong, that changed nothing. His path was set. If Neferata knew, and still permitted him to enter her palace armed, then her hubris was even greater than he had thought.

Mathas tore his eyes away from the mansion and started forwards again. The Black Knight watched him for a moment more before continuing onward.

Another hour passed before they reached the palace. They did not approach it along the main avenue. The door that waited for Mathas was on the opposite side from the grand entrance. The Black Knights took him through a maze of ever-narrower streets, weaving through an endless graveyard. Colossal, nitre-encrusted obelisks clustered like sentries, looming over the road. The passage was so tight, the Black Knights now walked single file. Mathas' shoulders brushed against the obelisks. Melting snow streaked his armour with gore. The road, slick with blood and slime, glowed faintly, giving just enough light for Mathas to see where he was going. He glanced behind once, and the way back was lost in impenetrable darkness.

The path narrowed still, winding and twisting. Mathas felt he had become a carrion worm, burrowing through a gigantic corpse. He lost all sense of direction; he had been unable to see the mass of the palace since entering the cemetery. A huge, squat monument reared up ahead, crouching over the path like an immense toad. The road entered a tunnel in its base.

The wind still blew inside the tunnel, whining in captivity. The crimson melt of the snow ran down the slope, and the low walls echoed with the footsteps of Mathas and the Black Knights. The tunnel ended in a wide antechamber, where the Black Knights brought Mathas to face a massive door. It was metal, but as dark and gleaming as obsidian. Its surface appeared featureless at first glance, but once he was closer, Mathas saw runes. They swam in the surface like oil on water. They shifted, flowed into one another and flickered on the edges of meaning. Mathas could not read them, but protean menace reached out from the door and wrapped tendrils around his soul.

The wind rose and fell. It hissed and rasped, and became the voice of the door.

'*Who would be pyre-bound?*' said the door.

For the first time, the lead Black Knight spoke. The cold that blew from his soul shaped itself into words, the syllables cut into sharp pieces by the rattling of teeth. 'Mathas Hellezan,' he said, turning Mathas' name into a foul incantation.

'*Mathas Hellezan*,' the door repeated.

'Firstborn of the house,' said the Black Knight.

'*Firstborn!*' the door exulted. '*Let him pass, and grasp his fate-thorn.*'

The door opened, swinging inwards into gloom with the sound of a mountain grinding apart. A faint glow wavered deep inside the stone tunnel. Mathas' eyes adjusted, and he realised a single torch hung on the wall, waiting for him.

Without looking back or glancing at his undead escort, he drew his sword and marched into the tunnel. The door closed behind him with the boom of hollow thunder.

Mathas raced down the tunnel, anxious that the caprice of the test might snatch the illumination away. The floor crunched under his boots. As he entered the circle of light thrown by the torch and snatched it from the wall, he saw that the floor was a pavement of bones. Skulls, femurs, pelvises and more, densely packed together into an uneven surface. There was no distinguishing between individual bodies. The floor was a compressed hecatomb, its brickwork stained the colour of old blood. Viscous fluid, too thick to be water, flowed down its length. The stench of corruption was foul. Mathas breathed through his mouth, and the smell scratched at the back of his throat.

The tunnel was about ten feet wide, and fifteen feet high at the centre of the rounded vault of the ceiling. It descended deeper into the foundations of the palace. Its slope was steep and its curve was sharp. Mathas could only see twenty feet ahead as he advanced down the spiral.

Echoes scrabbled upwards to meet him. Garbled and overlapping snarls. They grew louder, the voices becoming more distinct, and eager. They were unintelligible, as if the speakers had mouths full of bones. The noise of claws scraping against walls twisted Mathas' spine into a knot. The stench was almost overpowering.

He moved as fast as he dared, careful not to slip on the curves of skulls poking up like slick cobblestones from the floor. The gabbing, snarling voices were close now. He sensed the enemy around the next curve. Monstrous voices laughed. They could hear him, too.

There was no point in attempting stealth. Gathering himself, he raised his sword and charged. '*Withstand and prevail!*' he shouted.

There was an answering roar, and from around the bend came a trio of hulking monsters. Their flesh was pale as the underbelly of a dead fish, and was pierced by long, jagged bones, the trophies of former victims that stuck out of their limbs and torsos like spines. What had been mortal had become gargoyle, and they bared their blackened teeth in pleasure and drooling hunger.

The lead monster swung a misshapen bone-axe at Mathas before he was in range, missed and lunged clumsily, grasping for him with its filth-encrusted claws. Mathas dropped the torch, crouched, and drove his sword upwards with both hands, impaling the horror through the throat. 'I have not come here for you,' Mathas snarled as the monster staggered against him, its great weight almost bringing him down. 'I am here for the Queen, and you try my patience.' The monster choked on the blade. Dark, stinking blood gouted from its jaws, soaking his armour. One of its eyes burst from its skull. It dropped its axe and tried to grab him, but it was dying, and its claws slapped against his pauldrons, then fell to the side.

The other horrors gabbled at Mathas. Their words were nonsense, yet there was something in the rhythm of the yells that sounded like mottos, as if they were hurling the pride of their own noble houses back at Mathas.

'Your foul blood sullies a noble blade!' Mathas shouted back. 'But come. I will kill you just the same!'

The horrors clawed and beat at the body of the first. They were crowding forwards, and in the confined space of the tunnel, they could not reach past the body to sink their claws and blades into Mathas. Between their blows and the mass of the corpse, his knees almost buckled. He managed to step to the rear, sliding his blade out of the body. With a jerk, he leapt backwards. The dead horror fell. The monster on the right had jammed its claws into the corpse's flesh to pull it away, and the sudden shift pulled it forwards, off balance. Mathas slammed the point of his sword into the beast's eyes and punctured its brain. He threw himself to the side as the last of the horrors reached for him. It caught his helm with the flat of its axe blade. His head rang with the blow and his eyes blurred. He swung to his right, slicing open the ghoul's flank. It howled, dropped its axe and clutched at him with both hands.

The grip was powerful. His armour began to buckle under the pressure. The diseased claws sank into the seams. The beast gnawed at the front of his helm, breaking teeth on metal and suffocating him with the stench of its breath. It held Mathas' shoulders, its strength like a vice of iron. He managed to move his forearms up, stab the monster in the belly and saw upwards, slicing through muscle and viscera. The horror's snarls mixed pain and rage. It tore his visor off with its teeth, and the blood from its shredded gums and lips poured over his face and neck. Mathas gagged at the poisonous, rotting fluid. With desperate strength, he brought his sword up higher, and at last cut through too much for the monster to live. It stiffened, its snarl fading to a gurgle, and then fell, taking Mathas down with it.

Choking and coughing, Mathas broke free from the dead grip of the horror and squirmed out from under the hulk. He wiped his eyes clean of the thing's blood, and tried not to think about how he might have been tainted. He picked up the torch and moved forward again.

The spiral passageway ended after another few hundred yards, levelling out into a wider cavern littered with bones, scraps of flesh and piles of detritus. The stench made his eyes water. On the other side of the chamber was an iron door. It screeched as Mathas hauled it open, and the echoes of its scream were swallowed up by a choir of shrieks in the huge space beyond.

Mathas crossed the threshold and walked out onto a finger of fused bone which arched gently upwards, extending over an abyss. The light of the torch could not reach the walls or the ceiling. The bottom of the cavern was an unguessable distance below. Its deep night was broken by fitful streaks of light and the glow of apparitions. Phantoms glided over the pathway to circle Mathas, rising from the depths and dropping back into them. They keened in distress and hunger, in anger and eagerness, in grief and madness. Spectral hands, gnarled as talons, formed out of ghostly energy, reached for him as they flew past, but they did not come near enough to touch him. The bridge seemed to be forbidden to the wraiths, and they screamed in an intensity of pain and frustration as they passed.

From somewhere in the dark came the heavy beat of leathery wings. Mathas held the torch high and swung it from side to side, but the thing that made the sound remained out of sight.

Mathas kept to the centre of the bridge where the footing felt even more precarious than in the tunnel. There was nothing to keep him from falling off the sides if he stumbled too far – or if something hit him. The flapping of the wings passed overhead, closer now, as if the predator were closing in, making ready to attack.

Ahead, the bridge reached a platform. But Mathas' hopes that he had reached the far side were dashed when he saw it was a circular surface at the apex of the bridge's arc. The span continued on the other side. Shaped into a shallow bowl, the platform was ringed by stones twisted into gnarled forms, as if it were in the grip of a giant skeletal hand. The stones thrummed with sorcerous power. Wraiths clustered around, casting the bowl in the sickly green of their soul-light, but though the power of the stones seemed to draw them, it also held them at bay. The phantoms were spectators, Mathas thought, forced to bear witness to the struggle to come, but unable to affect its outcome.

The screams of hunger chilled Mathas. He was surrounded by the ghastly persistence of existence after death. To become such as these things was worse than oblivion. The nature of their captivity in this cavern was even worse. It was a display; a statement that his struggle for survival was nothing more than another's entertainment.

Your hopes are meaningless, it signalled. *You are but a plaything.*

Above him, the flapping of wings circled, waiting for him to reach the platform.

'Are you amused?' Mathas shouted at the unseen queen of Nulahmia. 'I come to bring an end to your delights! You are right to hide from me!' He ran forward. Let there be an end to games, he thought. Victory or death, let either come now.

Mathas crossed the ring of stones at a run. There was a sudden sharp flap from above, as of wings being tucked in for a dive. He changed direction abruptly, pounding around the curve of the bowl as the snarl from above became a roar. Unable to alter its trajectory quickly enough, the hunter smashed down into the centre of the platform, splintering the surface of bones.

The brute turned slowly, tracking him, its breath making like snarling bellows. It had the form of an immense bat. The talons on its wings were as long as his forearm; its massive torso furred and muscular – a body suited to battering through doors.

Varghulf, Mathas thought. The family chronicles made reference to such monsters in descriptions of past battles. Viscous saliva dripped from its fangs.

Mathas charged, aiming his sword at the varghulf's throat. It swept a wing at him, and in the moment before it struck, Mathas hurled the torch into the monster's face. His aim was true. The varghulf shrieked, its fur smouldering and its face blackened with the burn. Mathas threw himself to the right in the direction of the monster's retaliating blow, and though weakened, the impact knocked him off his feet and sent him sliding up the platform, smashing against one of the stones. His chest plate cracked. He felt broken movement in his ribs as he struggled to his feet.

The varghulf swiped at its eyes with one of its wings, and lashed out with the other with wide, sweeping blows as it stormed up the slope towards Mathas.

He ran to his left, away from the scything wing, then down along the monster's flank. Half-blind, the varghulf missed him. It paused at the ring of stones and sniffed for its prey, stopping just long enough for Mathas to plunge his sword into its spine.

The varghulf screamed and leapt. Blood streaming down its back, it flapped its wings and flew straight up from the stones. Mathas held tight to the hilt of the blade. He rose with the monster, his weight dragging open a longer wound. The varghulf climbed vertically, then looped, and Mathas fell.

He landed on his back. The impact knocked the air from him, and pain exploded down his spine. He could not move.

Above, the varghulf climbed higher yet, then dived for him, its jaws gaping in fury. For a terrible moment, the sight of those jaws and the blaze of the monster's uninjured eye held Mathas, extending his paralysis. Then, he thought of his family, and of his duty, and of the dream of freeing Nulahmia from the tyrant who arranged these battles for her amusement. Teyosa's face rose before his mind's eye. *You do not die here*, she said, her voice as strong in his heart as if she had really spoken.

With a surge of desperate determination, he rolled to the side and rose to his knees. The burning vision of the varghulf's face was still before his mind's eye. Its monstrousness was mesmerising, and though he had broken from its grip, it remained the vivid centre of his reality. It was the core of everything, and so when he rose, he stabbed at that centre with his sword. His instincts and reflexes knew where the face was even more than did his rational mind. He thrust, and the blade struck the eye of the varghulf. The speed and weight of the monster drove the blade deep into its skull. The varghulf's scream cut off. Its immense body shuddered, and then, with a crash, collapsed.

Mathas crawled out from underneath a wing. He staggered up the side of the bowl to the descending arc of the bridge. Wraiths shrieked at him, skeletal fingers of ectoplasmic energy reaching out in frustration. Mathas' stride steadied as he marched along the span, the adrenaline of victory coursing through his frame. It gave him the focus to work through his pain, and he moved faster. He raised his sword in challenge.

'I know you are watching!' he shouted. 'I know you can hear me. Your nemesis has come, Neferata. Your end is here!'

His words were lost in the wailing choir of phantoms. But to speak the words aloud was a form of power. He did not have to hide any longer. Here, in this monstrous place, his rage was natural. Who would not wish destruction upon Neferata after this? So he roared his truth, and raced for the far end of the bridge.

At the foot of the bridge was another wide platform. Five doorways led off it. Each of the doors was forged from the same obsidian-black metal as the one that had barred the entrance to this netherworld of slaughter. In them, too, runes appeared, disappeared, and shifted, threatening him with meaning, but withholding the blow. Understanding was an executioner's axe poised over his neck.

Mathas stepped onto the platform, and the door in front of him began to move. It stopped after a few inches, opening no more than a hand's breadth. Mathas regarded it with suspicion. The other doors were silent. This was the path of the labyrinth he was directed to choose, then. He did not like having his hand forced. *Then again*, he thought, *how much choice have we had at all?*

None.

Even so, he delayed the inevitable, rebelling to the extent that he approached the doors to the left and right of the open one. The wraiths shrieked with mocking laughter at the futility of his gesture. The other doors were sealed to the walls. They would not move for him. Surely, they waited for some other victim, concealing some other doom.

Mathas returned to the first door. He grabbed the edge and, with a harsh scrape of metal against stone, dragged it open. The space beyond was completely black. He held the torch forward, and the flame became a feeble red glow, illuminating nothing. Mathas hesitated, picturing himself stepping forward and plummeting to his death. But where would be the sport in that?

He crossed the threshold, and the darkness drew back like

a receding tide, settling into the recesses and corners of the chamber.

He was in a circular, domed hall. Sconces of skeletal human arms held torches on the curved wall. In the centre of the floor was a huge mound of bodies, the corpses of hundreds of warriors cast in iron, their death agonies and their shame of failure preserved for eternity. Limbs, armour, weapons and severed heads tangled together in a mass grave of humiliation. Would-be champions were now the tortured foundation for the throne that sat atop the mound. It was constructed of bone. It gleamed ivory-white in the torchlight, yet it was not as white, or as pure a thing of death, as the skin of the tyrant who now rose from it.

Neferata walked slowly down the mound of bodies, and Mathas felt his strength, his courage, his very ability to move, drain away. His sword arm hung limp at his side. The torch dropped from his fingers. He was paralysed. It was not mere beauty that transfixed him, but something far more terrible. It was majesty, a sublimity of command. Her presence struck him with awe, the true awe that was the supreme form of horror. Her being was too great for the hall, as if she were somehow larger than the space through which she moved.

She wore her tall, spreading crown of overlapping plates and gold-plated bones. It sat low on her brow, and beneath it her eyes glittered, eyes of devouring darkness that pulled Mathas' soul with the strength of a monstrous whirlpool. Her lips, dark as arterial blood, curled upwards slightly in cold amusement. Her armour, of the same black and gold plating as the crown, left her arms bare, as if they disdained such mundanities as protection. Her only weapon was a dagger, and it was sheathed.

'Well met, Mathas Hellezan,' she said. Her voice was low

and compelling, like a torrent dragging him to the heart of a glacier. 'But where is my promised nemesis?'

The taunt broke Mathas' paralysis. With a cry of hatred, he ran forward, sword raised. He reached the foot of the mound at the same moment Neferata did. She still had not drawn her dagger. He swung his blade at her neck.

Neferata's strike was a blur, too fast for Mathas to see, but in that fraction of a second, there was time for understanding. Her arms were unclad not from pride, but so that their speed was without fetters. The blow knocked the sword from his hand and sent it skittering across the floor. Neferata yanked his helm from his head and grabbed him by the throat. Black claws sank into his flesh. Mathas could not believe those were fingers that held him. Surely he was in the grip of an unholy device of ice and iron.

Neferata tilted his head to one side. She looked at him with impassive contempt. 'I'll ask you again. Where is my nemesis?'

Mathas tried to find defiance. He tried to curse. All he could do was choke.

'Not here?' said Neferata. 'That's what I thought.' Her lips parted, revealing fangs sharp as a serpent's. She pulled Mathas close and bent her head to his exposed neck.

Mathas' limbs twitched as the fangs slid into his flesh. His soul cried out though his voice was mute. He reached one last time for duty, family and honour. He saw Teyosa again, and his promise echoed back at him, cruel and mocking.

I will return to you.

Darkness closed over him.

Stability is a lie. It is the limning of a battlefield; the chance to prepare for war. Its risk is that it conceals the struggles already taking place. I am engaged in those struggles whether I am aware of them or not, and if I do not know it, then I will deserve my defeat. I must not be blinded by stability and its illusions of peace. I must never forget that peace has no reality, though its mirage can blind the gods.

– *Exhortations*

TWO

AGE OF MYTH
THE SEASON OF LOSS

The revels had returned to the Palace of Seven Vultures. In the centre of the great hall, Neferata presided over the festival from a vast, raised dais. She walked slowly around its periphery, circling her drakstone divan, watching her court unleash its desires. Her gaze let no detail pass ignored. In any corner, any shadow, or under any light, she might find that which her subjects tried to conceal.

High above her, wraith-light circled the great chandelier with urgent hunger, eager for her to find the guilty. The candles of human tallow blazed as if the souls of the executed themselves had caught fire, foreshadowing penalties to come. The volcanic glass and fossilised bone of the chandelier gleamed with a liquid brightness, a pure essence of corruption conjured from ancient, petrified death. Below, along the walls, flames rose high from the gilded bone braziers. Their burning light mixed with the colder, refracted light of red and green and blue from the jewels embedded in the crystal skull lanterns. The eye sockets were dark, yet they seemed watchful, joining their scrutiny to the queen's.

The darkness of the hall cavorted with the light. Beauty and horror were one. The shadows danced, their movements both angular and sensuous, a pantomime of the pleasure, the grace, the cruelty and the bloodshed that filled the hall. The vampire nobility of Nulahmia gorged itself. The feast of blood was a harvest of mortals, highborn and low, chosen for their youth, their beauty, their strength, their artistry, their wisdom. Some vampires delighted in the destruction of something precious. Others preferred the vintage of blood taken at its prime, when its possessor bloomed in the fullness of vigour. Gore and torn flesh spread across the marble floor of the hall, but thralls gathered up the remains and swept the blood into draining channels with such dexterity that the revellers were never conscious of their presence.

For all the mortals doomed this night, there were as many who would not be bled, and they knew it. Neferata read the dark joy in their faces. They had purchased their safety with the sacrifice of their kin, and had been rewarded with gold, jewels and heightened prestige in the court. They danced too, and if they regretted the price in flesh they had paid, if they grieved the loss of children, siblings, parents and spouses, they showed no sign. And so the grand ball of slaughter moved around the pillars, crossing and re-crossing the expanse of the hall with a flow that was frenzied, precise and elegant. The swirling movement of predators and prey had so much energy, it appeared to govern the melodies that came from the orchestra in the gallery above.

The musicians were mortal. On some occasions, Neferata commanded the presence of vampire players, whose centuries of experience had honed their skill to a perfection no mortal could reach. But that was a cold perfection. On nights such as this, the terror of the mortal players lent their music a delicious and delirious passion. They played as if their lives depended on their performance, as if this was their final hour. For some of them, it would be.

Neferata studied her subjects and analysed them, searching for treachery. At her side, Lady Raia walked attentively. Neferata's chief spy murmured quietly to the queen when her opinion was sought, and was otherwise silent, a useful shadow.

Neferata did not partake in the feast. She had satisfied her hunger earlier, when she had drained Mathas Hellezan. She still wore her armour, choosing to be a figure of dark command, the forbidding point at the centre of the maelstrom of riot. Her gaze returned again to Mathas, watching the newest vampire in the court fall upon prey for the first time, and weighed possibilities.

As the currents of the dance brought undead and mortals past the dais, they bowed to Neferata. When the music swelled, the multitude offered a choir of thanks and praise to her. The vampires were joyous in their savagery. The gift of blood she had given them was bountiful. And the spared mortals were giddy with survival and newfound riches. They had every reason to celebrate her reign.

Neferata did not trust their worship. Nulahmia had been safe from outside threats for some time. That safety bred complacency, which created fertile ground for rebellion.

A handmaiden approached the dais, lowering her head and clasping her hands together in respect first to Neferata, then to Raia. Neferata gave her a slight nod, and the vampire climbed the stairs gracefully.

'You have news, Mereneth,' said Neferata.

'I do, my queen. Should Lady Raia and I retire so as not to disturb you?'

'No. Tell me what you have learned.'

'It is not as much as either of us would like.' Mereneth spoke softly, too quietly to be overheard. Her words were almost an admission of failure. Neferata had executed underlings for less. But Mereneth had repeatedly proven her skill as a spy. She performed her visible role as handmaiden as expertly as she extracted secrets from Neferata's enemies. She was too useful to be discarded lightly. If she did not have all the information Neferata expected, then that lack would itself be significant.

'Go on,' the Mortarch said.

'What we suspected appears to be true. The Avaranthes were not alone in plotting against you. But the conspirators have concealed themselves well. The Avaranthes must have been far from the centre of the plot. They did not even know who their allies were.'

'You are certain?'

'Your necromancers have made sure. We continue to pursue the rumours, my queen, but for now we are chasing shadows.'

'Yet the rumours are plentiful.'

'They are, and they are proving to be of some use,' said Raia. 'They are giving us some sense of the extent of the discontent.'

'Which is?'

'Considerable.' It was brave of Mereneth to be so blunt. It was also what Neferata demanded of her. 'The stirrings of rebellion seem to be most widespread among mortals.'

Neferata had expected that. With no outside threat, the mortals would feel the predatory demands of the vampires more keenly, and with greater resentment. 'Vampires are also more adept at concealment,' she pointed out. Again, the absence of a threat was the problem. That was one less goad to find unity under her reign. She had rivals out there, even if she did not know who the dangerous ones were, yet. Their ambitions would be freer. Some would be toying with the idea of replacing her on the throne of Nulahmia. A select few would be moving towards making the idea a reality.

Nulahmia is mine. I created it. None shall rule it but me. Ever.

Raia said, 'I am troubled, my queen, by how successful the mortals have been at concealing their actions. The rumours are legion, but vague. We are finding very little that we can act upon.'

'That success implies considerable organisation,' said Neferata.

'So I believe, too,' said Mereneth. 'They are determined.' The spy turned her head to look at Mathas. 'The link of marriage between House Avaranthe and House Hellezan is suggestive.'

'We will pay greater attention to the Hellezans.'

Raia said, 'I am relieved that their firstborn is now your thrall.'

'He will be useful,' said Neferata.

Mathas took another offering, plunging his claws into the neck of a daughter of House Bantayre. Neferata noted how far he had progressed during the course of the revel. His initial kills had been frenzied, the work of a mad butcher. He had ripped the prey to pieces, shredding throats, ripping arms from bodies, bathing his face in huge jets of gore. So much flesh destroyed, so much blood wasted. Now he had calmed. He was no longer a wild animal. He attacked with precision, more like the warrior he had been. He had moved past mindless destroyer to discerning hunter. There was much promise in him. He would indeed be useful.

Especially once she sent the monster back to his family.

Neferata left the great hall before the end of the revels. The orgy of excess would continue until dawn, and she had accomplished her goals. She had been seen, reminding all present of who had brought the festival into being. More importantly, she had seen, noting well everything there was to observe. Now she retired to the most private of all her chambers.

The circular hall occupied the entire height of a narrow turret that rose from the centre of the Palace of Seven Vultures. It adjoined the great library, but its access was hidden, veiled by Neferata's spells and wards designed by necromancers she had killed as soon as their work was completed, so that she alone would know the passes needed to arm and disarm them. Even the tower, the Claw of Memory, for all that it was clearly visible from the exterior, escaped notice. The observer's gaze slid over it, all attention diverted to adjoining features of the palace.

Against the interior wall, a staircase of iron-clad bones spiralled up all the way to the roof. It climbed past shelves holding thousands of tomes bound in mortal flesh. The vertiginous chamber looked like another wing of the library. In a sense, it was a library, but one that held the works of a single author, who wrote for the eyes of a single reader. Here, Neferata wrote for the benefit of her future self, and consulted the wisdom of her past. The Claw held aeons of memories, and their analysis. In these books, she recorded all the means to power, to its preservation, and also the records of its losses, of the errors she had made, and of the inevitable blows of chance and destiny.

In the centre of the ground floor was a lectern. Its pedestal was a mummified body, strengthened by sorcery. Its jaws stretched wide by dried tendons into an expression of endless pain. The pain was no illusion, for the damned thing's soul was trapped in the withered, leathered flesh, cursed to support the drakstone slab of the lectern's top, and to feel the weight of every moment of eternal service.

The lectern held one of the bound volumes, open to a blank page, waiting. Neferata took up a quill, dipped it into a pot that was perpetually replenished in a fluid that mixed ink, blood and ectoplasmic ichor. She began to write, addressing a warning to herself for now and in the days and millennia to come.

A storm is coming. A storm is always coming, even for the gods. Where there is stability, there is ground awaiting disaster. Embrace the storm. If necessary, summon it.

– On the Crucible of Disaster

THREE

AGE OF SIGMAR
THE SEASON OF CREMATORY

The thin vampire sat on the throne atop the mound of iron-cast corpses. Torchlight danced over his armour of midnight-blue. He cast his eye around the circular chamber. It had been abandoned by its former mistress who no longer used it to receive and devour the firstborn.

It is mine, now, Venzor thought. *I decide its purpose.* He smiled, and his flesh pulled tightly over his narrow skull. Bit by bit, he was establishing his claim on the Palace of Seven Vultures.

The door to the chamber opened. The vampire who entered was injured, but she walked without hesitation. Her armour bore the marks of huge claws, and her drawn sword was slick with blood. She stopped before the great mound and looked up.

Venzor rose from the throne, his membranous wings folded beneath his arms. He walked halfway down the hill, stopped and bowed.

'I am Venzor,' he said, 'sworn to Arkhan the Black. I am his regent in Nulahmia, and I salute you, Dessina Avaranthe.'

The warrior's eyes widened.

'Yes,' Venzor said, enjoying himself, 'I know your hidden name. I am aware your splinter of that house has survived in the cracks and shadows until now. I have paid attention to the folklore of Nulahmia. I have heard the stories of the Avaranthes still fighting against Neferata, century after century.'

Dessina did not sheathe her blade, but she did not attack. She nodded, waiting for Venzor to speak again.

'I am not the one you expected to find,' he said.

'Nothing in these halls is what I expected.' She glanced back towards the open door. 'I did not expect to do battle with Blood Knights.'

'But perhaps you are not as surprised as you might be?' Venzor asked.

'Perhaps not,' she admitted. 'Who were they?'

'Warriors loyal to Neferata, seeking to undermine what we are doing here. We do not prevent their infiltration of this region of the palace. We find them useful.'

'And what is it that you are doing here?'

'Recruiting,' Venzor said with a thin smile. 'Our lord Nagash has punished Neferata for her overreach during the recent siege. It was not her place to choose to forge an alliance with Sigmar's immortals. For her presumption, she is punished.'

'She still reigns over Nulahmia,' Dessina spat, her voice filled with undisguised bitterness.

'She does, but only after a fashion,' Venzor reminded her. 'Her authority is diminished. After all, here I stand, deep in her beloved palace. By right of my master, granted to him by Nagash, I have unlimited access to the palace. Our forces do more than govern the walls and the northern sector of Nulahmia. We watch her actions in the heart of her domain. We watch, we see and we act.'

'Yet still she reigns,' Dessina insisted.

Venzor conceded her point with a shrug. 'For the moment. And so we recruit. We gather our strength. We prepare.'

'You think to destroy her?'

'Isn't that what you thought when you found your way into these caverns? Did you really think to challenge her single-handedly?'

Dessina didn't answer at first. At length she said, 'I had to try something. I am a firstborn, and I knew that would open this entry point to the palace for me.'

Venzor's fanged, misshapen smile became broad. 'And you have done something. You are here. Join your strength to ours, firstborn of the broken House of Avaranthe and last of that line. You fought well for Nulahmia against the forces of Lord Lascilion, and you fought for a ruler who did not deserve your prowess. Fight with all your passion now. Be the leader you are destined to be. Avenge your house at last.'

'You swear that Neferata will fall?'

'Her final defeat is my great purpose,' said Venzor. 'And you. Are you true to your fallen house?'

'I am.' She pulled a chain out from her gorget. A large medal hung from it. Venzor noted the Avaranthe coat of arms: twin dragons coiling their tails around a spear of gold. Dessina let the medal hang on her chestplate.

Venzor nodded with approval. Carrying that medal, even concealed, was a supremely dangerous act of loyalty to her slaughtered ancestors. 'Wear the honour of your house with pride,' Venzor said, and walked the rest of the way down the mound of the dead.

Dessina took a step forwards, bent a knee and presented Venzor with the hilt of her blade. 'My sword is for you, and for Arkhan.' She bared her fangs. 'Command me, so that I might drink the blood of Neferata.'

* * *

She had not lost the city. It had been stolen from her.

I will reclaim it.

The Queen of Shadows moved along the northern ramparts of the palace. Hate and determination swelled in her heart as she looked down the slope of Throne Mount upon the blemished vistas of Nulahmia. The blasting heat of the season of Crematory gnawed the bones of the towers. The wind was the breath of a forge, gritty with ash and blown dust. It was as nothing before the fire of Neferata's purpose.

This will be mine again, she thought. *All of it. All of you will be mine again.*

The city still bore the scars of the invasion by the Slaaneshi lord Lascilion. Mausoleums, towers, bridges and grand boulevards had been destroyed in the fighting. One wound, at least, was healing to a certain extent. Nagash's return had killed almost every living soul in the city, but mortals had since made their way back to Nulahmia. Even so, the metropolis of the living and the dead that had risen in answer to her will and her desire was marred. The aesthetic perfection of death that she had sought was cracked. The worst distortion was not the physical damage and a population that was still far from what it had been. The worst was the occupation.

Knowing how best to wound her, Nagash had decreed her punishment should be the loss of power, and he had commanded that the northern sector of Nulahmia be under Arkhan's rule. Forces loyal to him, under the command of Venzor, were cantoned in barracks below the wall. Neferata was nominally sovereign over the rest of the city, but realities of shared rule meant that Venzor's influence spread across Nulahmia. Mortal and undead powers were thinking through their allegiances. Neferata knew full well that there were those, even far outside the region controlled by Venzor, who saw advantages in allying themselves with Arkhan. As long as the other Mortarch had even a semblance of control in Nulahmia, Neferata could not be sure of her authority at any level. Nagash had undermined her from the foundations up. The city would not be hers until all of it bowed the knee to her again.

So she became a shadow, and made the Palace of Seven Vultures a tomb. There were no revels, no grand displays of power, artistry and blood. In time, when the Palace was truly hers again, she would remake it, too. For now, silence filled the halls. Venzor and his acolytes walked through the palace freely, but they encountered only the grey death of luxury. Her servants performed their duties, and members of her court came and went, but she refused to give Venzor the victory of seeing her daily humiliation. She passed from chamber to chamber like a breath of cold wind, seen only when she wished to be seen. She came upon courtiers when they did not expect her, emerging from darkness like a promise of vengeance. If Venzor wished to speak with her, then he must seek her, and if an encounter was absolutely necessary, it took place on her terms, where and when she chose. She was an absence, but a felt one. She was the movement in the corner of the eye, the footstep at the back. She was a whisper heard over all of Nulahmia. Every soul in the city, living or undead, tensed in the anticipation of her resurgence.

She had lost power, but she would reclaim it.

She walked the ramparts in silence, blending with the night, unseen by any of her sentries. She knew the rhythms of their patrols better than they themselves did. When she had had her fill of looking at what had been stolen from her, she withdrew into the interior of the palace.

Venzor went wherever he chose, but there was one door he had never seen, one chamber he had never entered. The Claw of Memory remained inviolate. When Nagash had returned from his apparent death, and she had been humbled on the point of turning the battle of Nulahmia into a great victory, Neferata had understood that punishment was coming to her, and that much would be stripped away. She had thrown all of her efforts into preserving her sanctum. It held the keys to her restoration. She would sooner burn it than have Venzor paw through its tomes, even though it was unlikely he would be able to interpret the ancient language of her writings. But the enchantments guarding its doorway had remained strong, and she had reinforced the wards since. Venzor's pleasure in entering every other chamber of the palace was such that he remained oblivious to his blind spot around the single tower.

She left the outer wall of the palace, and made her way to the Claw, and to the parapet at the top of the spire. Only the elect of her servants could reach this peak, and even they could not do so from inside. There she could speak with her spies with no possibility of being seen or overheard. On this night, Lady Mereneth waited on her, standing against the battlements, facing outwards, away from the centre of the roof. The vampire noble bowed low when Neferata came up behind her.

'Is there confirmation?' Neferata asked.

'Yes, my queen. Our scouts have observed the enemy force directly. It approaches from the north-west.'

'It is a large one?'

'Massive. Our initial judgement is that it is comparable to the army led by Lascilion, and its allegiance is to the Blood God.'

'It is heading this way?'

'We believe so, though it is still at such a distance that some doubt remains. There are also many obstacles between it and our walls.'

Neferata waved the matter away. 'They are no longer obstacles that will stop such an army. Not now.' Lascilion had pierced the veil concealing Nulahmia from the hordes of Chaos. Once found, the city could not be hidden again. Nor did Neferata wish it to be. 'Does Venzor know of its existence?'

'I don't think so. Not yet.'

'Very well.' Neferata was pleased. Mereneth had justified her elevation yet again. 'Tell me its location.'

Mereneth did, and then, dismissed, she dropped over the side of the battlements and scuttled, a shadowy spider, down the outer wall of the tower. Neferata looked up in the night sky and whispered, 'Come to me.'

Her words reverberated through the night itself. They were soft, a hiss of command intended for one being only, and they made distance meaningless. Moments later, a concentrated glow of aethereal energy descended on the tower. Answering the call of his rider, Nagadron the Adevore landed on the parapet, claws sinking deep into stone.

The dread abyssal whipped the length of his skeletal tail back and forth, eager to obey. Neferata had exiled her mount from the palace at the beginning of the occupation. Since then, Nagadron had flown over Nulahmia in wide circles, hidden in the ash-clouds that shrouded the land, waiting to be called upon. He was a thing of bone and claws. His huge rib cage was a prison for countless phantom skulls, souls all screaming for release, their agony finding expression in the sick, pulsating green of their ghost light. Nagadron was their eternal sentence, and the beast drew strength and pleasure from their pain.

Nagadron lowered his huge skull, and Neferata mounted his back. She touched his neck bones, and he leapt into the sky. The wind blew hard and cold against Neferata's face as they flew north-west, but it was not as hard nor as cold as she. Neferata stared towards the horizon, waiting for her first glimpse of the Khornate army, waiting for the first hint of the disaster she sought.

She did spare one glance for Nulahmia before it dropped behind. She looked at the expanse of the city that had been stolen from her. *This will be mine*, she thought again. No sacrifice would be too great in the name of power. *Disaster is the crucible of opportunity, and you will be mine once more, if I have to burn you to the ground.*

If I believe myself to be all-seeing, then I am lost. My sight has shadows. In them, enemies find shelter. To forget this truth is to offer my back to their blades.

– *Treatise on Blindness*

FOUR

AGE OF MYTH
THE SEASON OF LOSS

Mathas left the Palace of Seven Vultures at twilight. Gorged senseless on blood, he had slept after the revels. He had no coherent memories of what had happened since. He could not remember retiring to a chamber, yet he had awakened in a golden sarcophagus lined with silk. The chamber was illuminated by a chandelier of human arms. Their hands held candles, and their severed ends dripped a soft rain of blood into a bronze basin set into the centre of the floor. When Mathas rose, the arms moved with him, stretching to shine their light where he went. A wardrobe of the same golden design as the sarcophagus held fine clothes for him, their material rich beyond the means of any mortal in Nulahmia. He found boots and gloves made of the finest leather. His senses were heightened, and the touch of the leather was a sensual delight. He inhaled its scent, and learned that it was worked from the flesh of infants. Next to the wardrobe were his armour and his sword. They had been repaired, cleaned and polished. They gleamed in the light of the chandelier.

They were hungry, Mathas thought. Their hunger reflected his.

He dressed, donned his armour and exited the chamber. Servants bowed their heads as they passed him in the corridor. There were no guards outside the door. Mathas turned left, and surprised himself by finding his way to the grand entrance of the palace. As a mortal, he had attended court functions, performing the expected, worshipful homage to the queen, but he had never ventured beyond the great hall. Now he walked through the palace with the same assurance he had in his family's home.

Home. The thought rose, insistent, burning with the force of a command, when he passed beyond the palace gates. He did not just wish to go there. He *must* go there. There was no choice.

Mathas descended the Throne Mount along the Pathway of Punishment. He walked down the centre of the wide, switch-backing road. The mortals climbing up to worship at the gates of the palace gave him a wide, anxious berth. The bloody, iron architecture of torture lined the avenue. Victims cried out in pillories, atop elevated breaking wheels, and shuddered their last on impalement poles. Lines of pikes were topped with heads, freshly decapitated or rotten with flies. Before this day, Mathas had stared at the torture with horror and fear. Now the scent of blood made him heady. It didn't matter how much he had fed the night before. The thirst was always there, always ready. If the duty to return to the Hellezan palace was not so ferocious, he saw how easily he might pause to drink from one of the suffering mortals.

Or perhaps he would have chosen a richer, stronger vintage. He could sense the blood pulsing through the veins of every mortal he passed. He was a predator moving through a river of prey, his for the taking. The kills would take no effort. He had learned that last night. His strength was prodigious. His hands could puncture bodies, opening them wide and spilling their treasures for his delectation. He was walking murder. He knew it, and the mortals did. They glanced at him in terror, and he could see their desperate hope that they would pass beneath his notice, that they would escape his desire, because there was nothing they could do to defend themselves.

But first, *home*. Nothing else was as important as *home*. It called to him, thundering in his head like a heartbeat, *home, home, home*, and he marched to the rhythm of the summons.

Below the Throne Mount, he moved quickly through the streets. His stride was effortless, and he passed over the cobblestones as if he were flying. The temptation of blood was everywhere, but he found the mastery of his instincts becoming easier. And the closer he came to the Hellezan palace, the more urgent the drive to reach *home* became.

Within those walls was the blood that was truly *his*.

He raised a gauntleted fist when he reached the palace doors, and he hammered on them with the same force that had called him out what must have been an aeon ago. The bronze trembled, as if it too feared the return of its house's master.

Three streets away, overlooking the grand sweep of the Queensroad, a clock tower tolled the fall of night. It was a tall shadow, and twisted, a giant of tortured architecture, lit from within by a spectral glow. To look upon one of its faces was to see time as the inexorable approach of death. Now the hollow call of its bell sounded at the same moment as the doors of the Hellezan palace opened. Mathas could not but perceive an omen in that coincidence.

His parents and Teyosa were there, flanked by guards. The faces that met Mathas were almost as pale as his. He was white with death, and they with fear.

'We prayed for your return,' Verrick whispered.

'Your wish has been granted,' said Mathas.

Verrick blinked at his words, and turned even more pale.

In his father's stricken face, Mathas saw the truth of what he had become. He was the shape of the family's doom. Teyosa, Verrick and Glanath stood straight and proud despite their terror, and the guards did not flinch, though he could cut them down in an eye blink.

The people I love most are waiting for me to kill them, Mathas thought.

The thirst curled in his chest. He heard the hammering of pulses, smelled the blood that surely was eager to leap from veins into his mouth.

Mathas stepped across the threshold, into his moment of truth.

He looked at Teyosa, and reached out for her. 'Do not fear me,' he said.

She rushed into his arms, and they embraced.

'She did not take you from me,' Teyosa murmured.

Mathas groaned a sob of gratitude.

'And she has not made me kill all that I love,' he said. 'I did not destroy her, but it is she who has failed.'

'How is this possible?' Verrick asked when Mathas and Teyosa at last broke their embrace. The guards had withdrawn to give them privacy. 'You are…' Verrick did not finish. He winced, overcome by grief and relief at the same time.

'I am undead, father. We must say the truth, face it and use it. I am a vampire. But I am not her thrall.'

'But how?' Verrick insisted.

If he had been asked while he was still making his way through the streets, Mathas would not have been able to answer. He had not even known, then, if he was free. The thirst and the need to return were so strong, they had seemed to be the same impulse. He was thankful they were not. He was able to think more clearly now, and he understood at least in part how he had triumphed. 'Family,' he said. 'It is our ties that have made me strong.'

He remembered the darkness taking him as Neferata drank his blood. 'I could not fight her,' he said. 'She took me, and I fell into night. She stole everything that defines me…' He paused, the memory of dissolution sending a shudder through his frame. Then another memory came, the memory of salvation, and his strength returned. He looked at Teyosa. 'But she could not take you from me. At the last, I saw your face. I felt your presence, and your love – *our* love. It was the last thing that was mine, and I held it. You were the jewel whose light defeated the abyss.' He smiled. 'You are my truth. You are my duty and my defiance.'

The truth of love had sustained him in the hours that had followed, even if he had not been aware of its presence. He felt it now, in the centre of his heart. It was imperishable in its strength, eternal in its fire. His death had been as nothing to this truth. His body had died, but his self had survived.

The greater implication of that survival was not lost on him.

Teyosa saw it too. 'She failed,' she said, echoing him. 'She *can* be resisted. She *can* be fought.' What had only been a dream before was now a reality. Where there had been only determination, now they could add hope.

'And she will have to be fought *now*,' Mathas said. 'Our time is limited. If I was permitted to return, it is because she believes me to be her thrall, and that I have come to prey on this family and control it in her name.'

'Does she suspect us?' Glanath asked.

'If she does, she must be uncertain, and not see us as a threat,' said Teyosa. 'Or she would have destroyed us.'

Mathas thought of the destroyed House of Avaranthe, its inhabitants reduced to skeleton slaves reshaping their home into a monstrous image conjured by Neferata's will. Teyosa gave him a quick look. *She knows*, he thought. *If I had good news to give her, I would have done so.* He would tell her what he had seen, but when they were alone, and she had the space to grieve. He held her eyes with his, and her lips thinned as she braced herself to go on.

'We have her doubts in our favour,' Mathas said. 'But it will not be long before she realises that I have not done what she expects me to do, and that I am free of her control. We must strike before she takes further action.'

'Can we possibly be strong enough?' Verrick wondered aloud.

'No matter how long we prepare, the only way we will know is in the struggle itself,' Mathas told him. 'But she is weaker than we thought. Her failure to destroy my will is proof of that. She is weaker, and we are stronger.'

'He is right,' Teyosa said to Verrick. 'The time has come. The signs are all there. Tell him.'

'Tell me what?' Mathas asked.

Verrick smiled. 'In the short time of your absence, we have received help from outside the walls of the city.'

'What help?'

'Come. I will show you.'

The four of them descended into the vaults of the Hellezan palace. Past the wine cellars were the deeper foundations, older than the palace itself, riddled with tunnels linked to the honeycomb of underground passages that swarmed beneath Nulahmia. Mathas did not know how far down they extended, though there were whispers that their roots were so deep that unwary explorers would enter the true underworlds, never to return.

'She can still see us,' Verrick murmured, 'even down here.'

The tunnels, like every other aspect of Nulahmia, were part of Neferata's design. The city was so utterly her creation that every bend and branch and dead end, in every specific location, had come into being because she had willed it. The sense of security created by the maze and the depths was an illusion. If Neferata turned her gaze this way, there would be no hiding from her.

'She can see us,' said Mathas, 'but only if she knows to look.' *Her eyes cannot be everywhere at once. There must be some limits to her knowledge. There must be.*

At length they reached a low, wide chamber, lit by a handful of guttering torches. The stone coffins that lined its walls were empty. The people gathered in the space would have been careful to make sure of that. The tombs had been disused so long that their interiors were thick with cobwebs and dust.

Present were the heads of more than a dozen of the great mortal families of Nulahmia. This was the first time Mathas had seen them together, outside of court functions. Each of them represented a cluster of families. The cells of the rebellion were breaking the security of isolation. They sensed that the time to strike was fast approaching. There were vampires present too. They represented houses that were under Neferata's political control, but none were her direct thralls.

But among the vampires was one Mathas had seen only a few hours before. He was Jedefor, and he was a captain of the guard at the palace.

Mathas eyed him carefully. Jedefor gave him a brief nod. Mathas had not known he was part of the conspiracy. His jaw tightened with suspicion. 'I am surprised Neferata would choose as captain a vampire who is not her thrall,' he said.

'I am surprised one of her thralls can claim to be a rebel.'

Teyosa touched Mathas' arm, and he bit back his retort. 'Indeed,' he said, and forced a smile of acceptance. If Jedefor was here, then he had already proved himself loyal to the cause.

There was another vampire that Mathas did not know. His brow was heavy, his chin pointed, giving his face a pronounced triangular appearance. He was a noble, clad in fine armour of wightbone and leather. The insignia of his house, borne on his chest, was strange to Mathas. Jedefor introduced him as Lestor.

'We come from a friend outside Nulahmia,' said Lestor. 'He has taken an interest in your cause, and pledges his support.'

'Of what kind?' Mathas asked.

'Arms. Other reinforcements too, for when you march.'

'And what is his price?'

'Nothing you cannot afford.'

Mathas had his doubts about that. But the conspirators were not in a position to turn their back on aid.

'Please convey our thanks to your lord,' said Hasynne of House Nastannar. Broad of shoulder and thick of arm, the vampire seemed to have come into being to take to the battlefield in heavy armour. Hers was the most bellicose of the noble families. She brought great strength to the cause.

Lestor bowed. Jedefor looked pleased, and Mathas guessed what he hoped to gain from Neferata's overthrow.

But this is more than an exchange of masters, Mathas reminded himself. *Whoever replaces Neferata may be as cruel, but none will be as powerful.*

'This is very well, and we are grateful,' said Sethek, one of the vampire nobles. Her gratitude sounded perfunctory. 'But we are running out of time. Meeting like this makes certain the moment of our discovery is imminent. When do we attack?'

'Very soon,' said Mathas. 'I agree with you. We must make ready.'

'*Very soon*,' Sethek repeated bitterly. 'What does that mean?'

'It means what I said,' said Mathas. 'I doubt that anyone here is ready to march on Throne Mount tonight.'

'*We* are ready,' said the vampire lord Borzhas, standing next to Sethek.

'Ready to attack on your own?' Mathas asked.

Borzhas frowned at him.

'That is why we are here now,' said Teyosa. 'To coordinate, to know what must yet be done, and to set about doing it.'

'Let us be clear about my role,' Jedefor said. 'I will provide information about the Palace's defences on the chosen night, and I will do what I can to assist behind the walls. But I cannot be seen to do so until the last moment. I will not lead the uprising.'

There was disappointment in the faces around the chamber.

Coward, thought Mathas. Though he understood Jedefor's reasoning, and he wondered how certain the captain was of his troops. Mathas looked at the hesitation in the others. Sethek and Borzhas were still seething over the delay. They were reckless, he thought. Before either of them could step forward, he said, 'I will lead. I will carry the banner for mortal and vampire alike.'

The veins of Borzhas' face stood out in anger, giving him the appearance of cracked porcelain. Jedefor, though, was nodding. 'Yes,' he said. 'Good. Her newest thrall. The proof of her weakness.'

'The proof of our strength,' said Teyosa.

Mathas believed Jedefor was right. He hoped Teyosa was too.

She looked at him, her eyes shining and strong, and suddenly he felt he could throw the Palace of Seven Vultures down with his bare hands.

If strength is to serve power, its true form must be recognised. Strength is to understand limits. It is to see the power of the adversary. It is also to see the enemy's illusions of strength, and to turn them to advantage.

– *The Use of Enemies*

FIVE

AGE OF SIGMAR
THE SEASON OF CREMATORY

Ruhok turned at the sound of the rumbling grind and the screams. A stretch of land a score of yards across was eating more of his troops. The Mighty Lord of Khorne cursed the weakness of his men to let themselves be taken, and he cursed the ground on which they all walked.

His army was fighting its way through the Cremation Plain. The landscape looked like bare, jagged rock. In reality, it was composed of the remains of millions upon millions of beings. Their teeth were fused together in vicious clusters, jabbing upwards through densely packed ash. The surface might be solid for a long stretch, and then suddenly the ash would give way, insubstantial as a dust cloud, and the long, razored constructions of teeth would grind and slash. The Plain would take its victims one at a time, or it could devour a hundred at once. There was never any warning, and no way to tell where the unstable ground lay.

The teeth ripped flesh to shreds. Blood erupted in fountains from the dying men. And when blood touched the Plain, a new cremation occurred. Flames roared out and up from the collapse, incinerating the corpses, and washing over more troops as they fled the explosion. Ruhok stood without flinching as the fire engulfed him. His ornate bronze armour blazed crimson, shining brighter than the flames in the night. His flesh had become a blackened, scarred hide, so thickened and scaled with scabs that there was nothing left for the fire to consume. He waited out the fire. When the flames dissipated, it appeared to his troops as if he had defeated them. Shouts of anger and praise came to him, and the horde struggled on.

'We move ever forward, Lord Ruhok,' said Ghour, pausing with him.

'Too slowly,' Ruhok told the bloodsecrator.

Ghour did not contradict him. He bowed his head and, carrying Ruhok's huge icon high, marched forward.

Ruhok paused a moment longer, watching the huge siege towers sway back and forth. The casualties among the brayherds hauling them forwards were tremendous. Every few moments, new flames marked where the ground consumed tuskgors as they pulled the great chains, or the towers jerked as their wheels dropped into another collapse. The towers were immense constructions of brass. Their peaks were carved into grotesque faces with gaping jaws. The interior of the maws glowed red. The towers had their own fires. They were forges of destruction. Nations had fallen to their advance, cities reduced to ashes on the wind. Ruhok had sworn to Khorne that he would bring the same fate to Nulahmia.

At the base of the towers, Torsek the Skullgrinder raged at the tuskgors. His anvil swung on its chain, striking any slave who did not pull hard enough. The towers were Torsek's creation, and he rarely left them, as if his will alone was what pulled them to the walls they would destroy.

As Ruhok turned and marched forwards again, his slaughterpriest caught up with him. Vul's chest was marked by the last explosions. His flesh glistened with burns, and his horned helm was charred. 'Doubts are spreading,' he warned. 'Doubts that you know where you are taking us.' He lowered the point of his spear with a rattle from the skulls tethered to the shaft, and pointed into the distance. There was nothing to see except the next few hundred yards of the Cremation Plain, lit by the torches of the warhorde and the infernal blazes of the siege towers. 'By day and by night we march across this ground, and by day and by night there is only more of it.'

'Are my followers afraid?' Ruhok demanded. 'If they are, they are weak. Let the ground consume them.'

'It does, Lord Ruhok. It well and truly does.'

Ghour had stopped again, watching the exchange, his eyes narrowing with anger when he looked at Vul. Ruhok wasn't sure if Vul was merely reporting on the discontent, or indirectly issuing his own challenge. It did not matter. His message for everyone was the same. 'Let those who doubt me try themselves against the edge of my axe.' He swung the blade of the terrible weapon up and down. The rune of Khorne glowed white with heat, and the axe hissed in hunger. 'Spread the word!' Ruhok shouted. 'Tell them! Tell them all! Step forward if you defy me! Prove your leadership by usurping mine!' He lowered his voice. 'But tell them this, too. Tell them that their loyalty and their effort will be rewarded. Nulahmia will perish forever in a storm of fire and blood that will shake the entire realm.'

Vul bowed. 'I will do as you command.' His voice trembled with reignited fervour. The slaughterpriest believed in Ruhok's promises.

'Take my gospel to the warhorde,' Ruhok said. 'Fill the hearts of the Bloodbound with new fire.'

Ruhok marched on, thinking of the destruction to come. The visions of utter ruin had filled his thoughts since the Everchosen had given him the dispensation to correct the errors of that dilettante Lascilion and in some measure avenge the death of Bloodking Thagmok. Ruhok grudgingly admitted that the lord of Slaanesh had one genuine accomplishment of which he could boast, and that was finding the way past the magical defences that had hidden Nulahmia for so long. But once in the city, he had squandered his advantage, indulging too much in the pursuit of sensation rather than devoting all his energies to the complete annihilation of his foe.

Nulahmia was no longer inaccessible, but when Ruhok was done with it the city would have vanished again, this time forever. He would drown Nulahmia in blood, and leave nothing behind, not even the stones to mark where the city had once stood.

But first he had to reach it, and the land was seeking to grind his warhorde down before he could even be absolutely certain he was leading them in the right direction.

He felt the ground subside under his right foot. He sidestepped with a growl, while a spike of teeth ground futilely in his wake.

Movement in the sky caught his attention. A glow of wraithlight was approaching. He stopped walking and raised his hand to warn of an approaching enemy. There was just one, though. The appearance of a single foe made him far more suspicious than the thunder of an opposing army. An individual meant some sort of subtlety was being woven, and he despised such schemes. They were the delight of the followers of Tzeentch; all Ruhok asked of war was the endless spilling of blood.

The glow drew closer, and Ruhok's jaw dropped in surprise. Mounted on a dread abyssal, the Mortarch of Blood flew towards him. Ruhok had never seen Neferata before, but he knew this was she. No other being could have such presence. Ghour hissed, and Ruhok growled low in his throat, discomfited by the sensations Neferata provoked, even at a distance.

The dread abyssal stopped less than a hundred yards away from the Lord of Khorne, and some twenty feet up. It made lazy passes through the air, its bony tail whipping sinuously. Ruhok looked on all sides for signs of an ambush, but Neferata appeared to be completely alone.

Kathag, the Exalted Deathbringer of Ruhok's Gorechosen, came up behind him. The scars on his bare torso were so numerous, they had turned his hide into leathered armour. His face was barely human. He had cut his cheeks open, stretching his lips into a perpetual grimace of hate. The horns he wore completed his transformation into a beast of war, a thing of such coiled muscle and burning rage that he looked as if he needed no battering ram to shatter fortress gates. 'This is a trap,' he said. 'Do not let her spring it.' His voice was surprisingly soft. The anger of his words seemed to come from a source of instinct rather than wisdom. He adjusted his grip on his huge, ruinous axe. 'I will destroy her.'

'We shall present a fine skull to Khorne,' Ghour said.

'But *can* you?' Neferata asked. Below her, bloodreavers had rushed forwards. They strained upwards with their blades, shouting in rage and hunger. She ignored them. 'And will you?' she asked, her attention on Ruhok. 'When I offer you the keys to my city?'

'This is a trap,' Kathag said again.

'Is it?' said Neferata. 'If it is, wouldn't I have sprung it by now?' She cast her eyes over the army of the Bloodbound. 'It is done,' she mocked. 'The war is over. You are all dead.'

The warhorde screamed back at her.

Neferata shrugged. 'It seems you are not.' She turned back to Ruhok. 'I will speak with you alone,' she said.

Attack now, he thought. *Destroy her, and the siege is won before it has started.* The thought was not enticing. That was a victory unworthy of Khorne. Unlike Kathag, Ruhok was not foolish enough to think Neferata could be taken down so easily. If she was here, she was ready to fend off an immediate challenge. And her offer was interesting. After the endless march through the Cremation Plain, it was very interesting.

Ruhok nodded. 'I will speak with you,' he said.

'You are a fool,' Kathag snarled.

'Then I will not return, and you will be Lord,' said Ruhok. 'And so you will be spared a duel you could not win. You should be grateful to the vampire. Perhaps offer her a few skulls.' He pushed Kathag away contemptuously.

The Exalted Deathbringer's eyes narrowed, but he stepped aside, calm despite the insult. The spikes of the skullgouger on his left hand were motionless. He had not even clenched his fist in response.

'You accept insults too easily,' Ruhok said, trying to provoke a reaction. He did not like the depths of Kathag's self-discipline. He had yet to challenge Ruhok's reign and had fought loyally. But this ability to channel his anger into still waters was a profound threat.

'I ignore what is pointless,' said Kathag.

Ruhok growled and stalked forward, following Neferata as her mount flew slowly away, remaining low and visible.

Ruhok followed the flight of the Mortarch for over an hour. There were only slight rises in the Plain, and they would have had to travel for miles to be beyond the sight of the warhorde. Neferata had to content herself with pulling him far beyond the possibility of immediate action from his army.

Ruhok laughed. 'Do not think you are safe!' he called.

Neferata didn't answer. Her skeletal beast landed. Its head, covered with an eyeless mask, faced Ruhok, the jaws gaping slightly, perception deeper and more sinister than any provided by eyes focused on the lord of Khorne. Neferata descended and stood before Ruhok. In her hands were a black dagger and wide-bladed staff darker than the night. She held them casually, without threat. The danger they represented was clear. She looked steadily at Ruhok, and though her skull would be a supreme prize to offer to Khorne, he felt himself strangely reluctant to attack her. The low growl began once more in the back of his throat.

'So,' said Neferata, 'what lord of Khorne is it who seeks to capture Nulahmia?'

'I am Ruhok, and I will not capture it. I will burn it. I will grind it into dust.'

'Good,' said Neferata.

Ruhok snorted. 'Do you expect me to believe you seek to betray your city to me? Without reason?'

'I have every reason,' said Neferata. Her voice wrapped itself around his head, its music insinuating and intoxicating. 'It is not my city any longer. It has been taken from me, and what I cannot have, I will destroy.' As she spoke, her voice became colder, shot through with an anger of ice and steel.

That was rage he saw in her, and Ruhok had a deep understanding of rage. 'I will destroy your city with or without your help,' he said, but he was curious now. 'What could you offer me?'

'You are approaching the city from the north-west,' said Neferata. 'Yes, Lord Ruhok, you are indeed heading in the right direction. You will continue as you have been.'

Ruhok stiffened in anger that she dared to give him an order.

But he would hear her out. And, though he could barely admit it to himself, he wanted to continue listening to that voice.

'You will, as you begin your attack, make a convincing feint towards the north-west section of our wall and the Hyena Gate. But your main strength must be ready to strike instead at the north-east. Send a small force ahead, and they will find the Raven Gate open to them. Let them hold it, and the city is yours.'

'Why is this subterfuge necessary? Open Hyena Gate for us.' He was already displeased to be discussing a form of warfare that was anything less direct than a battering ram.

'I cannot,' said Neferata. 'That gate is too well guarded.'

'And the other is not?' Her tale was sounding more improbable by the second.

'The second is not guarded because the defenders of the northern quarters of Nulahmia do not know about it. It is small, and my arts have kept it hidden from all eyes but mine. It is a route for my personal escape. If Nulahmia is no more, I shall have no further need of it.'

You will regret giving that secret away, Ruhok thought. *You will die with the city you are betraying.*

'Once enough of your troops have...' Neferata paused as if searching for the right word. 'Once enough have *entered* the city, you may open whatever gates you like.' She smiled, perfect predator teeth showing through the blood-red of her lips.

'And what of your troops? You are sacrificing them on the altar of your displeasure?'

'You will not be fighting my forces. Your foes will be legions in the service of Arkhan the Black.' The smile vanished, and the terrible winter of fury consumed her features once more. 'Did you not understand that the city is no longer mine?'

'I do,' said Ruhok. 'And now so must you. I said that after I am done, nothing will remain of Nulahmia.'

'So I should hope.'

'My vow encompasses all that belongs to the city. Your betrayal is no protection. I will destroy you too.'

Neferata sheathed her dagger and stepped forward. She reached out slowly. Stunned by disbelief, Ruhok did not react. She dragged a nail down the scarred flesh of his cheek. The wrath of flame could not move him, but that delicate touch sent a shudder through his frame. 'Please try, Lord Ruhok,' Neferata whispered. 'Please try. Be my disaster.'

Properly honed, the blade of truth and the blade of lies are indistinguishable.

– Philosophy of Deception

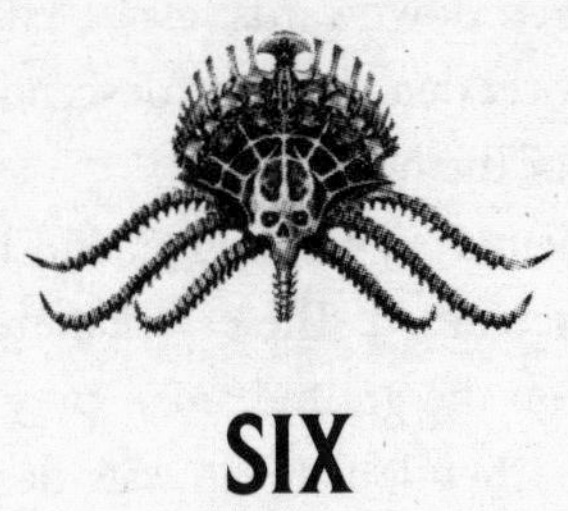

SIX

AGE OF SIGMAR
THE SEASON OF CREMATORY

Neferata headed back towards Nulahmia in a shroud of darkness. She was the unseen watcher in the night, and she was hunting. She flew in a search pattern, covering a wide area on the path between the warhorde and the city. She scoured the ground with her sorcerous sight, seeking those who would remain unseen, watching for the other watchers.

She needed Ruhok to advance as far as possible without Venzor knowing. The warhorde was an impressive one, but she would give Ruhok every advantage she could going into the conflict. She needed the full power of the disaster.

Twice she caught sight of her own spies moving swiftly through the night. Then, midway on her journey, she saw two figures who did not serve her. They were moving north, and on the western edge of a path that would bring them to a point where they would catch sight of the warhorde. If they deviated slightly from their current direction, they might miss Ruhok's advance entirely. But if they kept going, they would see what Neferata did not want them to see.

Nagadron plunged downwards, claws extended. Neferata's veil of darkness shredded, and she descended on the scouts with the full fury of the hunt.

The Adevore opened his jaws wide, and the souls trapped within his frame screamed. The cry shattered the night, and the two vampires on the ground froze, prey paralysed by the shriek of a raptor. They looked up, saw destruction coming for them, and ran, sprinting in opposite directions. Nagadron streaked for the one on the right. Just before he reached the ground, Neferata leapt from his back, arcing through the air for the other scout. She landed in a crouch a few yards ahead of the vampire. Ash puffed up between her feet. Though his eyes were wide with fear, the scout kept running towards her, choosing to fight rather than veer off. There was no escape. His sword was drawn, and he lunged at Neferata with the ferocity of desperation.

Neferata rose from her crouch and blocked the scout's blade with Aken-seth, the Staff of Pain. When the sword made contact with the staff, a crackle of eldritch magic arced from Aken-seth to the blade and down the arm of the vampire. He screamed, immobilised by pain that coursed through his tainted blood into the depth of his bones. Neferata stabbed him through the chest with Akmet-har. The Dagger of Jet pierced his heart. The scout's vitality, which he had taken from the blood of mortals, was stolen again, devoured by the ancient weapon. The vampire's face withered. His sword dropped to the ground, and then he fell too.

A short distance away, Nagadron was dragging his claws over the body of the other scout, spreading it over the Cremation Plain. A circle of fire erupted around the dread abyssal as the vampire's blood soaked the hungry ground.

'Take the body,' Neferata commanded. 'This one too.'

Nagadron obeyed, grasping his victim in curled claws, and seizing Neferata's in his jaws. The monster's teeth ground bones and organs to jelly. There had still been a spark of existence in the scout, and now he twitched his last.

Neferata mounted Nagadron again, and she directed him west as they flew off once more. They travelled for some time, and a murky dawn had come before Neferata brought Nagadron to land. They were in a region where the Cremation Plain transitioned to the Tombhills. The terrain became rolling here. The hills varied in size, but not in shape. They were all burial mounds. They held as little as a single grave, or many hundreds. There were so many that they overlapped, the upward slopes of some mounds emerging from the rounded peaks of others. Carrion grasses covered them: brown, razor-edged weeds that hummed and sang in the winds blowing over the hills. The grasses fed on the countless bodies buried beneath the surface of the Tombhills. They also added new bodies to the land, slicing the veins of any living thing that dared to enter the region.

Where they had landed, the grasses presented in thin clumps, dusted by the ashes blown in from the Cremation Plain. The ground here was hard-packed dirt, and stable. The reeds recoiled from the presence of Neferata and Nagadron, then leaned in hungrily at the mangled bodies the abyssal steed dropped. Tiny mouths opened along their lengths, puckering in hunger. A few stalks sank the sharp contours of their lips into chunks of flesh, but not enough of the grass could reach to entirely consume the corpses. There would be traces of the scouts for some time to come.

Neferata had Nagadron paw through the remains again. The violence done to the bodies must be massive in order to conceal the signs of her handiwork. Just as importantly, the extent of the injuries would suggest attackers of enormous ferocity. That would make it easy for Venzor to believe that Khornate forces had passed this way, moving in a direction that would make them miss Nulahmia. This one scene of murder would not be enough to convince him, but there would be others to come.

The following night, she spoke with Mereneth again on the roof of the Claw of Memory.

'I will have Venzor blind to the north-west,' Neferata told her spy, 'but believing himself to be clear-sighted. Draw his attention westwards. Hunt for his scouts. Lure them from the path that would lead to them to Ruhok, or kill them. Leave no trace of violence that would cause him to look in the direction of the enemy.'

'Sooner or later, he will know what is coming,' said Mereneth.

'I do not expect the forces of Chaos to take the city by surprise.' *At least*, Neferata thought, *not initially.* 'But I will have Venzor less than prepared. We will do what is possible. What is most important is that he does not suspect my hand in the death of his agents. Should he become anxious enough about the north-west to send a reconnaissance force that way, ignore those troops.' She would alter her tactics when that eventuality arose.

Five nights later, Neferata stood in a narrow fissure sunken into the outer wall of the Palace of Seven Vultures. Far below, the glints from torches and lanterns in the windows of Nulahmia's palaces were indistinguishable from the wraithlight of tombs. The city flickered with currents of light and darkness, and the night pressed down, heavy with the great heat. The anticipation of fire dwelled in the city, a fever-dream of catastrophe.

Mereneth approached down the tunnel behind Neferata. They were in the gossamer web of passages that gave her secret movement through the Palace's walls.

'Venzor appears to be satisfied, my queen,' Mereneth said. 'He believes the news he receives about the passage of the enemy.'

'I am less concerned with whether his belief is sincere or not,' said Neferata, 'than how he chooses to act.' She did not turn around.

'His energies remain concentrated on his position in the city.'

Neferata smiled thinly. 'He seeks to rule entirely. When he believes he is ready, he will move against me.'

'His ambition will be his doom,' said Mereneth.

'Do not be dismissive,' Neferata warned. Now she faced her spy. 'His challenge is real. The longer my rule is diminished, the stronger he becomes.' She could feel more and more of the currents of the city flowing away from her. Greed and fear were the engines of loyalty in Nulahmia, and she was no longer the sole controller of those passions. She was engaged in a race to reclaim her rule before it was taken from her once and for all. 'Loyalties are shifting, are they not? My subjects grow restive. They perceive a new master.'

'Some do,' Mereneth admitted. 'We have not acted against them, as you commanded. Do you wish us to punish them now?'

'Not yet. My judgement will fall on them, and it grows heavier with delay. For now, we wait. But we do not wait much longer, Mereneth. Ruhok approaches.'

'We cannot keep Venzor's awareness away from the warhorde much longer.'

'I do not intend to. Indeed, I will warn him myself. Where is the proud lord?'

'Holding court, my queen.'

'Excellent. Then I shall see him.'

She left the tower, and Mereneth followed, the loyal shadow following the great one.

Venzor had quarters in a palace near the north wall, one whose mortal inhabitants had been killed by the return of Nagash. Though it was close to the larger concentration of the troops under his command, Venzor had been spending more and more time of late in the Palace of Seven Vultures. He was growing accustomed to its surroundings. He was coming to see himself as the new master of Throne Mount. Like a monarch in waiting, he had taken, for his use, a magnificent suite of chambers adjacent to the grand hall. Neferata had not protested. She had remained the phantom in the halls of the palace, and it had suited her purpose that the only show of luxury and renewed energy in the palace should come from Venzor. Let him be the counterfeit ruler. His poor mimicry of the glory that had been hers would only be the more apparent.

Neferata threw open the doors of Venzor's receiving hall. The vampire lord was seated at the far end in a chair of gold and wraithbone, its arms constructed from fused, bejewelled skulls. It was very close to being a throne. Neferata had amused herself in the past by offering the seat to ambitious nobles and wealthy ambassadors from outside Nulahmia. Her amusement came precisely from the fact that the seat was so very near to being a throne, yet it was not. It rarely took more than a few seconds for her visitors to understand this truth, and to feel torn between the honour that was shown them, and the humiliation of the lesson. Venzor, it seemed, was immune to the lesson of the chair. Neferata looked forward to ending his delusion.

Neferata strode down the centre of the hall. On either side

of the central aisle, a procession of tall candelabra lit the room. They were bodies of mortals frozen in the moment of death agonies. Molten iron, and then gold, had been poured over them. The courtiers surrounding Venzor drew aside at her advance. Alarm crossed the faces of the vampire nobles. She gave each of them a quick, contemptuous look. Flanking Venzor were his lieutenants. One of them was Dessina Avaranthe. There, Neferata thought, stood the symbol of a family with a history deeply entwined with the currents of treachery that flowed through Nulahmia. Such turns of fate and chance it had taken for Dessina to exist at all. An age had passed since Neferata had ordered the extermination of the Avaranthes, yet here still was a representative of that house, clad in armour, and silent in power.

Venzor seemed entertained by Neferata's interruption. 'You honour us with your presence, Queen Neferata,' he said. He hesitated minutely before and after her title, underscoring its precariousness.

'It is not an honour I wish to bestow,' said Neferata. 'But your foolishness compels me to do so. I am here to demand that you explain yourself. With so much at stake, why have you concentrated solely on defence? I do not understand.'

Venzor's thin lids lowered and raised in a slow, reptilian blink of confusion. 'You have me at a disadvantage,' he said, his rasp steady and unconcerned. 'I do not know what you are talking about. Defence against what?'

Neferata stared at him, arranging her features into a mask of astonishment and anger. 'Why do you dissemble? What purpose is there in pretence? Defence against the Khornate warhorde, of course.'

Venzor shrugged dismissively. 'We have noted the evidence of its passing. The enemy has not located Nulahmia. There is no threat.'

Neferata maintained an icy silence for a long moment. Though she had engineered the deception, she still wondered if Venzor truly was as much the fool as he appeared to be in this moment. She didn't think he was. Some of his unconcern had to be for show. Even so, her pretended outrage took very little effort to be convincing. 'No threat,' she said at last, repeating his words with a precise mixture of contempt and disbelief. 'Evidence of its *passing*? Lord Venzor, what have your scouts been telling you? Where have you been sending them? My spies have *seen* the warhorde. The Bloodbound of Khorne will be at our gates in a matter of days.'

Now it was Venzor's turn to be silent. His left eye fluttered with a nervous twitch. 'You are certain of this?'

'Would I be here if I was not?' Neferata began to pace. 'We have been fools, both of us,' she said. 'You, for remaining ignorant of what is closing in on Nulahmia. I, for assuming that you were taking measures to protect the northern walls. I should have spoken sooner.'

'Why didn't you?'

She stopped pacing and rounded on him with a snarl. 'Because I did not wish to,' she hissed. 'Because your presence in *my* city is a perpetual humiliation. And because I *thought* you knew what you were doing!' Venzor fumbled for a response, and she kept going. 'At least my foolishness had limits. I have taken some measures to prepare for the coming war.'

'What measures?' Venzor asked.

Was that hope she heard in his voice? The irony was of a rich vintage. It was the first unalloyed pleasure she had experienced within the walls of Nulahmia in a long time. 'My agents have opened negotiations with Lord Ruhok,' she said, and the look on Venzor's face was the equal in delight to the irony of his hope a moment before.

'They have *what?*' he sputtered.

'They have promised, in my name, to ensure that the Hyena Gate will open to the warhorde.'

Venzor gaped. One hand clutched the arm of the chair, while the other clawed at the air, as if trying to catch the words that had failed him.

Until now, the rest of the vampires present had been silent, perhaps hoping to drop beneath the notice of the leaders in conflict and so be forgotten. Now they stirred. Whispers of fear circled the hall. Neferata felt their stares. None could understand what she was doing. All were reminded that in this room, there was only one being who had the right to inspire terror in their hearts, and that was their queen, not this ambitious lieutenant of the Mortarch of Sacrament.

'What have you done?' Venzor finally managed. Behind him, Dessina took a step forward, her gaze furious, her hand on the hilt of her sword. Venzor raised a finger, signalling patience and restraining her.

'What, it seems, was necessary.' She cocked her head and looked curious. When Venzor did not respond, she sighed in exasperation. 'Do you not see? I have set the terms of the battle in our favour. We know where Ruhok will direct his strength, and we have time to prepare our defences and our counter-attack.'

Venzor leaned forward, some animation returning to him. His eyes narrowed. 'And why would Ruhok trust you? Why would he believe you would betray your city?'

'Because rage is what he knows. My spies brought him word of strife in Nulahmia. Will you pretend there is none?' Venzor said nothing, and she continued. 'They told him a tale of usurpation. And of a queen willing to destroy what was taken from her.' There was no pretence of anger in her words. Her voice was the cold of vengeance, and the flames of the candelabra dimmed. The courtiers instinctively took a step back. No one in the hall doubted her sincerity.

'That is a tale to convince a lord of Khorne,' Venzor admitted.

'I'm glad you agree,' said Neferata. She strode forward until she towered over Venzor in his seat. 'Now,' she said, 'what do you intend? Are my efforts to be in vain?'

'They will not be,' said Venzor. 'If this is the situation we face, then we will make ready, we will break the siege before it even begins, and we will crush the forces of Chaos.'

Neferata read his eagerness and his determination. She was close to putting Venzor on the war footing she desired. *If*, he had said. *If this is the situation we face*. He was cautious. He knew better than to take her simple word as truth. He would seek certainty for himself. And look where she wanted him to look.

Once Neferata had left, Venzor turned to Dessina. 'How much of what she said would you believe?' he asked.

'I was never close to the queen,' said Dessina.

'I am well aware of that. But your life and your undeath have been spent in Nulahmia. You have been in and out of her court. Your insights have already proven valuable. I would have more of them now.'

Dessina bowed her head in respect. 'I believe most of what we have heard. A lie about the advance of a Khornate army would be too easy to disprove.'

'Then you feel we should act on the assumption that her information is accurate.'

Dessina grimaced. 'I would do so with reluctance.'

Venzor nodded, pleased. 'As would I. The question, then, is where we are to find the lie in her words. This is where we must find the trap and its nature.'

'She may not be lying at all,' said Dessina.

'Explain yourself.'

'It is a strategy I have witnessed the Mortarch deploy more than once, but one I have not been able to detect until it is too late. She may have told you the truth, but perhaps not all of it. Or she may have told you all the truth, but told it slant. For Neferata, the truth is the most powerful of all lies.'

'I see.' Venzor sank back in his throne. One fang bit his lower lip as he began to go over Neferata's words, looking for the gap in the story or the weakness in the reasoning that would show him what he must do to hold on to the city.

I know what lies on the other side of stagnation, of decay, of all forms of defeat. I have seen it. When I close my eyes, I can see it now.

– The Understanding of Annihilation

SEVEN

AGE OF MYTH
THE SEASON OF LOSS

Neferata was uneasy. Her impulse said, *Look in the north.*

Her discomfort came from more than the rumours of rebellion. It was acute to the point of pain. It was an instinct she did not dare ignore. Something was happening in the northern reaches of Nulahmia. From the highest tower of the Palace of Seven Vultures, she looked down the Throne Mount into the city, her witchsight revealing every street and courtyard to her. She saw nothing to warrant what she felt. The city pulsed with its nocturnal rhythms of cruelty and blood. Predators hunted prey, and the weak cowered behind locked doors and barred windows. The dance of the living and the dead continued as it had for millennia. She saw nothing to warrant her unease.

I see no rebellion, either, she thought. *Yet I know the conspirators are out there.*

And then again, *Look in the north.*

She would not ignore the instinct. So she seized the Staff of Pain and the Dagger of Jet, and summoned Nagadron. With

Aken-seth strapped to her back, and Akmet-har in hand, she flew off from the Palace. What she could not see from a distance, she would hunt out. She left behind her bodyguard of morghasts. For now, she would be the unseen presence in the night. She would find the source of her unease, and then decide on a course of action.

On Nagadron's back, she soared over the rooftops of Nulahmia. To the citizens, mortal and undead, who happened to look up, she would have appeared as no more than an eddy in the banks of fog that moved across the city. The Adevore flew low, grazing the peaked gables, flashing between the spires of mausoleums. Neferata was close enough to feel the pulse of the city, the throb of its lifeblood. No matter what discontent arose in her subjects, she was the creator of Nulahmia. Its being and its soul belonged to her, and whatever force now disturbed it, like an insect struggling in a web, she would find it, and preserve what was hers.

Deep into the northern region of Nulahmia, in the midst of the Silent Quarter, the disturbance grew stronger and clearer. The nature of the instinct that had driven her into the night became clear. She sensed the deployment of powerful magic. Its precise nature and location were still veiled from her sight, but its mere presence sent occult ripples through the aether. There was no question in her mind that this was connected to the stirrings of rebellion in the city, and it disturbed her that those who plotted against her had abilities on this scale. There was something familiar about the nature of the magic. Though she could not yet find it, and though she did not know what it was meant to do, it had a character. The closer she came, the more precise that character became.

The Silent Quarter was a vast cemetery. No mortals lived here, and no vampires held palatial homes. There were only the dead, entombed in mass graves, in humble tombs, and in sepulchres so vast they rivalled the Palace of Seven Vultures in size. Cobbled passages wound between the vaults and mausoleums in a twisting, tangled maze. The mortals who erred and wandered into the Silent Quarter soon became lost, and never emerged. The living who entered this region were doomed to fall into silence. At the centre of the Quarter was the Tomb of the Unnumbered. It was a colossal mausoleum, one of the oldest constructions in Nulahmia, and it contained legions upon legions of the dead. It rose from the surrounding tombs like a great, slope-backed beast, its spine covered with grim, black towers of basalt slabs and fossilised bone. The tallest were on its peak, twin spikes that reached hundreds of feet into the sky, clawing the fog into streamers.

Nagadron flew between the twin spires. Too late, Neferata realised this was the centre of the disturbance. Black, sorcerous energy lashed out from both of the windowless peaks. It enveloped both the vampire and her mount. Neferata's limbs convulsed, and her hand clenched with such violence around the hilt of Akmet-har it seemed that she should have snapped the dagger in half. Pain coursed through her limbs and her spine, and that agony was as nothing compared to the searing eruption in her skull. She could not move, or think. Her head was thrown back, her jaws locked open in an unvoiced scream. Nagadron shrieked, his tail thrashing in fury and distress. He clawed and flailed at the air, as trapped by the coruscating darkness as his mistress. The souls inside his huge body screamed too, and then he began to lose cohesion, to return to the otherworld from which he had been summoned.

Neferata sensed the imminent dissolution of her mount, and through the torment of her paralysis came the salvation of anger, of outrage that she should be attacked here, *here*, in her realm. She could not yet move, but she could think again, and she could see, though her vision was cracked by black lightning. The greatest drive of all, the drive to adapt, to do whatever was necessary to survive, took over, and in the incandescence of agony, she began to move.

Nagadron was still in mid-dissolution. The attack had begun half a heartbeat ago.

As Neferata took back control of her limbs, two figures leapt from the top of the spires. They were winged vampire nobles, Borzhas and Sethek. They each carried a sword in one hand, and a large, gnarled, talismanic cylinder in the other. It was from these objects that the energy coursed, lashing across the gap between them with unending fury. The two vampires dived at Neferata, blades out to impale her.

Take them, she commanded herself, and because that was the greatest necessity of the moment, she did. Nagadron's spine was the last portion of the abyssal steed to remain solid, and she launched herself from it in the moment before her mount vanished completely. Her leap was clumsy, her movements jagged with pain, but it was enough. She flew to meet Borzhas. Startled that she had broken her paralysis, he tried to veer out of her way, spoiling his blow. Neferata's armour turned his blade aside, and she collided with him. The impact knocked him down, and they fell, a tangle of struggling limbs. As they dropped, the link between his talisman and Sethek's snapped. The web of energy tore. Chaotic, weakened but still ferocious, the violent magic surrounded the combatants. Neferata's pain lessened, and Borzhas screamed in the shock of new pain. He tried to fly, but she stabbed Akmet-har through the membrane of his wing, tearing it into flaps.

Down they fell, and the uncontrolled storm of the spell

blasted through the roof of the Tomb of the Unnumbered. Neferata forced the pain of the energy further back into her consciousness and fought for control of her actions, but she was still awkward, still jerking wildly. As she and Borzhas tumbled over each other, she caught a glimpse of Sethek streaking down after them, her wings tucked in for the dive. She must have dropped her talisman when the magic recoiled. Her left arm was blackened and trailing smoke.

Neferata saw Borzhas' talisman clearly now. It bore a great seal, one she recognised. '*Mannfred*,' she hissed through her pain. The Mortarch of Night had lent his signature to the trap then. His hand was reaching into Nulahmia to attack her, mocking her from afar. 'You strike with borrowed power,' she sneered at Borzhas. 'It will always betray you.'

They dropped through the domed vault beneath the roof of the Tomb. The stone coffins below were laid out in circular rings, forming a funereal amphitheatre. Spectral light shifted like tattered lace over the graves. The shouts of the struggle and the crackling blaze of the sorcery broke the silence of millennia. Then they hit the centre of the vault, the floor disintegrating before them.

They fell, end over end, snarling in anger and pain, a dark comet plunging through the heart of the Tomb of the Unnumbered. Borzhas tried to break free, but Neferata jammed the Dagger of Jet between his ribs, and held it there. Her grip was iron, and she trapped the other vampire in her fall. There was no escape for him. She would take him with her into the abyss of their own creation.

The magic seemed to be growing weaker, or perhaps Neferata was inuring herself to the pain. Yet she was still caught in the midst of a black explosion, whirling and falling, seeing only fragments of the monument around her and of the pursuing

Sethek. Falling through level after level, ever downwards, through the foundations of the Tomb and its subterranean vaults, down through the tunnels and the caves beneath Nulahmia, and still down, Mannfred's monstrous spell burrowing endlessly into the earth.

Borzhas smashed his other wing repeatedly against her head, dazing her, and he started to pull away. She snatched at the membrane with her free hand and sank her claws into it, shredding the leathery flesh. Borzhas screamed anew as his blood sprayed, and she dragged him closer, forcing him to see the journey of the fall to the end.

And down, deeper and deeper through rock, Sethek still following, until the rock became of uncertain substance. They fell through caverns so huge they seemed to have no walls or floor. They fell through howling fogs of ectoplasm, and past legions of wailing spirits. They were plunging through regions that were the threshold of spirit worlds.

Neferata's head became clearer. The magic was weaker now, but it was still enough to tear through the substance of the realm. The thought came to her that perhaps this fall might never end. Then, as they fell through a maelstrom of whirling, howling, tormented souls, an instinct of terrible danger awakened in her, an instinct infinitely more powerful than the one that had led her to the trap, and one entirely hers. The deepest core of her being shrieked at her, that fundamental urge to survive howled that she must stop the fall, and she must stop it *now*.

With the Dagger of Jet still lodged in Borzhas' body, still trapping him to her, she released his tattered wing and reached behind to snatch the Staff of Pain from her back.

Below, the chamber floor rushed to meet them. It glowed with green wraithlight tinged with a strange, thrumming grey.

The stone of the floor was twisted into the form of a frozen whirlpool, as if wrenched and contorted into this shape by an immeasurable force below.

Neferata jammed the blade of Aken-seth against Borzhas' chest and sent a withering blast of magic into his body. A searing flash of violet, sorcerous light hurled her and Borzhas away from each other. His left hand had closed around the talisman as if fused, unable to let go of the source of both their torments, and the shock of Neferata's attack jolted his fingers open, dropping the talisman, and at last they were free of the corrosive magic.

Borzhas spread his wings. He tried to fly, but they were too shredded, and the festering wound where Akmet-har had pierced him slowed his movements. He could do no more than slow his fall. Sethek flew to his aid. She grabbed his arm, but his weight dragged them both down, towards the floor.

Her frame still jangling knots of pain, her mind filled with broken glass, Neferata straightened out of her tumble and focused her energies through Aken-seth and directed them at the floor of the cavern, hundreds of feet below. The stone surface rippled as if it were nothing more than a membrane ready to tear at the slightest touch. Feet-first, Neferata rode a pillar of magical fire, but she was too weak to reverse her fall. She slowed, dropping more like a feather than a stone, but still she dropped.

Borzhas' lost talisman hit the floor of the cavern ahead of the vampires. The rock crumbled away beneath the talisman. Cracks raced outwards, covering more than a league in every direction. The cracks became crevasses, and the stone tore. It became something thin and fragile, mere parchment. It flaked away to nothing, shreds of rock and the talisman falling into the horror that waited below. There was a moan as if all existence mourned its death.

Neferata gasped. She knew, with terrible, final certainty, what she saw. It had always been a legend, even to the Mortarchs. Nagash had only mentioned it in her hearing once, millennia ago, and even then speaking as if there were some things that, for the gods too, were better left as myths.

A huge whirlpool of grey nothing churned beneath her, swallowing the falling wreckage of the floor, and eating at the distant walls. The grey had texture, the arms of its vortex wrinkled like the surface of a brain. The movement of the currents was heavy, but not sluggish, massiveness whirling with inexorable strength. But the sense of spinning matter was an illusion. The texture and the movement were visible only because they were the dying gasps of consumed reality. The truth of the whirlpool was that it truly was *nothing*. It was the greatest and most terrible of devourers, because everything, at the last, became nothing. This was the Maw of Uncreation.

Shyish was the realm of death, yet it, like all the mortal realms, was still a thing of being. It *existed*. But down in that whirlpool was the final end, absolute entropy. It was there that even death would come to an end.

Above her, Sethek and Borzhas screamed. Sethek flapped her wings with the power of pure terror, and carried them both towards the cavern wall.

Neferata's slow fall was still a fall towards extinction. With the energy born of desperation, she called to herself a tangible wind of darkness. Its tendrils surrounded her and, at her command, threw her towards the cavern wall. As she flew, the dark disintegrated and fell into tatters, and she arced ever downwards.

The maelstrom was silent, its spiral movement of grey dissolution majestic in its indifference. She came closer and closer to it, the immense coils of the churn ready to consume her. In the seconds of her flight, she sheathed her weapons, freeing her hands. She reached out, a final act of denial. She *would* exist. And her hands gripped the rock of the wall.

Neferata's fingers drilled through stone, and she clung to the curving rock face. She was less than fifty feet from the relentless turning current of non-existence. She looked down into the terrible grey. It mesmerised and repelled. There were no true features, only the endless movement of matter dying. She looked away, conscious of the danger of meeting the gaze of pure blankness. But though she was dangling over her terminal fate, and though she had so little strength left with which to save herself, her curiosity was not dead. This was a wonder below here, and it was also a power. One that could not be reasoned with, and that could not be grasped. Yet power was what she understood. It had been the study, practice and purpose of her existence.

She would not turn from the study of the Maw.

She would learn from it. For where there was power, there was opportunity.

Neferata looked up, and saw that Sethek had managed to bring herself and Borzhas to a narrow ledge midway up the cavern wall from Neferata's position and some distance to her right. Borzhas was moaning in pain and fear, and Sethek was staring down into the whirlpool with fascinated horror. For the moment, they appeared to have forgotten Neferata in the extremity of their terror.

The Mortarch of Blood jammed her hands deeper into the rock. She kicked the wall, creating footholds. Certain, for the time being, that she would not slip, Neferata rested.

Cautiously, wary of the pull to dissolution, she studied the Maw of Uncreation.

The point at which the cavern wall met the whirlpool drew her attention. It seemed that matter did not so much disintegrate as *flow* into the current. The stone was not molten. It was as cold and grey as the rest of the walls, yet it was as if the rock had become a slow-moving liquid, a gradual cataract feeding the hunger of the Maw.

The extent of that hunger was another puzzle. Once in contact with the maelstrom, nothing could resist it. Still, the Maw of Uncreation had not reclaimed all being, devouring Shyish and the other mortal realms. It was both the end and the precondition of existence. It was ravenous, yet it was contained within the boundaries of the cavern. Neferata wondered what supreme enchantment governed this cavern, giving the necessary strength to hold back the ravenings of absolute destruction.

She looked back up at the assassins. Borzhas had quieted, and they were both staring at her, torn between the need to finish her off and the fear of moving even an inch closer to the whirlpool. Neferata smiled at them, taunting them with their cowardice. Sethek snarled. She let go of Borzhas and rose to a crouch. Borzhas scrambled back on the ledge, clutching at the wall. Neferata had stolen the power of flight from him. If he fell, he would have no chance, and he knew it. He clawed gouges into the rock as if he would burrow his way back up to the surface.

Sethek hesitated, alarmed by Neferata's smile. She looked back and forth between the Mortarch and the maelstrom, gauging distances and chances. Poised for flight, her balance on the ledge was precarious.

Thank you, Neferata thought. *You have made all the errors I wished you to.* Her strength renewed, she took up the Staff of Pain again and sent a sorcerous bolt blasting up to the ledge. It struck Borzhas and hurled him from the ledge, into the void. Borzhas screamed and grabbed at Sethek. He seized her ankle and she toppled over with him.

They fell, but Sethek reacted quickly. Her blade slashed down and severed Borzhas' wrists. Howling, he dropped away from her and plunged into the Maw of Uncreation. He vanished beneath the grey, his scream silenced on contact. The speed of the current increased suddenly, and the level of the whirlpool rose.

Sethek wheeled away from Borzhas' grave and flew straight at Neferata, eyes burning in fury. She came in with blinding speed, heedless of the cliff face, her blade extended, aimed at Neferata's heart. The half-moon blade of Aken-seth glowed with dark power, and Neferata thrust upwards, impaling Sethek through the upper chest. Sethek choked, gasping, broken by her own speed. She dropped her sword and clawed at the Staff of Pain. Blood foamed from her mouth. Her blade clattered against the cliff, and dropped into the vortex.

Effortlessly, Neferata held Sethek out at the full extension of her arm. She dangled the other vampire over the Maw of Uncreation. 'You did well,' she said. 'You may take pride in that. You also have my thanks. You have shown me just how dangerous my enemies have become. You came very close to achieving your ends,' she said, and paused, then smiled again. Even in her final agony, Sethek writhed in fear from the promise of that smile. 'Forgive me,' said Neferata. 'I misspoke. You did achieve your end after all.'

'No,' Sethek choked out. Now she clutched the shaft of Aken-seth as if it were her salvation.

Neferata lowered her arm and aimed the spear downwards.

Sethek slid off the blade. Neferata watched her fall into the whirlpool, eager to see the reaction. Sethek sank, leaving the surface of the grey untroubled, but again the speed of the current increased, and again the level rose. The maelstrom was now less than thirty feet away from Neferata, and the pull of its lethal fascination was stronger than ever.

'You feed, and you hunger for more,' Neferata whispered.

The wall of rock vibrated under Neferata's touch, and the entire cavern shifted minutely. The flow of stone into the Maw of Uncreation accelerated by the same infinitesimal degree, and the whirlpool receded, dropping back to its original level.

The sense of adjustment was profound. Touching the wall as the change happened, Neferata felt how far the change went. It was no spell, no magic as she understood it, that allowed the cavern to act as prison for the Maw of Uncreation. It was something greater. It seemed to her that Shyish itself acted to suppress the thing that was the destroyer of being. Neferata wondered how much of Shyish's nature was shaped and governed, however invisibly, by the need to keep the Maw buried.

She scanned the cliff above her, and spotted a ledge a short distance away. She climbed up to it, and then sat, exhausted, waiting for enough of her strength to return so that she might summon Nagadron to the realm again, and have him take her from this place.

She turned her face away from the whirlpool, resisting the dark fascination. She looked up instead, at the distance she had fallen, and was troubled. In their plunge, she and Borzhas had broken the seals that had kept the Maw hidden away. Now it was exposed. They had opened a wound in creation. The whirlpool was contained, but if it was fed again, it might grow and rise. Disaster waited in the wings. Her city was up there, exposed to the hunger of the final predator.

I am the nomad of power, holding not to the illusion of structures and stability, instead moving from node to shifting node. I do not fight the currents and tides. I am one with them. I make their strength my own. I embrace then, too, the fluidity of labour, the mutability of art, and the eternity of the task. If the project before me appears long, even after more than a century of progress, I must remember that this is the nature of all work. There is no end except in the Maw of Uncreation. Creation keeps the Maw at bay, and death is the purest form of creation. All this I write, I believe, and I remember. I will not expect the project to end, but I will see it to fruition. I do not concern myself with utility. Let potential be my beacon.

– *The Understanding of Annihilation*

EIGHT

AGE OF MYTH
THE SEASON OF LOSS

At Neferata's orders, an army descended on the Silent Quarter and into the deep foundations of the Tomb of the Unnumbered. The scale of the construction that began matched its urgency. The Silent Quarter was silent no longer, and no more did the Unnumbered dead sleep. The first contingent of the army to arrive was the necromancers who summoned the dead from their tombs to their duty. Their queen had commanded, and the living and the dead must obey. Thousands upon thousands of skeletons dragged huge slabs of granite through the streets of Nulahmia and into the depths of the Tomb of the Unnumbered. Tireless, they swarmed over the construction site to create a new seal over the Maw of Uncreation. It was higher than the final barrier that had existed before but it would be more solid, and closer to Neferata's watchful eye.

She had named it the Annihilation Gate.

Most of the slaves creating the Gate were skeletons. When chains snapped and slabs dropped through the shaft that had been created in the Tomb, crushing scores of workers in their descent, there was barely a pause in the work. Skeletons did not mourn their comrades who had been smashed to powder. They did not wonder what it was they were labouring to seal away. They were not slowed by curiosity or fear.

But not all the workers were undead. Neferata demanded the presence of hundreds of mortals. Her Black Knights rounded them up from all levels of Nulahmian society. Slaves, prisoners, tradespeople, artisans, merchants and aristocrats, Neferata's deathly guard took them all to the Silent Quarter.

The entrance to the Tomb of the Unnumbered was so wide, a dragon with its wings spread could have passed through. Neferata stood next to it, Raia at her side, as the stream of mortals entered the Tomb. The people bowed their heads as they approached her.

'They are struck with wonder to be walking these forbidden paths,' Raia said.

'Some of them have realised that the paths are still forbidden,' said Neferata. She looked at an elderly man whose face was pale with foreboding. 'They know they will never leave the Silent Quarter.'

Raia was quiet for a moment, then said, 'Rumours are raging across the city, my queen.'

'So I would expect. The tales vary, do they not? There is no consistency except that the city is in danger of destruction from below?'

'Precisely so.'

'Good. Do nothing to counter them. I want my subjects to know that doom came near, but is being held back.'

'I still do not understand the nature of that doom, my queen.'

'Nor can you,' Neferata said. 'Not without seeing it, and its sight would destroy you. Content yourself with the rumours, Raia. Imagine that they are all true, and you come close to the heart of it.'

The weeks passed. Neferata supervised the construction in person, and as she strode past the lines of trembling slaves, she saw their growing terror, and the dawning of bleak understanding. On the day the Annihilation Gate reached completion, she addressed the mortals from atop a high plinth next to the Gate.

As she mounted the platform, the assembled mortals looked up at her with terror. They had laboured hard for her, and now that their task was complete, she saw that they dreaded the reward she was about to bestow.

'You were right,' she said, 'to fear for your lives. But take this lesson into your hearts. You never had a choice. There was nothing you could have done to alter your fates. I command, and you obey. This is the plain truth of existence. The purpose of your lives has been revealed, and it is to serve the end you will, this coming night.'

The slaves trembled, their worst fears realised. A few, however, stood taller at her words, taking pride in the sacrifice they would soon make for their queen and their city. She noted who they were, each one. Their honour would see them through their deaths, and she would see that their families were rewarded. She regretted that she would not be able to reward their loyalty still further, and resurrect them as skeletons, that they might continue to serve. But even more than the strength of the great stones that made up its physical being, the Annihilation Gate needed the most powerful magic possible. The sacrifices would have to be absolute. Nothing could be held back, not bone, not flesh, not blood.

The dead who had worked alongside the mortals now surrounded them, herding them into a great circle before the Gate, to await the assigned moment of their doom.

The rite that would consecrate the Annihilation Gate was announced across Nulahmia. Vampires of the Palace

Guard and the Company of the Walls marched down the Queensroad and the other great boulevards, banners unfurled, fanfares trumpeting the event. Once again, the queen had seen to the salvation of Nulahmia. Neferata declared three days of feasting, and even the lowest-born mortals, many of whom would be those feasted upon, rejoiced, for she decreed too that great hordes of gold and jewels were to be showered upon the human populace.

For every citizen who died, and for every citizen who grieved, she knew there would be another who would rejoice in their good fortune and shout their thanks to the Mortarch of Blood.

For the hours that preceded the ritual, Neferata returned first to her court, and then flew with Nagadron over the parades. She heard the cheers and the roars of gratitude. And during these hours, she felt the danger of an insurrection recede. The conspirators would not have the support they needed for the moment. The city was celebrating. They required its seething discontent.

That would come again. She had no illusions about that. This was a false peace, an even more brittle and misleading form of stability. It would not last.

The hour of the ritual approached, and the vampire nobility of Nulahmia descended into the Tomb of the Unnumbered. A wide chamber in the shape of a shallow amphitheatre surrounded the Gate. There were so many sacrifices gathered on the floor and the lower slopes that there was limited room for spectators, and so Neferata decreed that only one representative from any of the aristocratic clans would be permitted to attend. Even so, many had to be turned away. Hundreds of vampires in their finery gathered in the chamber, eager to bear witness to the shedding of so much blood. Channels had been carved in the slope of the amphitheatre to bring the flow of offering to the granite Gate.

On the plinth, Neferata watched the crowd. She observed the nobles' eagerness and hunger. Most of them seemed to regard the event as no different from any of a thousand revels she had hosted in the Palace of Seven Vultures. Even if they were awed by the sight of what had been built, they did not appear to grasp the full import of why it was necessary. *How could they?* Neferata reminded herself. *They have not seen what lies beneath. If they have not seen it, then its existence must be suppressed from their consciousness.* As with the realm of Shyish, so with its inhabitants. She had not tried to tell the people the true nature of the danger. They would not understand, and she had no wish to see what sort of disintegration might ensue if they *did* grasp what the Maw of Uncreation meant. It was enough for them to know that a danger existed, and she had arranged for it to be locked away forever.

The Annihilation Gate was more than a hundred feet high, but was at such a low angle to the ground that it was several times that length. Its granite doors were inscribed with runes of imprisonment. Each of the runes was at least ten feet wide, and they overlapped, amplifying their individual power into a collective wall as powerful as Neferata and her necromancers could construct. At the centre of the doors was the seal, a multifoliate iron blossom of a lock, the edges of its petals honed such that the merest touch would cut deeply into flesh, flooding the trespasser's body with a poison lethal to mortal and vampire alike. Its convolutions were so complex that no key could ever be constructed to fit them. At the cardinal points around its circumference, baleful eyes of pure silver gazed forbiddingly outwards, eternal, unblinking sentinels.

Neferata wore black, hooded robes woven with runes in threads of crimson and gold. When she moved, the voluminous folds concealed and revealed the runes, throwing them into different conjunctions with each other. Her every gesture was an incantation. Her eyes were shadowed. Her lower face was visible, that all who looked upon her would see her lips move. The words of power she would utter this night must be seen as well as heard.

She spoke, and her voice echoed against the wall and ceiling of the chamber, but was absorbed by the inert massiveness of the Annihilation Gate. 'This is a night of celebration,' she said, 'but our celebrations are solemn. We do not mark a triumph. Instead, this is the moment of triumph. We have been engaged in a battle, and tonight we strike the final blow.' She swept her eyes over the vampire nobles. 'You who stand here before this great gate have not come to bear witness. You are here to act.'

She paused. The audience stirred uneasily. The vampires whispered to each other. Some of them appeared now to notice that the contingent of skeleton guards who surrounded the mortal captives was fairly small. It was enough to keep the prisoners contained, but it would take a long time for such a number to work through so many sacrifices.

At the front of the throng, Lord Tristallar stepped forward. He was a tall vampire, and ancient, though it had been many centuries since he had taken to any battlefield more dangerous than the ballroom floor. 'Do you mean for us to perform the sacrifices ourselves?' he asked.

'No,' Neferata said. 'Not at all.' She raised her eyes towards the back of the chamber.

The aristocrats turned to follow Neferata's gaze. At the rear of the chamber was a much larger force, with more skeletons arriving though the entrance. They were the most mindless of reanimated servants, summoned from their vaults in the Tomb of the Unnumbered. They were draped in torn funeral shrouds and mouldering armour. Their blades were pitted and dull, though they would serve their purpose.

A number of the mortals began to laugh. Neferata looked at them and smiled, sharing their mirth. They were pleased that those who had come to witness their deaths would instead become part of their sacrifice.

'You cannot mean this!' Tristallar shouted, his voice shrill with outrage.

Neferata glared at him, and the force of command in her stare made him take a step back. 'I cannot mean this, Lord Tristallar? Who are you to pronounce upon the nature of my intentions? How do you presume to know your queen's mind? No one but I can ever declare what I mean. But I will tell you this. I mean exactly what I do.' And she raised a hand.

The skeleton army descended the slopes of the amphitheatre. The warriors formed a solid wall. They marched slowly, steadily, without hesitation and began the slaughter. The vampires did not accept their destruction peacefully. They fought back. The air of the chamber burned with sorcerous energy, and scores of skeletons exploded into fragments of bone in the first few seconds. Against a single noble, even a dozen skeletons would not prevail, but they came in the thousands. No matter how many were destroyed, there were always more. There was no breach in the wall of bone and blade. A few vampires, motivated perhaps by rage, perhaps by panic, tried to fight their way back up the slope, throwing themselves deeper into the army. They managed to make some headway, but were always borne down and cut to pieces before they could reach the exit.

On her plinth, Neferata turned the Staff of Pain against the nobles. She selected for her targets the vampires who were holding their own most successfully against the skeletons. She hit them with withering black lightning. They doubled over in agony, their spells dissipating without effect. The skeletons closed around them and cut them down, bony arms rising and falling with unwavering, implacable rhythm, blades chopping through finery and flesh to unleash the stolen blood from undead veins.

The skeletons filled the chamber, and there were always more. There was no room for the vampires to fight. Many of the spells they cast crippled other nobles as well as incinerating skeletons, and the army of slaughter never diminished.

On a platform midway up the plinth, the necromancers chosen by Neferata to oversee the construction of the Annihilation Gate added their sorcery to hers, and it was not long before the throng of vampires began to thin. The thunder and crackle of magic diminished, giving way to the screams of the dying as vampires and mortals were united in becoming part of the great sacrifice. The blood ran in rivulets, then streams, then torrents. It overflowed the channels, and it rushed like a cataract across the entire slope of the floor. It lapped in waves against the stone of the Annihilation Gate, and the doors drank it in. The huge runes glowed fiery red, and the granite darkened. The blood spread through the grain of the stone as though it were sponge, changing its nature, transmuting the rock into a substance far stronger. The Annihilation Gate became the black of absence, an echo of the horror it concealed. The seal turned, its razor petals spiralling, and the silver eyes, now streaked with crimson veins, blazed with light. The Annihilation Gate sang as it came into its strength. Its voice was deep and grinding, and it was a choir of thousands of souls fused into unity, all individuality gone, its final trace in the multiplicity of the Gate's triumphant cry.

As the storm subsided, the blood lapped higher against the edges of the Gate. The vampires fell, overwhelmed, and the skeletons moved deeper into the mortal prisoners. Some still refused the honour of their sacrifice, and they tried to fight. Without weapons, without hope, their struggle was brief. But several mortals, and even a few vampires, came forward to stand next to the plinth, before the gate. They looked up at Neferata and bowed to her. She nodded, acknowledging the grace of their acceptance, and its importance. They could not know what they died for, yet they knew their deaths were necessary. Because their queen commanded it, they gave their lives willingly.

They faced the Gate, looking in awe at that thing they would die to complete. Then the skeletons came, and hacked them to bloody meat.

Such loyalty, Neferata thought, watching the sacrifices fall. *Would that I could see where it lay at all times.*

Then she thought, *I would be bored.*

The certainty flashed through her mind and then was set aside. She needed to focus her concentration on the ritual, and leave nothing undone. The contemplation of that truth would have to wait for another time.

Now the butchering was done. No mortals or vampires remained on the floor of the chamber. Mutilated bodies and shattered skeletons lay everywhere, but there was no blood. The Annihilation Gate had devoured every drop.

The Gate's song had dropped from its initial frenzy. Now it keened and whistled, through its stone throat. The seal turned and flowed, the petals of iron shaping the song like lips.

Neferata looked down at the necromancers. They looked back at her. 'The ritual is complete,' one of them said.

'You have done well,' Neferata replied. 'Who is left now, who worked on the Annihilation Gate, or who knows even partial secrets of its construction?'

The satisfaction on the faces of the necromancers faded.

'You are good and loyal servants,' Neferata told them. She pulled the Dagger of Jet from her robes. 'I receive your sacrifice with gratitude.' She dropped down onto the necromancers' platform, and slit their throats.

The Annihilation Gate sang as it accepted their blood.

When it was done, Neferata returned to the top of the plinth and contemplated her work. The angle of the doors was so low that from her position, she was almost at eye level with the seal. She watched its gradual, graceful revolutions and mutations, and listened to the grinding, rising and falling whistle of the Gate. The immediate risk to Nulahmia was past, but her efforts here were not truly completed. The Gate would require perpetual vigilance, and its strength would need to be renewed. The skeleton army would remain to protect the Gate, guardians as unflagging as the eyes that surrounded the seal.

At length, Neferata turned away, knowing she would return. There was also much to study here, even if she did not see the Maw of Uncreation directly. Much to learn. Much to think about. She had faced the hidden, obscene core of being, and had retained her sanity. There were lessons here. And where lessons could be learned, there was power.

On the following night, Neferata held court at the Palace of Seven Vultures, and the illusion of unity in Nulahmia was over. There was a mob of courtiers clamouring for her attention and for redress. There were mortals who had come to the great hall, though they were far outnumbered by vampires. Of that nobility, a few attended out of duty. Perhaps, Neferata thought, even out of loyalty, though she would not trust that possibility. What she trusted was the anger. She appeared before them on her dais, and waves of suspicion and resentment crashed against her. She was pleased by the honesty of the reaction. It told her where she stood. She was able to read the state of Nulahmia more easily when the anger was not hidden.

At first, she had intended to face her subjects clad in her armour. She changed her mind, deciding instead on robes of translucent emerald and red, their many layers so delicate that a breath made them billow like sails. Their voluminous sleeves and train exaggerated every movement she made. That exaggeration would be useful to her. So would their appearance of fragility.

She said nothing for a long time, letting the clamour grow. The demands were stated a hundred different ways, but they were all essentially the same. Why were so many of her most loyal – and here she understood the word to mean *important* – subjects massacred? The act was senseless, the nobles cried, though none of them truly knew the nature of what had happened. That their kin had never returned from the ritual was enough to stoke their rage.

Neferata waited until the shouting was at its peak. Then she stabbed again at the false stability of Nulahmia. *Let the blood flow*, she thought. *Let treason come to light.*

'I will not be questioned!' she shouted. She introduced a querulous note into her voice. *Give them frustration instead of command. Give them weakness.* The uproar in the great hall quieted enough that she could be heard. '*I am your queen!*' She swept across the dais as she spoke, throwing her arms out in melodramatic anger, and the robes became a storm of movement. 'How dare you stand before me in this way? Will you defy me?' She paused, as if out of breath or at a loss for words, giving her question time to sink in. Let them ponder the idea. Make them decide. Push them to come out into the open. 'You will not,' she said, and she deliberately undermined her authority with a petulant gesture. *Be weak*, she thought. 'And I will not answer to you,' she finished.

She threw herself down on the divan, and her handmaidens rushed to tend to her. The walls of the great hall vibrated with even more shouting than before.

Raia knelt beside her. 'You have fanned their unhappiness,' she said, looking at the nobles.

'Good. Let it spread. We will force the unrest in the city to the crisis point.' Sethek and Borzhas had taken her by surprise. She would not let that happen again. If the slaughter of the nobility beneath the Tomb of the Unnumbered did not push the rebels into the open, then her show of vulnerability would.

'Watch and listen,' she told Raia. 'When my subjects leave, you and your sisters will follow them, and see where the paths of anger take them. Most of all, observe those who shout the least. Beware the thoughtful. They are the ones we must guard against.'

She studied her restless subjects. The deeper truth behind the theatre she had mounted was that she *was* vulnerable. That was the lesson she had learned in the Silent Quarter. She hoped she was not acting too late.

Subjects belong to the ruler. Their happiness, their wealth, their lives, indeed every facet of their existence are the prerogative of the ruler. To believe otherwise is to march down the path that leads to the ruler being subject to the ruled. That end is ruin. It may be useful to allow the subjects to believe their well-being is the responsibility of the ruler. But in the end, they are but chattel.

– Dominion

NINE

AGE OF SIGMAR
THE SEASON OF CREMATORY

Once more, Neferata was a shadow in the Palace of Seven Vultures. She had chosen the role, adapting to her circumstances. Yet as she moved through halls, observing but unseen, she felt those circumstances more painfully than ever. She was running out of time. The longer it took for the disaster to arrive, the more devastating it would have to be if she wanted even the faintest chance of taking back her city.

She flowed through the Palace with Mereneth in attendance. 'Lord Venzor is spending more time at the wall, shoring up the defences,' the spy reported.

'So he has taken the bait. That is promising, but politically, he seems to be more active than ever.'

Mereneth nodded. 'He has been making overtures to the nobles outside the northern quarter.'

'Are they responding?'

'They are.'

Neferata paused outside the archway to Venzor's receiving hall. Shrouded by darkness, she and Mereneth observed the aristocrats who were speaking with him. There were a few who had been there before, and several new faces. Neferata's appearance in this chamber, then, the reminder that she was present and that she saw all, had done little to shift the political realities. 'They think they know which way the winds of power are blowing,' she whispered to Mereneth. 'And so they lay their plans. Mark them. Add their names to the register of judgement.' They would know a full measure of terror when she was no longer a shadow.

Her determination was unchanged. But she saw how badly Venzor had undermined her. 'He is no fool,' she said. 'He acts on two fronts. He assumes that I was telling the truth about the Bloodbound advance. And he assumes that I was lying. He seeks to counter both threats.'

Neferata withdrew from the doorway. 'Come,' she said to Mereneth. 'Lord Venzor is too divided in his attentions. He needs focus, and I will give it to him.'

Morbhend lay to the north-west of Nulahmia, in a region of arable land past the termination of the Cremation Plain. Before the forces of Chaos had burned their way across Shyish, it had once been a city of considerable importance in its own right. It had begun to recover in the wake of Lascilion's defeat, though it was a mere splinter of its former self. New walls had risen around the former keep, and its population, primarily mortal, lived within them. Beyond the walls lay miles upon miles of blackened ruins. There were just enough people in the reviving embers of Morbhend to have resumed trading with Nulahmia. Given time, if left in peace, Morbhend might truly rise from its ashes.

It was probable that Ruhok's horde would come across it, but not certain. It was some leagues to the west of the Khornate line of advance.

Neferata had taken up a position in the peak of a ruined tower. The north face of the tower's battlements had been destroyed, and the structure resembled a dagger plunged into the body of Morbhend. Nagadron was crouched on the edge of the remaining battlements, his tail coiled around the curve of the tower. In the night, he was an angular shadow, one more jagged piece of rubble among many. Even the glow of his imprisoned souls blended in. Wraith energies flitted over the smashed, burned streets of the city.

Neferata looked to the north-west, waiting. At last, she was rewarded. She saw her three scouts running across the fields towards the city. Some distance behind them came the torches and shouts of a Bloodbound raiding party.

Let yourselves be seen, Neferata had instructed the scouts. *Draw the Chaos followers to Morbhend.* They had done as they were told. Their mission was almost complete.

The scouts were running quickly, but so were their pursuers. The Bloodbound were gaining ground. The scouts sprinted past the rubble that had been Morbhend's outer wall. They reached the open space of a large square and paused. They turned around, peering at the falling houses and low heaps of stonework. One of them made an uncertain movement. The other two looked back at the Bloodbound, who were closing in. They were, Neferata knew, wondering if they had erred, if they had stopped in the wrong location. They had not. They were doing exactly as she had commanded. They had done everything she had asked of them. What she needed from them next was not something they could give. It had to be taken.

Too late, they realised they had been abandoned. They ran for the shelter of the ruins. Given a few more seconds, they might have been able to find hiding places. But Ruhok's warriors saw where they went. They ran into the shell of a temple, and the howling pack of bloodreavers followed. The Blood Warrior in command led a direct charge through the doorway. There would be no prolonged siege.

The three vampires fought hard. Neferata saw bloodreavers stagger back out of the temple, their throats sliced wide open, their jugulars spraying wide. The interior of the ruin flashed briefly with sorcerous energy. But her scouts had cornered themselves, and the Khornate savages were too numerous. Their frenzy only increased as their own blood was spilled. After a few minutes, the screams and roars faded. The Blood Warrior marched back out of the temple, the blade of his goreaxe slathered in vampire blood.

The Bloodbound explored the ruins for more prey. They passed by the side of Neferata's tower, ignorant of the fact that a much greater predator observed their progress. Then the Blood Warrior shouted and pointed to the south. He had spotted the torchlight on the inner wall of Morbhend.

The warband rushed towards the gate, lured by the promise of greater bloodshed. Neferata climbed onto Nagadron's back and they rose into the dark, invisible as she followed the progress of the attack. The first part of the martyrdom of Morbhend was complete. The next stage would require that she play an active role.

The defenders of the reborn city greeted the Bloodbound with arrows and boiling oil. Khorne's followers shouted threats and ran at the gates as if they could break them down with hand-held weapons. The Blood Warrior was almost strong enough. The entire portcullis shook when he seized it. It held, though, and the defenders began to take their toll on the bloodreavers. Without siege engines, the Chaos warriors were not going to breach the wall.

Neferata smiled. 'Such puppets,' she murmured to Nagadron.

The Adevore made a low, whistling sound, a hiss made from the cries of the damned, expressing pleasure at her words. 'They have no choice in their roles. There is no question about their fates. They believe in their own wills, but only mine is real.'

The Blood Warrior marched away in disgust from the gate. He shouted at his followers.

'Now they will choose to retreat,' Neferata said to Nagadron. 'They think they will return to the main army and return with a larger force. They do not understand that this choice is closed to them. I do not have time for Ruhok to be distracted by a siege here. Morbhend should be no more than further incentive for him. So take us down. Finish them all.'

Nagadron plunged to the earth, his skeletal jaws parted to issue a roar that was fashioned from the cries of imprisoned souls. The Bloodbound froze, then looked up, in time to see Neferata unleash an arcane bolt from the tip of the Staff of Pain. The blast struck a bloodreaver in the chest. It blew him apart, his body vanishing into ash, and the flash of energy knocked the Blood Warrior off his feet.

Nagadron landed, his claws crushing two other bloodreavers, and he lunged forward to seize another in his maw. The Blood Warrior rose and, with a roar, charged at Neferata. She looked down at him with contempt, and raised her hand. At her signal, her hidden forces joined the fray.

Despite the weakness of her position in Nulahmia, she still had a large army to call upon. For this night, she had chosen the troops carefully. She needed obedience and silence in equal measure. The foot soldiers were skeletons, and the commanders were her most trusted spies. The vampires and skeletons emerged from their concealment in the ruins of Morbhend and swarmed towards the Chaos warband. The Blood Warrior stopped before he reached Nagadron. He snarled when he saw the wave of skeletons descending upon him on both sides. He charged into them with a roar, his goreaxe smashing the undead troops into pieces. Neferata smiled at the frustration she heard in his shouts. His enemy did not bleed, and were a poor offering to his god.

Neferata killed a few other bloodreavers with fiery spells. They were no more of an irritant than carrion flies. The end of the struggle was decided before it began. Neferata's forces overwhelmed the warband. The skeletons kept coming, relentless and seemingly infinite in number. The vampires circled around the Blood Warrior, moving like wind, attacking like serpents, and they wore him down. He cursed them, blood from a dozen wounds pouring down his limbs. At last, he cried, 'My blood for you, Khorne!' and fell to the ground with a crash.

Cheers resounded on the ramparts of the inner wall when the last of the Bloodbound died. Neferata's spies gathered beyond Nagadron, the skeletons forming up behind them. Neferata mounted the dread abyssal again and flew to the height of the ramparts. 'Open the gates,' she commanded.

Her subjects were loyal, and they obeyed their queen without hesitation. The portcullis rose.

The skeletons streamed in.

The shouts of celebration from the people of Morbhend became cries of confusion. The new Lady of Morbhend had run forward to greet the saviours of her city. She stopped, frozen. 'Wait!' she shouted, a command of nothing to no one. She held up her hands, as if there had been a misunderstanding, and her plea could stop what was about to happen.

Now her citizens cried in disbelief, then in terror, and then in despair. The skeletal army marched through the reborn city. Their slaughter was cold and implacable. Under the command of the vampires, they put the inhabitants to the sword and set fire to the rebuilt structures. Neferata brought Nagadron in low over the massacre, weaving between the flames, judging the quality of murder.

'More savage,' she commanded her spies. 'Tear the bodies apart. Flood the streets with blood. And cut the heads off.' She let Nagadron join in the feast, his talons and jaws rendering the bodies unrecognisable.

On the steps of the keep, a hundred people were on their knees, their arms raised in supplication to Neferata. 'What have we done?' they cried. 'Have pity on us, our queen! Let us redeem ourselves in your eyes!'

Neferata looked down at them, and shook her head at the weakness of their plea. 'It is fascinating to me that dreams of mercy live on in Shyish,' she told the cowering sheep. 'You have committed no crime. But I am your queen, your lives are mine, and I have need of them.' Then she turned Nagadron on them.

What the Bloodbound had failed to do, Neferata's forces did for them. Two of her spies dipped the hair of severed heads into currents of blood and splashed the symbol of Khorne onto the walls of gutted buildings. When the last of the screams faded, and the fires died down to smoking embers, Morbhend had died a second time. Neferata walked the streets with an artist's eye, evaluating the authenticity of the illusion she was creating here. The slaughter was well-wrought. Everywhere she looked, she saw the remains left by frenzy and butchery. And in the outer ruins, any searchers would find the bodies of some Khornate warriors, clearly the ones who had fallen in the early stages of the siege. Present too were Neferata's scouts. She, too, was experiencing losses as Ruhok drew closer.

By the end of her inspection, she found no flaws in the evidence she was leaving in Morbhend. The story that would be deduced, that would reach Venzor's ears, was clear.

Her spies gathered at the gate, which the skeletons had now demolished. The vampires waited for Neferata's verdict on their work. 'This was well done,' she told them. 'This will concentrate Lord Venzor's mind.'

A force that passed through Morbhend was on a direct path for the Hyena Gate. As Neferata flew back to Nulahmia, she was pleased with the narrative she had constructed. She thought it would hold. She hoped it would gain her some time.

The race between disasters was narrowing.

Do not be bound by the chains of intentions. The intention of an act is unimportant when compared to its consequences.

– Exhortations

TEN

AGE OF MYTH
THE SEASON OF LOSS

Neferata stood before the Borzhas palace and watched it burn.

'Why have we waited until now?' Raia had asked.

'I wanted the families to wonder about the fates of their commanders. I wanted all the rebels in Nulahmia to wonder what had happened. I have made uncertainty their poison. Let them worry about what I know. Let them look over their shoulders. Let them squirm and make mistakes.'

Only the mistakes had not happened.

'The rebels are still hidden to us,' Raia said, frustrated.

'That is instructive too,' Neferata said. 'They are well-disciplined. And perhaps Sethek and Borzhas acted on their own. They may have attacked when the rest of the traitors counselled caution and patience.'

The north tower of the palace became a torch, flames roaring up its entire height and reaching up into the dark and falling snow.

'We must change strategy,' Neferata said. 'If the battlefield is not what it appeared to be, I will not cling to an illusion.'

In the end, her goal was to shape the field to suit her, but she would adapt to each reality as it presented itself. She would always adapt. 'We shall end the patience of the rebels. We will push them again and again, harder and harder, until they can no longer hide.' The anger in the wake of the sacrifice at the Annihilation Gate had not even begun to fade when she finally sent justice upon the Houses of Sethek and Borzhas.

Neferata turned from the blaze. 'Come,' she said to Raia. 'I would see all the fires at once.'

The palaces of the traitors were magnificent constructions, and they were huge – among the largest at the base of Throne Mount. It took a full night for Neferata's guard to put their entire households to the sword. It took three nights before the flames that consumed the palaces finally dropped to embers. Neferata watched the conflagrations from her parapets, reaching out with her senses to smell the burning flesh, to taste the blood and the ash on the air, and to hear the screams of thousands. The extermination was total, down to the servants. If there were beggars on the doorsteps, they died too.

On the third night she went down to the ruins of the House of Sethek. She marched through the smoking stones and blackened timbers. Withered, scorched arms reached out from the rubble in entreaty. Every so often, Neferata passed arms that were still moving. She spotted a hand that bore the high rings of Sethek, and she crouched beside it. She cocked her head, listening, and heard a faint, despairing moan. With a few quick gestures, she tossed away the cracked slabs that covered the victim. Harkhaf, Sethek's consort, dragged himself forwards. His legs were a jellied mass, and the blaze had charred away his silk robes, turning his skin shining red and black. His hair had burned away, and his scalp was split and suppurating. His hands were contorted talons, and he reached for the soles of Neferata's boots, begging for mercy with a phlegmy moan.

Neferata ground a heel into his wrist, and the moan became a scream. 'Your arrogance amazes me,' she said. 'You conspire against me, and now you turn to me for succour.'

'Nnnnn... nnnnnuhhhh...' Harkhaf gasped.

'You would contradict me too? Sethek would burn in shame. She, at least, fought to the last.' She took a step away from Harkhaf. The ruined vampire coughed, and tried to speak, but he no longer had lips. 'What do you have to say to me? Promises? Truths? Lies?' She shook her head. 'I will not waste my time trying to decipher your final gasps. There are others who will do that.' She gestured to two of the palace guards. 'Take him to the Pathway of Punishment. Have someone listen to what he says while he is on the wheel.'

Harkhaf thrashed weakly as they came for him. His agony would soon be supplemented by torture. He made a palsied gesture at his heart, begging to be put to death.

Neferata only smiled at him, and kept walking.

At the centre of the ruin, where the fires had burned down into the cellars beneath the palace, she found Raia. 'I would think it a kindness,' the Mortarch said, 'if you have found information of value to make up for your failure in not anticipating the perfidy of these houses.'

Raia hung her head, stung by Neferata's words and her failure. She had been anxious since the assassination attempt, and Neferata was concerned that she was spending too much effort on the possibility of redemption rather than simply doing her duty.

'Do not forget that I have other kinds of spies,' Neferata said. 'Some of them are so deep in the shadows that to use them is to sacrifice them. They are a precious resource, and there is no certainty that, even in their positions, they know more than you do. But I will consume this resource if you cannot serve me as I want.'

'I will not fail you, my queen.'

'Show me that you will not. Begin with what you know.'

'We have found little,' Raia said. 'Even under torture, it seems most of the family was ignorant of the wider conspiracy. That knowledge must have perished with Sethek.' She pointed at the tunnels below. Smoke billowed out of their entrances. 'The conspirators meet beneath the surface of Nulahmia.'

'Of course they do. That hardly narrows the location down.'

'It does not,' Raia admitted. 'But it must be a point easily reachable by both houses. That will suggest some regions in which to look. I will take charge of the search myself.'

'Do so.' Neferata paused. 'Explain your failures,' she said. This was a test.

'The rebellion is widespread,' said Raia. 'There are too many rumours to follow, and too many lead down unimportant avenues, to people who know little or nothing. We know our assassinations have had some effect. So did the sacrifice you performed, my queen. But the beast has many heads.'

'How many of the families do you think are now involved?'

'Of the vampire nobility, it is hard to say. I believe a majority of the families are still loyal to you.'

For the time being, Neferata thought. *If they see the wind blowing against me, their allegiances will shift*. There were very few she would trust, though there were more that she knew she could control.

'As for the mortal families,' Raia said, 'it is possible that they are *all* involved.'

'If they are, they will learn that they do not yet know what it is to truly fear me.'

'They will have earned that lesson, my queen.'

Neferata thought for a moment. 'What have you heard about the Hellezans?' she asked.

'Very little. Nothing since the thrall returned to his family. Is he not providing the information you require? Shall I dispatch a spy to that house?'

'No,' said Neferata. 'Leave that house to me. Tell me where you think we stand overall.'

'With regards to the wider conspiracy, decapitation will not be possible,' Raia said. 'Only extermination. For that, we need the rebellion to be in the open.'

'Granted,' Neferata said, still testing. 'And are we nearly there?'

Raia waved a hand to take in the smoking ruins. 'This kind of pressure will push them out of the shadows, or in the end, that is where they will die. It sends a warning, but it also breeds converts to the cause. Our task is to push them into the open before they are ready.'

'Then what must we do to ensure that result?'

'We must strike them where they feel safe. Even if we know we cannot find all their leaders, they must believe we can. So we must find their meeting places. We must make them desperate.'

Neferata nodded. Raia was thinking clearly. She had not tried to minimise the situation, and she saw what needed to be done. She had proved her usefulness, and so avoided execution. If Raia knew how close she had come to her doom, she did not show it. She demonstrated only her determination to serve her queen, which was as it should be.

'Go, then,' Neferata said, looking into the tunnels. 'Find them and make them panic.'

* * *

'You said we were about to act,' Hasynne Nastannar said to Mathas, 'and we have not. How many more will Neferata slaughter before we do?'

The meeting in the underground chamber was far more tense than the last one. Mathas could smell the desperation in the air.

'Sethek and Borzhas were too impatient,' Mathas said. 'Now they and their families have paid for their hurry and set us back.'

Hasynne growled, then she turned on Jedefor. 'And they were killed by you!'

The captain of the guard shrugged. 'Of course they were,' he said. 'I said I would not lead this rebellion. I most certainly am not going to openly defy Neferata while she still reigns.'

'Do not mistake his alliance for belief in our cause,' Mathas said to Hasynne.

Jedefor's smile was cold. 'That would indeed be foolish,' he said. 'But I see your strength, and it will get me what I want.'

'I am satisfied,' Mathas said before Hasynne could retort. To the others, he said, 'We are not defeated. By her actions, Neferata has driven more families to our banner.' There were missing faces in the chamber this evening, but there were new ones as well. He turned to Lestor. 'You promised us support from your master. When is it coming?'

'Very soon,' Lestor said, unconcerned by the anxiety in the chamber.

'It had better be,' said Hasynne.

Mathas agreed. *Anything less than* immediately *is risking disaster*, he thought. The sacrifice at the Annihilation Gate and the destruction of the Houses of Sethek and Borzhas felt like the beginnings of a purge. It was important that he remain calm and lead by example, but Hasynne was not far wrong. If they did not act soon, they might not be able to act at all. But Neferata was still strong. With the reinforcements that Lestor promised, they would be very close to being able to confront her.

'What are we to do then?' Hasynne asked. 'Have we gathered merely to talk again?'

'No,' said Mathas. She was right. One way or another, the moment of truth was close, and it was time to prepare.

There was a map of Nulahmia on the table in the centre of the chamber. He opened the large scroll. He studied it for the hundredth time, looking for the error in his plans. But the strategy remained firm in his mind. For all the doubts he was wrestling with, the plan of attack was one of his few certainties. He saw what must be done with such clarity, it felt like prophecy. 'Get your forces ready. When we strike, we will have to take the Queensroad.'

'Which is what will be expected,' said Jedefor.

'Of course, but there is no other way for an armed force to reach the palace, is there?'

'No,' Jedefor admitted.

'Can you slow down the response of the guard?'

'To an extent, yes.'

'That will be sufficient,' Mathas said. 'Even a small delay should buy us the time we need.'

'You're very confident,' said Hasynne.

'I am.' He had to be. That was part of the role he had accepted. He had as many doubts as any of them about their success. But Neferata had been weakened. She was lashing out, and though she had inflicted losses on the rebellion, they were not targeted ones. They were luck. So there *was* a chance of success. More than that, the need to fight back was imperative. The tyrant must be toppled, and now was the moment of possibility.

He had his doubts, but he had his certainties too. Victory *was* possible.

'The cave is ready, is it not?' he said. The massive natural formation lay several levels below the meeting chamber. Hasynne's guards had kept it under constant watch for months, and no one had gone through it.

'It is ready,' Hasynne confirmed. 'The tunnels between it and the houses are complete. Our forces may gather there at any time.'

'Good,' said Mathas. 'Now look at the map. Imagine our houses as ramparts. See how we come close to forming a line that can choke off the Queensroad at the near approach to Throne Mount. Once we march at full strength, we could be on the slopes very quickly. But I think we do not need to take that route.'

'I don't understand,' said Jedefor.

'Neferata will expect us to try to storm the palace.'

'Aren't you?'

'No. We take the city instead. We hold the Queensroad. We lay siege to Throne Mount. We force her to come to us. While your guard wastes time mounting defences that we will not challenge, we consolidate our positions below and spread the uprising.'

Jedefor grinned. 'And thus my loyalty is both unquestioned and useless. Our delay in descending will be considerable.'

Mathas looked around the chamber. The atmosphere had changed. There was eagerness now, and hope. They were on the edge of transforming Nulahmia.

'What about the keep?' Teyosa asked. The guard stronghold sat in the centre of the Palace Quarter. 'Do we have the strength to take it?'

'We will if that help arrives,' said Mathas. He gave Lestor a significant look.

'Be assured,' Lestor said. 'They will.'

'I will feel assured when they arrive on time,' Mathas said. 'We do not have the luxury to wait much longer.'

'Your patience will be rewarded,' said Lestor, his unconcern palpable and enraging.

'We no longer have patience,' Mathas told him. 'There is no space for it any longer. We...' He stopped. The back of his neck was suddenly tense. His skin prickled with unease. He had heard nothing, but he was ready to lash out. There was an enemy present, and he knew this with the same clarity with which he had visualised the plan of attack. He forced himself to speak again. 'We need to know *when* the support will arrive,' he said, and signalled to Lestor to keep talking.

The other vampire nodded. 'My master has not given me those details,' he said. 'It is not my place to ask. And the gifts of goodwill he has already given you were squandered by that premature ambush.'

Lestor went on, equivocating arrogantly and saying nothing at great length. Mathas held up a finger, warning the others not to question him as he turned away from the table and padded towards the doorway behind him. Teyosa looked at him in alarm. He gestured to her and to the other mortals to move to the back of the chamber.

He eyed the tunnel beyond the doorway. If they were being observed, then he was already at a disadvantage. If the intruder was only listening, he might have surprise on his side. He could see no one. His new sight pierced the shadows, down to the point where the tunnel curved. The passage was empty. *If I cannot see you,* he thought, *you cannot see into the chamber. I hope.*

He drew his sword silently from its scabbard.

The doorway was arched, which meant there was one place where an intruder could be close enough to hear every word and still be hidden. Mathas grasped the hilt with both hands and raised the blade. Then he lunged through the doorway and struck up at the low ceiling.

The spy was clinging like a spider to the roof of the tunnel. Mathas had seen her before at the Palace of Seven Vultures, always standing close to Neferata and whispering to her. It was Raia, and in the moment of Mathas' attack, he realised that if he did not strike true, then it would not matter when the help from Lestor's master arrived. The rebellion would end now.

Fate smiled. He stabbed Raia through the chest before she could react.

Raia shrieked. She dropped from the ceiling and rode the blade down. It protruded from her back as she grabbed Mathas' neck with her claws. She sank them into his flesh, and his blood poured down his chest to mix with hers. They were trapped with each other now. Her claws plunged deeper. Tendons tore, and Mathas started to choke before he forced himself to remember he did not need to breathe. The tip of a claw scraped against bone, and in another few moments, she would be able to snap his head off. He twisted his blade and sawed to the right, fighting to reach her heart.

'*Traitor*,' Raia hissed, spraying dark gore in his face. '*You will all burn*.'

'The tyrant failed with me,' Mathas grunted, the words liquid as his mouth filled with his blood. 'Now she will fall.'

Raia's lips pulled back in a feral snarl. Her hands began to curl deep inside and tear at Mathas' flesh. His physical being teetered on the brink of dissolution. He wrenched the sword desperately, and Raia stiffened. The blaze in her eyes dimmed, went dark. Her arms went slack, and her legs gave way. Mathas lowered her to the ground and released his sword. Carefully, he pulled her talons free from his throat. His blood was still pouring from his wounds and his mouth, and he felt a terrible looseness in his neck. He crouched and fed from her river of blood flowing from her severed heart. The vintage was rich with age and experience, and as he drank, his wounds began to close. This was blood stronger than any he had tasted before. His senses exulted. Savage, intoxicating pleasure roared through his veins.

A hand touched his shoulder, and he whirled, snarling, teeth bared to tear the throat from the rival who would dare drink from his kill.

Teyosa staggered back, eyes wide.

Her terror broke the feral spell. It stabbed into him, soul-deep pain much stronger than any murderous pleasure.

He rose from Raia's corpse, swaying and reached out to Teyosa. 'Do not fear me,' he pleaded. 'Don't ever fear me.' He stayed where he was, his hand open and waiting.

Teyosa met his eyes, and she came forward again. She clasped his hand. He pulled her gently to him, embracing her with one arm, protecting her and at the same time leaning on her for the strength of her love.

He turned to the others as they crowded in the doorway. Still dizzy from the power of Raia's blood, he pulled his sword free. He had killed a much older, more powerful vampire. It had taken luck to give him this victory. Yet the victory was real.

'You see?' he rasped. He could barely croak out the words. 'We can win. And we will.'

'Do you know who that is?' Jedefor asked, eyes wide.

'I do.' With Teyosa's help, Mathas took a step towards Lestor. 'There is no more time,' he said. 'We need your master's aid. *Now*.'

'You aren't returning to the court tonight,' Teyosa said. 'You can't. Not after this. She will know.'

'I must,' Mathas told her. 'She may not find out. But if I don't return, she will.' He paused, already anxious at the thought of being absent from his family. 'Be ready to take Kasten into the tunnels,' he said. 'The passages can be reached by a door hidden in the wine cellar.'

'We won't be safe here either.'

'But you will have hope.'

That night, Mathas took his place among the other vampire nobles. He composed his face into a mask of attentive humility whenever Neferata spoke, a thrall awaiting the pleasure of his mistress. He hoped Neferata would not look too closely at him. He hoped she would not perceive his thoughts of Raia's dust scattered through the tunnels.

There were few revels in the Palace of Seven Vultures any longer. Neferata's anger pervaded the halls, and Mathas took that fury as a good omen, another sign of her growing weakness. The light from the torches seemed dimmer, as if the fire itself were clotted with resentment and corrupted blood. Dark smoke coiled around the pillars of the hall and gathered, sullen, under the ceiling like a lowering cloud. There were no musicians, and no dances. In their place were terse whispers and the whine of complaints. The Mortarch of Blood still provided the court with fine mortal victims on which to feed, but the events seemed more like executions than celebrations. Over the course of the last several nights, Mathas had found himself looking carefully into the faces of his prey before he fed, increasingly worried that he might see someone familiar.

He watched the other nobles, too, careful not to hold the eye of fellow conspirators too long. The faces that interested him were the ones who were not part of the rebellion, but looked so unhappy they might well take part when the uprising began.

'Why are you displeased?' he overheard Lord Vasyth ask

Lady Casein. 'You ascended to control of your house thanks to that slaughter.'

'We are as decimated as you are,' Casein hissed back. 'Control means nothing if there is nothing left to control.'

Neferata presided over harsh sessions where the encounters with her courtiers threatened to draw blood through words alone. The nobility was becoming less obsequious and more demanding. The queen was becoming less willing to grant favours, and more savage in her denials. In the great hall, beneath the smell of incense and spilled blood, the air reeked of conflict and hate. With a spark, the atmosphere would combust into war.

The stars were aligning. An uprising was inevitable. All Mathas asked was that he be able to choose the moment when the spark was applied.

He hung back, keeping to the rear of the hall, saying nothing and requesting nothing from Neferata, doing everything he could to avoid her attention.

Casein reached the front of the line of supplicants. 'You have weakened us,' she said, paused, and then added, with bitter pretence of respect, '*my queen*.' Her hands were clenched in anger. 'Yet your tithes are unchanged. We cannot sustain them. We seek compensation… my queen. We seek justice.'

Neferata rose from her divan. She strode to the edge of the dais and glared at Casein, then at the entire court. Weakened she might be, Mathas thought, but she was still terrible in her anger. Majesty wrapped around her like a cape and thundercloud. Her eyes burned with deep, volcanic fire. 'You tire me with your needs,' Neferata declared, her words a hissing serpent. 'You would feed from my very veins if I let you. Your greed and your vanity would devour Nulahmia. I will not let them. Begone from my sight. I will see true fealty, or I will see no one.'

The courtiers pulled back from the dais as if burned and

filed out of the great hall. Mathas moved with them. The ragged ceremony was done.

Then Neferata called out to him.

'Mathas of House Hellezan, you will remain.'

He froze where he stood. With an effort, he forced himself to turn around. He stared across the empty space of the hall's floor to the dark figure of Neferata.

'Stand before me,' she ordered.

He obeyed. As he walked towards her slowly, feeling the pressure of her glare, the doubts returned. He wondered how he could think to challenge this being in whom beauty and command and death were fused.

Mathas reached the edge of the dais and stopped. He looked up into a cold, merciless mask.

'I hear little of your family,' said Neferata.

Mathas forced the tremor from his voice before speaking. 'There is little to hear, my queen,' he said.

'Isn't there? That is, I must say, a pleasant change from the chattering vermin that assail me in my palace. And how well do you feed?'

'Very well.'

'Your wife and child, were they succulent?'

His face turned numb with fear. He grunted, unable to answer. He could not lie. She would know. She must realise they were still alive. The question was a trap, and there was no way out. 'I...' he said, and trailed off.

Neferata smiled, showing her perfect fangs and perfect cruelty. 'You don't know? No matter. I'm sure someone else knows the answer now.'

Mathas stared, trying to pierce through the pounding clouds of horror in his head to make sense of her words, and then trying to deny their meaning.

Neferata waited, her smile sinking its venom into his veins. Then he turned and ran.

Guards closed in from the sides, but Neferata stopped them. 'Let him go,' she said. 'Run, Mathas! Run to your house of traitors! Did you think you could hide your perfidy from me? Did you think I did not see your pretence? Did you think I would let Raia's death go unpunished? You are a fool. Go now, and learn. Go, and burn.'

Mathas burst from the main doors of the Palace of Seven Vultures. He pounded down the Path of Punishment, and the martyrs to Neferata's will were a blur in the corner of his eyes. The wind of his flight blew his hair back. He barely saw where he was going. A howl rose from his chest. It caught in his throat, then squeezed out of his jaws, so huge it emerged as a long, constricted whine.

As he ran, he sought hope, and found none. The fact that she had not succeeded in making him her thrall now seemed nothing more than an extra layer of cruelty. Part of him wondered how much Neferata knew, but that part was drowned in the incoherent grief and terror of the rest. He could not think. He could not plan. He could only run, and run, and run, and try to free the scream that grew larger and larger as he drew closer to the Hellezan Palace.

He smelled the smoke before he saw it. It billowed up over the roofs of Nulahmia, rising to greet the dark of the night, spreading its annunciation of doom, the crimson glow of flame pulsing from beneath. Mathas drew his sword as he flew down the final streets before his home. He was ready to fight and kill and die for his family. *Jedefor*, he thought. *I curse your name, you coward.* He had no doubt the captain had led the attack on the Hellezans without hesitation, unwilling to take any risk until the battle was already met and decided.

Mathas rounded the last corner. House Hellezan was before him, a black shell of walls containing a maelstrom of fire. If it had been Jedefor's guards who had turned the palace into a torch, they were gone now. The streets were empty even of onlookers. No one wished to draw the Mortarch's attention their way. Mathas stumbled forward, his sword raised in desperate anger, but he was alone.

Fire billowed out of the shattered doors. It spun in furious cyclones from the windows. The dull, suffocating roar of the conflagration filled Mathas' ears. It was the cracking, rumbling thunder of the death of his family. Centuries of honour burned. Nulahmia might belong to Neferata. It was her creation. But the Hellezans had been part of it too. They had built a history and a tradition. They had placed their mark upon the city. They had helped shape it and its story, and surely what they had done was theirs to own and take pride in. Neferata was not a god. Some aspects of what made Nulahmia must be the work of its citizens.

Something must belong to them. Something must belong to a family that had stood proud and unbowed in this land of death, holding the line for an ideal of decency when decadence and cruelty flowed through the very air and ran in blood through the drains.

All gone now. History annihilated, symbols and flesh turned to fire and black smoke.

The walls trembled with the force of the firestorm. Mortar crumbled, and a portion of the upper wall collapsed inwards. No mortal could still be alive in the palace. Mathas knew that. Any who would not have been put to the sword would have burned alive. Yet he ran through the doorway, into the holocaust. He had no choice. It was the only action left to him.

'Teyosa!' he cried out in the great hall. He could not hear himself over the fury of the blaze, but he kept calling for his wife. The tapestries were curtains of flame, waving in the wind of destruction. Fire writhed and coiled along the ceiling, twisting into spectral shapes that mimicked the pain of dying souls.

Mathas staggered towards the stairs. 'Teyosa!' His cape caught fire and he tore it from his shoulders. His skin curled and cracked in the heat. He would already be dead if he were still mortal, and the violence of the firestorm could still destroy him.

A wall of smoking rubble crashed onto the stairway before he could reach it. The barrier stopped Mathas and jolted him back to rational thought. He had been racing on the wings of instinct, about to run upstairs to his and Teyosa's chamber. She would not be there. If there was any chance she and their son had survived, it would be down below, in the deep tunnels, far from the palace.

He turned to the cellar doors. They too were smashed. Fire and smoke roared out to meet him. He hurled himself into the choking, flickering darkness. 'Teyosa!' He took the steps three at a time. He did not fall. He cut through the howl of the fire with preternatural grace. He dropped through the cellars and vaults of the Hellezan Palace. Flaming timbers fell before him, and he battered them from his path. On all sides, the wreckage of his family's history blazed. Corpses lay under smashed shelves and overturned chests, and sprawled in his path. Their throats were cut. Their limbs were dismembered. They were eviscerated, decapitated. Every outrage of mutilation had been visited on their bodies by the command of the Mortarch of Blood. They were burned black, and beyond recognition to mortal sight.

But Mathas knew who they were. He smelled the nature of their blood through the smoke. His witchsight caught the residual agonies of their spirits still convulsing over them. Every corpse he passed, no matter how quickly, was a new stab of grief.

But none of the dead were Teyosa. None of them were Kasten.

There was too much horror for hope, and too much urgency for despair. Mathas ran faster yet. The fire was consuming even the deepest foundations of the palace, and it was here that he found Verrick and Glanath. His parents had died together, their mutilations fusing their corpses, and there was no telling one severed finger or fleshless skull from another.

And still he knew who they were. Their rings had not melted. His father's blackened seal of office hung from his charred neck.

Mathas stood over the bodies, his lungs raw from smoke, his throat tight with grief, his limbs trembling with rage. He tried to give voice to his horror. If he screamed loud enough, perhaps he would banish the reality before him. '*Nnnnnnn*,' he groaned. His teeth clenched tight, and his denial became an animal keening. '*Nnnnnnnnnnnn...*'

His parents had fallen in the centre of a corridor in the foundations. The hall led to the tunnels running under the palace, but not the important ones. Mathas entered the wine cellar, and gave a sob of relief when he found the entrance to the rebels' network untouched. The cellar burned, but the mechanism that opened the stone door was not damaged. Perhaps, in a final act of defiance, his parents had misled their killers. Perhaps they had saved Teyosa and Kasten.

Don't hope. Don't you dare hope. Look for them. Find them. But don't succumb to hope. It seeks to destroy us on this day.

Mathas closed the door, and he shut the fire away behind him. There was smoke in the tunnels, but much less. He ran through the maze, into a darkness that was ever cleaner, shouting his wife's name. He made for the meeting chamber, the floor outside its threshold dark with Raia's blood. Just before he reached it, he foolishly let himself think that perhaps, perhaps, Teyosa had found refuge there.

There was no one in the chamber.

Now there were no further destinations. Mathas had nowhere to reach, no sanctuary he could think of. There was nothing left to do except run, and run, fleeing the despair that at last closed in, its black pinions sweeping to embrace him.

'Teyosa!' he screamed. '*Teyosa!*'

Saaah-saaah-saaah! the echoes mocked.

He ran and shrieked until he no longer knew where he was, and his voice was hoarse. He sank to his knees. 'Teyosa,' he whispered, and the only answer was the susurrus of his pain rasping against stone walls.

Mathas hung his head, limp with despair. It was over. Some of the other families might still be committed to the uprising, but the battle would happen without him. Neferata had destroyed the Hellezans before they had begun to fight. He was spent. He thought that maybe, just maybe, he could will himself into nothingness right here.

Distantly, he heard the sound of marching feet. The palace guard, he thought. The coward Jedefor leading a sweep to finish his bloody work. Very well, then. He would accept his execution and be thankful for it.

As the boot steps drew closer, he realised he was mistaken. The marchers were approaching from the west, away from the palace. And there were many of them. Many more, he thought, than would have been necessary for the raid on his house.

He blinked, and rose slowly. He stood in the centre of the wide tunnel, waiting to face the arrivals.

Closer yet, he could hear the clanking of heavy armour and the grinding drag of heavy masses being pulled along the floor. Barely aware that he was doing so, Mathas tightened his grip on his sword. Deep in his soul, an ember glowed, and he was ready to fight one last time.

Lestor emerged from the gloom ahead. Behind him marched a seemingly endless column of vampires and skeletons. Their armour was dark, and shorn of all insignia. They were an anonymous army. There was no way to tell what master they served.

Lestor had drawn his sword, but put it away when he recognised Mathas. His smile of greeting faded when he met Mathas' eyes. 'Is all well?' he asked.

'It is not,' said Mathas. 'Neferata has destroyed us.'

Lestor bowed, acknowledging Mathas' grief. 'Am I too late, then? Have the other houses fallen as well?'

'No,' Mathas said. 'The others are not burning.'

'Then they have something to lose. Their leader must not.'

Mathas stared at Lestor. 'If you mean to say the murder of my family is a boon…' he snarled, and took a threatening step forward.

'I do not,' Lestor said. 'But fate has chosen you, Mathas Hellezan, and fate is rarely kind. You were preeminent in the rebellion. Now your command will be unchallenged. And you will lead with such fury the enemy will burn before your gaze.'

Mathas felt the brutal truth of Lestor's words. He thought about his wife and son. There were not even any bodies over which he could mourn. He had only his last memories of them to fan the embers of his soul, and ignite the ruins of his heart. Energy surged through his veins. Grief transmuted to anger, anger to strength. He was not done. He was not finished.

He looked at the army stretching into the gloom behind Lestor, and he was ready. He was ready to bring down a queen.

The anger of my enemy is to my advantage. I must be wary of mine serving my foe in turn.

– War and the Passions

ELEVEN

AGE OF SIGMAR
THE SEASON OF CREMATORY

Dessina at his side, Venzor strode through the Palace of Seven Vultures, seeking its shadow queen. He had sent word to her household that he wished to speak to her, but she had not appeared in his chamber. In frustration, he had left his throne to find her himself.

Though he marched past many of his underlings, the halls felt empty. At the same time, the air seemed thick, as if he were having to push his way through curtains of cobwebs. He caught himself several times about to raise his hands to part the invisible threads.

'Where is she?' he snarled.

'Spinning her web,' Dessina answered, as if she had read his thoughts.

'You feel its presence too,' he said.

'It is her nature to weave it. It is always there, Lord Venzor. It would be a mistake to think any of us are ever free of it.'

'I am not blind,' Venzor snapped. Arkhan had warned him about Neferata's skills, and he was not going to be lectured by a subordinate. 'I know that I have been at war with the Mortarch since I arrived in Nulahmia.' What he would not admit was that this was a war where he had difficulty perceiving even his own moves. The critical point was closing in. He had ceased any political activity not directly connected with the defence of the city against the Bloodbound. 'Somehow, she plans to use the coming siege to her advantage. I will prevent her.'

Pride demanded that he confront her, and show her he was not going to be her fool.

Yet when he found her, he flushed with humiliation. After more than an hour of searching, on the verge of giving up, he looked once more in the throne room.

Neferata was there, seated on the great chair of bones coated in black iron. Clad in black, she was perched on the edge of the seat, a predator on the verge of pouncing, but also a statue of infinite and dark patience. She smiled at Venzor. No doubt she had been expecting him, he thought.

'Leave me,' he snapped at Dessina, wounded pride festering. He composed his features and advanced to the throne.

'You were looking for me?' Neferata asked.

'I was.'

'You have come to discuss our plans for the defence of the city?'

Venzor shook his head. 'No. I am taking measures, and I will not seek your counsel.'

Neferata cocked her head. 'Then why are you here?'

'To tell you that I know your hand is at work behind the Chaos threat.'

Neferata laughed. 'How will Ruhok's conquest serve me? Do you think I plan to rule at his side? Do you think he plans to leave a single stone of Nulahmia standing?'

Venzor held on to his temper. 'It is enough for me to know

the attack will benefit you, even if I do not know how,' he lied. 'I will defend the city. I will defeat Ruhok. And I will defeat you.'

'If I said that you were fighting on a front where there are no enemies, would you believe me?'

'I would not,' said Venzor. The response felt weak in the face of that knowing smile, but it was the best he could muster. He turned on his heel and left the throne room with what dignity he had left.

He returned to the private chamber he had claimed for himself. Maps of Nulahmia lay on the huge oak table in the centre. He had been studying them obsessively ever since Neferata had come to warn him of Lord Ruhok's approach. He came back to them now, running a finger over the contours of the walls, searching for weaknesses in the defences, and trying to pry out the secret that could do him harm.

Neferata's smile slipped as soon as Venzor was out of sight. Torturing his pride had given her pleasure, and filling him with doubts was useful. It was good that he seemed uncertain. But the fact remained that he was strong enough to counter her. Venzor was more of a threat to her than he knew.

From a shadow in the Palace, she became a shadow in the skies. Mounted on Nagadron, wreathed by mists of darkness, she flew over Nulahmia. She combed the city with her witch-sight. She listened to the blood running through its veins. She pierced its secrets. And she flew north. North over a city that was no longer hers.

Along the southern border of Venzor's area of control, she saw lines of torchlight. Neferata's hands clenched in anger. Venzor was erecting barriers, sealing off the north from the rest of Nulahmia. Even the Throne Mount would be cut off once he was done. Barricades of wood and stone twenty feet high filled the streets. The houses along the line of the new wall had been emptied. Some of them were smouldering shells, their interiors burned and collapsed so they were an inert, impassable mass. Lanterns shone in the windows of others, where Venzor had stationed troops. Two of the broad avenues were still open. Through them poured the fearful of the south. Neferata flew low over them, glaring at the wretches with hate. They were all from the nobility of Nulahmia. She saw no one from the lower classes of the city, except the servants of fleeing households. Either the less fortunate had been turned away, or they still feared Neferata enough to know better than to make the attempt.

The faithless travelled from the south to the north in ragged caravans of wealth. Servants and horses pulled wagons overladen with gold, jewels, art, furniture, clothing and tapestries. The nobles sensed the coming of war, and they were trying to save their existence and their positions at the same time.

Neferata circled over them, her anger growing. She raised her head, looking away from the worms, seeking counsel with the darkness above.

Think about what you know you are about to do, she told herself. She worked to detach herself from the scene below, from the humming and whining of Nulahmia's blood and fears. She sought to read the currents of power. This was, in the end, why she had taken to the skies. *Remember what must be accomplished*, she thought.

I remember. And I will do this thing, too. There is no contradiction. There is no error. This will change nothing. The disposition of the forces is set.

The river of power was growing turbulent. She still believed she could ride the turbulence to her victory.

Is this reason or rationalising?

It does not matter. I accept the consequences.

She dispelled the concealing mist, and brought Nagadron down to land on the vast heap of rubble that would soon be moved to block the width of the Bloodway. Already the avenue was half its normal span. Venzor's troops were shepherding the refugees through the passage between the rubble.

Nagadron landed with a splintering crunch as his claws shattered stone. Soldiers and aristocrats turned in alarm. Neferata descended from the Adevore and walked slowly down the slope of the rubble. The citizens on the avenue winced at every step that brought her closer to them.

'You are cowards,' she said. She spoke softly, and she spoke so every soul in her sight heard her voice, and felt its hiss sink into their bones. 'You are ungrateful.'

One of the vampires dropped to his knees in a practised show of obedience. His robes spread out around him in a flourish. 'My queen,' he said. 'We wish for nothing but your eternal reign.'

'Do you? How kind.' She reached the bottom of the wreckage and walked over to the noble. People rushed to clear the way for her, stumbling into each other and against their wagons. Horses whinnied and bucked, their eyes rolling in terror at her presence. 'Tell me, Lord Bessein,' she said, standing over the kneeling vampire, 'why are you so quick to mention my throne?'

Bessein coughed, his smooth obsequiousness slipping away from him. 'I meant... That is... I did not presume to suggest...'

'Fear drives you,' Neferata said. 'It has brought you here. It speaks through you now. It defines you, and its stench is repugnant.' She turned around, catching hundreds in the scythe of her gaze. Venzor's warriors stood by uneasily, knowing better than to move against her. 'Fear drives all of you,' she said. 'Our city has suffered greatly.' She tempered the anger for a moment, yet made her pretence of understanding so transparent that many of the wretches, Bessein among them, began to whimper. 'Nulahmia will soon suffer again. Awareness of this truth will bring fear to the craven. This is the nature of things. Not all subjects are warriors. Nor do I expect them to be.'

She turned back to Bessein. He fell silent.

I will punish later, she thought. *And I will punish now.*

'Your fears are misplaced, Lord Bessein. You have forgotten how much you must fear me. This I cannot forgive, and must correct.'

Bessein's eyes widened. 'Please,' he said, and began to rise from his kneel.

Neferata whipped the Dagger of Jet from its sheath and plunged it through Bessein's neck. She lifted the choking vampire until his feet left the ground. He tried to pull Akmet-har from his neck, but his strength was fleeing, his energy pouring down the blade and into Neferata. His flesh contracted on his skull, withering and turning grey, pulling back from his fangs, thinning into tearing parchment. His struggles grew weaker, but the pain in his eyes did not diminish. He dangled from the blade, a whimper of agony bubbling up from his throat.

Neferata looked around. 'Lord Bessein has remembered to fear me. What of the rest of you?'

'Mercy, great queen!' nobles wailed, on their knees. 'We are loyal! We have been misled!' Others turned to run. Venzor's warriors, seeing what must surely come next, were pulling back, putting space between themselves and the passage to the north. There was nothing they could do here, and they saw no reason to let themselves be destroyed pointlessly. Neferata pulled back on the reins of her anger, marking a limit to her actions. She would not force Venzor into open war.

She waited, drinking in the screams around her. At the edges of the crowd, to the north and south, people were fleeing, carrying their renewed fear like a virus. Bessein trembled weakly, his pain still rich as his body contracted in on itself.

'Do you fear me?' Neferata asked. With a sharp flick of her wrist, she cut through the right half of Bessein's neck. His head flopped to one side, and he dropped to the ground. Already, his body was beginning to crumble to dust.

'We fear you!' the nobles cried. 'We fear you!'

'Not enough,' Neferata said, and at her signal, Nagadron the Adevore craned his neck down and opened his jaws wide. He breathed a fog of terrible dissolution on the crowd. Spectral green, it screamed with the voices of shattered souls. Vampires and mortals alike screamed back as their bones shed their flesh, and a pain beyond the corporeal tore through their beings. The street filled with the roiling light of rot and pain. Neferata strode through it, slicing throats and tearing heads from their bodies, consuming blood with savage contempt. 'To the living and to the undead I bring death,' she pronounced, her voice an echoing toll of doom. 'Death is no mercy, because I am a stranger to mercy. Death is merely the beginning of your unending suffering.'

Nagadron inhaled. The Adevore had no lungs, and he did not breathe, but he inhaled. A devouring wind howled up from the street, and with it new souls flowed, shrieking, into the dread abyssal's maw. He gathered new prisoners into torment, new screams into the cage of his body. He snarled, the glow of death blazing from his core.

Neferata stood in the centre of the Bloodway, surrounded by twisted, broken corpses. Blood washed against the heels of her boots. Screams of terror came from the north and south. The nobles who had managed to move beyond the scope of her massacre were fleeing further into what they hoped would be Venzor's protection. The ones to the south were cowering back, though she knew they would rush forward as soon as she left. She had given them new cause to fear, but it would not be enough to stop them. They still believed the south of Nulahmia would fall.

'It is accomplished,' she whispered, the flush of rage leaving her.

The satisfaction of punishment was a reward, and she would savour its taste for some hours to come. Her anger at the disloyal nobles was real, but the slaughter had served a larger purpose.

Venzor, do you see how weak I am? Do you see how I lash out to no purpose? Give me the gift of your contempt.

She returned to Nagadron and soared upwards. The site of the butchery dropped away, and with it the wails of the frightened. Neferata took Nagadron higher and higher, until all of Nulahmia was spread out below her. She reached out, the span of her fingers encompassing her city. *Mine*, she thought. *Now and forever. Mine.*

She looked to the north-west, and the night was burning. Flame and brass and blood was a day's march away.

Catastrophe was coming to storm the gates.

Knowing that the storm must come, I may choose to summon it. But because a crisis can be called into being, that does not mean it can be controlled.

– *On the Crucible of Disaster*

TWELVE

AGE OF MYTH
THE SEASON OF LOSS

'She has doomed herself,' said Hasynne.

'Yes,' said Mathas. 'Yes, she has.' Hasynne was speaking the simple truth. In the cavern that had awaited them, the rebels had gathered at last; Mathas was surrounded by strength, and the fire of vengeance burned in his blood. The Mortarch of Blood must fall. Fate could not judge otherwise.

The hour had come, and the army of liberation had come together with such speed that a surge of satisfaction and anticipation cut through the walls of Mathas' grief. 'She has galvanised us,' he said. 'She believes she has killed my family. In truth, she has killed herself.'

'The rest of us are not prepared to wait for her to decide when it is our turn on the executioner's block,' Hasynne said. 'I do not think she intended it, but she struck the first blow of the war when she attacked your house.' She paused for a moment, then said, 'Jedefor has sent word that he is ready too.'

'Jedefor,' Mathas repeated, his voice flat.

'If he led the attack, he had no choice,' Hasynne reminded him. 'I believe he is still loyal to us.'

'To us?'

She shrugged. 'Then to the promise of power. It has a powerful hold on him.'

Mathas grimaced, then nodded. With or without Jedefor, they were ready. 'The time of hiding is over,' he said. The warriors of a score of noble houses were assembled in the cavern. Their armour shone in the torchlight. Standard bearers held banners aloft. The colours hung motionless in the still air, barely visible in the gloom, but their presence was a brilliant shout of pride. Mathas smiled. 'This is our fist of defiance,' he said. 'Our sword to slay a tyrant. Once it reaches the surface, it will be a clarion call to all who would be freed from the yoke of their fealty to Neferata.'

'You are faring well, I see,' Hasynne said.

Mathas thought before answering. 'Yes,' he said. He nodded. 'I am well.' He pulled his lips back over his fangs. 'And I am ready.' His family was gone. There were no Hellezans for him to lead into the fray. Instead, he was at the head of an entire army. His heart was in agony, but his soul blazed with power. He could, he thought, break the foundations of Nulahmia with his bare hands. He was fire. He was wrath.

He was vengeance.

'We are ready,' Hasynne said. 'All of us are.'

'Then let us begin.' Mathas raised his sword, and the echoing din of voices and armour faded. 'You are the great families of Nulahmia,' he shouted. 'And you have never been as great as you are this night. Because this is the hour when we declare that this city is *not* the work of a single being. And we are not her property. We are this city!' A strange conviction took him, and he spoke the next sentence in full passion, before he could have second thoughts. '*We are its life!*'

'Life!' Lestor exclaimed in surprise. 'A strange boast in Shyish!' Yet he sounded curious in spite of himself.

Mathas wondered what had pushed him to speak those words. He felt as if he was tempting the anger of Nagash himself. He saw the irony in making that claim now, when life was no longer his. But the god of death did not strike him down. And he knew he was speaking the truth. *Life.* The word was strange, misplaced, yet it also felt right.

'Yes!' Mathas answered. 'Life! There is life in this cavern, and this army will bring life to Nulahmia!' He pointed his sword at the phalanxes of skeletons and zombies that had come with Lestor. 'There is no life in them, but not because of what they are. It is because they are here at the command of your distant master. He has no interest in the well-being of Nulahmia and its citizens. He cares only for the downfall of Neferata. Is that also true of you, Lestor? You, who spoke to me of fate?'

The other vampire didn't answer. A hesitant excitement spread over his sharp features.

'Life!' Mathas shouted again. '*Life!* It is in our passion for our cause! It is in our belief in what our city can be!'

And Hasynne cheered his words, as did all the other vampires in the cavern.

Mathas had had to die before this revelation came to him. He saw it now, and as the moment of the beginning of the march had come, he was alive in a deeper way than he ever had been before.

'The three great tunnels are our route,' he announced. 'They run in rough parallels to each other, and through them, we shall storm to the surface. We must use speed against the tyrant. Our first strike must be too fast and hard to stop.' He turned and aimed his sword at the exits from the cavern. 'To war!' he cried, and his army of followers obeyed.

At the head of his phalanx, Mathas marched, and then ran, racing back up through the underworld of Nulahmia, rising from the darkness, a blade reforged and made stronger by grief. He led his troops back through the tunnels that had marked his descent into despair, and then he was storming through the broken foundations of the Hellezan palace. Hasynne and Lestor followed closely behind him.

'You were right,' Mathas told Lestor. 'I was mindful of risk before. Now I have nothing left to lose.'

'You would be a martyr for the freedom of your city?' Lestor asked.

'For that prize? Willingly. And what of you? Do you march and die only for your master's pleasure?'

Lestor hesitated before answering. 'I am no longer sure,' he admitted. And he grinned.

The ruins were still smoking. The blackened timbers and stones were a further goad to action. With the companies of House Tennsein, House Gallatal, House Vernax and House Bretherel, Mathas climbed through the ashes of his home, and burst like a phoenix of rage onto the street. Now, truly, the time of secrets was over. Mathas roared, and his troops roared with him. They thundered their challenge to the reign of the Mortarch of Blood, and with a still greater thunder they made for the Queensroad. The tramp of boots and crash of armour filled the streets. The standard bearers raised trumpets to their lips, and the music of rebellion blared in Nulahmia for the first time in the city's existence.

The three corps merged together in the Queensroad. They hit the great avenue in a wave. The road was always crowded, as day and night the pulse of Nulahmia moved through it. Now Mathas severed the flow of merchants and serfs, pedestrians and riders, caravans and corteges. People fled in confusion and fear to the side streets. Dark towers of residences lined the road in this quarter, and faces crowded at their windows, looking down on an event that, until this very moment, had been unimaginable in the city of Neferata.

The army had advanced less than a mile up the Queensroad when it encountered the first guard patrol. The warriors stared, rooted to the spot for crucial seconds by the sight of the impossible. Mathas charged them, and the torrent of the army followed him. As the trumpets sounded again, Mathas yelled, 'I am the vengeance of the Hellezans! For Nulahmia! For freedom!'

For life! he thought. He did not put the great heresy into words.

Not yet. Not quite yet.

He fell on the captain of the guard as the other vampire broke through his paralysis and lunged forward. Mathas smashed his sword to the side and barrelled into him, a battering ram of fury. The captain stumbled back and Mathas decapitated him with a single stroke. The rest of the guards planted their pikes and tried to stand fast against the wave that came for them. They were swept away in moments, trampled and cut to pieces by the unwavering tide of freedom.

'First blood!' Mathas shouted. 'First victory!' He paused to look up at the people in the windows. 'You know us!' he called. 'We are you! We are Nulahmia! Join us! Together, we will seize the night from the tyrant!'

He ran forward again, taking the charge up the Queensroad. People were leaving their windows and emerging from doorways and side streets. 'Join us!' Mathas called. 'Become the birth of hope in Nulahmia!'

At first the citizens hesitated. Before long, though, a stream of new recruits joined the rebellion.

The further Mathas went up the Queensroad, the larger his army became. Already it covered the width of the avenue, and it was so long he could barely see the end. It advanced relentlessly. Vampires and mortals marched side by side, supported by unflinching ranks of skeletons and zombies. Before long, a pale green cloud drew Mathas' gaze upwards. A spirit host flew overhead. He readied himself for an attack, but it did not come. Faces emerged from the roiling mass of ectoplasmic energy. Their eyes were empty gaps, their mouths contorted howls of pain, but their anger was directed towards the Throne Mount. When they looked down at Mathas and his army, there was no anger.

It was tempting to believe he saw hope in the forms of the tortured dead. He knew better. Yet it was very tempting.

The crowd ahead of the rebels thinned quickly, and more and more of it became part of the march. The wave overwhelmed the individual squads of guards it encountered. There was still no coordinated response, no larger cohorts of troops loyal to Neferata.

Hasynne joined Mathas. Behind her, her troops of House Nastannar followed in a solid wall of armour. 'Captain Jedefor is true to his word,' she said.

'So it seems,' Mathas said bitterly. They were almost at the foot of the Throne Mount, where their stand would begin. Already, it was too late for Neferata to prevent the siege.

'You sound disappointed,' Hasynne said.

'I would have welcomed the chance to kill him for his treachery.'

'He will be careful, no doubt, to remain safely above the fray.' Hasynne looked up towards the Palace of Seven Vultures. 'We cannot surround the Mount,' she said. 'We can't trap Neferata up there.'

'We don't have to,' said Mathas. 'Even if we did surround it, what does that mean to someone who can fly? We block her strength, though. We do not need her. It will be enough to take her power.' It was a lie and he knew it. This might have been true a few nights before. He would not be truly satisfied now unless he could destroy Neferata. The souls of Teyosa and Kasten demanded it.

Be content with what you can achieve, he told himself. *Look around you. You have made the impossible real.*

Then why not a bit more? Why not one more impossibility?

He glanced up at the spirit horde, half-expecting to see the traces of his wife and child. There was no sign of them. They had vanished absolutely, and for that, he was grateful. His last memory of them was not of their burned corpses. He would have no new memories of their tormented, raging souls, or so he hoped.

The front ranks of the army reached the base of the Throne Mount.

'Houses Tennsein and Vernax,' Mathas ordered, 'barricade the bottom of the Path of Punishment. The rest of us will move west.' As the barriers went up, he eyed the slope. There was a formation of several squads of guards at the first sharp bend of the Path. Even from this distance, Mathas could sense the uncertainty in the troops. Whatever orders Jedefor had given them must have been contradictory or vague, at the very least unsuited to the circumstances. The guards held their position.

Sink into your doubts, Mathas thought. *The longer you wait to act, the stronger our barrier will be.*

Then, with Hasynne and her house at the fore, supported by Lestor's undead hordes, Mathas turned the march to the west. Two thirds of the rebel force went with him. They left the Queensroad and plunged back into the Palace Quarter of Nulahmia, making for the guard keep at its centre.

'Now comes a true test,' Hasynne said. 'There will be more than a matter of a few isolated patrols at the keep.'

'We are strong enough for that,' said Mathas. 'But I agree. There is a test. It will be how the rest of the population of this Quarter responds to us.'

'You think we will be defeated if they turn their backs on us?' Lestor asked.

We? Mathas thought. *Interesting.* 'I refuse defeat,' he insisted. 'But the fight will be hard without them, yes.'

He had his answer before long. The trumpets called, and the people answered. They shouted from windows and rooftops, and then they came running. From doorways and side streets, from alleys and markets, from courtyards and from the grand houses, the rich families of Nulahmia came running.

'The moment has come!' Mathas shouted to them. 'We shall overthrow Neferata and make the city our own!' He picked up the pace. 'Move fast,' he said to Hasynne and Lestor. The street was narrower than the Queensroad. 'We must not become trapped by the crush of our own numbers.'

The larger the crowd, the faster it grew.

Despite the risks of the massive crowd, Mathas laughed. 'Do you see?' he asked Lestor. 'Do you see the people taking courage from each other? Our movement will not be stopped. Did your master foresee something this vast?'

'I don't know,' Lestor admitted. He did not seem to care what Mannfred had anticipated or not.

'How many of our new recruits are believers, do you think?' Hasynne asked.

'I am not asking myself the question, because it doesn't matter,' Mathas said. 'Even if most of them have joined us to be part of the victorious side of the conflict, I can accept that. The victory is important, and they will help get us there.'

Though Mathas kept his force together, concentrated on a single street, the march spread wide. Soon, it seemed to him that the entire Quarter was on the move. The immensity of the wave stoked his internal fire even higher. A new thing had come to the city. He would not call it *life* yet. With pride, he would name it *hope*. After untold centuries of decadence and excess and exuberant murder, *hope* was here. It was a strange, disturbing, disorienting emotion in Shyish, yet it was here, and Mathas exulted in its arrival. He did not know where it would take him or how the thing he had become could encompass it, yet he also knew that he would, just as surely as his thirst for blood would never be truly slaked. He hungered for the hot spray of salty gore in his mouth, and he was consumed with the determination to protect the citizens of Nulahmia. Perhaps the paradox could not be resolved. If so, he would be content. He would embrace it as the new truth of his being, and see defining unity in division.

The road ended, opening into a wide square that surrounded a squat, glowering keep. Mathas had expected to see defenders on its roof, for arrows to streak from the crenels and finally test the mettle of the rebels. Yet he saw no one. There were no shouts, no alarms; there was no attack of any kind. There were no torches on the roof, and the windows were dark.

'Surround the keep,' Mathas ordered. 'Seal the exits. We'll turn their fortress into their prison.' Hasynne and Lestor repeated the commands. The rebels filled the square and flowed around the walls of the keep, a sea of arms enveloping an island of stone.

The keep remained silent.

'Front ranks, torches,' Mathas commanded. 'Throw them through the windows.'

Flaming brands arced through the air and into the apertures. The interior began to burn, and still, there was no reaction.

Mathas, Hasynne and Lestor regarded the keep with growing concern.

'Why haven't they shuttered the windows?' Lestor wondered.

'Where are they?' Hasynne said. 'They can't be hiding.'

'That would be an odd strategy,' Mathas agreed.

'They have had time to prepare,' said Lestor.

'We always knew they would,' Mathas told him. 'We had no surface access points nearby. Better to seize the Queensroad and have that strong point than to be bogged down in the Palace Quarter while Neferata sent her reinforcements unchallenged down from the Throne Mount.' He shrugged. 'We expected this would be a hard fight.'

'We did not expect nothing,' said Hasynne.

'We must assume they made ready,' Mathas said, thinking aloud. 'Why would they abandon their keep? This is their strongest defensive position.'

'They can't have simply retreated,' said Hasynne.

Look to the west! The mental warning hit Mathas with the force of a physical blow. His body jerked as if struck by lightning, so intensely did his instincts shriek with the premonition of imminent danger. He spun around.

The exit from the north of the square was the Doomwood Way. The wide road reached the square at a hard diagonal, angling so sharply north-west that he could see nothing more than fifty yards of the Way.

'They haven't retreated,' his said. 'They aren't defending. They're going to ambush us.'

The vulnerability of the rebels' position chilled him, and he saw the magnitude of the trap they had entered. His army was spread around the empty keep. A powerful strike from the Doomwood Way could hit without warning and smash the coherence of the rebel force before any defence could be mounted.

In the distance, they could hear the sound of marching boots.

'We are fools,' Hasynne groaned.

'We are not destroyed yet,' Mathas said. 'They have already missed their chance. As long as we're moving, then we have the offensive. He raised his sword. 'With me!' he shouted. 'To the Ten Sepulchres!'

Warriors cleared a path for him and then followed. The distance across the square seemed infinite, an attack before he could reach the Way inevitable. And yet the wings of war supported him and he ran like the wind. Behind him, the forces of the rebel houses turned to the new direction of attack with the fluidity of a river.

We are not destroyed yet, he thought again. Hope refused to be extinguished, and he would not let it die. It was too precious a flame in Nulahmia.

At Mathas' side, Hasynne bore a fierce, determined grin. *You feel the flame too*, he thought. Lestor kept pace with them, the commanders of the three largest forces hitting the Way together. Lestor was grinning too, and the smile was much fiercer, much more impassioned than earlier, when the first hint of excitement had crossed his features. Lestor, who had nothing truly at stake in this war. Lestor, who acted as his master's tool, a master who saw the rebellion merely as a useful weapon against Neferata. But Lestor was grinning, his eyes shining with a fire that had nothing to do with cold calculation.

The rebellion of hope rushed into the Doomwood Way. The torrent thundered up the cobbled pavement between the façades of palaces and high walls bordering the grounds of great mansions. The army was well engaged in the street when the enemy came into view, less than a mile away. If Mathas had wasted another few minutes, staring at an empty keep, the trap would have closed. Instead, two juggernauts raced towards each other. Wide as the avenue was, it still constrained the armies.

'How many, would you judge?' Mathas asked Hasynne.

'More than what would have been in the keep. Beyond that, I cannot tell. I cannot see as far as their rear flanks.'

Mathas glanced back quickly. 'They will say the same of us,' he said.

'The queen is with them,' Lestor said. He pointed up. The sinister glow of Nagadron flew above the front ranks of the guards. He moved back and forth across the width of the Way, his tail slicing sinuous wounds in the night. From her wraith-bone throne on his back, Neferata looked down at the rebels. The golden crown of Lahmia caught the infernal light of the Adevore and shone with the majesty of cruelty. Mathas could not see her eyes, but he could feel her reptilian gaze strike him.

'It is good that she is here,' Mathas said, forcing himself free from the terror of those eyes. 'It is *good*,' he said again, exhaling the word in a long hiss of anticipation.

'She means to end this war at a stroke,' Hasynne said.

'She will fail,' said Mathas. 'The victory will be ours. Nulahmia will have its freedom.' *I will have my vengeance. My family will have justice.*

A bronze statue of Neferata stood at the intersection with a narrow cross street. The figure was posed in stern triumph, its head inclined downwards to judge all who passed beneath. Mathas leapt high and landed on its shoulders. Visible now to all his followers, he stood atop the image of the hated queen whilst he pointed at the real one, and shouted over the rumble of the two armies. 'Behold the tyrant! Behold her fall! She has her power, but we have hope!' And then the moment finally came for the greatest heresy, the challenge to all of Shyish, the roar of the most impossible, and most powerful truth. 'We have *life*! Charge the enemy! Seize your victory *now*!'

The words were lightning. From them followed thunder: the thunder of voices raised in triumph and fury, and of boots slamming against the ground as the rebels hurled themselves forwards. Mathas jumped back to the ground and sprinted forwards, leading the way, leading the hope.

Like clashing oceans, the armies came together.

The study of enemies means more than learning their tactics. It means learning what they call themselves. To learn the names and the ranks by which they exult themselves is to learn their cultures and this, in turn, is to learn their souls. The souls of Chaos are the most crucial. Whether forces are to be used against each other or must be fought directly, their names must be known, and with them the strengths and desires and madnesses of the armies of the Dark Gods. Then the truth can be perceived. Truth must be mine. From it, I will craft the strongest illusions.

– *The Orders of Chaos*

THIRTEEN

AGE OF SIGMAR
THE SEASON OF CREMATORY

'She did not lie,' said Venzor. On the north ramparts of Nulahmia, he and Dessina observed the approach of the monstrous horde of the Bloodbound. The air shattered with the blasts of brass horns. Towering siege engines made their slow, implacable way towards the Hyena Gate. Lit by torches, energised with hate, a surge of the crimson warriors of Khorne moved towards the gate with the destructive force of a lava flow. The first exchanges of arrow volleys between defenders and besiegers had begun, though the targets were still just out of range. 'They are coming for the gate, just as she said.'

'Truth is the most powerful of lies,' Dessina reminded him. The words sounded like an incantation, as if she had survived as long as she had only by branding the sentence onto her soul. 'You would do well to take that fact to heart, too.'

'Yes,' said Venzor. This moment, when events were definitively proving Neferata to be honest were when he should be most suspicious.

If he was going to alter the disposition of his forces, he had to act quickly. There would soon be no more time to manoeuvre. There was no doubt that Ruhok was attacking the Hyena Gate, and Venzor had prepared for that battle. And yet…

The Bloodbound horde was so vast, it stretched to the east and west as far as Venzor could see, the horizon turned to brass and blood, coming to embrace all of Nulahmia. The army was too huge for all of Ruhok's warriors to assault a single portion of the walls.

Venzor cursed. The inspiration he had been pursuing for days finally came to him, when it might be too late. 'Come with me,' he told Dessina. He strode quickly to the command tent he had ordered erected on the battlements. Inside, a table held the same maps that had obsessed him in the Palace of Seven Vultures. He snatched the one he needed and unrolled the scroll. He stabbed a finger at the north-east section of the defences. 'What do you see?' he said.

Dessina studied the map. 'Nothing. The wall is unbroken there.'

'Exactly.' He opened another scroll that showed the quarter of the Hyena Gate. 'There is nothing when there should be something. The wall is unbroken, yes. For so very long a stretch. Why? Where is the gate?'

'Should there be one?'

Venzor nodded. 'The lack of one creates a delay for travel to the north-east that does not exist in other sectors. It makes little strategic sense, unless there is a greater reason for there seeming to be nothing here.'

'An escape,' Dessina said. She spat the word.

'Would that not be in character?' Venzor asked. 'A secret egress for the queen rather than a passage for her troops?'

'It would be,' said Dessina. 'That duplicity defines her.'

'And I have been a fool not see this earlier,' Venzor said.

'Go,' he said. 'Take your warriors to the wall. Find the gate if you can, but at all costs defend that region of the wall.' He looked outside the tent at the monstrous siege towers still closing on the Hyena Gate. 'You were right,' he said. He pointed at the towers. 'They are the truth that concealed the greater lie from me.'

Dessina bowed. 'I will do what I must. I will not fail. This I swear.'

She hurried from the tent. Venzor watched her go, then advanced to the front of the battlements again to command the defence of the Hyena Gate. This attack was still a truth he must contend with. It constricted his actions and shut down his choices. He cursed Neferata and her corrosive truths, and he cursed himself for coming to understanding so slowly. His hope lay in the hate he saw in Dessina's eyes. She would fly to the north-east in a fury that would match the rage of the Bloodbound.

A huge figure rode at the head of the legions below. His helm was a crimson skull of bronze, and from his shoulders rose a massive rune of Khorne. His dark cape swung heavily in the night wind. On the armoured flanks of the monster he rode, rows of spikes impaled skulls, and every death's head wore a crown. A destroyer of nations advanced to the gates of Nulahmia. He came within the range of archers, and rose higher in the saddle as arrows struck against his armour and broke. He raised his axe and roared with a voice so loud and full of rage, it seemed to Venzor that a volcano had found a tongue and the power of speech.

'Nulahmia falls this night!' Ruhok shouted. 'Do not seek mercy or flight – stand and die! I am *war*, and I have come to throw your towers down! *Blood for the Blood God! Skulls for the Skull Throne!*'

The horde behind him echoed his shout, and the Bloodbound charged.

The parapet vibrated under Venzor's feet. An arrow of doubt pierced him. *We aren't ready*, he thought. It was as if Ruhok's voice alone was shaking the walls. They felt thin as parchment, and weak as hope. Venzor pictured them cracking apart. He pictured himself falling through shattered stone to savage axes below.

Storm clouds had gathered over Nulahmia. They hung low, grazing the highest spires of the city. They glowed a dull red, reflecting the fires of Ruhok's army. The architecture of Nulahmia cast angular, wavering shadows in their light.

Neferata moved through darkness in the far north-east of the city. Wreathed in a mist of shadows, she passed between two high, broad monuments. They were engraved with colossal representations of her image, seated in judgement, dispensing death. Their black, polished granite was cold to the touch, and they held all habitations at bay. They shouldered close to the city's ramparts, allowing only a narrow passage between them and the wall. The darkness of the passage was eternal. The cobbles were slick with moss and slime. The alley was nameless. It was never used, and led nowhere. Except to the Raven Gate.

Neferata approached a featureless expanse of the wall and placed her palm against it. The stonework vibrated beneath her touch. A split ten feet high appeared, and two sections of the wall rumbled apart. She entered the tunnel, advancing a dozen yards before she reached an iron door. When she touched it, it ground upwards into the rounded ceiling.

She kept going. One barrier after another opened at her touch. No other key would open the Raven Gate. She moved through Nulahmia's outer wall, a faint aura of sorcery surrounding her.

It reached into the walls of the tunnel, holding at bay the wards that would destroy any presence that sought to pass the gate without her permission.

She had conceived of the Raven Gate as a means of escape. She had never intended to use it to permit entry into Nulahmia. She found the alteration of its purpose interesting, not distressing. The currents of power flowed in this direction, and so she had adapted. So she always would, or she would fall.

The outer stonework of the wall parted, and the gate was open. The land beyond was steep slope, broken by curved boulders, the fossilised claws of an ancient leviathan that had become its own monument. Neferata stood in the archway. She let the shadows flow away from her. 'The city awaits you,' she said. 'Do not keep it waiting.'

The warbands emerged from behind the stone claws. Ruhok had clearly commanded them to do as she had instructed, and conceal themselves until the gate was open. Even that minimal gesture towards stealth ran against their natures and the warriors who came towards her were consumed with new rage. She smiled at them, fuelling their anger and confusing them at the same time. They did not understand what she was. Their instinct to attack her was, for the moment, troubled.

She wondered idly what orders Ruhok had given them concerning her.

'Come,' she said, and walked back through the open gate. The Bloodbound followed, running now, the promise of unleashed violence and mountains of skulls urging them on.

Ruhok's warriors were savages, Neferata thought. That savagery would be useful to her. So would their strength. They entered the tunnel, and the walls seemed too small to contain their muscle-contorting wrath. Neferata knew the kinds and ranks of the followers of Khorne.

Most of the troops entering Nulahmia were bloodreavers. Many of them disdained armour, taking violent pride in the fresh wounds and old scars that covered their bodies and faces. The Blood Warriors who led them dwarfed their underlings. They were huge, mountains of crimson armour clanking with every step. At their head was the largest of them all. His helm, surmounted with massive horns forming the rune of Khorne, concealed his face. There was nothing human visible beneath the mask of rage. The spikes on his shoulders were coated in blood, and some of it was very fresh. He had, Neferata thought, anointed himself with the gore of a subordinate who had displeased him. She approved of the excess. She had less patience for the crude application of force.

'And what do you call yourself?' Neferata asked the Blood Warrior.

'I am Wrahn,' he said. The massive double blades of his goreglaive moved back and forth as he walked. 'My name is the name of your destroyer if you betray us.'

Neferata laughed, making him jerk with surprise and anger. She tapped a finger against the edge of the glaive. 'That would be singularly pointless on my part, don't you think? Betraying you inside these walls would not serve my purpose at all.'

'We are not here to serve you,' Wrahn growled.

'Aren't you?' She looked back at the long line of Bloodbound following her through the wall. There were over a hundred of Wrahn's warriors already inside, and more were following. A very good start, she thought, for the work ahead. She was pleased with the size of Ruhok's detachment. 'I rather think you are,' she said. 'Lord Ruhok is too, though no doubt it will please him to believe otherwise.'

Wrahn growled. 'Jest while you can.'

'I do not jest.'

As she spoke, they reached the other side of the Raven Gate, and the Bloodbound spilled into Nulahmia.

Neferata took a step to the right, and crooked her hand in summoning. The mist of shadows rushed around her again at the same moment that Wrahn turned with her and swung his goreglaive at her neck.

The attack was as predictable as the fall of night.

'Blood!' Wrahn yelled. 'Blood for the–' His swing went wide, cutting trailing darkness. Then Neferata seized him from the whirl of shadow, tearing his helm from his head and clutching his throat, cutting him off in mid-shout. His features were a mass of scar tissue, huge parallel claw gouges running from forehead to chin. He gasped for air, but her grip had closed his air passages. He lashed out with the glaive again, and she grabbed its shaft, immobilising the weapon.

In answer to her will, sorcerous energies rose from the ground at her feet, lifting her and Wrahn into the air. Her attack was so fast that the other Khornate warriors were only just starting to react, and already Wrahn was out of their reach. The Blood Warrior had doomed himself the moment he had thought of turning on her.

Wrahn could not speak. He kicked at the air. His lips mouthed the words *Blood God*.

'*No*,' Neferata hissed, her voice tearing the air like lightning, blasting down to the army below. 'Here, there is no blood for the Blood God. Here, the blood is *mine*.' She snapped her head forward, a striking serpent, and sank her fangs into Wrahn's neck. His blood flooded her mouth. She drank deeply, draining his strength in moments. She pulled back while the gore still pumped, letting it rain down, and tore Wrahn's head from his shoulders. She crushed the skull to powder, brain matter and eyes squeezing from between her fingers. 'This is *my* city,' she thundered at the Bloodbound. 'All that exists inside these walls belongs to *me*. Every life, every death, every drop of blood. *You* are mine. Now go, and wreak your havoc. Go, and do your worst. *I* command it.'

She dropped Wrahn's corpse and rose higher, vanishing from the sight of the warriors as the shadows embraced her completely. She listened to the Bloodbound scream their outrage and hate and then, the target of their wrath gone, turn to punish the city in her stead. Neferata's spell carried her to the roof of the tallest monument. She perched there, watching the Bloodbound bring their rampage. The first fires began to spread, and the stream of warriors was still passing through the gate. The Bloodbound raced through the streets, their path of murderous conquest fuelled by the even greater hate that was her gift to them.

Two fronts had opened in Nulahmia, and Venzor was caught between them. Catastrophe had come to the city, and the flames were the start of its great blossoming. Her fate – and Nulahmia's – hung in a balance of destruction.

The currents of power had become a torrent, hurling everyone in the city at the rocks that could and would tear them apart. Exhilarated, Neferata laughed, her voice the crack of doom sounding over the city at war.

*The blood is **mine**.*

Never accept defeat. Never doubt its possibility.

– Exhortations

FOURTEEN

AGE OF MYTH
THE SEASON OF LOSS

Below Neferata, the Doomwood Way was awash with blood. Rebels and guards cut each other down in a war of passion against discipline. The skills of the guard slowed the advance, but no more. The rebels outnumbered them, and though their formations were more ragged, there were enough veteran warriors among the houses to make the difference. The ranks of the skeletons had a greater effect as the battle wore on and they moved up, bringing their unflinching relentlessness to bear. The defeat of the guard was more than predictable. Neferata could anticipate the moment of their collapse down to the second.

She took Nagadron high above the rooftops and looked down upon the panorama of the uprising. Most of the Palace Quarter was in turmoil, the streets filled with marching, chanting traitors. In the regions furthest from the combat, the rebellion had taken on the aspect of a carnival, the people celebrating a victory that had yet to occur.

I see you all, Neferata thought. *You have revealed yourself to me, and my judgement will spare no one.* Her anger would scorch the streets with the fury of the sun. The celebrants would curse their existence. Their deaths would be eternities of torment.

But the punishment could not come yet. She would need her victory first.

She took Nagadron back down, swooping in on the march a short distance behind the front lines. As the Adevore closed in, talons extended, she noted each banner and coat of arms. She had wanted to know who plotted against her, and here was that triumph at least. She had pushed them into the open, and there they were, defiant in their treachery, howling for her blood.

You see them all. Now crush them.

Nagadron struck the centre of the Way, crushing rebels under his talons, then raking more apart before leaping skywards again. Neferata turned Aken-seth on her enemies, blasting a storm of dark magic through their ranks. Rebels fell, twisting in death agonies, withered to emaciated mummies as the Staff of Pain drained their life forces in an instant.

She took Nagadron up again, leaving a score of rebels destroyed. But the gap in their formation closed almost at once. Nagadron dived again, and again, this time dragging long gouges through the army, shredding mortal, vampire and skeleton to pieces. The march did not slow. If anything it moved faster, as new warriors raced through the spaces Neferata and the dread abyssal opened. The rebels' commitment to the struggle was absolute. *They must know the only outcomes for them are victory or annihilation,* she thought. And so they attacked with a fusion of belief and desperation.

There were so many. The line of rebels stretched all the way back to the Queensroad, and it seemed to be growing all the time. The guards were able to slow the march down only because the confines of the Doomwood Way limited the width of the front lines. And the reinforcements were massive. She had no doubt who had sent them. *I survived the trap of your spell, Mannfred, so you try this instead.* He had played his hand well. The skeletons and warriors he had sent were a small fraction of his strength, and represented no risk for him. Had they been besieging Nulahmia, Neferata would have exterminated them effortlessly. In the streets of the city, they were a much greater threat.

But that isn't enough, she thought. Mere physical force was too crude an approach for Mannfred. *There must be something more.*

She soared up and down with Nagadron, attacking without cease, to little effect. The brief stalemate began to break down as the remainder of the guard made a last stand. When they fell, the rebels would be able to spread far and wide. There would be no front. The other guard formations would be isolated islands in the raging sea of the uprising. The rebels' advance had to be broken in the Doomwood Way, while it was still concentrated. She needed a death blow.

And she still could not find Mannfred's trap. 'I know it's there,' she said to Nagadron. 'You can feel it too, can't you?' Unease tensed her shoulders, and the Adevore hissed in distress. Something was concealed from her, forcing her gaze to slide over what she sought.

Neferata climbed again, and Nagadron banked towards the front lines as they began to move faster. As the Adevore turned, a sudden, violent movement of shadows caught Neferata's eye. It came from partway back on the Way, far enough to the rear of the rebels that those marchers had not come under her attack yet. At first all she could see was a vague swirl of movement in the dark. The motion slowed, coalesced into a thick, pulsating dome of fog. The spell faded, and the fog dispersed, revealing a mortis engine. The ornate, necromantic throne was held aloft by a swarm of bound spirits. It had been travelling low to the ground, camouflaged by magic and the crowd of marchers. It rose now, Mannfred's banners unfurling from its spikes to the howls of banshees. Standing on the throne, a robed corpsemaster pointed at her, thrusting his arms forward as if he were hurling a great weight. The mortis engine shook with a build-up of dark energy.

The mortis engine had been concealed until it was ready to attack. Now it did, and there was no time to react. Yet Neferata had all the time she needed to think, *you wanted this.*

The corpsemaster made his gesture of attack, and the power in the engine lashed out. The violent release shattered the throne apart. The corpsemaster disappeared in the black lightning, howling in the triumph of his sacrifice.

You wanted this.

The lightning struck Neferata, and pain eclipsed the world.

Then she was falling.

Mathas stared, dazzled by the jagged flare of black, and the war took a breath. The combatants on both sides looked up, their gaze seized irresistibly by the sight of a burning star plummeting to earth. Nagadron burned with green and black flame. The dread abyssal screamed and hurled himself back and forth across the avenue, smashing into the building façades, smashing spires down into the street. Neferata streaked to the ground, a comet of fire and darkness. She struck the Way a few hundred yards up from Mathas' position. The pavement shook, and stone bubbled. A fountain of molten rock splashed outwards from the crater left by the Mortarch's fall.

'The tyrant falls!' Mathas roared, and he attacked the ragged line of the remaining guards with the fury of imminent victory. He brought his sword down in a diagonal swipe at the throat of the guard before him. The other vampire's block was too weak, Mathas' strike too fast and too strong. The blow shattered the chainmail gorget as if it were glass. Mathas' blade sliced through the guard's neck and shoulder and down into his chest, severing his heart. Mathas gulped down the jetting blood, and strength built upon strength.

The guards went down beneath the surging wave of rebels. The sight of Neferata falling shattered their morale and energised the rebellion. Mathas fought and killed, but his spirit was already past the guards, and in moments his body was past them too, racing down the Doomwood Way to finish Neferata while the chance was there.

The Mortarch of Blood emerged from the crater. She was limping and bent over in pain. She moved quickly to flee, but Mathas and his comrades were faster. The distance between them narrowed.

'She cannot escape,' Hasynne said.

Beside her, Lestor grinned ferociously. He burned with the fire of the cause now, as fully as if it were his own. He had caught the scent of an epochal triumph, and of glory that went beyond being his master's servant in this war.

Above, Nagadron flew uncontrollably. The sorcerous fire still consumed him, and the monster howled. Rubble fell to the street as he smashed back and forth across the avenue. Mathas threw himself to the side as a slab smashed into the street before him. A hail of shards exploded in his face, and bounced off his armour. He wiped away the blood that ran down his face and kept running. More wreckage crushed rebels running on the sides of the Way, but the losses were trivial now. The guards were destroyed, the way was clear, and Neferata was in desperate retreat.

The rebel army pursued. From the grand apartments bracketing the Way came shouts of jubilation, adding to the liberation chorus that resounded across the Palace District.

Mathas climbed a mound of rubble with Hasynne and Lestor, pausing at the vantage point for a moment to see the sweep of their triumphant force.

'The citizens of Nulahmia are unanimous,' said Lestor.

'Can we truly be this unified?' Hasynne wondered.

'Let the perception be the truth,' said Mathas. 'If it is not true now, it will be after our victory.' No one would dare admit to standing with Neferata after she was destroyed.

They ran forwards again, leading the hunt for the tyrant.

The huge statue of the queen stood in the centre of the Way. Mathas saw Neferata stumble as she passed it, steadying herself against a plinth twenty feet high. The obsidian statue was imperious, its chin raised, its eyes staring with merciless impassivity into the distance. Its heroic posture mocked the hunched, diminished figure beneath it.

Neferata pulled away from the plinth, and with a burst of speed, passed into the storied heart of the Doomwood Way. The rebels followed, and Mathas suddenly thought: *it ends here. She can go no further.*

In the middle of its length, the Doomwood Way widened into a circular plaza a mile wide. Surrounding it were the sepulchres that gave the road its name. They were colossal, hundreds of feet tall, constructs of black marble streaked with crimson, and each holding thousands of graves. They were built in the shape of immense trees. Their branches, thick as the temple spires, reached out to one another around the periphery and across the centre of the plaza, forming a grim, latticed dome. Iron sculptures of dead, drooping, ten-foot leaves hung in the tens of thousands from the branches, turning and grinding in the wind. They filled the plaza with the sound of unnatural, heavy foliage trapped in an eternal autumn, always about to drop, but never falling. To look up from the plaza was to see the twisting reminder of the imminence and immanence of death. To stand in it was to feel oppressed by gargantuan presences. The sepulchres were vast shadows of stone, their shapes mockeries of life that crushed the soul with the weight and majesty of death.

It was here, in the centre of the plaza, that Neferata stopped running. She turned to face the rebels, straightening now, in her hands the Dagger of Jet and the Staff of Pain. As small as her figure appeared in that space and at that distance, Mathas felt the force of her presence strike at him. Wounded, at bay, doomed, she yet seemed greater than the towering sepulchres.

Mathas' mouth dried, and the fiery song of victory that flowed through his blood stuttered for an instant. Beside him, Hasynne's smile faltered. The chant of the rebels dropped.

But only for an instant.

'We have her,' Lestor said.

Mathas heard his total commitment to the rebellion, and he took up the shout. '*We have her!*'

Furious that even now the queen could make him hesitate, Mathas ran even faster, his cry of vengeance tearing his throat.

His army ran with him.

The rebels howled the refrain of victory. '*We have her! We have her! We have her!*'

This spell. It would be wrong to say I hope never to cast it. I know the currents of fate and misfortune too well to preserve such an illusion. I have thought of the spell, and so the day will come when I shall cast it. Disaster will call upon a greater disaster. I do not know if this spell will work. I do not know if I can survive its casting. I do not know if I will be able to control it, once I have unleashed its force. I do know that I will not hesitate when the time comes. Certainties are tedious lies. Only mortals, caught in the narrow span of their existence, can believe otherwise. Power requires risk, and the casting of this spell will be the greatest risk. I will embrace the risk. I will revel in it.

– *The Understanding of Annihilation*

FIFTEEN

AGE OF SIGMAR
THE SEASON OF CREMATORY

Blood before and fire behind, Venzor thought. He ran back and forth on the battlements, shouting orders no one could hear over the monstrous clash of arms and the roars of the Bloodbound. He could not fathom the true nature of Neferata's trap. 'She can't have chosen to destroy her city!' he exclaimed, turning to speak to Dessina, forgetting for a moment she was no longer there.

'Trapped, trapped, trapped,' he snarled to himself and cursed Neferata. 'Where is Dessina!' he shouted. 'Where are her forces?' Had she not reached the wall in time? Had she been overwhelmed?

No one answered, and the Bloodbound rampaged through Nulahmia. To Venzor's rear, fires raged as the enemy cut through the streets towards the Hyena Gate. To the front, the horde was pushing through the volleys of his archers and the flesh-destroying spells of his necromancers. The ground at the base of the wall was awash with the blood of the fallen, but every death only drove the followers of Khorne to greater ecstasies of rage. They raised ladders as fast as the defenders could hurl them down, and the monstrous siege towers had reached the wall, and loomed over the battlements.

The towers' maws gaped wide, unleashing cataracts of molten brass onto the parapets. The burning river spread wide, incinerating Venzor's troops and driving them back from the defences. Skeletons stood their ground and vanished under the flow. The necromancers fled, but not all were fast enough. Their robes burst into flames and they screamed, drowning and burning at the same time as they were engulfed.

On the upper flanks of the towers were thick arms of bronze, fists raised to the sky. Now they slammed down onto the parapets. Stone shattered under the blows of the fists, and the arms became bridges onto the wall for the forces waiting inside the towers. Gates opened at the towers' shoulders. They unleashed the hordes of Khorne. Brayherds and bloodreavers charged down the arms. At their head, swinging a blazing anvil on a chain, was a skullgrinder. Just before he leapt from the fist onto the parapet, he paused for a moment, bellowing with delighted hate at the sight of the destruction his engines had wrought.

Venzor jumped over the river of brass and landed on the crest of the battlements. He leapt from merlon to merlon, making for the skullgrinder. He gestured as he leapt, issuing silent commands. They were obeyed at once. Flights of vargheists and fell-bats swarmed out of the battlement towers. They swooped low over the parapets, talons and fangs tearing into the horde of Bloodbound. The parapet became a storm of wings and blades, of blood and molten flame. The spread of the enemy's army slowed. The rush down the arms of the siege towers stopped as the Khornate warriors struggled against the ripping death that descended upon them, screaming, from the sky.

'We are holding them!' Venzor shouted to his troops.

We are holding them, Venzor thought. His satisfaction evaporated in the next moment. 'Holding them for what?' he said to himself. 'Hold, hold, hold, and then? And then?' Unless Dessina performed a wonder, all he had gained was a brief stalemate. The fires were raging higher in the city, and already much closer to the gate. Ruhok's two forces were tightening the noose, and Neferata's troops were all in the south of the city. 'She won't send them,' he said, and startled himself with his high, bitter laughter. 'She told me the truth, and I didn't see it. She *does* want her city to die. She *does*. But I won't let it. I won't. I will make it mine. I will. I *will*.'

The skullgrinder marched across the bronzed corpses, using the dead as a causeway to keep him just above the killing flow. He wielded his anvil with the dexterity of a whip. Skeletons exploded into smouldering fragments on impact. As Venzor closed with the skullgrinder, the huge warrior hurled the anvil into the face of Akthal, one of Venzor's captains. The vampire's head burst apart, vanishing in a gritty spray of red. The skullgrinder saw Venzor and swung the anvil at him. Venzor feigned hesitation, then launched himself up at the last moment. As the anvil destroyed the merlon that had been his perch, he spread his wings and soared over the skullgrinder's head. He came down behind the Gorechosen warrior's back. The skullgrinder whirled, too slow to block Venzor's daemon-possessed blade. With a vibrating hiss and a flash of violet, the sword sank deep into his shoulder and cut off his left arm. Howling, the skullgrinder threw himself against Venzor, swinging the anvil with his right hand. The chain wrapped itself around both combatants, pulling them into a bloody embrace, two corpses in a single coffin. The heat of the anvil whipped past Venzor's face, and its momentum toppled him and the skullgrinder into the molten brass.

The jaws of fire and pain seized Venzor. They shook him, taking away his control over his limbs. He managed to jerk his head forwards and sink his fangs into the skullgrinder's throat. The flow of rejuvenating blood healed him as fast as the stream burned. The skullgrinder thrashed, but was tangled in his own weapon and weakened quickly, his flesh sloughing off his bones. It took all of Venzor's will not to scream, to keep drinking, and then the chain of the anvil snapped. He shoved the dying skullgrinder away and shot up out of the river of brass, howling in agony and anger.

His armour was scored and melted. His flesh hung in tatters. But he was healing, and he was in command of his powers. He flew up, shedding the burning metal and flying towards the peak of the nearest siege tower. He channelled his pain into a withering blast of magic that he aimed into the maw. The upper portion of the tower exploded, and an eruption of liquid brass drenched the battlements, falling on attacker and defenders alike. The huge engine became a torch. It collapsed with the roar of a dying monster.

Soaring over the battlements, Venzor looked into the city and his moment of triumph vanished. The Bloodbound infiltrators had reached the Hyena Gate, and were slaughtering its defenders.

To Ruhok's left, the siege engine fell and unleashed an ocean of molten brass across the Bloodbound, hundreds at a stroke. The edges of the killing sea lapped at the feet of Enteth, Ruhok's juggernaut. The armoured monster growled, but held its ground. The air roiled with the heat. Ruhok gave Torsek the skullgrinder's fallen achievement only a passing glance.

'The queen has betrayed us,' said Kathag. The Exalted Deathbringer stood beside Enteth's right flank, the eternal grin-snarl of his face more threatening than ever. He was as ready to attack his lord as he was the walls of Nulahmia. Nearby, Vul the slaughterpriest and Ghour the bloodsecrator said nothing, waiting to see how the confrontation would evolve. 'She made us come here only to hurl ourselves against the strongest defences,' Kathag insisted.

'This is what she said would happen,' said Ruhok. 'This is not defeat. This is victory. Look. Look beyond the wall.'

Kathag hesitated, then obeyed.

'See those flames,' said Ruhok. 'The city burns. Neferata should have lied, because she has sealed her doom. But she did not lie. Nulahmia is ours, and we will destroy it so utterly, it will vanish from memory.'

Ruhok had barely finished speaking when he heard booming sounds from the other side of the Hyena Gate. It was the knocking of fate. The time had come for him to raise a mountain of skulls in Khorne's name.

As if in answer to his thought, the sound came from the other side of the walls of the Bloodbound chanting their praise of Khorne. Through the screams and clash of arms on the battlements, the words were still clear.

'*Blood for the Blood God! Skulls for the Skull Throne!*'

'Now!' Ruhok shouted to his legions. 'Take the gate now! Take the city! Drown it in its blood!' Enteth thundered across the last of the ground that separated Ruhok from the Hyena Gate. Kathag and the other Gorechosen warriors kept pace. There was doubt in the Exalted Deathbringer's eyes, but he obeyed.

Ruhok bellowed, exulting in the charge. There was nothing to hold back the legions of Khorne, and they launched at the Hyena Gate like a terrible, crimson fist. The defenders on the ramparts were either dead or locked in struggle. Forces still descended from the other siege tower. Torsek's chained anvil no longer swung above the crenellations, but his creations carried his bloody work forward.

The great charge grew stronger with every step. 'Give praise to Khorne!' Ruhok commanded, and Vul picked up the chant, shouting prayers and imprecations that fired the blood of the attackers with a force greater than frenzy. He called upon the Blood God's blessings, and his prayers were answered. Ruhok felt new power spread through his limbs and gather in the air itself. Ghour reacted the most violently. He raised his standard high, and the huge rune blazed with energy. Mouth agape in religious ecstasy, the bloodsecrator gathered the building fury into the icon. As the Gorechosen reached the arch of the Hyena Gate, the reality of Shyish grew brittle. Chaos itself was on the verge of breaking through.

The Hyena Gate glowed angrily as its wards sought to kill the attackers before they could strike the huge portcullis. 'Weak!' Ruhok shouted. 'Show them, bloodsecrator! Show them the strength of Khorne!' He urged Enteth forward as, with a howl of praise, Ghour unleashed the stored power of his icon.

In this small region of Shyish, the reality of the realm tore and crumbled. '*Skulls for the Skull Throne!*' the Bloodbound raved, a thousand voices united in rage, and Chaos roared through a rent in the air. The anger of the Blood God lashed out, Khorne's hatred of magic made manifest. The Hyena Gate's glow turned into a death blaze, and then darkness. Enteth slammed into the portcullis, a living battering ram. Weakened from the other side by the attacks of the infiltrators, the gate flew apart before the incandescent rampage of the Bloodbound. Iron and stone shattered and melted.

Howling in the unstoppable glory of rage, the legions of Lord Ruhok stormed into Nulahmia.

* * *

Let me be on time, Dessina thought. *Let me be on time.*

She felt the weight of the city on her shoulders, and she took the burden gladly. The mission was the greatest honour of her existence. The prospect of its failure was her greatest horror. And failure was a possibility as likely as it was dreadful. Let her be on time? There *was* no time.

The tunnels through which she led her forces of vampires, skeletons and zombies were damp, and their echoes were old, dull with abandonment. They had not been used in an age. Every step she took down them was fateful. That she was here, that anyone was here, marked the day as a turning point.

'I question again why we are here,' said Felsein. Venzor had made her Dessina's lieutenant, and she had served without hesitation until now. 'Why are we here?'

'We will take the enemy by surprise, from below.'

'So you said. But, it will be impossible for us to reach the surface quickly. We are very far below ground, and we keep going down.'

'Yes,' said Dessina. 'It is necessary.'

The other vampire tried a different tack. 'We are urgently needed.'

'I know that even better than you do.'

'Were we not supposed to be making for the north-east portion of the wall? I think we have been going south at least some of the time.'

'We are going where we must. I have never made so crucial a journey, and neither have you.'

The passion in Dessina's voice quieted Felsein for a moment, but did not put an end to her doubts. 'Did Lord Venzor order us to take this route?'

'It was commanded,' Dessina said, and her voice almost broke as she thought of the trust that Neferata had placed in her. *I will not fail you, my queen.* This would be her greatest act of loyalty, and the fires she would unleash would at last burn away the final traces of dishonour to cling to her name.

The destruction of the House of Avaranthe, in another age, had been deserved. It was the punishment due for treachery, and the Avaranthes had dared to rebel against the Mortarch of Blood. The destruction, though, had not been total, because not every Avaranthe had joined the Hellezans and the other conspirator houses. When Dessina's direct ancestors had discovered the treachery, they had gone to Neferata, and condemned their kin to the flames. One of the few comforts Dessina could take from the history of her family was the knowledge of its punishment. Even now, centuries upon centuries later, she sometimes saw enslaved wraiths and skeletons that she recognised as the ancient rebels, still suffering their punishment.

Dessina had inhabited the shadows of Neferata's reign for hundreds of years, unknown even to her sister spies, her every action having the sole purpose of projecting her queen's will. She was Neferata's hand, striking in the dark and at a distance. She proved her worth a thousand times over.

And it was never enough. Not for her. The shame of her family followed her, always in her consciousness. It found her no matter how deeply into the shadows she ventured.

On this night, though, with this task, she hoped at last to purge the shame.

One more descent, one more tunnel, one more passage through the emptiness and dust and silence of age, and then they crossed under an arched doorway. It was the last threshold.

Though she could not know if she was in time, and the doubt tormented her, Dessina smiled when she saw what stood before her. 'We are here,' she breathed. She could have wept in gratitude to Neferata.

'What is this place?' Felsein asked, shaken. The other vampire troops were murmuring, distressed. 'We are not at the wall.'

'No, we are not.'

'And who are they?'

'Reinforcements.' *Of a kind,* Dessina thought.

Tens of thousands of skeletons awaited them. The tens of thousands of skeletons who guarded the Annihilation Gate.

The night was heavy with the heat of the season of Crematory. The sky was low, ash and dust falling in curtains over the rooftops, swirling in the desiccating wind. And a silence spread across the city from the Tomb of the Unnumbered. It smothered voices. It muffled the din of siege in the north. It was the silence of final anticipation. It was the silence that came before the roar of ending.

Nagadron circled above the Tomb of the Unnumbered. The Adevore moaned eerily, in sympathy with his mistress. Neferata's eyes were half-closed. Her fingers combed and braided the air through which she flew. Her consciousness was divided between the work of her hands and her senses that reached down into the bowels of the city. She was waiting, waiting for the slightest touch on her web. The thrumming of a single strand.

In the north, the city burned. The flames had spread over entire districts, and the night crashed and boomed with the sounds of war. Two armies struggled for ownership of the city, one to control it, the other to destroy it. She would break them both.

Neferata's gestures carved runes and summoned powers, shaping the most terrible of spells. The powers that she called to her were not hers alone. She drew upon the energy of the entire city. Her rule had been weakened, yet Nulahmia was still hers, by right of creation. It was as she had told the Bloodbound. All blood within the city's walls was hers. *All* within was hers.

The power built. The spell trembled on the verge of completion. Neferata ground her fangs in the effort to keep it contained. *Not yet*, she thought. *Not yet.* If she unleashed it too soon, it would miss its mark, and all would be lost.

Then it came. The thrumming of a single strand. The presence of the loyal servant.

The arrival of the willing sacrifice.

Now, then, *now* was the time of the spell. And it was ready, howling to be unleashed.

'Nulahmia is mine!' Neferata shouted. 'Mine to rule and mine to destroy. *I reclaim it*!'

She hurled the monstrous force of the spell down through the peak of the Tomb of the Unnumbered. A coruscating beam of starlight silver and void black roared towards the Annihilation Gate.

As if sensing the catastrophe to come, the city began to shake.

Against defeat, no sacrifice is too great. Beside defeat, all pain is trivial.

– A Call to Purpose

SIXTEEN

AGE OF MYTH
THE SEASON OF LOSS

On the Doomwood Way, in the plaza of the Ten Sepulchres, Neferata stood alone and faced the army she had come here to destroy. The deathly snow of quietus was falling, draping the monuments in grey and trickles of blood.

'The city is mine,' said Neferata. Did they think they could take it from her? Did they think they could destroy her? Did they not understand the arrogance of hope was theirs only because she willed it?

Pain still wracked her from the blast of the mortis engine. But the pain was inconsequential. It was the price she had paid, the price she had sought, to bring this moment into being. She had prepared for a blow that might be strong enough to fell her. The risk was necessary. The injury had to be real, so her flight to the plaza would be real.

The truth was the most powerful of lies.

Mathas and his army of traitors raced to finish her off. They filled the grand plaza of Doomwood Way. Their roar of triumph was deafening. Fifty yards away, Mathas slowed in his charge. He raised a hand, and the army slowed with him. He was looking at her wounds. She saw him take in the tremor in her limbs. He could read the extent of her injury. He could see the truth. He could see the importance of this moment, and how it would determine the fate of Nulahmia.

Neferata saw that he had learned well, and had determined, as his forces surrounded her, to savour his triumph. She could see the fire that burned in Mathas' eyes. The fire she had ignited and carefully nurtured.

'We have come for justice, tyrant,' he said.

'You shall have it,' she said, her voice rough with pain.

Mathas walked forward slowly. Hasynne and Lestor followed a few steps behind. The last Hellezan advanced with determination, and a stern purpose worthy of a king. 'Justice,' he said. 'For all your victims. For my family. For my son. For Teyosa.'

Neferata smiled, and Mathas hesitated. A cold wind rushed through the sepulchres. It blew harder and harder, a freezing annunciation that turned the snowfall into a stinging punishment. Neferata's cloak billowed in the blast. Her hair streamed out from beneath the crown of Lahmia. The blood running down the sepulchres shot across the plaza to surround her, obeying the will of its absolute ruler. The burns on Neferata's flesh faded away. Her wounds vanished.

She ceased to smile. She opened her eyes wide, and showed to Mathas and all before her a fury that was colder than any tomb, and colossal beyond measure.

'The city is mine,' she said again. *'The city is mine!'*

Her voice, the great tolling of judgement, boomed across all Nulahmia.

And she raised her arms, and she took the city back.

Thunder drowned out the roar of the rebels. The thunder

of Neferata's true army. The strength that she had held back until now, the strength that she had concealed, poured out from the huge sepulchres. Cavalries of Black Knights and blood knights led thousands of skeletons and vampires upon the rebels. From the upper branches of the monuments came another cavalry. Mounted hexwraiths galloped down through the air, leading hosts of spirits, an unending storm of glowing ectoplasm descending upon the plaza. Flights of fell-bats swooped through the deathly green, hunting for the blood of the queen's enemies.

Flying on skeletal wings, Neferata's morghast guards landed beside her. The monsters of shadow, monsters of bone, they raised their massive blades to slaughter in her defence.

She barely needed them now. Her will had called absolute destruction upon her enemies, and that rejuvenated her as much as the richest blood. She strode forward, Aken-seth held high. Mathas and the other leaders of the rebels were still making for her, but there was only desperation in their run now. Their uprising had no chance, and they knew it. Their shouts of triumph had turned into screams of despair, and the massacre had only just begun.

'*Life?*' Neferata taunted Mathas. He staggered as she turned his deepest thoughts into words. '*Hope?* You thought to bring them into *my* city?' She laughed, and invited them to battle.

The morghasts fell on Lestor, chopping his limbs from his body before he could even begin to fight. Mathas and Hasynne brought their blades in at opposite angles, and at the same moment. Neferata blocked Mathas' strike with the Staff of Pain. Hasynne's sword cut through her wraithbone armour and into her side. Neferata snarled. With the speed of a mortis scorpion, she stabbed the hooked blade of Akmet-har into Hasynne's right eye, cracking her skull open with the force of the blow.

The powerful warrior slumped to her knees as the Dagger of Jet pulled her undead vitality out of her.

'*Life?*' Neferata repeated. She blocked a flurry of blows from Mathas. 'What is life except the prelude to the power of death. Do you see its power now? *Do you?*'

'I do,' Mathas growled, granting a truth without admitting defeat. He came at her again and again, his fire undimmed.

'Do you not know what you are?' she asked.

He backed away and circled her, looking for an opening, trying to exploit her injuries. 'I am not what you would have made me,' he said. 'I am free, and you are fallible. If you destroy me tonight, another will come, and your end will come.'

'Free?' Neferata said, speaking softly now, and smiling.

Mathas hesitated. The blaze in his eyes faltered. Perhaps he suspected what was coming.

'I did not fail,' she said. 'You were never free. I have given you the illusion of freedom. I planted the venom of hope in your blood. I needed to know my enemies, and you led them to me. You have been, truly, a loyal servant.'

'No,' Mathas whispered. His eyes were wide, the fire gone, in its place a shine of horror. 'I will not believe your lies.'

'Then believe the truth.' She smiled more broadly, showing him the pleasure his hope had given her. 'Stop,' she said, as if he had been overfilling a chalice, and he froze in mid-lunge.

'Drop your sword.'

The blade clattered to the cobblestones.

'Give me your neck.'

Mathas' scream as he obeyed was the exquisite sound of perfect despair and absolute loss. It was a sound that took time to craft, and Neferata was pleased by her work. The scream went on and on, a perfect accompaniment as she drank his blood one more time. She turned her thrall into a husk as she washed her pain away with pleasure.

'All blood is mine,' she whispered to him.

The truth was the most powerful of blades.

The power of balance can be immense. I witnessed its strength in the chamber of the Maw of Uncreation. The matter of Shyish flows into the Maw at a rate that keeps it quiescent. If the balance is disturbed, whether through a sudden influx or through a withholding, then the vortex rises. Once the matter at the circumference of the vortex asserts the flow enough, the Maw will recede to its original point. So I believe. One day, I know, I will have to put that belief to the test. If I am wrong, then I will doom everything.

– *The Understanding of Annihilation*

SEVENTEEN

AGE OF SIGMAR
THE SEASON OF CREMATORY

'Reinforcements.' Felsein sounded doubtful.

'Yes,' said Dessina, and strode forwards. She no longer needed Felsein and the others to trust her. The few moments that their doubts would grant her would be enough.

She marched into the ranks of the skeletons. As they raised their swords to strike her down, she said, 'I must see Karvent.'

The skeletons paused, then stepped back, clearing a path for her to the base of the Annihilation Gate's plinth. A Black Knight awaited her there. As she walked, Dessina grasped the medal that hung from a heavy chain around her neck. It was the coat of arms of the Avaranthes. The symbol was a hated one, an embodiment of disloyalty. Now she broke it in half. Inside it was another, smaller, obsidian medal, carved to match the seal of the gate. She had been carrying Venzor's doom in plain sight.

Dessina reached Karvent, and showed the Black Knight what she carried.

'Has the time come, then?' the skeleton asked with a voice like wind over sand.

'By the command of our queen, it has.'

Dessina carried Neferata's authority with her, but not the Mortarch's power. The key would not, by itself, be enough to complete her task. But Dessina had her loyalty and her love, and for her, they were enough.

She had faith Neferata would provide the rest.

Dessina gestured at Venzor's forces. She raised her voice so that all could hear. 'They are the enemies of Neferata. Kill them all.'

'Traitor!' Felsein shouted.

'No,' Dessina said as Karvent led the skeletons forward. 'My loyalty is greater than yours could ever be.'

She watched as Felsein and Venzor's forces charged the skeletons. Their attack was futile bravado. Venzor had given Dessina strong warriors to command, but there were only hundreds of them. They could not hold out long against Karvent's many thousands of guardians. Neferata had designed the Annihilation Gate's defences to be impregnable to all but her or her chosen servant.

The chamber shook with the clash of steel and crack of bone. The vampires' screams of rage became cries of distress as the skeletons overwhelmed them. Dessina turned her back on the slaughter and climbed the plinth.

She stood before the seal, and savoured the moment Neferata had given her. *So great a boon*, Dessina thought. *I am not worthy, but I am grateful.* 'I am the hand of your will, my queen,' she said, and touched the key to the seal. The seal began to move. She felt a thrum rise from within the Annihilation Gate, passing through her body, and up through the underworlds of Nulahmia. For a brief moment, Dessina was closer than she had ever been to her queen.

And the power came down.

Storm of night and storm of light, destruction had arrived to release annihilation. Dessina came apart in a blaze beyond the reach of fire. In the last fraction of a moment of her existence, she felt not pain, but ecstasy. There was joy in martyrdom, and finally there was honour in her name.

Neferata stood beside Nagadron on the peak of the Ossa Spire. Constructed entirely of fused bone, the tower was a thin, jagged spike stabbing hundreds of feet in the air at the northern edge of the Silent Quarter. Here she could witness the totality of her action. Her work of centuries was coming to fruition.

Not completion. Nothing ever ends.

Except that tonight, that was not true. Tonight, there would be endings. Tonight, the end itself would rise.

The time had come. She unleashed catastrophe, and the great engine of sorcery and stone roared to terrible life.

The tremors, centred at the Tomb of the Unnumbered, radiated across Nulahmia. Towers swayed and crumbled. As far away as the southern wall, spires collapsed in a thunder of rubble as the surface of the streets rose and fell like ocean swells. Spirits beyond counting rose from the splits in the ground and the shattered mausoleums, hurled from the underworlds as the shattering spread through the material and immaterial domains of Shyish. The engine opened a great wound in the Realm. This was the beginning of its work.

The shaking of the Tomb of the Unnumbered reached a new intensity. A cleft appeared, running vertically down from its peak, between the twin spires, through the centre of the structure. With an immense grind of tortured stone, the gargantuan mausoleum began to rise from the Silent Quarter. Sorcerous light of crimson and violet burned at its base, and the two halves of the Tomb began to part. The monument gradually took on the appearance of an opened claw. The mausoleum floated hundreds of feet above the streets.

Then the streets fell. The Silent Quarter dropped into an abyss. The pit widened quickly. Its edges moved towards the flames of battle. The hot wind blew straight down, air and dust called to their destruction too. Tombs and monuments disappeared, and then the Maw reached the border of the Silent Quarter. The Ossa Spire swayed. Neferata waited a moment longer, drinking in the immensity of what she had done, her gaze called by the darkness below, because she knew what waited in the depths. The Spire began to lean, and she experienced the vertigo of delicious, absolute destruction.

The gods themselves fear what I have freed, she thought, and then leapt onto Nagadron's back. They flew to the skies, fleeing the jaws of the most perfect of disasters. The Spire toppled, snapping in half, and in half again. The great lengths of bone tumbled end over end into the pit, small as needles before they vanished.

Neferata gazed down, her witchsight unveiling every detail of the cataclysm. The abyss consumed the Crepuscular Road. Its citizens filled the street, tramping each other in panic as they tried to flee. The distant sounds of their screams reached Neferata's ears. Individual voices merged into a single, collective shriek. At first, the scream was barely audible beneath the rumble of collapsing architecture, but soon it grew loud as more and more of the city joined in. Habitations, grand manors and palaces vanished. Thousands of the living and the undead perished in moments, and as great as the scream became, a greater silence followed, rippling outwards with the pit, putting an end to hope and despair alike.

And the war waged on, the armies ignorant for a short time yet of the doom that was coming for them.

The darkness in the abyss began to swirl and turn grey. The Maw of Uncreation was gorging itself into a frenzy. Its level rose and rose, the secret that could not be confronted becoming visible. Now madness outgrew and outpaced terror, as the inhabitants of Nulahmia beheld the absolute. The great scream took on a new tone. Madness and awe and terror became one.

'So great a symphony,' Neferata said to Nagadron. 'And it is my creation.'

Neferata watched and looked away, watched and looked away. She did not gaze on the Maw of Uncreation long enough for it to seize her with its devouring blankness, yet she needed to see.

The work unfolded in all the glory of horror. The pit was miles wide now, and its circumference was spinning, pulling more and more of the city into the vortex of the Maw. When it reached the streets of the north, torn apart by battle, the firestorms plunged inside, the flames sucked away by a force of destruction that rendered theirs meaningless. The Maw of Uncreation rose higher yet, and it devoured the war.

Neferata took Nagadron north, the better to see the end of folly, the shared folly of Venzor and Ruhok that they had any right to the city.

The usurper was fighting with the Lord of Khorne. They had come to grips, and Ruhok was trying to snap the vampire in half while Venzor lashed at him with a frenzy of sorcerous bolts. To their rear, Bloodbound fled from the onrushing collapse. They cut each other down in their panic. Those who were close enough to the edge to see the Maw were frozen. They understood, to their cost, what they saw. No being could behold the destroyer and not know it for what it was, for it nestled in the deepest recesses of every thought, every belief, every consciousness. Every reality.

Neferata heard the glorious sound of the Bloodbound screaming in fear, and she laughed. Her laughter rang across the city in agony, clear and strong and merciless.

Venzor and Ruhok stopped in mid-strike. They stared at their doom. Not far from them, Kathag, alone among Ruhok's Gore-chosen, had understood the nature of the maelstrom in time to turn away. 'Do not look!' he cried. *'Do not look!'*

His warning was a whisper in a gale. Only Neferata heard it, and she smiled.

The bloodsecrator and the slaughterpriest did not run. Neferata witnessed the crumbling of their faith. Their muscles went slack. Their faces went dark with monstrous comprehension. At the last moment, just before the ground beneath their feet dropped away, the bloodsecrator hurled his huge icon into the pit. Then they vanished, unable even to curse.

Ruhok, too, was paralysed. He stared directly into the face of doom, but when it came for him, he raised his voice in a thunderous roar. His pain and his rage would have hurled fortress walls to the ground, but the Maw of Uncreation took his anger, and so this too, only Neferata heard. Then he fell, a meteor of crimson armour plunging into the terminal grey.

Venzor tried to flee, gabbling in terror. But he turned his head away too late. He was too slow, and when the Maw came for him, he looked at it again, all choice stolen. His last scream was high and long, rich in all the shades of terror.

Only Kathag moved fast enough. He tore through the struggling hordes of Bloodbound, trampling them into the ground, sprinting for the outer walls. He looked back only once, from the top of a hill of rubble. Instead of staring at the Maw of Uncreation, he looked up, and Neferata met his gaze.

'Run!' she called to him, and laughed. 'Tell them!' she shouted, as the Exalted Deathbringer turned and ran again, fleeing the collapsing city, the all-destroying hunger at his back. 'Tell them all! *Tell your god what you have seen this night!*'

Whirling, growing, whirling and growing, the Maw of Uncreation swallowed the armies, casting the legions into final silence. It pulled the outer walls of the city down, and the northern edge of the abyss stretched into the land beyond. There were no fires now, no defenders and no attackers. The Maw had claimed them all.

The glow from the base of the Tomb of the Unnumbered sent tendrils to the circumference of the pit. They were the arms of disruption, and they prevented the material of Shyish from restoring the balance that restrained the Maw of Uncreation. The strain on Neferata's sorcerous engine was enormous. The Tomb of the Unnumbered began to crack. Slabs of dark rock fell from its sides. Splits webbed across its façade, turning it into a broken eggshell. Foul light gleamed from inside. The engine was on the verge of flying apart.

Neferata did not know what would happen if it destroyed itself. And its work was done. Balance must be restored. So she turned the Staff of Pain towards the hovering monument and jagged sorcery crackled across the night to the Tomb. The force was powerful, but it did not drain her as before. She was not unleashing magic now. She was releasing the strain.

The spell struck the Tomb of the Unnumbered. The tendrils of light flared, then vanished. Now there was a rush of new material into the Maw faster than its hunger could grow. The vortex began to withdraw. The grey sank down into the darkness, receding to its chamber.

The Tomb of the Unnumbered began to descend. The open claw closed, the two halves returning to one another and, as far below the Annihilation Gate shut once more, so did the Tomb come to ground with a boom that shook the city. Destruction slumbered again, covered by the sleep of death.

The tremors ceased. Silence fell over Nulahmia. The silence of dread, the silence of rubble, the silence of Neferata's rule. The northern quarter was a slumped pit. Phantasmal energies floated over it, a nimbus of green and loss. Mile after mile after mile of the city was utter ruin. The destruction was more complete than anything that had happened during Lascilion's siege. What Neferata had created, she had destroyed. What she destroyed, she could create anew.

She brought Nagadron down into the wasteland. She dismounted and began to walk, first through what had been the Silent Quarter, then onwards, into the ruins of the north. The sound of her boots on broken stone rang sharply in the quiet. The wind gradually picked up again, keening with grief. And then, though the end of the furnace season of Crematory was still far in the future, it began to rain.

The rain fell up. It rose from the rubble, droplets darkened with ash. Neferata stretched out her hands, and the mourning of stone pattered up against her palms. She smiled, followed the flight of rain to the sky, where clouds turned sluggishly in aftershocks of pain.

At her back, she felt the sudden gathering of night. She wheeled around to see the coming of a god. She had expected his arrival. That did not make it any easier. Now she would see the ultimate consequences of her risk.

The ropes of night became limbs and armour. The cold fire of the gaze appeared, and then the terrible skull. In glory and might, he who was dread incarnate, he who was death incarnate, materialised before her. His armour was ribbed in golden wraithbone. Long spurs rose from his shoulders, symbols of his grasp reaching out beyond his form. In his hand he held

Alakanash, the great Staff of Power, his authority captured in blade and bone.

Nagash was here to render judgement.

'You risked my Realm,' said the god of death.

'I was not reckless with Shyish, master,' Neferata answered, her tone humble and respectful, but not cowering. She must stand by her actions. 'I knew, once I permitted it, that the balance would be restored.'

'You knew, or you believed?'

'The line between the two was insignificant.'

'Yet it exists.'

Neferata bowed her head. 'I do not believe that you did not know the Maw of Uncreation lay below Nulahmia, master. I do not believe you did not know I would, in time, make use of it.'

The eyes of the death's head glowed with what she hoped was amusement.

Nagash swept his hand, taking in the devastation of Nulahmia. 'The city was a different risk. You sacrificed much.'

'It is mine to sacrifice. Is it not?'

'Yours? Yours by my dispensation.'

Neferata said nothing, waiting.

The cold fire in Nagash's gaze grew brighter, and she was sure, now, that she saw dark pleasure there. 'Yes,' he said. 'Yours. Through your skill at deceit, you have destroyed a legion of Khorne and reclaimed the right to your city entire. I revoke Arkhan's claim.'

Neferata held her face still. She kept her triumph in her heart, though she had no doubt Nagash could see it. She lowered her head again. 'My thanks to you, my lord. My service, eternally, is yours.'

'So it must be,' Nagash warned, and he faded from view, death returning to the night. The sense of his gaze lingered, a call to obedience.

Neferata turned back to Nulahmia. The city was wounded, bleeding. *Her* city. To wound and to heal as she saw fit.

Her city. Bleeding at her command.

For all blood is mine.

ABOUT THE AUTHORS

Josh Reynolds is the author of the Horus Heresy Primarchs novel *Fulgrim: The Palatine Phoenix*, and two audio dramas featuring the *Blackshields: The False War* and *The Red Fief*. His Warhammer 40,000 work includes *Lukas the Trickster* and the Fabius Bile novels *Primogenitor* and *Clonelord*. He has written many stories set in the Age of Sigmar, including the novels *Shadespire: The Mirrored City, Soul Wars, Eight Lamentations: Spear of Shadows*, the Hallowed Knights novels *Plague Garden* and *Black Pyramid*, and *Nagash: The Undying King*. His tales of the Warhammer old world include *The Return of Nagash* and *The Lord of the End Times*, and two Gotrek & Felix novels. He lives and works in Sheffield.

David Annandale is the author of the Horus Heresy novels *Ruinstorm* and *The Damnation of Pythos*, and the Primarchs novels *Roboute Guilliman: Lord of Ultramar* and *Vulkan: Lord of Drakes*. For Warhammer 40,000 he has written *Warlord: Fury of the God-Machine*, the Yarrick series, several stories involving the Grey Knights, including *Warden of the Blade* and *Castellan*, as well as titles for The Beast Arises and the Space Marine Battles series. For Warhammer Age of Sigmar he has written *Neferata: Mortarch of Blood*. David lectures at a Canadian university on subjects ranging from English literature to horror films and video games.

YOUR NEXT READ

KORGHOS KHUL: THE RED FEAST
by Gav Thorpe

On the Flamescar Plateau, a time of peace and prosperity is threatened by a distant sorcerous power. Can Athol Khul bring the tribes together to keep the peace, or will war claim them all – and destroy their future?

For these stories and more go to **blacklibrary.com**, **games-workshop.com**, Games Workshop and Warhammer stores, all good book stores or visit one of the thousands of independent retailers worldwide, which can be found at games-workshop.com/storefinder